Oileán na

Island of the Dead

David A Dunlop

Copyright © 2014 David A Dunlop

All rights reserved.

ISBN:1500241423
ISBN-13:9781500241421

For my children

*Marie-Claire,
Niall,
Ciara,
Michaela,
Conall
& Danielle
(who is waiting for us)*

CONTENTS

1	The White Strand	1
2	"The Lark on the Strand"?	10
3	The Hooded Crow	17
4	The Washing of Hands	24
5	A Slow Night Air	37
6	Shadow in the Water	46
7	An Island Burial	57
8	Sad News is Carried	71
9	A Clergyman's Sorrow	82
10	My Thoughts Before Leaving For Ireland	98
11	My Observations Concerning My First day on Irish Soil	108
12	My Dear Parents	120
13	Reflections on the Dunfanaghy Public Meeting and My Continuing Journey West	122
14	Reactions in the Manse	139
15	My Thoughts on Diver's Donegal	146
16	Light and Dark	151
17	My Unanswered Questions	157
18	Another Letter Home	160

19	My Thoughts on a Wonderful Mountain	171
20	His Darkness Grows	180
21	A Further Letter From Roberts	186
22	My Thoughts on the End of the Line	188
23	A Dream Fulfilled	193
24	My Hopes for Today	200
25	My Thoughts on Today's Wretchedness	210
26	Hard Pressed	213
27	My Thoughts; my Darkest Thoughts	217
28	An Exchange of Letters	221
29	Home From the Wars	228
30	Johnny Goes Downhill	243
31	A Nameless Hornpipe	258
32	Expectations	274
33	Confrontation	288
34	Decisions in the Night	301
35	Flight	322
36	Aftermath	331
37	Railway Workers	338
38	The End of Waiting	351
39	In-between	366
40	Letters from Home	377
41	Oileán na Márbh	387

Acknowledgements

To all the many friends who have helped me in the writing of this my first novel I offer sincere thanks. Some will know who they are; among those who may not are the many good folks of Carrickfinn, the Rosses and Gweedore who told me stories, lent me books and have never tired of my appetite for the local historical trivia of this part of west Donegal. These are the "cultural gatekeepers" who have welcomed me in to some of the traditions of the area.

Frank Sweeney's excellent history of the Letterkenny to Burtonport railway extension, "That Old Sinner", (Irish History Press, 2006), has been an immense help in setting the background context to the narrative of the novel.

Thanks to several friends and family who have read the text at various stages and offered helpful advice. In this respect I should like to especially thank Ruth Morrison and Julia Carroll. Thanks also to the best of neighbours, Máire agus Dónall Macruairí, for their assistance with 'the Irish' in the text.

Thanks to my good friend Deirdre Tasker for her beautiful whistle tunes which very much enrich the iBook experience and the promotional video which can be viewed at http://vimeo.com/81494239

My daughter Marie-Claire has a great eye for a photograph and I should like to thank her for the poignant study of Oileán na Márbh which appears on the front cover of the book. Another daughter, Michaela, provided me with valuable information in her professional role as a midwife. Thanks to my son Conall for his ideas and expertise in e-publishing the book.

Thanks also to a former pupil of mine, William Allen, who produced several fine sketches for the novel.

Finally, thanks to Mary, my patient wife, who has been a constant support and encouragement and upon whom I have relied so often for her perceptive criticism and advice.

Author's note

While several of the names of characters in the novel are those of historical persons, the portrayal of all characters, actual or imagined, is entirely fictional. Any similarity to persons dead or alive is accidental.

Oileán na Márbh

Island of the Dead

Section 1

Chapter 1

The White Strand

From a distance he thought it was the carcass of a "muc mhara", left behind by the receding tide just short of the sand banks; an out-of-place dash of distant whiteness in the freshly strewn tangle of dark seaweed. "Muc mhara" translated as "sea-pig"; it was the Gaelic name that local people put on the harbour porpoise which could occasionally be seen as a fleeting shadow in the waves around Inishfree Bay.
The morning on his skin, gentle after the storm of the last two days, a pleasure to him. He took in deep breaths of Atlantic-washed air, happy to be away from the tightness of the home cottage and the yard. He was his own man out here! Away from the stifling clutter of collected paraphernalia, driftwood of the ebb and flow of lives lived out on this western seascape. Away from the intensity of relationship and expectation, temporarily free from the apparent pre-ordination of the pattern of his life. A slow-beating rhythm of season and cycle, regulated by clan and creed and punctuated by occasional fairs and wakes and ceilis.
The September sun above the Derryveigh Mountains away on the eastern horizon competed half-heartedly with a covering of misty cloud, mottled cream and slate-grey, still undecided as to whether or not to shed its load upon the already saturated bogland. And yet he walked under a clear blue heaven; he wasn't the first to notice this idiosyncratic aspect of the local pattern of weather in this part of The Rosses; the western coastal strip was often bright and clear-skied, whereas a couple of miles

inland towards the heathered hills, rain would be bucketing from a peat-slab sky.

The roan heifer he was leading slowed to urinate, its back arched slightly, its eyes bright and wild in the throes of hormonal stirring. He paused, let the hemp tether rope slacken and looked back along the half-mile length of An Tra Ban, the White Strand, towards the rise of the shore-rocks. The lonely tracks of man and beast meandered randomly on the wide, virgin sand, testimony to the spasmodic tuggings of the animal as the heat took her. This would be her first time, he thought. She didn't know what was ahead of her with Stewart's bull. He wondered what was going through this heifer's mind. Does she have any idea what is bothering her this morning? Has she any sense of sex, or is it just a simple, basic driving instinct to produce offspring? Does the animal think in its head something along the lines of, "Get me to the bull quick!" In cow language of-course. Is that what her low moanings mean? Longing? Lust? He smiled at himself, at his own stupidity for thinking such incongruous thoughts. "Animals can't express themselves in language," he reasoned to himself. "That's what makes us different, the way we can communicate what we want, the way we feel about things, like love and desire and....." He stopped his train of thought abruptly as he was hit by a moment of self-realisation, clear as the sharpness of the sea-scented air.

"Who am I to pity the cattle that they can't put words on their feelings when I struggle to work out what my own feelings are in the first place, never mind putting language on them to tell to her? A right ejit, am I not? Twenty-one and as tongue-tied as when I was a wee lad.... But not as tongue-tied as her, God love her."

A ripple of a breeze from the north-west flaffed an unruly shank of long fair hair from the brownness of his brow. Like most folk around the coast, his complexion spoke of an outdoor life, long hours of work on sea and land. And, as his father sometimes joked, he had the figure of a greyhound.

The heifer sniffed distractedly at a twisted branch, lately washed up and now entwined in a rosary of slimy seaweed. He jerked the rope in impatience and resumed the journey. The view to the north and west was the same as always but he never failed to take it in and wonder at it; ahead of him, the huge sand hills thrown up some sixty years earlier during the night of the big storm of 1838, known all over Ireland as "An Ghaoth Mhor". He remembered his grandfather, Francey Pat, telling him that a couple of houses in Carnbui had been completely buried in the sand thrown up by the storm that night. All along the western coast it had been the same; villages wiped out by the mounds of sand deposited by these hurricane winds. The extensive area of sand-hills just around the headland at Mullaghdearg had been formed that same night. Whole clachans of houses had had to be abandoned, their inhabitants relocating in townlands further back from the shore. There were tales of rivers filling up whole valleys, sweeping everything before them to the sea, horses and cattle and even houses. People said that in one part of Ireland, miles from the coast, fish had rained down from the sky. Maybe it was in County Louth, he thought he remembered. The people weren't sure whether to eat them as a fortunate windfall, or leave them lying in case they were part of some kind of evil curse on the place. "They wouldn't have thought twice about it ten years later," Francey Pat had said, "When the hunger was on them the folk would have eaten them fish before they hit the ground."

He looked away to the north, to the tip of Oileán Ghabhla. Gola Island in the English. He had always thought that if you half-closed your eyes and squinted at Gola, it looked like the head of an ancient giant resting on the sea, as if stretched out in sleep, the hill of his nose sniffing the ocean air, his beard the creaming of Atlantic waves smashing into his granite jawline. Then beyond the jutting chin, a stark guardian rock which the people called Tor Glassen, high, hay-stack shaped; a plug of Donegal's oldest rock, wearing a spread of early autumn grass with the pride of an elderly man still holding onto a reasonable head of hair. Further to the west of these outcrops the sea rose in mighty, foam-topped rollers. The swell out there, still stirred by the recent storm, breaks over a submerged reef and is feared and avoided by the locals who fish the plentiful shoals of herring and mackerel beyond Gola and Inishfree. A precarious occupation at the best of times, no matter what stretch of sea they would be fishing in. As he should know. His cousin, Colm Cavanagh, was lost in the bay years ago, on his first occasion to go out with Bartley O'Donnell to lift lobster pots. Bartley's curragh was never the safest; flimsy and with far too many strips of poorly-repaired canvas; everybody but Bartley knew it;

one or two of the braver ones had even had the temerity to tell him but, being the thrane character that he was, he wasn't ever going to listen to them. And so the sea took its own, as the old people always believed it did. It took the pair of them on a July evening when a southerly breeze got up quickly from behind the headland and met the swell of the filling tide head on, whipping up the surface of the ocean into a lumpy, churning cauldron and drowning a boy of twelve and a husband and father of thirty four years. Husband of a much younger woman, Maggie Dan. Father of an eight year old boy, his friend Johnny, and father of a three year old girl who, as far as anyone could tell, never really remembered the big, open-faced, red-haired joker of a man who was her father; or maybe never really recovered from the loss of him.

Her! His mind back to her yet again; like the deepening rut of a turf-ladened cart in a soft area of the bog, he couldn't fight it.

Deliberately he thought of Colm. His mother's sister's only son among six daughters, which made it all the worse. They had lived further along the lane into the hills; that was before they all emigrated to Scotland or England or America. He'd had a certain awe of his older cousin in the way that younger boys do. He was about seven when the double tragedy had rocked the town-land of Ranahuel. It wasn't the first and it wouldn't be the last but, with everybody married through each other in a kinship web of supportive intricacy, the whole community helped to pull the two families through.

"What age would he be now?" he wondered. "Must be fourteen years ago, so he'd be twenty six. Around about the same age as my sister Mary. Well, for me he's forever twelve and he'll never be any older than the way he looks in my mind's eye the last time I saw him in his mother's kitchen."

A little band of black and white Oyster-catchers scuttled out of his way towards the safety of the breaking waves, their red legs flashing rapidly across the gloss of the wet sand. He counted seven of them and watched as they paused to scavenge where the tide had deposited clumps of seaweed, their long orange beaks dabbing among the wrack for molluscs and larvae. In the distance he heard the bawing of Stewart's cattle, and he wasn't the only one! The heifer responded, straining ahead of him, its head jerking at the tether until his hand hurt.

"Easy now! Go easy!" he said. "We'll get there; there's no rush. You'll get what's coming to you. Take it easy!"

He changed his grip on the rope, catching the halter closer to the lightly frothing mouth of the yearling, his knuckles pressed aggressively into its long jaw. She settled again and he scanned the bluey greenness of the sea over her bobbing head. The Stag Rocks stuck up from the horizon with angled, defiant arrogance. Three prongs of rock, maybe five or six miles out to sea, but a constant and clearly visible reminder of the rugged durability of the local rock to resist even the most violent thrashings of the ocean. He'd seen them closer up once, from the cliffs at the back end of Owey Island, proud, craggy projections that looked about forty or fifty feet high, rising up precociously from the sea-bed, the focal point of an area of swirling foam and spray; and to think they been there since the beginning of time, or, if he was to believe the local folk-lore, since the three witches of Tory had been driven off the island by Saint Columcille and turned to stone as they escaped! "Big lumps o' witches they must have been," he smiled to himself.

On along the beach they trudged, veering this way and that to avoid the areas of freshly laid sand where the heifer's feet dug several inches into the coarser-grained, corn-coloured deposit. Thin skitters of yellowy-green foam, reminding him of day-old calf scour, lay ribbon-like on the sand where they had been abandoned by the dissipating wavelets. The millions of shells, some strewn in colourful random patterns and some washed into low crescent-shaped ridges by the lapping of the waves, were so much part of An Tra Ban landscape that he didn't really take notice of them. But he did keep his gaze on the sand for a time and eventually saw what he was looking for, an object which had long held a fascination for him. He stopped to pick up a perfectly shaped razor-shell, at least nine inches long and without a blemish.

"What kind of thing is this? What kind of animal can make something as beautiful as this?" he wondered, as he had wondered before. He studied its delicate profusion of parallel curving colours, pastel mauves, greys and beige-whites, turning it over in his rough farm hands. "I'll give it to her....she'd like it. Now that she's back home from her granny's," he thought and placed it carefully in the bottom of his jacket pocket. His father, who of late had taken to his bed, surrendering to the chronic rheumatism which had plagued him for years, maintained that such shells were the home of a type of clam that burrowed a tunnel down deep into the sand. Once, on a Sunday afternoon walk on the strand, he had tried to dig down to find one to prove his point to his children, but without success.

"Good memories," Sean thought. "I hope to God those days aren't gone forever. He loved walking the strand."

The heifer's patience wore thin and it pulled on the rope. Sean resumed his trek towards the farmstead of the Stewarts. As he did he realised that he must have passed the carcass of the Muc Mhara which he thought he had spied earlier. A quick glance over his right shoulder and there it was, fifty paces away on the high-tide line, with the seaweed.

Except that it was no sea creature.

"Jesus, Mary and Joseph!" he breathed.

He dropped the tether and stood stock still, hand to mouth, his heart beating a rhythm totally new to him.

Not a sea pig!

Not a seal nor a shark nor a young whale!

Not a fish of any description!

The naked body of a man lay stretched out, face down on the sand.

The heifer took off along the strand in a crazy gallop but he didn't notice. "What do you do now, Sean Ban Sweeney?" he thought. After a paralysed pause he shuffled towards the pale corpse with the awful dread in his head that when he looked at the face he would know this person.

There wasn't a mark on the body. It was the colour of buttermilk. Young looking skin; sturdy legs and hips; a stockily built body; short black hair, very short. With relief he thought that this was a stranger; nobody around here has hair like that, or would be that white of themselves surely. There was an almost religious symmetry about how the body was laid out; head towards the northern end of the strand, feet splayed out towards the south, arms near enough by the sides of the body, as if carefully placed there for best comfort. But it was the face that worried him. It was staring directly down into the sand and he couldn't make out a single feature of it, though he tried looking at it from both sides, with his own face stooped low to the seaweed. The ears were very pale, he noticed; grey, blueish white.

"God help me, I'm going to have to turn him over," he said aloud. "To see what sort of a face is on him," he thought.

Slowly he got up and wandered around looking for a stick or anything that he could use to use to lever the body over. So he wouldn't have to touch it. To no avail. Nothing but the rows of fresh seaweed. He would have to just do it with his hands but he shuddered at the thought. These hands have delivered manys a calf and even more lambs, some of them dead, but this was a different matter. He tried his foot, shuffling the toe of his right boot into the sand under the body where the leg met the hip; the corpse was rigid of itself and, although it lifted an inch or two, he pulled back his foot with a shudder of self-disgust.

"He's a human being, whoever he is," he thought. "He surely deserves more in death than to be prodded with the same boot that I kick the cat with."

So kneeling down again he took the corpse, one tentative hand under the shoulder and the other at the pelvic, and gently lifted it. The feel of the dead flesh on his hands sent a shiver through him and at the same time the smooth tautness and coldness of it made him think, for some reason, of the marble statue of Christ on the cross, behind the altar in Annagry church. He muttered a prayer as the stiff body reached tilting point and flopped over on its back, soundlessly onto the soft sand.

"Hail Mary, full of grace; blessed art thou among women and blessed is the fruit of thy womb, Jesus. Hail Mary, Mother of God; pray for us sinners now and at the hour of our death."

The front was caked in sand; the face like that of a well-weathered gargoyle whose features have dissembled in the passing of time, so sand-encrusted were they. The chest, even the genitals, were similarly adorned. It crossed his mind suddenly to wonder why there wasn't a stitch of clothing about him; what was the meaning of that? Who was he and where did he come from and why, in God's name, were there no clothes on him?

Still curious about the face, he raised his hand to brush off the sand. But he couldn't bring himself to do it; something about the intimacy of the action prevented him.

"That's his mother's job," he thought and then grimaced at the irrationality of it.

"Water," he said getting up. "I'll wash it off. Sea water."

He set off at a run towards where the waves were breaking shallow on the gently sloping sand. "But how will I carry it to him?" He pulled off his well-worn boots and plunged out into the chilling sea-water before dipping both under the wave. One had a hole in the leather at the side and so wasn't a lot of use but the other stayed well-filled as he jogged back. He doused the whole boot-full over the stranger's face, still hoping it was a stranger. The sand washed away and confirmed that these were indeed unfamiliar features. He had never seen this fellow before.

"He's not local," he thought. "Of-course he isn't a local! What would a local be doing lying completely naked and cold-white dead on the white strand at this time of a September morning? They'd have more wit about them. Kept their trousers on at least."

But it was the eyes! He had never expected that, when the sand was washed off, the eyes would be anything other than closed. He was wrong! They were fixed wide open in an intense stare which he found shockingly disconcerting and fascinating by turn. He wanted, needed to look away, desperately wanted them to close, but couldn't bring himself to look anywhere else, such was their magnetism. He wouldn't dare touch them to try to close them and suspected that it would be pointless anyway. They were dead eyes but they retained a certain residue of vitality so that when he moved around the fellow's head he fully expected the eyes to follow him. They didn't of-course, remaining in a fixed stare upon some infinite point in the azure sky above, so he went back to look into them straight on, his bare feet astride the torso.

They reminded him of mushrooms, the colour of mushrooms, dull, browny-grey; bulging slightly like the shape of a mushroom…. maybe it was the effects of his time in the sea or maybe that was how he always looked. And the resignation of a mushroom too. There was in these eyes a pathetic sense of peacefulness bordering, he thought, on piety. And at the same time a despair of unfathomable depth.

The rest of his features were comparatively insignificant. Hair dark and much shorter and tidier than most of the young fellows around here. No beard, indeed remarkably close-shaven. Normal nose and mouth and chin; a small red scratch where he had recently nicked himself shaving; square shoulders and shallow-chested....he looked no further but stepped back from the body. The initial shock had been replaced by a strong sense of sympathy for this unfortunate and mysterious stranger.

"I'll go and tell the Stewarts. They'll know what to do," he thought. "But I'd need to cover him up first."

He looked around for some idea of what to use for the purpose but could think of nothing other than a few strands of seaweed. He set a straggly wreath of it over the face and, out of decency, another handful to cover the fellow's privates. Then, with a last backward look at the tragic figure, he picked up his soaking wet boots and set off barefoot at a jog towards the northern end of the strand.

He'd forgotten all about the heifer. She was nowhere to be seen but if he'd taken time to climb the tallest of the sand-hills he would have been comforted that she had found what she was after of her own accord and could have watched the satiation of her urges, courtesy of Stewart's obliging black Angus bull, in a lovely little area of deep grass and rushes at the end of the lough.

Chapter 2

"The Lark on the Strand?"

The melody is lark-like, soaring up and down a musical staircase of sound, the familiar arpeggios of traditional Irish dance music. The reel is both dance-step and tune, but only the reddish-brown stalks of white-topped bog cotton on the rough ground beyond the narrow meadow are actually dancing this morning, and not in any obvious relationship to the rhythm or energy of the tune.
She sits on the stump of a long-dead fir tree. The tune is coming from deep inside her. It is not self-created; few of the tunes that she plays on her battered whistle are. It has a genesis and a history which she knows nothing about. A more knowledgeable devotee might speculate concerning its origins and might ascribe it to such and such a town-land or to this or that renowned fiddler or uilleann piper. She just plays it. She knows it because she's heard it. Sometime, somewhere.

"Maybe she heard it in another life," the priest thought. He repented of this heresy at once and instead said to her mother, "Don't you wonder where she gets it?"
The mother, a short, wiry woman with a wad of grey hair and a ruddy complexion, continued to stir the contents of the soot-black pot as they boiled above the blazing turf fire in the open hearth. The smell of potatoes and fish drifted past Father Dunleavey. He stood full-square in the small frame of the door, arms behind his back, blocking a good percentage of the light that the smoky room cried out for.
"She'd be better fitted to be seeing something to do," muttered the mother through sparse, yellowing teeth, resignation underlying the tone of her voice and reflected in her grumble of a head. "She hasn't done a hand's turn since she landed back. It wasn't good for her being away all summer. All she does is sit and play that damned whistle."
"She could be doing worse, Maggie Dan. It's strange though, when you think about it; am I not right in thinking Johnny doesn't have a note in his head? And him her brother! But then, didn't Bartley have the odd tune in him, if I remember rightly?" And then he thought to himself, "What am I doing mentioning the drowned husband to her, as if she hasn't had trouble enough?"

Head tilted back, the priest inhaled the wholesome cooking aroma, salivating. As he listened to the melody from outside part of his mind performed the auditory equivalent as the tune burst up into its second section, in the major key this time. He found himself whistling along, not a proper fully-formed whistle, more a breathing of the notes at the front of his mouth, his full lips pursed as if to kiss. There was a simple, fulfilling joy in this melody; it was a nicely organised tune; always seemed to know where it was going. Self-confident of itself; and boy but she can play it. Oblivious to anything in her surroundings and at the same time so much part of them as to be one in essence with the bleak beauty of this countryside.

"Aye, her father could play a tune alright. It's his whistle she's playing. I bought it for him myself not long after we were married." Maggie Dan rolled her eyes towards the yard outside. "Whiles I wish now that I hadn't bothered. Aye, Bartley was a good enough player, to be fair. But Johnny? Not a note! More tune in a crow than in our Johnny. But he can work, I'll say that for him. A lot more use to us than a fistful of tunes. I have that to be thankful for in the middle of everything."

"Well, your mother will miss Annie. I'm sure she was glad of her. And she's a lot better you say?" Back to his whistling.

"She is, thanks be to God, Father. She's back on her feet. Able to get about the place again. Agh, it's lonely for her you know…."

"It is, I'm sure. Bound to be lonely."

"But there's no moving her. She'll never leave Cloughglas. 'I was born in this house and I'll die in this house! If it was good enough for my father and mother to die in, it's good enough for me,' says she."

She heard him whistling low for a while, looking out across the street of the cottage to the tree stump. "And she wouldn't think of coming over here for you to look after her, would she not?" the Priest asked and then, in her hesitation, realised that she had probably said something about that very subject while he was away in the tune with the daughter. "As you were saying yourself," he covered, turning back into the house by way of tacit apology.

Maggie Dan kept her head down at the hearth. "She'll not come this way," she said simply.

The whistle finds the end of the melody and fades reluctantly in a long, slowing cadence. The final note is sustained in a gently triumphant trill before the tune turns around and disappears to safety inside her again. She continues to sit on the tree stump, legs crossed. Her foot is still tapping out the rhythm of the jig as it plays on silently in the mists of her subconsciousness. She is puzzling about something in the deep recesses of her mind. Where has she heard this tune, she is wondering. Was it one of the tunes that those two old fiddlers played? The McConnell brothers, wasn't that their name? How she loves those surprise visits from itinerant musicians and tinkers; how she enjoys the long hours of sitting at their feet, listening to their yarns, playing along with them and then trying to remember and reproduce the tunes when they had moved on. She is without a trace of awareness of this unique and highly-developed ability that is inherent in her; this gift that fixes these melodies in her mind so easily that they can be recalled and played so perfectly, so beautifully, long after the event. She never forgets a tune; it's just how she is.

Father Dunleavey left the door and ambled bow-leggedly across the cobbled stones in the direction of the fir stump. His eyes lifted to the panorama of coastline stretched out below. He took in the sweep of headlands and islands, from the cliffs of Owey and Cruit in the west to the distant hump that is Bloody Foreland in the north east. The sun catching the squat peninsula of Carrickfinn at the end of the white strand, jutting north towards Gola.

Her head goes down as she sees him coming, her face secluded behind the veil of her shoulder-length, blonde hair; a curtain to the sanctuary of her eyes. The whistle in her left hand laid flat along the length of her thigh. The other arm tight across her stomach, with the right hand awkwardly clutching a fold of her shapeless, navy dress near her waist. One foot continues to pulse with the tune that only she is now hearing.

He began his monologue. "Lovely playing, Annie. Lovely altogether."
Nothing, but the slight swaying of the head.
"Do you know what it's called, that tune? Is it 'The Lark on the Strand', is it? Maybe not. Certainly sounds like a lark, doesn't it? The way it rises."
His hand fluttered up and down in mid air in his best imitation of a bird. She didn't see it.

"Maybe you don't know what it's called?"
Not a flicker.
"You can handle it well anyway."
The mother in the cottage, hammering something briefly in the short silence. Just a hollow thumping. Not another sound on the hillside.
He continued, accepting the silent punctuation of the conversation. "Did you play much to your Granny when you were over? Does she like the music, does she? I'm sure she loves it…she always loved it; used to dance like a dervish on the kitchen floor when your Granda Dan was alive, God rest him! So I'm told anyway."
Belatedly, a small, slow smile; but just what you'd notice; if you could see beyond the hair.
"Did you miss being away from your Mammy? I'm sure you missed her alright. She missed you too, Annie. And so did the Sweeneys. One of them especially."
One eyebrow raised as he looked closely at her for a reaction. Disappointed again. Impassive. A slight breeze played with her hair, flicking it back from her cheek. At the top end of the yard his mule snorted and shook its head at the midges and cleggs. Further back, whins, fuchsias, red-berried rowan bushes and straggly Scots pines decorated the side of the low hill.
"Ah, Sean Ban is a fine fellow now, isn't he? The Sweeneys are the best of God's good folk."
He watched a bee attacking a bright yellow dandelion at his feet.
"So what else did you get up to over at Cloughglas?" he asked, expecting no answer. Certainly not expecting the reaction he received.

She turns her head and looks at him with her big stark blue eyes. Looks him in the eye first, then stares at his neck, his clerical collar. It lasts but less than half a minute. And then she stands up. Just stands up. Doesn't make as if to go anywhere. Just stands placidly by his side, and looks with him down towards Mullaghdearg Lough and the rise of the green ridge of land beyond it.

The clergyman made no sense of her stare. Her body language defeated him, always had. After a bit he pointed towards the bay and said, "Do you see Rabbit Rock out there in the bay? Do you see? That one there, half way out to Inishfree? Don't know

why it's called that, mind you. It doesn't look like the shape of a rabbit to me. Then there's one closer in to Mullaghdearg strand that you can only see at very low tide; it's called Carraig-na-Spainneach, the rock of the Spaniards. And do you know how it got its name?"
Ever aware that Annie had not been able to attend the local parish school, the priest was in the habit of trying to develop her mind with local stories and folk lore.
"No? Have you never heard that story? Your mammy never tell you that one?"

The slightest movement of the head. Then she holds the whistle up to her right eye and looks down its length, across the holes, as if it was some form of a telescope.

The priest frowned slightly, wondering if she is mocking him in some childishly devious way. Staring at her, he cannot decipher anything of the devious, so he continued.
"Well, years ago there was a Spanish galleon, a big ship all the way from Spain, and it was trying to sail round Ireland to get away from the English. Not the first to be doing that. Anyway it got caught in a storm and was blown off course. The next thing, it hit that rock there and ripped a hole in the side of it. So it sank and drowned a lot of Spanish sailors. Some of them managed to hang onto bits of wood and got washed up on the sand. And some of their horses swam ashore too. So for years, it's said, there were gorgeous Spanish horses running wild among the bogs of the Rosses. Now that was big excitement for the local mares." He laughed in a stunted way at this his own risqué angle on the old story.
Annie looked at him again. Quickly.
"Twice in one day", thought Father Dunleavey.
Then her head bowed a little and the whistle came up to her lips.
Although he told a good story and used his hands in a most animated way to illustrate it, he could see that she was starting to lose concentration. He could sense the impatience in her fingers, flexing over the holes. So abruptly he turned, as if to move off, then paused for dramatic effect.

"There you are Annie. Spanish horses and handsome Spanish sailors all connected to that wee lump of rock sticking up out of the sea by Mullaghdearg strand."

He looked at her a long time, the sorrow rising in him like indigestion. What did she understand of Spanish horses or Armada ships? What did she understand about a lot of things? A beautiful creature of seventeen, the loveliest daughter of God, innocent as a baby and silent as a statue of the Blessed Virgin.

"There, that's the end of my story Annie. Not many people know it, so don't you be telling it to a soul," he said with a smile which immediately froze on his face as he repented at the idiocy of his attempted joke. Not that she gave any sign of understanding or annoyance, the whistle still at her lips and the breeze teasing with her hair. He left her abruptly, trundling back up the yard to the half-door of Maggie Dan's house, scattering a group of speckled hens dabbing in the stony grass.

"I'm away on here, Maggie Dan," he called into the peat smoke. "I need to see Sean Ban up above, for he's the best of the young ones with those ewes of mine, with your Johnny away gallivanting in the Lagan."

"Sean Ban is not there, Father," echoed back Maggie Dan's high-pitched tone.

"Where in the name of God is he then?" A hint of exasperation as he paused beyond the door.

Maggie Dan's upper half appeared above the lower section of the door, like a down-at-heel Judy in a rustic puppet show. Her face now even more ruddied by the glow of the open fire. She cleared her lungs raucously of smoke and dust and spat the resultant phlegm accurately into a flowerless flowerbed by the door.

"I saw him after dawn, leading a heifer down towards the lough. From the antics of her, I'd say he was taking her to the bull. But he should've been back by this time," she added by way of afterthought.

The clergyman shook his head in mock consternation. "The Protestant bull at it again, is it? Wouldn't you think that somewhere in the Rosses some good loyal farmer of the true faith would have the money to do the decent thing and buy us a sound wee Catholic bull for our springing heifers, rather than having to parade our poverty out to that black, bastardin' bull at the Point every time the heat comes over a cow?" he preached as he made his way to the mule.

"Lord save us but you're in some form the day," thought Maggie Dan, disappearing back into the fuggy gloom of her two-roomed abode. "Is it any wonder our Johnny christened him 'Father Don't-Leave-Me', the way he can eat up half a day on you with his rambling on and on."

Astride his ageing mount, the priest began to wind his way down the rutted lane between spiky, grey-green whins towards the hollow of the lough. Many feet above him, a lark hovered and flitted, fluting its carefree tune in the still afternoon air. Grasshoppers clicked in the dried-out grass beside the path. Before long though, he heard the sound of Annie's whistle, fragrant as the turf-smoke, following him around the twists of the path; he strained to catch the melody, another urgent-sounding jig but one unfamiliar to him. "Not to her though," he thought to himself and dug his heels into Saint Vincent's ribcage.

"Gid up, girl!" he grunted.

At about the same time the Stewart boys and Sean Ban Sweeney arrived at the body on the white strand.

Chapter 3

The Hooded Crow

The Hooded Crow was careless of the consternation and anger it caused the sheep-owning farmers and peasants of West Donegal, indeed of all parts of the county and the country as a whole. Also known as the Grey-backed Crow, its more sinister title better reflected its reputation as one of the nastier members of the Crow family species. "Hooded" suggested intentions of menace from behind a cloak of anonymity. Farmers didn't like the Grey-backed crow; they said it was "worth watching".

Crows on the whole were not an issue. Jackdaws were problematic only insofar as they created a bit of noise and tended to build straggly stick-nests in unused chimneys; such chimneys tended only to exist in the unused quarters of the "big house" or in vacant, dilapidated houses, forsaken during the famines of the forties. Their cousins, the regal, strutting, crawing Rooks, would feed communally on tilled ground but then feeding opportunities on such land were few and far between in the bleak Rosses. Rooks tended to stay in the fertile Swilly Valley and the arable countryside further east, known to the people of the west as "the Lagan". Arrogant thieving Magpies chattered incessantly in the mornings when you should have been up and about. If there was such a thing as gossip in bird-world, these black and white jesters were the most likely tell-tales. For all their opportunistic scavenging traits though, they were so intimately associated with superstitious notions of luck that they were given a fool's pardon.

"One for sorrow, two for joy
Three for a girl and four for a boy
Five for silver, six for gold
Seven for a secret never to be told"

But the Hooded Crow was public enemy number one for most farmers... for this good reason. The Hooded Crow considered that, amongst its extensive diet of garbage, there was one special delicacy to which it was entitled, almost as a constitutional right, it seemed.

The eyes of newly born lambs!

Up on the rough bog-land pasture in the hills, where shepherds had hundreds of acres to keep watch over and where sheep gave birth to lambs in the same pre-domesticated isolation as their antecedents, the Grey-backs had a field day. They took advantage of those first few hours of vulnerability just after the ewes resumed feeding, leaving their feeble offspring for the briefest of moments. By the time the bleating of the new lamb had penetrated the mother's hungry consciousness it was often too late, and the lamb was doomed to a short life, stumbling in blindness towards the waiting bog-holes! It was little wonder that the collective noun for these rascals was the word "murder"!

Down on the coast it was the same. Although more difficult for the Grey-backs, due to the closer proximity of the farmer to his patchwork of meagre, stone-ditched fields, they would attack lambs at any opportunity. Sometimes they were put off by the wind-blown, flapping carcasses of a few crows unfortunate enough to be caught in the line of fire of a farmer's shotgun and strung up around the fields as a macabre warning to relatives.

The lamb-eye delicacy was seasonal, springtime being the high point. At other times, the Hooded Crow scoured the landscape for carrion, searching the fern-covered scrub land, the rocky shore, the sand-flats and the beaches.

The beach! What was that on the beach? The crow flapped around again and landed cautiously a few yards away from the white body, alert, watching for any sign of response. Nothing! He hopped closer, in side-ways mode, sensed the coldness of the corpse, brushed the seaweed away with a sweep of his dirty grey beak and made his instinctive decision to have those big brown eyes, in season or not. Up onto the chest he flapped, then the face, his splayed claws on either side of the tight line of the mouth. Scattering the protective seaweed, he began his feast in the right eye, dabbing up and down in vicious rhythm, like a hooded worshipper in a spasm of ritualistic prayer.

Sean Ban Sweeney saw him first as he led an inquisitive posse of Stewart family members around the rock outcrop at the end of the strand. He swore under his breath and broke into a run, shouting curses at the hungry bird. Taking immediate stock of the situation, the crow resolved to live to feast another day and took to the air to watch from a safer distance.

"He'll have the eyes ate out of him," shouted Sean Ban in anguish.

"Calm yourself, Sean," said Robert John, father of three curious sons now running ahead with Sean. "It's not as if he's going to be needing them."

They gathered around the body, a reverential silence gradually overtaking their natural youthful ebullience as they stood and stared down at the blanched body of the stranger. The Stewart father was last to arrive. In middle age, his wispy grey hair struggled to cover the dome of his nut-brown head. Sharp blue eyes peered from his wind-scoured face. The prominent jaw-line, characteristic of his whole clan, seemed to jut defiance against the violence of this climate. Now jaw and head shook slowly from side to side as he looked at the corpse. A sort of awed quietness was broken by Jacob, a handsome young fellow and the oldest of the Stewart sons.

"Look at him!" he said, the black humour getting the better of him and breaking the tension. "Like Balor himself. Just the one eye left on him."

"Who's Balor?" quivered Richard, a scrawny rake of a boy who wouldn't be left behind at the house despite his mother's protestations.

"You'll be giving him nightmares, taking him to see a washed-up corpse. The wain's only ten; he has time enough to be seeing the likes of that," she had intoned in the lilting sing-song accent of the area.

Jacob recognised the terror in his young brother's voice and regretted the bravado of his attempted wit. He grabbed his younger brother playfully from behind, ruffling his hair. "Never worry; just an old legend. He was a one-eyed God on Tory Island years ago. He's long dead," he said.

"If he was a God, how come he is dead?" he asked, struggling to free himself from his brother's grip.

Robert John lifted his hand abruptly to demand attention as he circled around the body. "Stop it you two! You're in the presence of death. Show a bit more respect. No more of your nonsense."

Bobby, the middle son, turned away, his curiosity now replaced by sobering, white-faced shock. His father went to him, put his arm around his fourteen year-old's shuddering shoulders and said, "Run you back to the head of the strand and see what's keeping your granda with the cart."

Bobby took his advice with relief. A more delicate lad by nature, he had always seemed to lack the instinctive kind of virility required to embrace the cruder earthy essence of the farming life. The idea of cows and sheep and pigs, for example, giving birth to the bloody, goo-covered splodges of their young revolted him, so, after a couple of fainting fits during his initial experiences of animal birth, he had been excused further involvement. Now he set off at nothing short of an ungainly gallop, head tilted back, his longish hair strung out behind him, like a filly newly freed from its stable. By the time he had rounded the rocks at the end of the beach he was retching, out of breath and very sorry he had come at all. He threw up by the rocks, kicked sand over the mess and climbed to Condy's Well, a natural basin of fresh-water in the rocks at the end of An Tra Ban which was fed by a spring somewhere above in the cliff-face. Lying flat on the pinky-coloured granite, he plunged his head under the still surface of the cool, fresh water.

"I never want to see another dead body as long as I live," he thought as he climbed up over the bank to look for his grandfather. There he was, with the donkey and cart, plodding through the 'bent', the tall marram grass which spiked up in such profusion on the sand-hills. Bobby duked back down into the foliage and stayed hidden there until the ageing man had led his donkey and its traditional blue and orange painted cart well past him, descending to the beach. Then he trotted back in the direction of his home which nestled in the comforting clachan of Stewart houses at the reedy head of the lough.

"Have you ever seen the like of this before, Robert John?" Sean Ban was asking.

Robert John's brown, leathery skin wrinkled up around his eyes in thoughtfulness. "Seen a few bodies washed up over the years, but this one's different," he said in a quiet, slow whisper, as if unsure of whether to continue or not.

"What do you mean, Da?" Jacob picked up on his hesitancy at once.

"There's your granda coming, Richard. Go and give him a hand with that donkey for he's taking all night and Bobby seems to have disappeared off home."

Richard was slow to move. "Go on with you now," said his father. Then, when the boy was out of ear-shot "I've never seen a body washed up that didn't have clothes on it."

"What do you make of it?" asked Jacob, looking over his shoulder at the approaching donkey struggling to pull the cart with its narrow wheels through the deeper sand.

"Every other body we've had washed up around here….you could tell generally if it was a seaman or a soldier….. you could tell something about the man by what he was wearing. And it was always a man. Never saw a woman washed ashore."

"There's nothing we can tell about this fellow," said Sean Ban. "Not a damned thing."

"We don't know if he's a sailor or a soldier or a farmer; if he's Irish or English or what! Don't even know what religion he is!" observed Jacob.

"Well, sure doesn't everybody in the graveyard think the same, as the man said."

Sean's response was cut short by the approach of the grandfather with his straining ass. Out of breath and seemingly in ill-humour, the old man was lashing the animal's rump with a yellow-headed ben-weed while Richard tried unsuccessfully to balance on the back of the cart as it ploughed its shapeless furrows on the beach.

"Away outa that, son!" gruffed the grandfather. "Is it not hard enough for my dying old donkey without you making it worse for her?"

"What kept yous? We were starting to think you'd had to shoe the donkey, granda" said Jacob.

John Stewart ignored the taunt. "And who's this poor young fella?" he asked peering down at the body. "Nobody we know from round here anyway. Dear goodness, what happened his eye?"

"There was a crow at him when we arrived," answered Sean Ban. "A grey-back."

A knowing nod of the head. "Wouldn't you know," he said.

Robert John stared down at the blanched face. "God love him. He's some mother's son, the poor fellow."

"He is that. He will be missed around the table in somebody's house."

"I wonder will they ever know what happened to him; where he finished up," said Jacob.

"More than likely not. How would they find out? That's the thing about being lost at sea, they say. The big question that can never be answered. Where did he end up?"

"It must be a terrible way to die, you'd think,"

"Right boys, get round him and lift him onto the cart. We'll take him to the barn and he can lie there until the police and the priest make up their minds what to do with him," said Robert John, taking control and gripping the corpse firmly by the left arm.

"Father Dunleavey won't want to be bothered with him if he's not Catholic, and we've no way of knowing that," offered Sean Ban. "What about your clergyman?"

"Away at Synod meeting in Derry," replied Robert John. "He won't be back till next week, he tells us, so we'll get no help from that quarter."

"And the RIC are going to wash their hands of him, if there's been no reports of a missing person or no foul play about the place, so we might just be left with him," pronounced the grandfather. "It won't be the first time we've had to dig a grave for a seaman on Oileán na Márbh."

"Here, wrap this bit of canvass around him and put that tether in under his oxter. Tie it to the cart at your side to stop him sliding off," said Robert John, handing Sean Ban the end of the rope.

Sean Ban took the rope and stood for a second, looking at the tether. "Mother o God!" he exclaimed, "I forgot all about the heifer!"

"What heifer?" asked Jacob.

"Our roan heifer. I was bringing it out to the Point to your bull. That's what I was doing when I came on this fellow. I had it on a tether. My father will kill me for I let go of it."

"Frank will hardly kill you, Sean," smiled old John Stewart. "Sure he's the mildest mannered man in the Rosses."

"Maybe, but he'll not be pleased, especially after the time it's taken me already. And I still have to catch the heifer, once I find her."

"Where'd she go, Sean?" asked Robert John.

"I've no idea! Must've headed away to look for the bull by itself."

Granda John smiled wryly. "Well, if she found him I would say it's going to be twin calves you'll be having by this time."

The corpse now lay face down on the rough, sloping floor of cart, the cold flesh of its belly grating on the raw oak timber. The donkey leaned into its harness and the men helped push the load through the softer sand towards Condy's Well at the end of the beach.

As strange a procession as had ever been seen on An Tra Ban.

The Hooded Crow cawed hoarsely in defeat. Its grey head jerked back and forward a few times in protest or resignation. Then it stretched those charcoal wings and flapped itself from its boulder perch into the air to continue reconnaissance for scavenging opportunities elsewhere.

Chapter 4

The Washing of Hands

The sound of the oak-panelled grandfather clock dominated the atmosphere of the hall in the Parochial House. Sean Ban wasn't used to such constant, invasive noise; he wondered how a person could sleep anywhere within the sound of it. Every wooden thump of it increased an eerie sensation in his mind of doom, of destiny and death; a paradoxical sense of ongoing finality. He stood by the hat-stand, cap twisted in his hands, his short, athletic body tense and awkward. He surveyed the staircase; a lovely piece of work, in darkly-rich mahogany wood. "Whoever made that knew what he was doing," he thought. Not many houses in these parts had staircases, nor had any need of them. One-story cottages on the whole. Except for Captain Arthur Hill's mansion of a hotel beside Dunlewy Lough. Sean Ban wondered what rooms there were upstairs. And what need the priest has of them.

Mrs Gallagher had opened the door for him with her usual economy of conversation and enthusiasm. He never had met anybody who could talk so little and say so much. She did not tell him but somehow he gathered by reading between the lines on her well-tracked face that Father Dunleavey was indeed at home and would see him. "Wait there!" she mumbled, pointing to a small, grubby mat on the floor by the hat stand, and he did, as precisely as the house-keeper commanded. She dragged her lame leg away down the panelled passage beside the staircase towards the kitchen and disappeared to continue whatever vital culinary task had been interrupted.

The big clock tocking. Not tick-tocking, just the low, bassy, wooden tock-tocking clunk. "What happened the tick? Did it get excommunicated from the Parochial House for being too frivolous? Only the more serious tock was permitted," he thought.

He wondered if the priest was in the study beside him to his left and, if so, how did he know he had a visitor? Had he misheard the woman? Was he meant to go in? He stepped forward and listened at the door but heard nothing except the thudding time-piece. Then, from under the staircase, he heard the sound of water gushing and an empty, metal bucket being

set down roughly on the stone-flagged floor. A small wooden door creaked open and Father Dunleavey stepped out into the corridor, drying his hands on a towel. His long, black coat was hanging dejectedly on a hook behind the door and the white sleeves of his shirt shone in the gloom of the passageway. His waistcoat bulged over the lower reaches of his pear-shaped stomach to the extent that the bottom three buttons had not had any meaningful contact with their adjacent buttonholes in years. Below his dark grey britches, his bootlaces straggled along carelessly behind him on the wooden floor. Sensing that he was being watched, he looked up and saw Sean Ban waiting. He threw the towel inside and closed the door of his water closet.
"I was looking for you when you were out at the Point. What kept you anyway? There's a couple of those ewes need a dose." He crossed the hall and opened the parlour door. "Come in here and tell me what you want. Did you get the heifer served?"
"How'd you know about that, Father?" Sean asked of the older man's back as he bustled on into the room.
"Have you never noticed that I'm a priest? Sure I know everything that goes on in this God-forsaken parish and don't you ever let that slip your mind." He shifted a couple of chairs with his knees as he spoke and then stooped to lift a scattered newspaper off the floor, folding it into a tidier form and placing it on a small, ornately carved table beside a comfortable looking, green-upholstered sofa. "So, did the boul heretic bull do its dirty business for you?"
"To be honest, I don't know," confessed Sean sheepishly, following him with some reluctance into the parlour and getting his first sniff of its particular smell, a dusty dampness that cried out for an opening of the windows which looked out to the tide, ebbing and flowing in the estuary.
"You don't know? How do you not know? Did you not take it out to that bull o' Stewart's?"
"I did but…….I found a dead body along An Tra Ban."
The clergyman looked at him in surprise for a second. "You found a dead body along the white strand?" he echoed, as if to make sure he had heard everything correctly, as if to give himself time to process this unusual nugget of information. "What sort of a body are you talking about?"
"A man; a young fellow about the same age as myself. Just lying on the sand."

"A sailor likely, do you think?" quizzed the priest.

"I don't think so," said Sean, "At least we couldn't tell.....there was no way of knowing."

"Who's the 'We'? Who went with you? What do you mean you couldn't tell?"

"I went and got the Stewarts. We took the corpse up to their barn for the night, to see what to do about it," said Sean. "And we have no way of telling what he is because….. because he was wearing no clothes or anything."

"Ah!" said Father Dunleavey thoughtfully. "No clothes on him. Nothing at all?"

"Not a stitch, Father. Naked as a baby."

"What sort of man goes into the sea with no clothes on him?" puzzled the clergyman. "Either he was swimming that way and got washed out or….. and this is the more likely story…. since there aren't many fellows about who'd be at that game, thank God. No Sean, my guess would be that the reason he has taken off his clothes before jumping into the sea is that he didn't want anybody to identify him. What do you think? An anonymous suicide is what I'm thinking. That's the only explanation."

A short silence and then Sean Ban said, "That's likely what it is, Father; and none of us could see it. He doesn't want anybody knowing him. Must have just wanted to disappear."

"Looks like that to me."

The priest sat down on the sofa and leaned back, arms behind his head, his pot-belly rolling back on the thighs of his bandy legs which he spread ridiculously wide. Sean stood awkwardly in his glare. "Now what did you want me for?"

Sean shuffled and looked down at his cap which had by now stopped twisting in his nervous hands. He thought it was obvious why he was here but Father Dunleavey was playing some sort of game with him. "To tell you about the body. You'll want to see it surely? Before you bury him like?"

"That's where you're wrong, young Mr Sweeney. I won't be seeing "it". Nor will I be burying "him". I have enough to be doing with my own flock, and I don't just mean my parishioners either," he ranted. "Sit down there son and listen and learn."

He pointed to a high-backed chair by the table and Sean obeyed stiffly, wishing by this stage that he was elsewhere in the parish, in the county. Father Dunleavey continued. "You will no doubt be wondering why. Well, let me enlighten you. A man washed up on An Tra Ban without so much as the consideration of a pair of trousers to protect his nakedness is making a statement to me. He is saying this to me. One, he is no member of the Roman Catholic church… if he was he would be showing more respect for the laws of God and human decency by covering himself from the gaze of the world; two, he is trying to hide his identity, and successfully too, so he has shown himself to be ashamed of the Christian name he was given in the holy sacrament of baptism; if he's a Christian at all, that is; and three, he has separated himself from his God by taking into his own hands the right to end his own life. It is a suicide, clear as day. As such, the person concerned has shown no respect for the eternal principle of our faith, that life is given by God and can only be taken by God. So he has separated himself from the church, whatever church that is, and from its holy ordinances; he has denied himself the right to a Christian burial. And as such, he has nothing to do with me."

The clock beyond the door was suddenly battering loud in the silence as Sean Ban sat thinking of what to say. Eventually he simply said, "Right!" and left it at that.

"You may see if your friends on the Point can get their clergyman to bury the stranger. He likely will have no objection. He would bury anyone he can get. Take him over to Hill's graveyard in Bunbeg and sure nobody will be in a bother about it."

"That's not going to work either; the Stewarts tell me he is away in Derry for a week at some church meeting. Long meeting, if you ask me, and too long to be leaving this body stinking in a barn." Sean Ban sensed that the conversation had been closed.

Father Dunleavey sat quiet for near enough a full minute before sitting forward with a start which drew Sean's eyes back up from the floor and his mind back from wondering if he should ask another question or just get up and leave.

"Would you like a cup of tea, Sean?" His body slanting forward, hands on knees, in a manner that boded no argument.

"No, no, I wouldn't…. I'm alright Father, thanks," he stammered.

"You would. Good." He smiled schemingly, then going to the door he bellowed, "Tea, Mrs Gallagher, for the two of us!"

Sean stood up and protested, "I said "No" Father, I'm needing to be going ….I just came to see about the…."

The long arm of the cloth firmly on his shoulder. Back down onto the chair with a slight jolt. He didn't even like tea. Tea with the clergyman he liked even less.

"What about your father, Sean? Just the same?"

"Aye, much the same as he's been these past two years. Hardly ever out of bed with the pains. And when he is, it's not for very long. Any work at all around the yard and he's done."

"Ah, poor Frank. That rheumatism! It's a curse of a disease, and that's a fact. And what about Dermot? Any news from America?"

"Aye, the odd letter every now and then. He's alright I think."

"Good," said the priest and then seemed to drift off in his own thoughts, eyes looking out over Sean's head to the evening sky.

"Something I want to talk to you about, Sean."

"What's that Father?" wondered the younger man.

"We'll wait until the tea comes. Have you heard anything from your friend Johnny O'Donnell?" asked Dunleavey.

"Not me personally, but he's sent money back to Maggie Dan, along with a wee note that I had to read to her."

"Aye, I heard that. But that was weeks ago, was it not? Nothing since?"

Sean scratched his forehead as he tried to recall when his friend's letter had come. "Must be weeks ago alright; I can't rightly remember when," he said.

"What did he say? Is he getting on alright?"

Sean was cautious but answered openly, "He's doing grand I think. He didn't say much. The people he's working to are decent enough I believe; he has a clean place to sleep and plenty of porridge and spuds to eat. He'll be home before Christmas."

"Good!" replied the priest. "He's a good strong chap but innocent of himself; you'd hate to see him being exploited or not getting the right money. What sort of money did he send his mother?"

"I don't honestly know. I didn't count it." The thought of his friend Johnny as "innocent of himself" amused Sean greatly but he showed nothing of this reaction, thinking, "Innocent is he? Little do you know. And I know right well why you are asking about how much money he's sending home, you greedy oul reprobate."

A defensive shift back on the sofa and the clergyman said, "No, of-course you didn't, Sean. I was just wondering. Where's that tea at? That woman of mine is slowing down over the years you know."

"So what did you want to talk to me about, Father?" Sean's confidence and impatience were returning in equal measure. "For I'd need to be going."

The priest looked at him from under his bushy white eyebrows for a few seconds, eyebrows that reminded Sean of a couple of wisps of sheep's wool caught on a barbed wire fence and blowing in the breeze. He was remembering that "Eyebrows" was one of the nicknames the boys used to call him after he arrived as the new parish priest when the clergyman suddenly said, "What do you think about the railway?"

"What railway?" Surprise and consternation now joining impatience in his voice.

"What railway? Mother o' God listen to him! The blessed Letterkenny to Burtonport Extension Railway that I have been agitating about for the last half dozen years. Have you all been asleep up there on the mountain? The railway that is going to change our lives here in the Rosses; going to bring a bit of trade and prosperity to you poor, miserable, bog-dwelling paupers."

Sean Ban resented his tone and it showed in a darkness around his eyes. "That's your affair, you and Lord Hill and the business people in the towns. It's got nothing to do with the likes of me," he said gloomily.

"That's where you are wrong, so wrong, Sean Ban. It has everything to do with you. Sure weren't we just talking about your friend Johnny, away working his guts out in the County Derry or wherever he is; there's dozens like him from around here. Young men with so much to offer their own community. But the way that the local economic situation is here, they have to travel every spring to work in Scotland or the Lagan just to send enough money back to support their families at home. Look at how many men of this parish have emigrated to America, for God's sake. Instead of exporting fish we export people, young people, the best resource we have. You yourself are trying to scrape a living from a couple of acres of scraggy bog on Ranahuel mountain, dragging your heifer out to the Point because none of your own kind in the district can afford a bull."

"So?" retorted Sean Ban. "It's always been this way. It's our way of life. It's all we know."

"That's my point," continued Father Dunleavey, getting up stiffly and starting to pace the floor. "While you sit here in your ignorance, stuck in your 'way of life', some of us have been fighting the Board of Works and the Government with every bit of energy we have to try to get some development into this dead-end of a parish. That's why I am so passionate about this railway extension. Just think of the work it's going to bring to the area. Fellows like Johnny won't have to go east to Derry or anywhere else. He'll be able to get a job here that'll keep him going for several years. You too if you wanted it, if you weren't stuck to the farm on account of your father. If we get the go-ahead for the extension, there's every chance it'll come in this direction on its way to the Port; they'll need all the labourers they can get to level the route and put down the track. Then they'll need maintenance men and gate-keepers and the like. Two years ago the line to Glenties opened up and sure look what it's done for the parish there. Far less young ones having to leave, more employment in the area. And there will be jobs here too, later on, as our economy starts to pick up."

"What sort of economy would ever pick up around here? Sure it's the poorest area in Ireland."

"Exactly! You make my point for me, don't you see!" The Priest warmed to his argument like the amateur politician that he was. "North West Donegal is officially the worst of all the Congested Districts. Cloughaneely parish, Gweedore parish, the whole of the Rosses. We need the railway to bring jobs to the area. You see the fish that we catch all along this coast? The railway will be able to transport them fresh to the cities of England within a couple of days where now they take several days by steamer."

"Great! The English will get fresh fish out of us." Sean's sarcasm rose like bile. "As well as everything else they get out of us. How is that supposed to help us?"

The Priest was undeterred. "There will be work for local women, gutting them and packing them, in places like Burtonport and Bunbeg. Save our girls having to walk to Strabane to the hiring fairs to look for work."

"Aye!" retorted Sean dryly, "Now they'll be able to take the train to Strabane."

"They won't need to if they have a job making carpets or clothes here in the west. Knitting clothes for the markets in Dublin and Belfast and the cities of England." enthused Father Dunleavey.

Sean held his peace, eyes to the window.

"And what's more, the railways will bring more travellers and tourists from the far-away places to spend money in our district. So money flows this way from the better-off areas in the east, rather than the other way around, don't you see?"

"Sure what is there here to spend money on? They'll stay in Hill's Hotel and catch his trout and salmon; he'll make money out of them but I can't see it doing the ordinary people much good."

"Agh, Sean Ban Sweeney. You're so short-sighted. Who'll be making the food for these tourists, or making their beds and cleaning up after them, or rowing them out on Dunlewey Lough? You can rest assured it won't be Lord Arthur Hill anyway, will it? Ordinary people will get the chance of work, all over the place, just you wait and see."

Sean pursed his lips as he thought about this. "What stage is it at now? Sure there's no guarantee that they are going to give the go-ahead for this extension anyway."

"No, that's where you're wrong. The Grand Jury of Donegal gave its blessing in July. Now there might be an appeal to the Dublin authorities, I hear; from various objectors. But after all their promises and discussions it's going to be hard to back out of it now. Sure they've had a party of surveyors going over the whole route for the last six weeks; did you not hear tell of them? They were in Kerrytown and Meenbanad a week or two ago, not three mile over the bog from your own place. They're just finished and away back to Dublin to write their report."

"Well, good luck to them. I was too busy to be noticing them," said Sean, standing up to leave, shaking out his stiff limbs like someone about to break into a jig. "Is that all you wanted to talk to me about, Father?" he asked.

The priest looked at him strangely. "Where the hell is that tea?" he shouted. Then he smiled, a milky undertaker's sort of knowing smile, and said more quietly, "Sit down again Sean. I want to talk to you about ……. about Annie!"

The name hung between them like a wreath of freezing fog on a January morning. Sean swallowed his shock and tried to cover his rising tide of embarrassed annoyance by studying the faded sea-scape water-colour above the side-board.

"The oul bastard," he thought, "He's set me up. And I have to survive this, and his railway lecture, and his blasted tea." He cleared his throat and said, "What about Annie?" It came out far too high-pitched, too tense, the exact opposite of what he was after. He wished it was himself was dumb instead of Annie. "Are you not thinking of marrying her soon?"

"Jasus! As stark as that," thought Sean, standing motionless like he'd just been thumped in the chest. "The man has as much tact as his knackered oul mule."

A little rapping at the door as the tea arrived on a time-stained, silver tray. Good timing, for once. Thinking time. "Should I make a run for it, now that the door is open?" he thought, but his legs refused to obey this instinctive urge. Instead he sat down again, reluctantly. The Gallagher woman gave him a small cup of dark black tea, full to the top, and he wished it would stop vibrating on the stupid wee saucer he had to hold in his hand. He had always wondered what was the point of these saucers that the better-off people put below their china cups; now he thought he knew. To catch the wash of tea he was jibbling over the rim. He was glad of the saucer, for all its rattling in his hand. He drank quickly, to get it over with and get out of there; too quickly. The brew was just off the range and the heat in it caught him unawares. He spluttered the first mouthful back into the cup and onto the saucer. The priest looked over with a hint of amusement but said nothing. Neither did Sean Ban. He could think of nothing to say and he was hoping furiously that the question had somehow dissolved into the musty parlour air and joined the other ghosts of pointless conversations floating around in the house. He was to be disappointed though, and the clergyman picked up the thread of his unwanted counsel as soon as the door closed behind the limping old housekeeper.

"Look, I know this is a difficult thing for you to talk about, but you have to admit that it's not something you haven't thought about. I'm right, am I not?" No answer from Sean, looking down into his tea, his tongue feeling gingerly around the scalded skin of his mouth. "Let me tell you how I see the situation. The girl is what? Seventeen or eighteen? She has a problem; she's had it all her life. Her father's dead a long time.... She's never had a father, or at least one that she can remember. Her mother's not getting any younger, her grandmother will soon go to a better place, please God. Her brother will most likely work somewhere far away from here, unless we get the railway and he gets a job on it. What's going to become of her? She is going to need somebody to take care of her."

"And why do you think that should be me?" interrupted Sean, an edge of bitterness in his voice.

"Because it will be you. I have no doubt it will be you. You have been close to her since she was at her mother's knee. You are the only friend she has got; and you're far too good a fellow to abandon her, if you want me to tell you the straight truth."

Sean sat head down, silent in his entrapment. A cold, dark wave of despair rose up over him. After a moment, strategically left empty of words by the priest, he said, "Of-course I will look after her....but I won't marry her, Father."

"Why won't you marry her? What have you got against marriage?"

"I have nothing against marriage; how could I have anything against marriage? It would be like saying I don't agree with eating. Sometime in the future I probably will get married. But I can't marry Annie ama...." He cut off the word like it was a nettle on his tongue.

"What did you say?" Father Dunleavey sat forward abruptly.

"I didn't say it! I didn't say anything!"

"You were going to say "Annie amadan", you worthless git!" Dunleavey was genuinely angry. "Amadan...a simpleton. A fool. Annie's no fool. She can't talk. The girl can't help it, she was born that way, and you have no cause to be adding that nickname to her like the common village ejits do. Do you think she chose to be like that, do you? Isn't it bad enough her not having a word in her mouth without you taking that word in yours to be describing her. And you the best hope she has. Your mother would be disgusted by you. Brid Sweeney didn't bring you up to disrespect people like that."

"I didn't mean anything by it. Everybody knows her as Annie amadan, the same way that I'm Sean Ban. She knows it herself and she doesn't mind."

"Oh right, so she hasn't said a word about it, is that it? No complaints from her?" His priest's sarcasm wounded him and put him deeper into the brown bog-hole he was drowning in. Father Dunleavey continued. "So that's what you think about her then? You've thought that all along? When you'd be working with her up on the mountain, watching her bending over lifting the turf? Slapping the midges on her bare arms and you laughing at her? You'd be thinking to yourself, 'She's just a stupid lassie who can't talk.' And when you take her walking to Mullaghdearg strand and sit tight beside her on the top of the sand-hill watching the sun setting over Cruit Island? You're thinking all the time, 'I'm just being kind to this poor handicapped girl, 'cause let's face it, she's just dumb and daft and can do nothing but play a whistle to herself! Annie amadan, God love her!'"

"I don't think that. It's not like that." Sean protested quietly.

"How do you think of her then?"

Sean Ban shrugged his shoulders, said nothing and waited for the interrogation to end.

"Let me ask you this, Sean. Do you like Annie?"

Indignantly, "Of-course I like her."

"Would you go further? Would you say you love her?" pursued the priest.

"Do I have to answer this?" Sean stirred forward in his seat. "I need to be going."

"Answer my question!" It was a firm command and hard for the younger man to resist without being disrespectful, rude even. After a pause he murmured a response.

"Annie's always been like a sister to me; if I love her, it's like she's my sister."

The clergyman bored on into the nub of his case. "Now think about this next question, Sean Ban, and before you answer it remember that I have been hearing your confession since your confirmation when you were nothing but a snotty-nosed wee lad from the bogs o' Ranahuel. Think about that and be honest with yourself, and with me as your priest."

Sean looked up at him, an even deeper sense of dread arising around his throat. Why had he not just run out when he had the half chance? He felt resentment boiling up in him at the turn this conversation was taking. "Just shut your ears and your mouth for a minute," he spoke to his inner consciousness. "Don't let him trap you any further. Don't let him push you into saying anything stupid. He's too damned clever. Just be calm and careful."

The priest struck on with it. "Have you ever thought of Annie in a way that you shouldn't have? Like in a way you wouldn't be thinking about your sister?"

"What do you mean by that?" Sean instantly regretted speaking. In his mind, "Didn't you tell yourself to shut up? What are you doing encouraging him to go on, with a daft question like that?"

"Annie is seventeen. She is turning out to be a very pretty lass, Sean. Very nice hair. Lovely blue eyes. Her figure's filling out. She's not a girl any longer, she's a young woman and she's ready to be married. Now, I'm asking you, as your priest, have you ever had any impure thoughts about her? Have you lusted after her, at any time, in any way? Have you ever touched her in a way that you wouldn't want Maggie Dan to see you doing? And before you worry any more about what way you're going to answer my questions, I want you to stop. Stop there! You don't have to answer the question to me. I don't want to hear your answer, because I know full well already what it would be, if you were being honest. So don't say another word to me, but talk to yourself. Tell yourself the answer to the question I asked you. Go on, sit there quiet for a minute and answer the question to yourself.... Don't say a word."

He got up and went to the window. "And I'm going to stand here and give you a minute to think about it, alright?"

The fustiness was nearly choking him, a decaying smell like that left in a room by long-dead flowers. He felt he was a fly entangled against its better judgement in what should have been a fairly obvious web. He glanced quickly at the black back of the priest, blacker against the late evening sun demanding entrance at the window. The dust formed iridescent veils in the thin shafts of light which eluded the cleric's sentry-like bulk. Sean waved his cap viciously through the closest of these and watched the particles dance madly for a second before settling sedately again into the staleness of the atmosphere. He thought nothing of Annie. That could take care of itself in the course of time. He thought instead of entrapment. He felt the burden of the priest's words, yes, but also of the expectation of those he loved. And he tore at it like he would at a garment infested with crawling lice against his skin. He swiped the dust veils again and stood up abruptly. Father Dunleavey turned from the view of the sun across the full tide in the estuary beyond. He waited for Sean to speak, but no words came. Sean's calves pressed back against the seat of the chair like he was stuck to it. He did not look at Dunleavey. Then he moved slowly towards the door.

"You know what you should do, don't you Sean?" the voice followed him into the hall. He didn't notice the clock. "Thanks for the tea, Father," he muttered and, leaving the front door open behind him, walked mechanically out into the orange autumn evening.

Chapter 5

A Slow Night Air

By the time he reached Maggie Dan's, Sean was aware of a dull tiredness in his legs; he'd covered a lot of ground in the course of this eventful day. His walk back to Ranahuel from the Parochial House had taken him along the side of the estuary, the long way round by the hump-backed bridge over the narrowest stretch. Had the tide been out, he would have waded the shallow water and crossed the mud-flats, where the blackened stumps and roots of long-dead fir trees fingered up from the underlying peat like drowning men clutching at air. That would have taken half a mile or more off his journey and at the same time would have cooled his aching feet. But you couldn't risk it at full tide. Not with the memory of Finnbar Murphy fresh in your head. Why Finnbar ever thought he could swim across the inlet to Rannafast, and in the middle of the night, was beyond understanding; he hadn't been a great swimmer at the best of times; ah, but "in drink" nothing was beyond Finnbar, especially on a stout-anointed Saint Patrick's Day when he felt he could near enough walk on water, never mind swim in it. And now he lay in the cemetery behind the church in the village with the summer flowers fading above him.

A skull-like full moon had risen from behind the hill, a huge slice of turnip with darkened hollows gouged in its flesh; it hung in a mackerel sky between bars of bottle-green and smudged purple cloud and made him think of Halloween and the candle inside the scobed-out vegetable. He'd met not a soul on the road home and now he stood undecided at the end of O'Donnell's short lane, looking down on the low struggle of a cottage. Both sections of the half-door were shut against the night air and he could see a flickering candle-light in the small, square panes of the kitchen window. They would both be in the kitchen, he thought; mother and daughter, draining away the dregs of the day in some dimly-lit task. Not a word between them, for Maggie Dan had little to say to anybody and even less to Annie. He understood the feeling from years of experience.

The hillside was very still; he stood listening to the near silence, oblivious to the low, incessant noise of waves washing the beaches, breaking against the rocks in the middle distance and churning the banks of rounded stones and pebbles trapped in the horseshoe-shaped bays. He didn't hear it; it was just there as the constant and pervasive drone which the people of the shore lived their lives against, natural as the sea-smelling air. Only when a storm was raging might a neighbour notice the roar of the waves assaulting rock and remark, "The sea is fairly battering down there today!"

Still he stood, his tongue running around the sensitive areas of his mouth which had been scalded by the priest's unwelcome cup of tea. He waited for himself to know what to do next. Normal instinctive behaviour was now complicated by the import of the clergy's words; he was surprised at himself, at the sharpness of this newly focussed inner struggle. As he watched he thought he saw a faint light in the window of the one bedroom of the house, Annie's room. "It's early for her to be going to bed," he thought. He saw the shadow of her briefly and indistinctly through the tiny opaque window; he stood still, resisting the temptation to which he normally yielded, the Priest's sermon now a barrier between him and the natural course of action which had so often taken him closer to that window at around this time of night. Not that he had ever watched long enough to have his curiosity satisfied; it was another of those situations which seemed so hopelessly typical of his feelings about Annie. Fascination and self-disgust.

"What to do next?" he thought. "Go home or go in?"

From behind him an owl loomed up in the dusky stillness, its snub-nosed, shadowy bulk taking him by surprise. It deviated in its course and flew past, clear and intent on its nocturnal mission. Looking back at Annie's window he saw her head silhouetted by the candle and guessed that she was watching for him in the little light that the day had left in it. And he watching her, watching for him. He lifted his hand to wave but she disappeared and the candle went out. Seconds later the cottage door opened and he waited to see if she would appear; she didn't; just an open door. Maggie Dan's voice from the dull darkness of the house, "What are you doing opening that door to be letting the midges in?"

Sean stirred and headed towards the mother and daughter, and the growl of the dog welcomed him from the bottom of the yard. He shuffled self-consciously into the kitchen and pushed the door shut behind him. The fire in the hearth was all but out and Maggie Dan made no attempt to re-kindle it at this late hour. He sat down on a three-legged stool beside it, opposite the woman of the house. There was little conversation, just a stilted version of the tale he had already told the priest, with a few questions from Annie's mother. When he mentioned that the body had been naked she quickly covered the impact of this revelation with the strange observation that, "He must have been very cold in the sea!" A motherly sort of concern, he thought.

"Aye, he would've been that," he said, disguising a smile. Annie didn't appear to be listening anyway. She just sat on the settle bed in the shadowy corner, her head tilted down and her hair hiding her eyes in characteristic manner. Above her head, last year's St Brigid cross; its dried-out rushes had gathered a few dusty cobwebs but it had the distinction of being the only wall decoration in the kitchen.

The silences were winning over the conversation and during them he watched Annie from the corner of his eye until she suddenly got up and wandered in that aimless way of hers to the other room. She closed the door behind her and Sean Ban said, "What's wrong with her?"

"How would I know the answer to that? How would anybody know the answer to that? She's just herself, Sean, and there's no telling what's going on in her mind, whether she's happy or sad, or what she's thinking in that head of hers; that's the way it has always been, as you well know, and the chances are that's the way it will always be, for I see no betterment for her now at her age."

"I just meant....she wouldn't be usually disappearing like that..."

"Well, why don't you go and ask her?" Maggie Dan couldn't help the touch of annoyance in her voice, thinking, "Can't he be the right young ejit at times, for all his goodness."

Sean pushed open the flimsy door and, bending his head down below the low lintel, stepped a little way into the bedroom. "Annie, I brought you this shell from An Tra Ban. It's got great colours in it," he said into the darkness, taking the razor-shell from the depths of his jacket pocket and holding it out to her.

She stands with her back to him looking out through the window and she doesn't turn for him; there is a distance to her bearing that he doesn't recognise, a resistance which, expert and all as he is from reading the subtleties of her body language for so many years of growing up together, he is aware of but cannot understand. She senses him wait; her head goes down and her whistle comes to her lips and when the tune comes, a slow air, of her own making, confused and painful, it says to him, "Go away and leave me be; I am at a place where not even you can reach me." And it's a long tune, modal, haunting and not without beauty, but why wait for the end of it when there will be nothing you can say in response. He throws the shell onto the bed for her. It lands with a rattle on her rosary beads. "Oíche mhaith Annie." He breathes his "Goodnight" with something between resignation and exasperation and shuts the door slowly behind him, the dry screigh of its hinges strangely complimenting the high cadence of the whistle beyond it.

He walked slowly towards his home through the hushed night air; the last of the midges in his hair unnoticed; swamped by thoughts of her.
"What is it about her that has me so held by her?"
Eyes the blue colour of Forget-me-nots, that is if you could ever see them, the way she has always hidden behind that veil of hair. And if you do see them looking at you, you don't forget them in a hurry. You wanted them looking at you, saying something to you the way you could read something from most people's eyes. Not Annie though! Blank as the space between two summer clouds; blank and beautiful. Eyes looking through you more than at you, he thought. You wanted to put a story in them, a laugh or a tear, a bit of life; but the absence of response was painful to him, more now than ever.
The way her skin was tight on the shape of her face now, now that she was that bit older and had lost the girlish plumpness. Pale, creamy skin, stretched over those high cheekbones and the jaw the way that the skin of a bodhran would be when you pressed the palm of your hand or your knuckles against it from the inside. It was a pretty face, perfect lines that you would think somebody had really taken their time over the planning of, and a bit of care in the putting together of; the proportions, the distances between the parts just so perfect; the eyes just the right space apart, not like some of the girls around the Rosses whose eyes seemed to have been thrown at their faces from a

distance and just stuck where they landed. Some of the lasses around here you'd meet in the Main Street in Dungloe and you'd take one look at their wee squashed up faces, God love them, smiling at you the way silly lasses do, and your eyes would bounce away like waves bouncing off a cliff face, and you'd be suddenly gazing up the street, taking an interest in whether or not O'Doherty's was open at the top end of the town.

The shape of her chin and the arc of her eyebrows, and that pretty nose; the dimples by her mouth that you really only notice when she's playing that whistle of hers; and that mouth. That mouth that never had he heard a single word from; those lips of gentle red, like the petals of a wild rose that, despite his long attraction to her, he had never had the courage to kiss. The way the lips were always just slightly parted in the centre, a small dark space seemingly always ready for her whistle. He had often fantasised that maybe if he was to kiss those lips he would somehow break the spell of her silence which had bound her tongue since childhood; he wondered what her first words would be. Would she tell him that she had been waiting for that kiss to free her, like in a fairy-tale, and that she loved him and wanted him the way he wanted her? But he knew in his heart of hearts that such a fantasy was pointless, that she could never respond to his kiss in the way that normal girls would. Not that he had a great deal of experience of normal girls. A couple of times there had been a courting session in a darkened alley in Dungloe after a dance, or after a night in Sullivan's public house, and once after a wake in Keadue when himself and Johnny had found themselves walking the strand with a couple of grand-daughters of the deceased, two busty Letterkenny girls. While Johnny headed his solemn, dark-haired lassie up into the sand-hills, he himself had had a bit of a tangle with the shorter blonde one who giggled a lot; she brought more to the notion of a walk on the beach than he had bargained for; he had told Johnny afterwards that he was afraid he was going to be eaten alive. He had been to dozens of wakes in his time, as was the country custom in Donegal, but this was one that stuck in his mind, one of the more productive he had been to.

How delicate and vulnerable Annie was by comparison. The characteristic way she flicked her hair with just a wee toss of her head when she was in the middle of a tune; that was definitely when she was at her most animated, ironically when she was away in her musical world, the whistle in her fingers a natural extension of her hands, her body. Her body! The tallness and shape of her. He had noticed such a difference in her when he went to collect her from her grandmother's cottage in Cloughglas, a few days ago. He had been waiting her return like you would wait for a letter from America, having not set eyes on her for near enough two months, the whole summer, the time she was at her prettiest. In the end he had to go and get her himself, at Maggie Dan's request, her coming along as well to see the ageing grandmother. As he had done to deliver Annie to her granny back in July, he had again borrowed the pony and trap from his uncle, Joseph Cavanagh, to bring her back home; arriving in the late afternoon, they had discovered that Annie was nowhere to be found. The old granny had said she could be out along the coast; apparently she had taken to walking the cliffs and bays of an afternoon, if the weather was good. So Sean Ban took a walk out himself to see if he could find her. Find her he did, but only after a long search, and after he had shouted for her. He was still a way off when he saw her appear over the sand-hills; he saw her before she saw him and he stared at her like he had never seen her before. Whatever it was she was wearing wasn't the usual dark, heavy, dowdy material her mother used to make her clothes with, cloth more suited to a fifty year old spinster who was trying to avoid attention. This dress was the colour of a September oat-field, matching that of her hair. It seemed to be light and thin of itself, because the breeze was catching it, blowing it back against Annie's body so you could see her shape, the breasts and the thin wee waist of her and it clinging to her legs as she walked. But what he noticed most was the face, because her blonde hair, grown longer than he'd seen it, was blowing back behind her, like the mane on Cavanagh's pony when they were trotting west along the country lanes today. And she didn't seem to be aware that her hair wasn't covering her face and hiding her eyes in the manner which was her habit. Her defences seemed to be down that day in Cloughglas and Sean Ban realised he had never seen her like that before, not in all the long years of growing up together. There was something of the pony about her, not just the mane of flying hair but the confidence, the stride of those long legs across the sand, the figure and poise of her and the swivel of her hips as she leaned into the slope up from the beach and into the breeze pressing against her; she seemed oblivious to his presence and to the effect she was having on him after this summer of separation.

"Is this the Annie I have played with since we were children?" he remembered thinking in the trap on the way back home, his eyes averted from her in a most self-conscious way for the first time in his life. "The Annie I have talked to near enough everyday for the past seventeen years? The Annie who'd dawdle along beside me around the lanes of Ranahuel and go for walks on Mullaghdearg strand? I have been either half-asleep or too close to her to see her beauty, but now it speaks to me in a way that she never has been able to. Probably never will be able to. But what am I to do with it? She's not in the least bit aware of what she's doing to me. And I can't tell her either because it's not fair to her. She can't respond, like a normal girl could. And although she looks like a normal girl she's not normal in the way other girls are….God, what am I saying? She looks anything but a normal girl….she looks like the prettiest girl I have ever seen or am ever likely to see. And that's the pain of it. I can't tell her, it wouldn't be fair. I can't court her….it would be taking advantage. She can't respond to anyone else's feelings, never has been able to, locked away in her own wee world of silence with no way out."

Sean Ban went to his lumpy bed that night but not to sleep, despite the tiredness that was on him, and it wasn't the lumps that were keeping him awake. Even when he did drift into slumber he found himself reliving some of the events of the day in that dreamily distorted world of skewed images and half truths. Thoughts diffused and metamorphosed into a kind of reality. Memories began to reincarnate themselves, taking on the substance of a three dimensional painting, one with an inbuilt time signature which warped and leapt forward without regard for normal linear convention. He was back on the stippled canvas of the white strand and he was grappling with some sort of seal-like creature on the sand, fighting against the oily coldness of its wet pelt as he struggled in vain to turn it over. Why wouldn't it turn over? Why did it keep slipping in his hands? Father Dunleavey was somehow present, muttering inaudibly, the proximity of his knobbly blackthorn stick to Sean's face an annoying distraction. What wouldn't he like to do with that stick? When the thing on the beach did eventually flop over onto its back he was startled, horrified to see that it had the face of his long-dead cousin. Colm was looking up at him after all these years, even though, incongruously, his eyes were closed. Close-cropped hair now, but other than that he looked very like himself. The Priest was drawing everybody's attention to that fact as he blessed the drowned youth. "He looks very like himself, doesn't he?" he droned amidst his prayers and incantations. Annie was there, at the edge of the crowd that had gathered around the body. And strangely he was kneeling in the sea, the waves having gathered around him too. He stood up and he was following Annie. Wading, trudging through the water after the shape of her back as she strode along the strand. Trudging, struggling against the current. The undertow of swirling water. Waves breaking against him, pressing the air out of his lungs. Legs getting heavier, making no progress after her. Boots full of water. Her back to him. Neck. Hips. Breathless. Pumping. Why won't she turn? Look at me? Hair floating like blown smoke. Legs seeming to float too, gliding her over the glisten of the sand. Why is she hurrying? The swing of her. Disappearing. Up over the sand hills, through the tall grass. The colour of her dress blending with the fairness of everything. But he is sinking, into the soft sand now. Battling up the incline, panting, feet slipping back down as soon as he has taken a step up. Getting nowhere. This dreadful recurring feeling of numbing non-fulfilment, of being destined to struggle eternally against the quicksand of clawing failure. Climbing, still dragging one foot after the other up this hill. So steep it must be Errigal mountain itself he is on. And somehow he is on Errigal now but it's not Annie he is following. It's his lost heifer that has somehow strayed beyond the black bull at the Point and must have swam across the estuary to Gweedore and run all the way to Errigal, the stupid animal, and how on earth it ever got this far up the scree slopes of this God-forsaken hill he will never know, but he has to catch the damned beast. Otherwise how is he going to explain its absence to his father. And what has brought his father here to Errigal to be climbing this brute of a mountain with him, and him with a mountain of pain within himself to be climbing every day that he lives? "What are you doing, coming after me, father?" he calls. "Could you not have trusted me and let me go to do this on my own for once?" And now he is standing at the highest point on the mountain and his father is shouting but it is too late and he is falling, falling, falling...... and the light of the morning hits him in the eyes as he springs bolt upright in his bed.

Chapter 6

Shadow in the Water

Jacob Stewart had little heart in his present task, that of digging a grave for the drowned seaman. And to be left on his own to do it while the rest of his family gathered potatoes in the field by the side of the lough, that long, narrow sliver of shining fresh water that split their land in two. Across the evening air he could hear the others at times, laughing and calling to each other as they worked.

This was his first time to dig a grave, for that he was thankful. Local tradition had it that the men of a family undertook that task when one of their number passed away and Jacob had sometimes wondered how he would feel about the job when it came to his grandfather's passing. He was too young to be involved in grave-digging at the time of his grandmother Eliza's death but he did remember the funeral; a sad, slow procession across the fields and lanes to the pier at the east of Carrickfinn; then the coffin placed precariously in a fishing boat; his father and uncles rowing it cautiously across to Bunbeg for the burial in the Church of Ireland graveyard opposite the old church. Hill's Church and Hill's graveyard, as they were known hereabouts; sixty years ago, the local landlord by that name had been responsible for the construction of a building which doubled as both church sanctuary and school-house. Souls and minds his chief concerns apparently; the bodily welfare of his tenants could look after itself.

No such luck for this unfortunate sailor, he thought; he'll be laid to rest in the thin, sandy soil of this unconsecrated island, this place apart. Oileán na Márbh lay in a beautiful bay on the jagged western edge of the Carrickfinn peninsula. A tidal island, it stood tall and stubborn in the path of the eternally roaring waves, unable to make up its mind whether it was belonging to the sea or to the land. At low tide it could be reached across a beach of the finest sand but at high tide it was completely surrounded by clear green sea-water. A tall man could just about wade out to it if the tide wasn't too high for him; very few locals were swimmers so if you got yourself stranded on the island after high tide it was either wade, shout until somebody heard you and rowed over for you or stay put until the tide ebbed again. There were plenty of fireside tales of nights having to be spent on Oileán na Márbh; they usually involved a courting couple who had lost track of time, or so they claimed, or a sleepy fisherman who woke to find himself cut off from the beach. The fact that the island was an unofficial graveyard, with the hint of the spirits of its dead still prone to stir of an evening, tended to deter the Stewart children from ever being caught out by the incoming tide.

Oileán na Márbh was indeed the 'island of the dead', but only of a certain class of 'the dead'. For as long as anybody could remember the island had been a burial ground for babies who had been still-born or who had died at birth. During the terrible famine which had brought such pain to the people of the Rosses and had decimated the population of Ireland as a whole during the late 1840ies, a large number of babies in the local parish died at or soon after birth. Not having been baptised before they died, they could not be given a Christian burial or laid to rest in the consecrated ground of a church graveyard. The clergy had firm rules about such matters and the faithful understood that no priest, no matter how sympathetic to the sorrow of the parents, would bury the body. Instead they would advise their parishioners to take the little corpse out to Oileán na Márbh, dig a shallow grave and place the dead infant there to await whatever lay on the other side of Limbo. So the island was a Cillin, a shadowy burial place to serve the needs of those in the whole locality whose bereavement was deemed to be beyond the church's remit of care, spiritual or practical. There were dozens of these Cillins scattered randomly around the Irish countryside. Most seemed to be found in locations that could best be described as marginal places. They would be situated between two town-lands or parishes; 'in-between' places. Appropriate, given the nature of the thinking about the souls of these poor departed ones who ended up being consigned to burial in such peripheral situations. 'In-betweeners' that nobody was prepared to wrap a claim of comfort around, in terms of their state of grace or their eternal destination. And a tidal island like Oileán na Márbh, for all its rugged beauty, was such an ambivalent location. Many's a sorrowing couple had left their baby to the care of the island, to the spray of the ocean swell and the cry of the seabirds.

Jacob had never been present at any of these bizarre ceremonies of-course. He had heard about them though and had been moved and disturbed by what seemed to him the double grief of the family of the deceased child. He had never witnessed the burial of a sailor, or any other adult, for that matter, whose body had been washed up on a nearby shore. He did know that there had been one or two such cases; he had heard his grandfather speak of the body of a 'fir gorm', a black man, who had been washed up somewhere in the estuary; he had been buried without ceremony in the banks below Braade. Now he himself was having first-hand experience of the whole thing, actually digging a grave for that poor, naked fellow who was staring blankly up at the rafters in the barn and was now beginning to create such a stench there that the very animals in the yard were starting to protest.

His father had come with him to the island in mid afternoon when the tide was well out. Over his shoulder he had carried a shovel; his father, in the same manner, a spade. They matched each other stride for long, slow, swinging stride across the beach, their boots kicking up the little spirals of sand left by the hundreds of lugworms; any onlooker would have had no doubt that they were watching a father and son. This would have been confirmed by a closer inspection of the facial features of the two; the teenager shared the same protruding mandible as his father, his dark eyes deep-set in a similar boot-brown complexion.

Robert John had led the way up over the boulders and broken granite rock-face onto the island itself where, in contrast, a carpet of deep, luxuriant grass welcomed them. Less than half an acre in size, Oileán na Márbh was owned by the Stewart family but was never used for grazing in the way their more distant island was; boat loads of sheep were rowed the mile journey out to Inishfree for the summer grass every season and fetched back in the late autumn before the winter storms made such a journey too hazardous. But apart from a couple of wild goats which occasionally held court on Oileán na Márbh, no animals were ever permitted to graze there to enjoy the lush pasture; the dead were left in peace!

"Come over to the far side where there's more of a depth of soil," the father had said. "To the best of my knowledge most of the babies were buried on the south side, nearest the shore and where they get the full circle of the sun; the O'Doherty baby was the last one and it was laid here." He indicated a small green hollow between the rocks. "I remember the mother saying she wanted it buried where they could see it from their front door. Sure their house is at Ballymanus on the shore! Near enough two mile away. Strange the things people will say...."

He had walked on another twenty paces across the spongy surface of the grass, bleached to a flaxen colour by the summer sun and combed flat in one direction by the prevailing western wind.

"I could be wrong but I don't have any recollection of a grave being opened over here next the channel. Not in my time anyway," he had said and he thrust his spade into the turf a few feet from the cliff-edge.

"You're very close to the edge, da."

"Aye, well just take care you don't fall over. You'd better get started if you're to beat the tide," the father advised, turning to go back to join the potato-gatherers.

"What size am I to dig it?"

"What size? You saw the fellow the same as I did. He's about your height and build so.... dig it about the length of yourself."

"Can you not be a bit less gruesome?" Jacob had thought, "I'm hardly likely to be lying down in it to check."

He couldn't say this to his father though; instead he said, "Alright, but....how far will I go down? And what if I hit rock? Or if I come across another....?" Jacob had dropped his shovel and had taken a step or two after his father. "Would you not dig it and I'll go to the field?"

His father had walked on without even a look back at him. "You don't need to go any deeper than two or three feet," he threw back over his shoulder. "You'll have no bother with it for it's nothing but sand, once you get the scraw grass off it; and if you hit rock just start again in a different place. And keep an eye out for the tide coming in."

Jacob was left between task and father and it was a familiar feeling.

It wasn't that it was a particularly difficult job. Once you got through that mat of long grass and the two or three inches of light earth it was pure sand underneath. He dug out lumps of turf about a foot square and set these precisely to one side in an orderly pattern so that they could be placed neatly back over the grave hole after the burial. What a job to be doing! He took the longer-handled shovel and began lifting the sand out, tipping it to the other side. He worked in a steady rhythm with measured enthusiasm, back angled to his task, and his thoughts travelled widely as he worked.

He wondered about this dead fellow. What was the reason for him being washed up on the Carrickfinn's White Strand? What was behind it all? Why no clothes on him? How long had he been in the sea? Where had he come from.... had he been swimming and got washed out? Or was he in a small boat that got coped over by an unexpectedly large wave? Surely there would have been word of it if he had been lost locally. More likely he had come off a ship further out, whether he jumped himself or was thrown over. Maybe that was it....a murder at sea! That would explain the lack of clothes, wouldn't it....they had wanted to humiliate him as well as kill him. But why? What could have been their reason? He looked a civil enough chap, for a corpse anyway, as far as he could judge. Maybe he'd been caught at something terrible and that was the only way to deal with him, strip him and throw him overboard? Quick justice....and then they could say to the authorities that they knew nothing about it, that he must have jumped himself. That would likely be it....either that or a suicide.

But a suicide wouldn't explain why he was naked, would it? Why would a suicide strip off his clothes? Daft! But either way, some poor mother somewhere is going to get the news that her son is missing at sea, believed drowned. That wasn't going to be easy for her. Maybe he had no mother...or father? Maybe he was depressed because he was an orphan and he couldn't face it any more? He wondered if the fellow had left any message, any explanation. "What would the note say? Will it ever get to his mother? Will she ever find out that her son is buried here in Oileán na Márbh? And that I am the one who dug his grave?"

As he worked Jacob started to conduct a conversation in his mind with this imaginary mother. He gave her an account of how the body was found by Sean Ban Sweeney; how they brought it to the farm; how his father had informed a disinterested sergeant of the local constabulary in Bunbeg who had rowed across to take a statement, smoke a pipe and share the latest gossip; he hadn't even asked for the body to be lowered in its hammock from the rafters to have a look at. And then how Robert John had tried and failed to get a clergyman to come to bury the body. That part would be a very difficult blow to her, if she had any Christian belief at all. "But," he was saying in his head, "You couldn't ask for a more beautiful place for your son to be buried than here on this island, surrounded by the little corpses of dead infants; they couldn't be buried in proper graveyards either and sure look at them...never did a thing wrong in their wee lives. This is a special place for him to rest, whatever happened to him and whoever...."

He froze halfway through a thrust in his shovelling. The blade of his shovel had come into contact with something a bit more solid than sand; there had been a rasping sound, not quite the resistance of a stone, definitely not as substantial as the bedrock.

"What have I hit?" he said aloud.

For a while he stood in petrified dread of what he might see if he lifted this shovelful and dumped it on the growing pile of sand by the grave. He talked to himself in his mind.

"Take a hold of yourself, Jacob Stewart. It might be nothing. A lump of stone; or a shell or something. And even if the worst comes to the worst and it is a wee skeleton, sure what harm can it do me?"

He gentled the shovel back out of the sand and dropped to his knees in the trench. Tentatively his hand flicked the sand to left and right until it encountered something more solid; through the grains something white, rounded and smooth like a sea-potato, smaller than the shell of a sea urchin. Hesitant to touch with his fingers, he reached out and pulled a handful of the long autumn grass and used it as a light broom to brush away the remaining sand.

He found himself looking into two tiny, hollow eye-sockets. Lifeless and empty, but strangely serene and beautiful. He felt the dread seeping out of his body, being replaced by a reverent fascination. How could a baby's skull be so small? Is it any wonder it didn't survive. His finger stroked the little, toothless gums in wonderment.

"Maybe never even got to taste your mother's milk, you poor wee thing, whoever you are," he breathed. "Who were you? Who were you meant to be? Were you a girl or a boy? Why did they not put up some sort of headstone for you? You haven't even got the decency of a name. What sort of people are we in this country that we couldn't put a name on you?"

As he spoke he found his hands move into the sand under the little corpse, lifting it slowly out of the shallow grave and holding it up to the clear evening sky, as if in offering. The skeleton started to fall apart immediately and he placed it beside him on the grass, retrieving the scattered fragments of bone and trying in vain to piece it all together again.

"I'm sorry, little one," he said. "I'm not used to this kind of thing at all. You are the first ....", and then he thought, "What am I talking about? As if this baby can hear me. Well, maybe it can, for all I know. For all anybody knows. Maybe its wee spirit is still floating around here somewhere. And where better?"

Surprised by his own tenderness, Jacob resumed his digging with a passion. In a short time the trench was a couple of feet deep and, he guessed, long enough to house his body. He checked by using the length of the shovel, in preference to stretching out either in it or beside it. Satisfied with his first grave-digging achievement, he dug a deeper hole in the middle, about a foot square. Into this hollow he carefully placed the remains of the child; reluctantly he covered it with sand and patted down the bottom of the trench so it would be tidy for its second occupant tomorrow. Then, standing back to survey his handiwork, his eyes strayed beyond the rim of the island down to the sea and the incoming tide. To his dismay he realised that he had lost track of time; the sun had disappeared behind Inishfree to the west; the tide had silently filled the bay. He needed to move quickly unless he wanted to spend the night here on the chilly rocks of Oileán na Márbh. But something else caught his attention and held him fixed in a mesmerised curiosity.

There was a strange dark shadow in the sea!

Below the smooth, unruffled surface he could make out what looked like a grey cloud moving in the deeper water at the mouth of the bay, in the channel between his island and the pier on the mainland. The cloud's edges where ill-defined, a ghostly spectre gliding silently through the depths of that green other-world, moving and changing shape constantly in obedience to some common, exterior brain, some shared social instinct. It reminded him of a flock of starlings in anarchic flight above the farmstead in the purple dusk of an autumn evening.

Jacob realised what he was witnessing and a surge of excitement ran through him, overtaking his feelings of fear and vulnerability at being stranded on the island. This was an unusual sight but he recognised the shadow in the sea. It was, he realised, a shoal of 'seainns'! 'Seainns', the local name for the young fry of pollock or 'glashen'. These were seldom seen in water so close to the shore but once in a while, every couple of years, such a shoal would stray into the bay. Nobody could say why, or what weather or sea conditions brought them in so close to the shallows but tonight was obviously a perfectly suitable night for them to visit here. They tended to stay only for a short time, escaping to the deeper water again long before the turn of the tide.

Jacob's people had a special interest in the seainns. For many generations the Stewarts had watched every autumn on evenings such as this for the arrival of these mysterious little fish in their bay. It provided an ideal opportunity to land a big catch, a huge bonus of tasty rich food to feed the family in the hungry winter months ahead, supplementing the diet of potatoes, fish and the diary produce of their small herd of cattle. But it was all so unpredictable; nights on end one of the Stewarts could sit by the channel, keeping a lookout for such shoals and see nothing; a breeze stirring the surface of the sea made the task a pointless one. Every so often some of the more patient elder members of the family would be lucky and have a sighting; they tended to be more tuned in to the weather clues and the subtleties of the tides; but it was generally a fortunate coincidence that the seainns would be seen. Jacob was delighted to be the witness on this occasion of such a coincidence.

"If I hadn't come across that wee skeleton," he thought, "I would be off the island already and would never have noticed them."

He could barely contain his excitement as he began his descent down the rocky shoulder of Oileán na Márbh. He threw down both shovel and spade; "They'll be safe there until the morning," he said to himself; "I'll have trouble enough getting through this water to the shore without them."

He tore off his boots and left them on a flat rock above the high-water line. The chill of the water took his breath away as he lowered himself into it, thigh-deep at the side and likely to be up to his chest before he reached the beach. Careful to move as gently as possible so as not to disturb the seainns, should they come near, he waded slowly shore-ward. Halfway across it was deeper than he had imagined; he had to fight to keep his mouth above the salty water lapping around his neck. He was scarcely aware of the beautiful pattern of red and black triangles flickering on the water as the swaying surface of the sea reflected alternately the fiery horizon and the dark bulk of the island behind him.

Arriving on the beach, he crept carefully to the shadows of the sandbanks before straightening up. The seawater dripped from his clothes as he ran home, his barefooted sprint reminding him of earlier days of childhood before he graduated to wearing a handed-down pair of leather boots.

Half an hour later, as dusk began to take a firm control of the late September sky, a group of shadowy figures could be seen emerging from the small clachan of houses as the extended Stewart family made their way towards the pier. All carried something; creels, pots, baskets and basins. Robert John had two oars over his shoulder and old John, a twinkle of anticipation lighting his rheumy eyes in the twilight, was helping Jacob and Bobby to carry a large net and an attached coil of rope.

All the family was present, even the neighbouring uncle, William James by name, and not simply because tasks such as this required all available hands to be there to help. More significantly, traditions like this needed to be learned and shared and kept alive for the generations to come, both for good economic reasons and because.... well, because that's what traditions are for; learning, sharing, perpetuating; a vital part of the family's cohesive culture. And they are the best of craic of-course.

Everyone was under strict instructions to stay quiet, to remain in the shadows away from the skyline and to make no sudden movements. The shoal could be spooked so easily by the cry of a careless child and the chance to make a big catch be lost in an instant.

The boys shuffled slowly, noiselessly to the pier with the huge net, while the baskets and containers were set back by the rocks, gape-mouthed in anticipation of swallowing a bountiful fish harvest. Robert John took a long look at the waters of the bay, trying to discover if the seainns were still present, but the growing darkness of the water made it difficult to be sure. The grandfather and William James arrived at the pier carrying the family curragh from its nook in the sandbank, upturned on their heads in the normal fashion of the west of Ireland; in the gloom they looked like some sort of giant crab, the crust of long, black shell on top and spindly, scuttling legs underneath. Effortlessly they righted the canvas-covered craft with long-practised expertise and placed it on the surface of the water with barely a splash.

John Stewart rowed seaward at first, towing the net out across the channel. This was an exercise which, even after his many years and several similar experiences, he still took a great deal of pleasure from. Tentatively he stroked the curragh forward on an almost imperceptible swell, thinking back to a similar night when he was newly married; on that occasion he had headed much too close to the shoal of fish and had disturbed them, possibly with the speed of his craft or with a rough bit of rowing; all he could do was stare down into the water as the millions of small fish streaked below him towards open ocean, leaving behind some open-mouthed and swearing would-be fishermen and a very disappointed new wife. He would not make the same mistake again.

Turning the curragh towards the forbidding shadow of the island he felt the increased tension on the rope as the net dragged through the resisting current; silently, smoothly along the side of the island's cliff-face with barely a ruffle of oar on water, the net now stretched tautly right across the bay. Success was all about stealth and timing. If the seainns were still there they were now doomed.

The curragh was coming closer to the beach. Robert John's waving arms signalled for the two boys on the pier to begin to drag the net towards the shore. He himself helped pull the curragh ashore. It was all a matter of speed and brute strength now. William James plunged out into a couple of feet of water and joined his brother in beginning to pull on the net. Martha ran to help the boys at the other end, Richard out-sprinting her. The grandfather pulled the curragh up on the sand and added his strength to the haul. Slowly the net dragged through the water towards the beach.

"Feels heavy, doesn't it?"

"I think we've got a good catch here," said Robert John.

"Keep pulling! They're not in the creels yet," warned the grandfather. "Don't be counting your chickens."

"What's chickens got to do with it? It's fish we're catching. You're getting confused again, granda," teased Jacob.

But, as the middle of the net emerged in the shallower water, the writhing and jumping of thousands upon thousands of the little fish was confirmation that this was indeed a substantial catch. It rolled up onto the shore like the dark carcass of a beaching whale. The heaps of seainns grew, their tiny bodies splinters of silver light in the gloom of the evening. Whoops of delight rose from the younger members of the family.

Robert John brought them back down to earth.

"Come on boys," he said. "The job's only half done. Get the baskets and start filling them. We still have a load of work to do before morning. Need to get this catch safely into the barn and salted down in barrels."

"What about the body in the barn?" asked Bobby.

"What about the body in the barn?" repeated his father. "He's not going to be in a bother about a heap o' fish down below him, is he now?"

"Dead sailor, dead fish," thought Jacob. "He just can't seem to get away from them."

"I'll go for the donkey!" said grandfather. "We'll need it for the creels."

He hobbled off up over the sandbank and down the lane towards the farmyard feeling a deep sense of satisfaction in his bones. A smile played at the corner of his thin lips and there was a warmth of nostalgic cheeriness in his mind, tinged with just a hint of sadness as he thought, "Agh, but Eliza would have enjoyed that tonight. I wonder how many more I'll see before my time comes?"

Chapter 7

An Island Burial

Unlike the Stewarts, who slept long after their labours of the previous night, Sean Ban Sweeney was up with the cock-crow at dawn. His mother, Brid, wondered at him as he sat by the rough kitchen table.
"What is the hurry on you today?" she asked as he downed a draught of buttermilk from a tin mug, washing down the plain soda farl.
"I have a bit to do before I head over to Carrickfinn."
"What's taking you there again?"
"I need to be at the burying of that fellow I found on the strand," he said. "They're going to lay him to rest on Oileán na Márbh at noon; it's only right that I be there for it. There'll not be many more at it. Not even a clergyman."
"Well," she said, "they can't be burying every Tom, Dick and Harry that washes up on the shore, I suppose. Have you Father Dunleavey's sheep to see to? He was in looking for you again."
"Aye, they can wait. I'll go over to him after I come back. There's likely not a whole lot wrong with them."
"You'd better go to him first. You know what he's like."
"He'll hardly deny me the Mass now, will he?" Sean muttered to his feet as he tugged at his stiff boots. "If he'd just stop trying to run my life for me. Keep his nose out of my business and let me be. An oul ejit, he is."
"That's no way to talk about your priest, son. Your business is his business, that's what a priest is for....giving you good advice and that. Especially if you don't see things for yourself."
Sean straightened up and looked hard at his mother, unruly strands of her curly, grey hair falling over her face as she bent to the cooking pan. "Has he been talking to you?" His brow furrowed in frown.
Brid's eyes stayed low to the pan. "Sure he's always talking to me. What about?"
"About me....you know what I mean."
"He's often talking about you Sean; sure he needed you for the ewes."

"Ah, so that was all he said then? The ewes? Right! Well then, I'd better be off to see about his ewes." and he headed out to the farmyard towards the out-house.

"Did you speak to your father this morning?" Her voice trailing after him like a bad conscience.

"I looked in. He was asleep, I think. I'll talk to him when I come."

He climbed the hill which brooded protectively over the Sweeney homestead, counting and checking the sheep that grazed on the sparse grass between rushes, gorse and heather. From this vantage point he had a wonderful view down over the moorland to the waking village, where yellow-thatched roofs were now beginning to respond to the near-horizontal rays of buttery sunlight seeping in between cloud and distant mountain. He stood for a moment and watched thin tongues of shell-grey turf-smoke from the low-set chimneys of several cottages rising reluctantly, it seemed, almost as an afterthought. Straight up into the still air they rose until, at a common elevation, they seemed to curl off tangentially, as if to lick the pink under-belly of the morning. He went back into action.

By ten o'clock he had accomplished most of what needed to be done around the farmyard, the feeding of housed animals, the forking out of their soiled bedding straw. He washed his hands in the animals' drinking trough and shook the water off as he crossed the street.

In the corner of the kitchen he pulled off his working clothes and dressed instead in the only other garments he possessed, an ill-fitting, well-worn suit of dark, shabby material normally only worn at Mass or funerals. He gave his boots a quick wipe with a floor cloth, pulled them on and rose to go.

"I'm away on here mother," he called to the other room where she had gone to tend his father.

Her voice followed him towards the street. "Don't forget Father Dunleavey." she called.

"How could I forget Father Dunleavey?"

A lone seagull glided serenely above Mullaghdearg Lough below him, riding effortlessly on the air as it rose towards the hills of Ranahuel. It was a fine still day, white puffy clouds on a slow drift in over Aranmore Island from the northern Atlantic, looking like they had been painted on the morning indigo-blue of the sky by some watercolour artist trying to create the perfectly idyllic, Irish sky-scape. Not far along the lane he approached O'Donnell's cottage and again it struck him how differently he felt about the simple matter of walking past this house that had been his second home since childhood; the strange sinking sensation, the flutter somewhere in his abdomen.

"Ridiculous," he thought, "What the hell is wrong with me? Hurry on past. I haven't time to call in every time I walk down my own road past her. And why would I call anyway? What would be the point? Sure she's like an oyster in her own wee shell-world...I get nothing from it but frustration. Maybe it will be easier when Johnny gets back home. I'll have him to talk to, like old times, and I can ignore her. We'll have a lot to talk about, all his stories from the Lagan, and I'll be telling him about this fellow on the beach, and it'll all be back to normal again...and she'll be out of my head."

But he still paused at the end of the lane; and listened; and looked. No sign of anybody about, not even the dog. Just the faint trace of a tune escaping from her bedroom window. Another sad sounding melody, like last night's.

"Where's all her happy jigs and reels gone?" he thought. "Nothing but dirges and slow airs at the minute."

The seagull above uttered a series of plaintive cries, human-sounding, like a woman with an unfortunate strident laugh. Sean glanced up at the circling bird.

"Even the birds are mocking me," he said to himself and, to pre-empt any further temptation, he headed down the lane towards the lough and beyond, across the sand-flats to Carrickfinn. A couple of curlews were enjoying their autumn feeding rights ahead of him, their long curving bills excavating shellfish from the muddy sand. They quickly scuttled off to a safer distance down by the tide line as he approached.

As he strode out he was thinking back to some of the escapades that he and Johnny O'Donnell had gotten up to in the past. And he was wishing that his long-time friend was here now to share this particular journey, because he wasn't sure that he was going to enjoy it. What sort of funeral would it be anyway? Would there be religious rites involved, seeing as there wasn't going to be a Protestant clergyman there either? Would he have to do anything? Johnny would have an opinion on the proceedings, that's for sure, and would most likely make little attempt to conceal his usual irreverence. Maybe it was as well that he wasn't around at the minute.

In the street between the closely built homes of the Stewart clachan, old John was backing the donkey into the shafts of his cart, assisted by a couple of his grandchildren. They quickly secured the straps and chains, binding harness to load. From around the corner of the barn Robert John and his brother emerged carrying the enshrouded remains of the unfortunate stranger on a thin plank of rough timber. The children held their noses and backed off to a distance where the air was purer. By this stage it took a strong stomach to stand the odour of decomposition; even William James was looking sickly as he manoeuvred the head-end of the body onto the cart. The stiffened cadaver had now been wrapped in a makeshift burial garment, a piece of old unwanted sail-cloth, also washed up on the shore some time back. It had had to be tied up to the beams of the barn roof using a rope sling, to keep the decaying body out of reach of hungry rats around the farm. At least he was still in one piece, apart from a missing eye, although no-one was going to look too carefully.

There was no question of a coffin for this burial. Timber was a scarce commodity in these parts, for the twin reasons of poor soil quality and the local weather patterns. Only low-set bushes were able to survive the western gales. Good wood was such a prized commodity that to find a pile of driftwood, such as ships' timber, washed up on the foreshore was something to celebrate. Such finds were jealously guarded and quickly hitched up to a pony to be dragged back to the homestead. There it would be used in the construction of future houses or barns, carts or furniture. Most cottages close to the shore had a hoard of such reclaimed timber piled by the gable wall, saved for whenever it was needed.

Burying an unknown corpse was not such a time.

Sean Ban met the sparse-looking cortege on the lane to the beach and fell in behind the sombre procession. The donkey ambled sedately towards the strand. Old John gripped the bridle in a hand gnarled and twisted from years of holding reins and breaking horses. Across the sand they travelled, to the edge of the tide, still receding. Nobody was talking, out of respect to the deceased, but Jacob sidled up to Sean Ban, impatient to describe the events of last night, the catch of seainns. A stern look from his father silenced him almost as soon as he opened his mouth.

With some difficulty the adult men struggled up the shoulder of the island. Heads were turned away and noses pinched involuntarily at times, as they bore between them this foul-smelling body. Once on the grassy top, they wasted no time in laying it, none too gently, in the shallow grave.

Jacob watched anxiously in case he had misjudged either the length of the thing or the necessary depth. No-one offered him any rebuke, nor indeed any confirmation that he had done a good job. The sailor fitted, relief! And no-one else was aware that inches below lay the confused bones of a tiny infant skeleton. Jacob's secret, and he would keep it that way; a unique and arcane memory to which he, and he alone, could return when he wanted to; an occasion of mystically primordial sacredness to the young man, and one which he was already beginning to imbue with an almost religious significance. He only had to stare at his fingers to sense the smoothly delicate feel of that little egg-shell of a skull, cupped in the hollow of his hand.

Bobby picked up Jacob's abandoned shovel and handed it to his father. "Cover him up quick Da and save us from that smell!"

Robert John picked up a handful of sand and dropped it on top of the swaddled stranger.

"Dust to dust, ashes to ashes; we commit this body to the ground from whence it came," he said.

"Amen," came the mumbled response from behind him. He turned to the others.

"We'd better say the Lord's Prayer for him. You say it in Gaelic, Sean, and we'll say it in English, for we don't know what tongue he had at him."

"That'll do," said Sean stepping forward; he blessed himself hastily and began in a rush of words, "In aimn an Athar, agus an Mhic, agus an Spioraid Naomh.

Ar nAthair, atá ar neamh,

Go naofar d'ainm,

Go dtaga do ríocht,

Go ndéantar do thoil ar an talamh mar a dhéantar ar neamh.

Ár n-arán laethúil tabhair dúinn inniu, agus maith dúinn ár bhfiacha mar a mhaithimidne dár bhféichiúna féin

Agus ná lig sinn i gcathú, ach saor sinn ó olc. Amen."

The Stewarts joined in solemnly in English, the two languages twisting together like the strands of a mended rope.

"Our father which art in heaven; Hallowed be Thy name; Thy kingdom come; Thy will be done on earth as it is in heaven; Give us this day our daily bread; And forgive us our debts as we forgive our debtors; And lead us not into temptation but deliver us from evil; For thine is the kingdom and the power and the glory; For ever and ever, Amen."

Heads lifted again and faces looked each other with blank expressions. "Should you not say a prayer for his poor mother and father when they get the news, Robert?" murmured Martha, wiping the side of her eye, watering from the effects of the freshening sea-breeze.

"I will if you want. We'll pray again, alright?"

"Will it do any harm if you cover him up first?" complained young Richard in nasal tone.

"It'll not do you any harm to stand there and respect the dead," replied his father firmly and he bowed his head again and prayed, hesitantly, "Almighty and everlasting God..... Father of us all, we commend this.... young man here buried....whoever he is....to your care. May he rest in peace! And may you have mercy on his soul... and upon his grieving parents.... wherever they may be.... when this news comes to their door. Glory to the Father and to the Son and to the Holy Spirit, as it was in the beginning, is now and shall be forever. Amen."

As the others "Amen-ed" Richard sighed, a strange sounding noise through his firmly held nose. The sand was quickly shovelled over the body and soon the unpleasant traces of the odour had blown away over the waves. The grass sods were set back on top of the grave and firmed into place by the flat of the spade. As the corpse decomposed further over the next few months these cuts of turf would sink back level with the surrounding grass and in no time at all would no longer be noticeable. Not even a stone would mark the spot.

"Did you hear about our catch of seainns last night, Sean?" Bobby was first with the question, to Jacob's annoyance, and soon several different versions of the event were being told at the same time, each embellishing the tale until it was reaching epic proportions.

"If his story gets any bigger it'll be a whale I was after catching last night in my curragh," laughed grandfather John as he turned the donkey along the beach towards home.
"Come with us up to the house, Sean, and take a basket of them home to Brid. I haven't seen your mother in years." Martha took his arm. "With your father the way he is and not able to go to the fishing any more, I'm sure she'll be glad of them. They say fish is good medicine for the pains."
Sean needed no second bidding. "She will be more than glad of them, thank-you Martha," he said and they made their way back along the lough-side to the barn, where the smell of freshly salted fish was already wafting up from the barrels.

~~~~~~~

It was a full two hours before Sean Ban was making his way back towards home, a full basket of seainns under his arm and a sally-rod swinging in his other hand. He had managed to carry the basket in such an angled manner that no fishy fluid had dripped on his clothes. Climbing the steepest part of the hill, he rounded a tight bend in the lane and found himself semi-blinded by the late afternoon sun. As he squinted into it, he became aware of the silhouette of someone coming down the hill towards him. He paused, hand up to his eyes to defeat the glare, trying to identify the figure.
"Sean Sweeney, I was looking for you," grated the voice of Father Dunleavey.
"It's yourself, Father; I couldn't make you out....with the sun."
"What the divil is keeping you out at the Point till this time of the day? Didn't your mother tell you I was needing your help?"
Sean suddenly remembered. How could he have forgotten that he was meant to go to the priest? His mind had been everywhere else on his leisurely walk back from Stewart's place but he wasn't going to admit that to Father Dunleavey.
"I was going to you, after I take these fish home to my mother," he bluffed. "Mrs Stewart sent them to her. You didn't have to come all the way up here on one end's errand to remind me."
The priest bristled, eyebrows twitching like they had a mind of their own. "I didn't come to remind you. I had other business that brought me in this direction. But, when I was finished with that, I did call in with your mother to see if you were home or

if you had had another lapse of memory. Will you come with me now? There's two or three ewes needing seeing to."

"I'll be down straight away, Father. I'll just leave these fish in to the house first; they need to be out of the heat of the sun and into a basin of salt as soon as possible," said Sean, starting up the hill past the priest.

"Well, go on then, but don't be long!" complained Dunleavey. "These sheep of mine have been needing a cure for a couple of days and if they don't recover from whatever's got into them it'll be your fault and I'll hold you responsible." And he turned to waddle down the lane towards Annagry.

"Where's Saint Vincent?" Sean shouted after him. "A man in your position shouldn't be having to stretch his oul legs climbing up to Ranahuel. What's the point in having a mule if you have to walk?" And no sooner had he said it than he thought, "That's my priest I'm talking to. What sort of cheek am I saying at all?"

"Agh, no more of that disrespectful chat out of you, you ruffian," came Dunleavey's retort, thrown back over his shoulder like the tail of his clerical stole. "Saint Vincent is about to be de-canonised. That cantankerous oul animal and I had a bit of a row yesterday and it has decided not to cooperate with me today. You and the mule have a lot in common. You're both thick sort of beasts. I think it is a Sweeney too." And he rounded the bend and went out of sight, leaving his barb to irritate Sean like a wasp sting.

"So what was he doing up here, if it wasn't looking for me?" he thought. "Which of the people up our road would he have been coming to see? He was very private about it all and that makes me suspicious. Well, I'm sure it won't be long until I find out."

His mother was delighted to see the basket of seainns and straight away separated some out for the evening meal before beginning to place the remainder in a bucket, surrounding them with handfuls of even more rough salt. Sean watched her as she worked at the table and answered her questions about the burial, and about the Stewarts in general. They were a family that she seldom saw, now that she was living up on Ranahuel mountain. She had good memories of them from years ago, before she was married, when she worked in that little shop in the village. The Carrickfinn islanders used to come across on foot at low tide. They would do their business in Annagry, see whatever neighbours needed to be visited and buy their groceries in her shop, prior to returning across the sand-flats before the tide would cut off their retreat. She had memories of some of the older Stewarts bustling their way to the front of the queue in the shop, grabbing their supplies with obvious impatience, much to the annoyance of other customers who were waiting to be served. Their mumbled excuse was always the same. "The tide! The tide!" The phrase had become a bit of a standing joke with the locals. Whenever something was needed in a rush it was not unusual to hear the facetious rationale trotted out, "The tide! The tide!"

When he was satisfied that she had heard all she needed to hear about Carrickfinn Sean casually said, "So Father Dunleavey was telling me he was up on business today? Did he call in here as well?"

"Aye, he was in here looking for you again. Did you meet him on your way? He's getting desperate about those sheep. Get you away to him now before he has heart failure." Despite her agitation, his mother's head never lifted from her task.

"I'm going, I'm going. Was it O'Donnell's he was in at?"

"It was. He had a letter for Maggie Dan; he'd likely have to read it for her. Didn't seem best pleased about it either, whatever was in it. But it's none of my business, nor none of your business, so just you get yourself down to his ewes as fast as you can now, do ye hear?"

Sean said nothing as he left his house but already his mind was running ahead of himself. Another letter from Johnny, more than likely. Probably containing a few more pounds of Johnny's hard-earned cash. Hadn't the priest made some comment or asked some question about the money that Johnny was sending home during the last conversation that they had had together? That conversation, the one he would not, could not forget in a hurry. And why was Father Dunleavey bringing the letter from the post office this time? Why not Sean himself as usual? He had read the two previous letters from Johnny without any problem, short and scribbly and expressed in the very limited written Irish that Johnny had. And what would be in the letter that would have annoyed the priest, if his mother's observation had been accurate?

The whole thing became such a mind-clogging mystery to Sean that he found himself turning in O'Donnell's lane on his way back down the hill. His curiosity needed to be settled, indeed his suspicions needed to be either verified or laid to rest....otherwise how could he, in good conscience, go and help his priest to tend some of his other flock? He pushed open Maggie Dan's door, ducked his head and entered the gloom. Maggie Dan sat with her back to him, her feet at the hearth. There was no sign of Annie; he was surprised to realise that this was almost a relief to him; what a change that feeling was.

"Father Dunleavey was telling me he was up to see you, Maggie, with a letter?" he began. "Is everything alright with Johnny?"

Maggie Dan turned to look at him and there was desolation etched in the lines of her face. A grey pallor of worry underlay the flush that the glowing turf had raised, measling her wrinkled countenance. She said nothing, just stared at Sean before slowly turning back to the fire.

"He never sent a brass farthing," she muttered

Sean's mind jumped to immediate conclusions. He joined her at the hearth. "Had Father Dunleavey the letter opened when he brought it to you?" he blurted out.

Maggie Dan turned slowly turned to stare at him again. "Sean Ban Sweeney! What are you saying? The letter wasn't from our Johnny."

"The letter wasn't from Johnny? But you said he hadn't sent any money. What did.... Who was the letter from?"

There was a strange rebuke in Maggie Dan's look which Sean had only seen at such times as when he and Johnny had been caught out at some wrong-doing, back in the days of their childhood rascality. He realised he had over-stepped some line that he was unaware of and he stammered an apology.

"I'm sorry, Maggie Dan; I shouldn't be asking. It's just that Johnny's my friend and....well I'm confused. This isn't making any sense to me. Usually I bring you his letters from the post office, and usually you want me to read them for you. What happened to change that?"

"Father Dunleavey must have been in the post office this morning and Charlie Duffy saw there was a letter for me and asked him to bring it up to me. Father Dunleavey looked at it and saw it was in the English and he knew I would need the priest to read it for me.....sure you don't read the English, do you Sean Ban?"

"That I don't, you're right, other than the odd word of it. I can speak a good bit of it but reading it is a different thing altogether."

"So I would have been stuck if he hadn't opened it and read it for me, wouldn't I?" argued Maggie Dan.

The picture was clarifying itself for Sean, like a sea-mist blowing off the sand-hills, but the main point was still shrouded in as dense a fog as ever. He pursued this elusive truth.

"Of-course. He did right. But if the letter wasn't from Johnny, why did you say that he hadn't sent you a brass farthing? I'm still mixed up about that part."

Maggie Dan produced the letter from somewhere about her bosom and held it out to Sean. He took it reluctantly and examined the envelope carefully, holding it up so that the meagre light from the one small window and the open half-door would fall upon it. The hand was not Johnny's, that was immediately obvious; it had a much bolder, grander style altogether, that of someone who was much more used to writing letters, someone who was comfortable with writing in the English language. He took out the folded pages and looked at the top one. There was an address, neatly written in the top right-hand corner, followed by a date. Sean could just about read and understand the address as "Magilligan, Limavady, County Londonderry." He looked for the signature at the bottom of the letter and deciphered the surname.

"Rob-in-son", he said.

The scrawl of the first name defeated him entirely. How he wished he could read what it said. He made a mental promise to himself to learn to read English properly at some stage in his life. People had always encouraged him, Father Dunleavey especially, to learn to speak the English and to get as good at it as possible, because, of-course, it was the way to succeed in work and business, should you ever find yourself in need of a job in the eastern part of Ireland or in Scotland or England.

"It's from a man called Robinson," he said to Maggie Dan. "But I don't know what it says. What did Father Dunleavey say it meant?" He couldn't hold his curiosity in check any longer.

Maggie Dan gave a little sigh. "The Robinson man is the farmer Johnny has been working to. There was an accident. Johnny stepped on a nail that was rusty and it went up through his boot into his foot. He didn't know to do anything about it, maybe there was nothing he could do. So he just kept working. But a while later the foot had swollen up so much that he couldn't get his boot on, and he couldn't put it to the ground. The farmer found him one morning with his foot all swollen up and red, so he sent for the doctor. They got him medicine, likely very expensive, for you know what doctors are like all over. I don't know who paid for it. They put poultices on his foot but it is taking a long time to heal up. He has had a fever on him at times. He still can't walk yet, so he can't work. He's no use to the farmer, so he's not getting paid. But at least the farmer is a decent sort and hasn't put him out. He is letting Johnny stay there till he mends up, then if he can work again there's a job for him there, otherwise he will just have to get home some way."

Sean was stunned by this news and not a little rebuked at his own misinterpretation of the whole matter of the letter. He could think of nothing to say, so he said nothing, just looked at the peat smoke rising to the open chimney.

"There's a wee note from Johnny behind that page," said Maggie Dan, indicating the letter which Sean still held in his hand. He looked at the second sheet and recognised Johnny's childish scrawl.

"Mother I am alright," it said in Irish. "Do not worry about me. The worst is over. I still have my foot, though it was touch and go. Soon I will be walking and able to work and send you some more money before Christmas. Say Hello to Annie. Your son Johnny."

"Never one for using a sentence where a word would do, our Johnny," observed Sean Ban. They stared at the hearth together for a while, the silence unbroken, the concern shared as tangibly as the letter in Sean's hand. Eventually he folded the pages and put them back in the envelope. Rising from his chair he said, "You never have too far to go to seek your troubles, Maggie Dan."

"That I haven't," she replied. "And poor Annie is the least of them now. How we'll manage for money and food, I just do not know."

"Where is Annie anyway?" Sean asked, noticing her whistle abandoned on the rough kitchen table.

"She went out for a walk with the dog when she saw Father Dunleavey coming," replied the mother.

"She had a bit o' sense then," thought Sean. "I wish I could escape him that easily."

"I'm away to see to his sheep now. Don't worry yourself, Maggie Dan. We'll never see you stuck."

He left the house with her heartily warm thanks embarrassing his ears.

As he descended towards Annagry and the tribulations of Father Dunleavey's other flock, Sean Ban wondered about the strange way that ill-fortune seemed to follow some folk, some families, while others, no more deserving and no more pious, seemed to escape such troubles. As a family, the O'Donnells had had to endure more than most, with the loss of Bartley years ago and the effect on Maggie Dan who had never really got over it, then the handicap that Annie has had to carry all her life and now Johnny injured and not able to earn at such a vital time in the cycle of the year. It wasn't as if they had any more resources to fall back on; the usual hand-to-mouth existence of the rural peasant class of Donegal. The family was trying to eke out a living from a couple of acres of scrawny mountain pasture and bogland. The land was barely able to support the half a dozen sheep, the single cow and her calf, when she had one, and Maggie Dan's old brown donkey who had been on his last legs for as long as Sean Ban could remember. A near impossible task for the ageing woman, endeavouring to rear two needy children on her own over so many poverty-stricken years. Little wonder Johnny had been pushed into going away to work in the Lagan for the first time when he was as young as thirteen. Others did it of-course, but that wouldn't have made it any easier for the boy himself. But for the charity of the neighbours, Maggie Dan and Annie would have gone hungry on numerous occasions during those lonely months when he was away, before he managed to have some money sent back to his mother at home.

"They are going to have a tough winter financially if Johnny can't get back to work soon. What a pity that Annie isn't capable of doing something to earn a bob or two," he thought to himself. "My poor Annie. What's to become of her? I hope to God their luck changes soon for they deserve better."

And he continued between the rough stone ditches by the side of the lane. The evensong of thrushes and blackbirds, the chirping harmonies of tits and sparrows and finches, sweet to his ears. The warm, seasonal scents of the autumn countryside rising wholesome to his nose. Above all, the vivid memory of the shape of Annie in that summer dress that day in Cloughglas was completely flooding his senses with incompatible, yet inseparable, emotions; the joyous oil of human desire and the deep, dark waters of hopeless melancholy.

Section 2

Chapter 8

Sad News is Carried

The Callander to Oban train thundered its way along the edge of Loch Lubnaig making more noise than speed. Grey smoke belched up from its stack into the mid-day air, in seeming affront to the still purity of the green water and the heather-rich slopes rising steeply towards Ben Ledi to the west. A rust-red bull of the Highland cattle breed raised its classic, shaggy head and stared momentarily as the four carriages grumbled northwards. Watching from the window of the fourth carriage, Captain Murray Brownlow thought that something about the animal's form resembled a street fighter in the back streets of his native Glasgow, such was its squat, belligerent presence. Those magnificent horns, curving a full eighteen inches in front of its invisible eyes, were soon lowered again into the deep rushes of the marshy loch-side ground as the bull lost interest and resumed grazing. Brownlow wondered at those impressive horns, and not just those sported by the bull but by each of the five cows in his harem. No two pairs of horns appeared to be the same in design or curvature. The need for the bull to have such weapons might be understandable, but why these fiercesome attachments on the heads of the females of the breed, particularly when their general appearance and aura was one of disinterested placidity? They barely noticed the train rumbling past their field. Those that did stared into the middle distance with such statuesque boredom that they might have been delft miniatures in a shop-window in one of the winding streets of Stirling town, through which he had passed earlier that morning.

This was not an area familiar to the Captain, indeed he had never before been in Perthshire. He had not had occasion to travel up through the central interior of his country; instead, his fifty-four years had been spent either in and around the city of his birth or on the western seaways beyond the Clyde. There were very few areas of that western coast with which he was not acquainted; indeed, in the past decade he had become increasingly familiar with the coast of northern and western Ireland, as skipper of "*The Mary Ellen*", a cargo steamer which plied its trade between those parts and his native city.

Brownlow had looked after himself over the years and was still a well-built, even burly gentleman, pushing six feet in height. His muscular legs filled his suit trousers and his shoulders gave evidence of much physical hard work during a long career at sea. Clean-shaven for this journey, he possessed a fresh, ruddy complexion in which were set eyes of the clearest sea-blue; these peeked out from beneath neatly maintained grey eyebrows, the latter matching in texture his tidily-trimmed hair.

Leaving the loch behind, the train pushed further up Glenogle towards the head of the glen, slowing to cross a precarious-looking viaduct, its twelve, tall arches wonderfully engineered to support the path of the railway many feet above the valley floor. Brownlow leaned forward to peer down from the steamed-up window at the rocky river on its winding southbound journey so far below. There was only one other passenger in this second-class carriage, a semi-awake gentleman of rustic appearance who had barely uttered a word since boarding in Stirling, so the Captain's three pieces of luggage claimed the opposite seat. One item was a well-used, leather suitcase, secured with an extra leather strap to which was attached a brownish label bearing a name and address in watery, blue ink; then a wooden box with two clips and a handle which, by its shape and design, was obviously a protective case for a musical instrument, most probably a violin; finally there was what looked like a largish school satchel, the latter bulging with whatever contents were hidden inside. The Captain's gaze fell upon the satchel again, as it had done on numerous occasions during this journey, and it seemed that he winced around his piercing eyes as he looked sadly at this item. Yet again, his thoughts sidetracked to the object of his present journey.

How to approach this task? How much to say and what not to say? He had planned his conversation several times since he knew that he had to make this trip and each time he returned to the subject in his mind he changed tack, so that now he was entirely confused in his intentions and in his tactics. How do you talk to an ordained clergyman of the Church of Scotland about a matter like this? The disappearance of his son, no doubt much-loved and deeply mourned. The letters which had been exchanged between the two men had been brief and fairly matter-of-fact in content. Such brevity and such a dispassionate tone was unlikely to continue when the two would meet in an hour or so, given that the Captain was, in all likelihood, the last person to speak to the missing son before his disappearance.

Brownlow's letter to Reverend Gordon W Mackay had been scribbled with a hand more accustomed to steering his coaster than to composing letters of this sensitive nature.

"Dear Sir," it began, "It is with much sorrow and sympathy that I write to you on this day, the 21st of September, 1897. The sad tidings of news which you received by telegram in recent times does concern me as skipper of the vessel "The Mary Ellen" in which your son did travel for a brief time. It was I who discovered his absence from the ship on the morning of 15th of the same month. It was also myself who communicated this news by telegram to a Mr William Roberts, the same who had contracted us to have your son taken on board as passenger from Burtonport in Ireland to Glasgow on September 12th.

I report, Sir, that I am in possession of 3 items of personal belongings of the aforesaid passenger, your son. Would it be your intention to reclaim these items at the office of my company in Glasgow, namely Mackenzie and Sons, Limited, of Argyll Street? Or, should it be your wish to meet and speak to myself regarding the unfortunate circumstances about which I correspond, I will endeavour to make myself available to you for such discussion and will transport the luggage to a place of your choosing.

I await, Sir, your instruction at the above address, my home, where I shall be resident for a period of ten days, during which I am on leave of absence.

I remain yours faithfully,

Murray Brownlow (Captain)

As the train clunked rhythmically through a sudden shower of rain, Brownlow took from his pocket a slightly creased, cream-coloured envelope; removing the clergyman's reply he re-read it for the umpteenth time.

The Manse

Main Street

Killin

Perthshire

26th September 1897

Dear Captain Brownlow,

I acknowledge receipt of your letter of 21st September.

My wife and I thank you most kindly for the sympathy you express at this time of difficulty and uncertainty. There are so many questions that we wish to ask and to have answered that it is a comfort to hear from one who may be competent to help assuage our distress. I note also that you may be willing to travel with the belongings of my son. I would be most grateful to you if you could see it in your power to deliver them to us here in Killin. Given our current circumstance, you will understand that my wife does not desire me to travel to Glasgow, so leaving her alone. Should it be acceptable to you to do so, I will receive you here at my address. You may stay overnight, if it suits you so to do. You should travel by train from Glasgow Queen Street Station to Stirling, and via Callander to Killin Junction and onwards to Killin, a relatively straightforward journey. Be assured that whatever expenses you incur in this matter I shall more than recompense to you.

I await your reply.

Your humble debtor,

Gordon W Mackay DD (Reverend)

"One who may be competent to help assuage our distress," the Captain thought. "Hardly likely, your reverence, given what I suspect."

Rain splattered furiously against the window, so loudly that the second inhabitant of the carriage awoke, rubbed his eyes and swore under his breath at the downpour. The door of the compartment slid open and a very tall guard inclined his head inwards, speaking to both men.

"Five minutes tae Killin Junction," he lilted. "You'll baith be wantin' tae change there and tak' the extension tae Killin itself. Platform two, I believe."

"Platform twooo," repeated the agricultural gentleman disdainfully through a few discoloured teeth with a mildly mocking emphasis upon the vowel. His shanks of faded ginger hair pointed wildly in variable directions, as did the straggled grey tufts of what was intended to be a beard. "There only ir twa platforms. You mak' it soun' like Glasgow Central."

"Just dain' me job," droned the guard, withdrawing the top half of his lengthy frame from the narrow doorway like a cat curling around it's mistress' leg. A parting shot, though, to the farmer. "Wouldnae want you tae fa' asleep and waken up in Oban again." He was gone before the rasping excuse followed him out the crack of the sliding door.

"I was in drink thon day, ye lanky rascal."

The thundering of the train against the silence of the carriage again.

"You're going tae Killin as weel, I take it?" asked Brownlow eventually, more to distract his thoughts from his mission than out of any genuine interest in the destination of his travelling companion.

"That I am," came the answer. "It's me ain wee toon, so it is."

"How far is it .... frae Killin Junction, I mean?" Brownlow's thickly guttural Glaswegian accent contrasted with the high-pitched, rather sing-song tenor of his fellow passenger.

"Nae mair than three or four mile. But it's a slow four mile, fir the wee engine haisnae much power aboot it. Couldnae pull yer cep aff unless ye had grease in yer hair."

Captain Brownlow smiled at his quaint neighbour's sudden coming to life after a silent journey, and at his turn of phrase. He persisted.

"Seems strange tae me that the main line didnae just go through the toon o' Killin in the first place, rather than hae a five mile extension frae this Junction place. What happened there?"

"Aye, ye wud wonner aboot that. But when the line was built bac' a lot o' year ago, it wasnae built wae Killin in mind at al'. It was built tae carry kettle an' sheep frae the Heilans an' Islands doon through Oban, a' the wie doon tae Stirling an' Glasgow. Up tae that, it was a wile lang drive fir the drovers. I wis wan mesel', so I should ken. Walkin' fir mile after mile behin' a herd o' bullocks fir days on end. Naw the brawest view in the worl', when ye think o' it," said the neighbour.

"How dae ye mean?"

" I mean, lookin' at the dirty arse-en' o' fifty, o'er-exercised bullocks. Ye wud swear ye could see the beef drappin' aff them. I walked that journey mair times than I care to remember. That's why me legs are sae short."

The freckled drover warmed to his story as the train ground to a screeching, juddering halt by Platform One of Killin Junction Station. Brownlow stretched his body, massaged his back and shook the pins and needles out of his stiff legs. Grabbing the battered suitcase, he stuffed the violin case under one arm and took the satchel in his other hand.

"Here, let me gae ye a hand wae al' that," offered the drover warmly, shuffling forward on ancient-looking boots.

"Not at all," refused Brownlow firmly. "It's very light, I can manage, thanks."

The shower had splashed itself out but puddles gleamed all over the platform, the light creating miniature rainbows where oil had been spilled on the wet pavement. The two travellers had crossed this platform together and boarded the first of the two carriages; they would be pulled by a small, insignificant-looking engine which Brownlow recognised as a Pug, a saddletank engine very much like the kind of locomotive he would frequently see working along the docks in Greenock or Clydebank. Then, amid much hissing and groaning, the little train shuddered its way forward along the narrow track. The two men, quiet for a while, examined the gently passing countryside, the sheen of the recently abated shower still fresh on the pasture and the impressively built stone ditches. The landscape had flattened out here at the head of the glen and the river, running companionably along beside the railway and fed by numerous streams from the hills above, flowed wide and strong. Its sinuous path led it through some luxurious, deciduous woodland, where leaves were already changing to autumnal orange, vermillion and brown.

The drover, having had opportunity to study the label on Brownlow's luggage, could contain his curiosity no longer. "What brings ye tae these parts, if it's naw an ignorant question?" he asked with what seemed to be his usual degree of reticence.

Brownlow had been hoping they could get to Killin without being asked this question. The last thing he wanted was to be the instigator of any local gossip, particularly when the story was as morbid as the one he was bearer of. At the same time, his traveling companion had been friendly and informative and he had no wish to appear rude.

"Well," he began, then paused, "It's a personal matter really. I hae a visit tae pay tae a certain gentleman. Maybe you could tell me how tae fin' ...."

"The Manse yer lookin' fer, is it?" interrupted the drover.

"How did you ken I was goin' tae visit the minister?"

"The label on the case," admitted his companion without compunction. Then, a little more penitently, "I couldnae help seein' it. I can read the odd word, ye ken."

The captain looked out the window, across the river to the steepening hillside.

"The Manse is easy tae fin'; it's naw far roon the road. Ye may see it frae the train in a minute or two," continued the local man. "A big, grey, two-storied barn o' a hoose."

"Thank you."

"I'm thinkin' it'll be aboot thon son o' his. I hear he's missin' at sea?"

"Ah, so the news is oot aroun' the community?" said the Captain.

"This toon is like every ither place; word gets oot! Folk ken things, an' what they dinnae ken they mak' up."

A short silence, meditational. Brownlow, staring from the window, suddenly sat forward, his attention drawn to something of interest outside.

"What is this waterfall?"

From its patient lethargy, the river had suddenly burst into a riot of turbulent, tumbling foam, white and brown froth, cascading between stark slabs of jagged, grey rock as it fell from the elevated plain into a narrow gorge. Beyond the falls, on the far bank of the river, stood a picturesque old mill, it's huge wheel turning sedately.

"This wud be the famous Falls o' Dochart. Hae ye no heard o' them?"

The Captain shook his head as he watched the impressive cataract slide slowly out of view. "I haven't, no. And is that the name o' the river as well?"

"Aye, that's the Dochart, and we are just aboot tae cross o'er it. They had tae build a new viaduct.... This is it noo," he said with some pride, looking down at the swirling torrent some forty feet below as the train chugged slowly over the imposing construction. "It's built o' that new concrete stuff, you ken. Brought up frae Glasgow, I believe. I just hope it lasts like they say it does, but I hae me doobts. It's hard tae bate God's guid rock, that's what I say!"

If Brownlow was relieved that the conversation had veered away from his mission to Killin he was soon to be disappointed; the drover worked the topic back into their discussion, pointing to a large house just above the road, more or less on a level with the elevated position of the train.

"And thoner's the manse o' the Reverend Mackay like I toul ye," he said. "A gran' big hoose, compared tae al' the ither wee cottages aroun' it, as ye can see. The clergy need their comforts here the same as every ither place. I could show you the wie frae the station if ye like. It's nae bother. Specially after the trouble yer takin' tae bring the young laddie's belongings back tae his feather."

"Not at all! I can manage frae here. It doesnae seem very far," assured Brownlow as the train trundled to a halt in Killin's tiny Station.

The raggledy little man looked somewhat hurt by this rebuff to his generous spirit but, undeterred, he was at once back on the offensive.

"And what did you say happened to young Mackay?"

Brownlow set the suitcase down on the platform and adjusted the fiddle case under his arm. "I didnae say anythin' happened tae him, as a matter o' fact," he said firmly. "Maybe naethin' happened tae him. Maybe he'll turn up."

"Maybe he will. Please God he will. He was a harmless sort o' a laddie, so he was, an' his mither an' feather dinnae deserve this."

It was Brownlow's turn to ask a question. "So you knew him then?" He regretted it straight away, as the cattleman took him by the arm. With surprising quickness of step he led the way out of the station and along the road. The seaman struggled to keep up, despite having age on his side and the benefit of a superior physique.

"Aye! Sure everyboody kens everyboody aroun' here. An' everyboody kens the clergyman, whether they're o' the same kirk or no. Ye see the kirk o'er there?" He indicated a large white church nearby, apparently built in the shape of a cross. "So aye, I wudda seen the young laddie aboot the toon be times. Never had ony conversation wae him or that. Be al' accounts he was a quiet sort, maybe a bit lonely o' himsel', some wud say odd a bit. They say he wud sit fir hours oot be the river and he'd be drawin' that viaduct that we came o'er, or he'd be drawin' the train sittin' in the station, or as it came doon beside the Falls. Aye, a grand drawer he was, they say, but then what guid is drawin' tae anybody? Ye cud hardly make a livin' oot o' it, cud ye?"

"Probably not," agreed Brownlow, but he was thinking about some of the excellent drawings he'd seen when he had taken a surreptitious look through the young Andrew Mackay's journal the previous night. He would deny doing so if asked of-course. Despite his best efforts not to yield to the temptation, he was driven by a deep curiosity to try to discover what sort of fellow his passenger had been and what lay behind his sudden disappearance from the boat on the night of that storm off Aranmore Island. But he wasn't going to admit that to his present companion, nor indeed to anyone, least of all the boy's father. What he had seen in there had shocked him and wild horses could not drag from him either the fact that he had opened the satchel or that he had examined some of the journal's incredible contents. Enough to say that he fully intended to be well away from the minister's presence when the grieving father began to peruse the diary of his missing son.

"Did you meet the laddie yoursel'?" inquired the curious local.

"Aye, that I did, but only for a short time, so I didnae really get the chance to make any judgement aboot him. Tell me," he continued, "As you can see, I am carrying a fiddle case here; was he a musical kind of lad, to the best of your knowledge? Did he play the fiddle?"

This to change the subject and draw a veil over the circumstances of his own encounters with Andrew Mackay, as far as his present companion was concerned at any rate. He had a suspicion that whatever information he gave away to this happy traveller would be around the locality like a contagious fever. In no time the bones of his account would be fleshed out with angles and exaggerations and down-right lies in a manner that would render it unrecognisable to himself, should he ever hear the tale again. Discretion was his best friend here.

"That I cudnae say noo. It's mair than possible he was, fir his feather wud be a great man fir al' the oul traditions. Oul airs an' songs, oul stories; some o' them he'd tell in the Gallic. An' hardly a soul amang the locals cud understand' a word o' it. He might as weel a' bin talkin' double Dutch fir half o' them. The young wans, anyway."

Brownlow picked up on this point of interest quickly. "Oh really? Mr Mackay is a Gallic speaker, is he? There canny be too many o' them in the clergy, this far south at least. Was he frae up north some-place?"

"I believe he was. A Sutherland man, frae what I hear!"

"And what beseeched him to come to a wee, oot-o'-the-way place like Killin, I wonder?"

The drover paused for a moment as they neared their destination, wondering whether or not to take offence at the last remark. In the end he countered.

"Oot-o'-the-way are we? Just because a Glasgow man has niver bin here before, nor canny fin the place when he does come, doesnae make us oot-o'-the-way."

Brownlow smiled, conceding the point. They had stopped short on the road to look up ahead at what he guessed was the manse.

"I'll leave ye here, mister," said the drover. "I'll naw go tae the door, fir the last thing I need is anither lecture frae his reverence aboot the dangers o' alcohol. The only danger I'm worried aboot is naw being' able tae afford it. So I'll say goodbye tae ye Mister."

With that he turned on his heel and took off back along the street in long, loping strides, nearly falling over himself in his hurry to escape the possibility of an encounter with the clergy. Looking after him, Brownlow called a warm "Goodbye and thank you!" to the little man who had been such an unwitting mine of information in such a short space of time; at the same time he worried about what sort of a tale was already being woven around his own comments, and how they might be echoing around the public houses and the cottages of the village before the night was out.

He turned, ascended the grey, stone steps to the former residence of young Andrew Mackay and knocked on the door.

Chapter 9

A clergyman's sorrow

A cup of strong tea, served in a set of rose-patterned china cups; three heaped teaspoonfuls of sugar for him from a similarly patterned china bowl and a long, solid finger of traditional shortbread, resting snugly between cup and saucer lip. He stirred the dark brown brew with more noise and vigour than would have been normal in the quietness of this mausoleum of a manse. Even the chiming clock on the ornate sideboard behind him was silent and still, whether through mechanical fault or failure to rewind he could not guess.

The clergyman, now sitting impassively opposite him, beyond the pristine linen tablecloth, had greeted him at the door with pained formality some twenty minutes earlier. The handshake had been warm enough, as had been the gratitude expressed regarding his current mission of mercy. There was, however, a perceptible reserve in the minister's bearing; perhaps this was his normal modus operandi when dealing with parishioners, a cultivated social distance, or perhaps the present circumstances placed a constraint upon him with which he was struggling internally. His wife, on the other hand, could not contain her confused emotions and wept silently, handkerchiefed hand to her trembling mouth, when her gaze had fallen to her son's suitcase and satchel and violin case. She had appeared from a half-open kitchen door, timid and hesitant, staying deep in the dull shadows of the hall until her husband had beckoned her forward with a barely-perceptible gesture and introduced her to the visitor.

"This is Captain Brownlow from Glasgow, my dear. He has delivered...." He had tailed off; no need to go any further with that sentence, the lady already catching a sob in her throat. "This is my wife.....Andrew's mother." An involuntary bow of the head and fingers manipulated his clerical collar in the region of his Adam's Apple.

Brownlow had offered his hand. "Good-day tae ye, Ma'am. I'm right sorry tae be bringing his things....." Hard to know what to say. Her two hands had grasped his with gentle delicacy and stayed there, as if to absorb some understanding and comfort from the mutual touch of this stranger to whom she was now

mysteriously connected. The sea-hardened captain had felt her despair in a way that surprised himself; he sensed a deep need in her; it strained to soak support and sympathy from him, as a cut flower would draw sustenance from a vase of water. He had not been able to think of anything to say, indeed she did not utter a word herself, just stood there holding his hand in her two, staring at her son's belongings through tear-glazed eyes. The minister had waited patiently for several moments before taking her arm and sidling towards the kitchen.
"You'll make the captain some tea, dear?" he had suggested. "He's travelled a long way and I'm sure he is in need of some refreshment."
She had turned wordlessly towards her duty.
Leaving the three items of luggage by the ornate, darkly-stained cloak-stand in the hall, Brownlow had followed Mackay into the adjacent dining room. A dining room but obviously a study or library as well. Brownlow's eyes were drawn immediately to the bulging bookcases lining three of the walls of this room. A window above the sideboard looked out over the town to the grey waters of Loch Tay and the mighty bulk of Ben Lawers beyond. On either side of the window, gilt-framed water-colours, typical Scottish highland scenes, mountains and lochs, delicately painted by a more than competent hand. In one, an eagle surveyed its bogland kingdom from an outcrop of rock on the craggy side of a hill, above a green-blue lake; in the other, a stag stood belly-deep in purple heather, its antlered head lifted arrogantly as if to declare its monarchy of the surrounding glen. Beautiful and all as these two works of art were, Brownlow noted the fact that both pictures had Bible verses printed in bold, brassy letters across the sky. In the first, the text read "God is our refuge and strength, a very present help in trouble. Psalm 46 V1", and on the second a similar reference, "As the hart panteth after the water brooks, so panteth my soul after thee, Oh God. Psalm 42 V1."
"They are going to need all the refuge and strength they can get," he thought.
"Take a seat please. You must be tired after your walk up from the station, especially carrying.... You found your way alright? Obviously."

"Aye, there was nae problem wae that. I had help frae a local man who came up on the train alang wae me. Said he was a cattle drover; showed me up tae the manse!"

"A cattle drover, you say?" Rev Mackay pondered, tugging at his left ear in an idiosyncratic manner. "I wonder who that could have been? Ah, a short wee man, ginger hair?"

"That description fits him well; short and ginger; could use a comb. And a bath wudnae go amiss ither," answered Brownlow smiling. "Dae ye ken him? Sorry, I didnae think tae ask him his name, but I'd think he's a bit o' a character."

"I would say we are talking about a certain Archibald McNab, and you are right, a character he is. Maybe not of great character," said the minister, emphasising the 'of'. "He would be well known locally, maybe better known in certain public houses than in any house of prayer. Certainly never darkens the door of my kirk; well maybe once in a while for a funeral, but he's a right reprobate."

"I wudnae doobt that."

"And he would be full of information for you, I'm fairly certain. For an uneducated man he knows these parts like the back of his hand, aye and from here to Oban and Stirling too. He knows all the gossip, keeps his ear to grindstone, rather than his nose, if you know what I mean. Did you find him curious yourself, Captain?"

Brownlow tensed, sensing the clergyman's concern before he had even voiced it. "He wudnae be behin' the door in asking questions, that's true. But content yourself, I wasnae forthcoming wae much information when he tried tae fin' oot what I was daeing coming tae Killin."

The minister was pensive, and a short silence ensued as both men, sub-consciously reticent to approach the real subject of their encounter, sought for some small-talk to spread on the stale silence that separated them. The captain surveyed the vast ranks of stiffly-backed books which seemed to him to oppress the room and contract the space in on top of him. "Theology nae doobt," he thought dismally, but instead observed, "I see ye hae the odd book aboot ye."

"You could say that," said Mackay, looking around his shelves with a mixture of pride and affection, appreciative of his visitor's question. "Are you a reader yourself, Captain Brownlow?"

Brownlow thought instantly of the last thing he'd read, young Andrew Mackay's journal, and he hoped the guilt didn't show in his face. Instead he said, "Oh aye, there's naethin' tae beat a guid book when yer sailing the seas."

"And what sort of book would you be reading, may I ask? Are you interested in religious writing at all? How about the Scriptures themselves?" quizzed the clergyman, with more than a hint of evangelistic opportunism.

"Ah naw, Not for me! The time was maybe I would hae been. Used tae read the Psalms be times." He nodded towards the paintings. "But noo I enjoy a good story, something tae lift the mind. Sir Walter Scott used tae be me favourite but in recent times I hae been reading al' the Dickens books I can get me hands on. Some grand stories he wrote, that man. The last one I read was called 'Martin Chuzzelwitt'; he aye comes up wae these rare names fir folk. Whoever heard o' the name...." he broke off as Mrs Mackay backed into the room, pushing open the door of the study with her rear, and deposited a tea-tray on the table.

Looking across the top of his cup at the clergyman's wife, Brownlow realised that he had yet to hear her speak. Her brown eyes had a dull, hooded look, continually directed downwards, and her whole posture was one of patient subjugation. The slightly stooped shoulders and the rounded back; the barely perceptible forward hunch, from her slim waist up. He could imagine that once she had stood tall; on her wedding day she would have stood erect and proud to be marrying a promising young minister of intelligence and culture. Now the pallor of her skin, despite the recent summer, spoke of closure indoors, perhaps even of more long-term hibernation away from the kind of social company which would have invigorated her. And yet, looking at her, he could see that she had once been a pretty lass. There was still a shadow of decayed beauty in the lines of her face. Something about her spoke to him of a withered rose, prematurely dried and wizened, perhaps by worry, perhaps by a lifetime of serving a domineering and inflexible minister-husband. He liked Mrs Mackay, or maybe he just really felt a strong sympathy for her in the present circumstances.

The clergyman himself, now reaching to take his wife's hand as she sat beside him at the table, was an austere gentleman. Tall like a beanpole, with a strong impression of angularity about his whole persona, Reverend Mackay was pointy and physically awkward. A heron of a man! He sported a pair of fairly large and protruding ears, above which his dark hair was tightly cut and meticulously parted at the side. His gold-rimmed spectacles, which he seemed to wear all the time rather than just for reading, gave him an intellectual look. But his most striking feature was that of his substantial, well-manicured moustache which descended from right below his handsome nose, parted in the middle and flowed outwards to tapered points well beyond the corners of his invisible mouth. As he looked at the minister now, he was aware already of several crumbs of the good lady's shortbread taking up residence in the outer foliage of this feature, no doubt to be visited and retracted by his reverence's tongue for ingestion at a later, less public stage.

Reverend Mackay cleared his throat of similar crumbs and spoke, his wife shuddering momentarily by his side.

"So, Captain Brownlow, what can you tell us about Andrew and how he disappeared?"

It was the Captain's turn to clear the frogs from his throat. All he had planned to say, the order of things, the phrases he had conjured up to take the edge off the starkness of the tragedy....these all drained away from his mind. He stammered uncharacteristically as he began.

"I can tell you.... I would begin by saying....This is really hard, you understand, Mrs Mackay. I would rather be tellin' you anythin' else, I'd rather be anywhere else in the world. I just wish.... I just wish that I had got to ken the lad better in the wee while he was on my ship. Then I might be able to answer the big questions you are bound to be askin'."

He paused. The crypt-like silence of a manse study lay between them like a thick Glasgow smog; an intense heaviness, pregnant with unspoken disappointment and despair.

"Go on please."

It was the first time the lady of the house had spoken, a small tremble of a voice, brittle with fear.

"I believe you are aware that your son had been havin' some....problems, let me say, durin' the latter part of his time in Ireland. At least, that's what I was informed by the harbour master at Burtonport when he came to ask me if I would agree to giving him passage back to Glasgow. Would that be your understandin' o' the matter, Sir?"

Reverend Mackay nodded and sat forward in his chair, both forearms now on the table edge.

"That is something we are aware of, Captain Brownlow. We had a letter from our relative, Mr William Roberts, a few weeks ago. That letter explained the fickleness of my son's health and its apparent deterioration. You didn't meet Mr Roberts yourself, did you?"

"That I didnae, but I did hear his name mentioned; I suppose it was by Hughes, the man he had contacted in Burtonport. I dinnae really ken the background, but then I dinnae need tae. He just told me that the lad wasnae well. I didnae even think tae ask what was wrong wae him," Brownlow lied.

The clergyman looked long at his wife and, whatever query was contained in his look, Mrs Mackay nodded, almost imperceptibly, the pain in her eyes something dreadful to behold, Brownlow thought.

"I suppose I ought to tell you a little bit of the background; it is not easy to tell to a stranger but you have been very good coming up all this way to see us and bring Andrew's things. You could have waited and spoken to us at the inquest, whenever they get around to holding it, but you have shown a good deal of humanity and much kindness to us in making this journey, and in your own time too. So I feel I can share my burden..... our burden, because," and he took his wife's hand again, tenderly, "Maureen has carried this burden every bit as much as me over the past few years."

Tears trickled down the mother's face as he continued.

"Our son Andrew was.... is, a very special boy. He was our only son....well, only surviving son. We lost a couple of children during Maureen's confinement, but that we always accepted as in the Divine Plan, as part of God's will for us, and "His Will be done", as we always said. Andrew was blessed with huge talents, extremely clever, musical, a great artist, certainly a very promising draughtsman."

The captain thought of the drawings he had seen in the boy's journal.

"Aye, he seemed to be that alright....." His sentence tailed off as he mentally rebuked himself for interrupting with this inane observation. The couple looked at him curiously for explanation. "That's one of the things yer man McNab said aboot him, that he was a great drawer." And then he thought,

"What am I saying? Just shut up, Murray, and let the clergyman talk."

"How would McNab have known that? Sure he never even met Andrew," complained Mackay.

"True enough. He said he didnae ken the lad. Ah, but he did say that he had heard frae the local folk that he wud sit oot be the railway line an' draw things. That's what he told me. That's all!" But in his mind he thought, "Fool! I dug a hole for mesel' there."

"So you and this ungodly reprobate were discussing my son on your train journey here?" The austere face had reddened and creased into temper, and Mrs Mackay stroked his hand in a feeble attempt to reduce his tension.

"It's alright, Gordon," she whispered, "they were likely just talking."

"Just talking, indeed. About my son. My poor drowned boy. When it is no business of theirs to do so. Two strangers. Discussing my son's abilities...and no doubt much, much more."

"Don't say that, Gordon," wailed his wife, talking over her husband's outburst. "Don't dare say that! We don't know if he's drowned. He's maybe safe in Ireland somewhere, maybe on his way home to us right now."

She stood up and made as if to leave the study, but the minister caught her by the arm, firmly but gently, and spoke in a more reasonable tone.

"I'm sorry dear. I shouldn't have said that. Only God knows what has become of our boy and whether he lives on earth, or in heaven. I lost my temper. Sorry, Captain Brownlow, it just seems that the whole village is discussing matters to do with my household behind our backs, and yet nobody really knows what has transpired on your boat in Ireland. You can see why I would resent Andrew's life being discussed by someone like McNab, especially if he was trying to elicit information about him from you. Can you assure me that you told that scoundrel absolutely nothing about my lad during your conversation with him?"

Shocked by the clergyman's vehemence, not to mention the quickness of his temper, Brownlow defended his own integrity and the discretion of his conversation with the cattle drover. "Naw a single word o' information did I gae him sir, of that ye may rest assured," he vowed. Now, in retrospect, he was even more glad of his wisdom in saying little to McNab.

Mackay looked doubtful but his wife spoke soothingly into the tension.

"Go on, Gordon. Tell the gentleman about our Andrew."

He began again. "For all his remarkable abilities though, Andrew, as he left boyhood behind, began to develop some problems, problems of personality, of a ... problems of the mind. He had always been a shy lad, far too quiet, really. He was a deep thinker, and a worrier. You might say he was overly turned in upon himself. An introvert, and prone to periods of what I can only call anguish of the soul. He was such a good boy, so mannerly, and so quiet around the house that you would hardly have known he was there....and I appreciated that at the time because, believe me, it would have been very difficult for me to study had he been more.... more demanding, more noisy and assertive. So I always felt he was a model son really, until I suppose we noticed that he shied away from all social contact..... and, I suppose, until it dawned on us that he was without friends. He was strong in his faith, always had been since he was a bairn, but he couldn't cope with some of the challenges of his life in school. This despite the fact that he was more often than not at the top of his class in almost every aspect of study. He is an avid reader, and a reader of a wide variety of material, much of it way beyond his years. He knows the Scriptures backwards, he has studied many of the great classics of the faith, and, indeed, other literature. Sometimes his turn of phrase astounds me, for such a contemplative boy, I mean. It always brought great pleasure to his mother and I that he was such a diligent student."

The mother joined in. "And this was especially true of his art work. His teachers always spoke so highly of his achievements and praised his drawing skills to the highest. We were so proud of that, weren't we dear?"

"Indeed we were. We encouraged him at every opportunity, to develop this talent. In a sense that is what led to his going to Ireland."

"Before you explain that, dear, tell him about the music," suggested Mrs Mackay.

The minister considered this momentarily, twisting the end of his moustache. "I'm not sure how relevant that is, but... yes, I will briefly say that, because of his lack of social opportunity and his lack of confidence, his mother and I thought to introduce him to the violin. In earlier times I had played the fiddle myself; I have always had a strong devotion to all aspects of our cultural traditions, the Gallic language, the tales of our Scottish heroes and our traditions of dance and song and such like. But I suppose that, in the busyness of the ministry, I had not really continued to involve myself in the practice of these traditions. I had, in a sense, left all that behind me; in pursuit of higher things you could say."

Mrs Mackay cut to the point. "So we bought a fiddle for Andrew and got a teacher for him. Paid for lessons twice a week, and he was making..... fairly good progress, considering that he didn't begin until he was twelve."

"I blame myself for that," confessed her husband, "Twelve was just a bit too late. I should have been playing with him myself from away early on, to give him a love for the tunes. Although he could play well, it always sounded a wee bit mechanical, maybe like he was playing to please us. He never really threw himself into it as I would have liked. But he did take it with him to Ireland, as you can see."

"Ireland is a grand place for music, and Donegal especially," the captain said. "Some o' them fiddlers are as good as ye'd get anywhere in Scotland. Aye, an' they play a lot o' the same tunes."

"I believe you're right there," agreed Rev Mackay, "and that was one of our motivations for sending him there with his uncle."

"His uncle is really my uncle," said Mrs Mackay. "William Roberts, from Inverness where I come from too. He's a very good man, kind and generous in spirit. He spent a lifetime planning and designing railways all over Scotland. We heard that he had been asked to go to Ireland to assist in some dispute about the building of a railway in that county you referred to, Donegal. We had met him at a family funeral and he was describing the job to us, how he would be surveying and making drawings of the territory that this controversial railway was proposed to run through. When we discussed it later that night, it seemed like a God-given opportunity for our Andrew to go along with Uncle William, as an unpaid helper, developing his drawing and learning the trade."

"I understand. A good idea," nodded the captain.

"So we thought. You see, Mr Brownlow, Andrew had a strange fascination with railways; everything to do with railways but especially the bridges and viaducts that they had to have built. When we moved down here from Sutherland, he developed a complete fixation with the Dochart Viaduct and the river. He was only about ten at the time, and frequently he would go missing, hours at a time, but we always knew where to find him. Down along the river bank drawing that viaduct. Gordon even took him down to Glenoglehead, didn't you Gordon, to see the really big one they have there. You came up that way today so you must have crossed over it. He loved it; he drew it on the day and copied it so many times afterward. Beautiful sketches they were too. We never thought that there was anything wrong with this.... this preoccupation. We didn't regard it as unhealthy. The opposite, in fact. We encouraged him. So that is really the reason that we decided to write to my uncle William and beg that he take Andrew under his wing and take him on this surveying trip, to give him more guidance and help with his talent, at our own expense."

Reverend Mackay joined in. "You see, Andrew had not been able to move away from home as we had anticipated, to go to University, nor indeed to take employment....after he had completed school. So this seemed to us a perfect solution to the problem. We felt he needed time away from us, time and opportunity to become his own person and discover what God would have him do in the future. How we regret that decision now!"

Brownlow had the strange sensation that somehow there had been a reversal of roles, that he himself was now the priest, hearing the confessions of a couple racked with regret and doubt. He had a feeling that this was possibly the first time that this rather severe clergyman and his lovely little wife had ever verbalised their reflections about their son to another human being, possibly even to each other. In listening he felt somewhat empowered and he warmed to his role.

"Can I ask what age the lad was?" he inquired.

"He had just turned nineteen when he left," his mother said, "Just nineteen, and now it's...." She broke down again into barely-controlled crying, a shadow of annoyance passing over her husband's face as he reached for her hand again.

"That's much older than he appeared to me," Brownlow said. "I had him aboot sixteen. He seemed a very nice young laddie, though I have tae admit that I didnae talk much tae him, as I said."

"Captain Brownlow," said the minister, "We have given you some background, but we really need you to tell us about those days he had with you on the ship. Any light that you can throw upon his state of mind and what actually happened, we will greatly appreciate."

Brownlow paused to drain the last of the cold tea from his cup before beginning.

"He came tae the ship with Hughes, the harbour-master, aboot six o'clock on that Sunday evenin', twelfth of September. I had known he was to join us, frae talking to Hughes earlier. So we shook hands. He seemed fine tae me, as I said, a nice, mannerly lad, certainly on the shy side. I took him on board and showed him his berth. It's a very small space, just beyond the crew's cabin. As you ken, '*The Mary Ellen*' is a cargo boat, generally carryin' Irish fish tae the Glasgow market. But it was nae problem to offer passage tae your Andrew. There were nae crew aroun' at the time, they were al' away tae the pub, so I couldnae introduce him tae anyone. An' after that he kept himsel' tae himsel', didnae talk to a soul. Not even when he was eating. I made a point o' askin' the crew after he disappeared an' naebody had heard a word oot o' him. Maybe that was our fault but the men were busy an' they niver thought .... Ye understand?"

"Of-course. No blame attached to them or to yourself. But can I ask why the ship didn't come straight home to Glasgow? It seemed to take a lot longer than the usual."

"That's a fair question. Normally we would sail straight hame on the Monday mornin' but I had received a telegram, through the harbour-master again, tae tell me tae sail south tae Killybegs tae pick up a load o' lobster and crab that were going' tae go bad if they weren't shipped at once. So we had to steer a course doon there first. That took the maist o' a day. We picked up that load, just took a couple o' hours tae take on board, and then we put oot tae sea again. As we came round Slieve League cliffs and swung north towards Rossan Point, we saw that we were headin' intae a right fresh wind frae the North West. This was beating' us back the whole way up tae Aranmore Island an' were makin' very little headway. It was gettin' late in the evenin' and the storm was blowin' up into a typical Atlantic gale, so I made the decision tae pull intae the shelter o' Carricklea Bay, where the bulk o' Aranmore would shelter us frae the worst o' it, an' drap anchors fir the night. Then we'd set sail in the mornin' early and hope tae be back in port by nightfall. That was the plan."

"And is that the night Andrew went missing?" asked Mackay.

"That's right. I had been on deck, checkin' wae the watch if all was well, maybe three or four times durin' the course o' the night. The boat was takin' a batterin', but naethin' she couldnae handle. The anchors held the best, but it was rough noo, I'll have tae gae ye that. And whether the storm panicked young Andrew or not, I canny say; it's possible it did, fir it would have been scary fir someone naw used tae the sea. Anyway, I came on deck at first light and that's when I saw his clothes. I nearly walked past them for he had them so neatly folded and wedged in at the side o' the wheelhoose, on the starboard side, next the shore. Shoes an' al'. I looked at them, an' I asked the watch if he'd seen anythin'. He said that he hadn't. He didnae ken how the clothes had got there; must hae been when he was port-side. But I had a bad feelin' aboot it, a sort o' an instinct, I suppose. So I went doon tae the crew's quarters and looked in the berth beyond it, where he had slept, an' there was Andrew's things, al' neatly packed an' left, one beside the other on the bunk. It was a terrible discovery."

"Was there any note left with his things?" asked the mother.

"None at all I am sorry to say, Mrs Mackay. I did look very carefully."

"How was the storm at that stage?" asked the minister, a strange question, in the circumstance, Brownlow thought.

"The gale had largely blown itsel' oot," replied the captain and continued his account. "I raised the alarm at once, shoutin' "Man overboard!" and the crew came runnin'. We looked in the sea aroun' aboot, we searched the ship, but there wasnae a thing we could dae. It was just too late. I am sorry."

Another of those strained silences. No one spoke for almost a minute. Then Maureen Mackay asked the obvious question.

"Why were his clothes found on the boat? I don't understand."

Not an easily answered question and nobody tried.

"What did you do with the clothes?"

That was an easier question. "I put them into his suitcase, on top of his other things."

"Ah, good," said Rev Mackay, and he stood up and went into the hall, returning in a moment with suitcase, fiddle case and satchel. He opened the suitcase first and a sour, sickly odour rose to his nostrils. Delicately he lifted his son's shoes, trousers, shirt and jacket, setting them on the table, still in their folds. His wife watched, leaning back against the chair, shoulders shaking silently, hand at her mouth. He then turned to the satchel and, opening it reverently, removed a thick, well-bound notebook and a sheaf of loose pages which were obviously drawings of some sort. These the boy's father set in the middle of the table, emotion beginning to show in his eyes for the first time.

"His journal," he said softly. "And some drawings."

Finally he placed the fiddle case in front of him and clicked open the twin fasteners. He lifted the case-lid and stood back from the table in an involuntary movement of surprise. Mrs Mackay also stood up, pushing her chair behind her, its legs scraping on the wooden floorboards. Brownlow, from his position at the table could not see through the opened lid, so he also rose to peer into the violin case from a better angle.

There was no fiddle in the case!

He had never thought to check, the case feeling like it contained a light-weight instrument. He had just presumed, understandably, that it still contained a violin.

Instead of its usual occupant, there was a single sheet of white paper, ragged at the edge, probably torn from the boy's journal.

"A note," breathed the mother through her handkerchief.

Reverend Mackay picked it up and read the broad pencil inscription in a trembling whisper of a voice.

"Then Moses cried out to the Lord and the Lord showed him a piece of wood. He threw it into the water and the water became sweet.

There the Lord made a decree and a law for them and there he tested them. He said, If you listen carefully to the voice of the Lord your God and do what is right in His eyes, if you pay attention to his commands and keep all His decrees, I will not bring on you any of the diseases I brought on the Egyptians, for I am the Lord who heals you.

Then they came to Elim, where there were twelve springs, and seventy palm trees, and they camped there near the water."
Exodus ch 15 V25-27

THE WOOD TO THE WATER FOR ITS HEALING

That was all it said.

~~~~~~~

Captain Brownlow left on the 8.20 train the following morning, having accepted the hospitality of the manse and spent the night there in the chilly guest-bedroom. He had formed the impression that he might well have been the first person ever to have actually done so. And he slept only lightly, conscious on several occasions of a murmur of conversation, punctuated by stifled sobbing, coming from the bedroom next door. Mrs Mackay had looked a dreadful sight at breakfast and the atmosphere in the house was so tensely brittle that he could barely wait to escape into the fresh morning air and the wakening stir of the village of Killin.

The clergyman insisted on reimbursing the visitor for his train ticket and giving him a ten pound note for his troubles; now he further insisted on accompanying him to the station, a kindness that Brownlow felt he could have done without. He suspected that Mackay was glad of the opportunity for a walk and a break from the intensity of the grieving hearth; indeed, he might well be welcoming the chance to postpone the pain of opening and beginning to read his son's journal. In this suspicion he was more than correct.

As the little Pug engine strained its every rivet to shift the train up the narrow tracks towards the Dochart viaduct, Rev Mackay stared after it, hands behind his back, a forlorn and tortured statue. Standing in the brown shadow of the station goods house, his dark hat forward on his brow, his long coat motionless, his dog-collar was the brightest thing about him. The Station-master trundled towards him pushing an empty trolley with one well-practised hand, while the other hand shuttled a morning fag back and forward to his thin lips. He half paused as he approached the minister, as if to stop and chat, but instinctively thinking better of his intention, he merely nodded and mumbled, "Morning tae ye, yer reverence," then shuffled on past, a curl of sweet Woodbine tobacco smoke trailing behind him, not unlike the Pug on its way up the glen.

Reverend Mackey eventually moved, almost stumbled, staccato-like, towards the street. He kept his head down, his hat at a defensive tilt, as he made his way back up the hill. Ignoring parishioners who looked to him for his usual morning recognition, he reached Craignavie Road and kept on walking towards the mill and the roar of the Falls. He had no plan, his jumbled thoughts did not allow a plan; just walk until .... "Until I pick up the courage to open his diary. Until I have the wisdom to handle Maureen. God give me strength to get Maureen through this!"

He crossed the narrow, old bridge over the rushing river, just beside the wild, white water of the Dochart Falls, but he barely registered the sound. Beyond the bridge he turned to walk east, back along the high, tree-lined riverbank, past the gate-lodge and through the tall gateposts of the Kinnell estate, towards the decaying mansion that was Kinnell House. He stood under the dark, twisted branches of an old witch of a tree, staring emptily at the ancient circle of standing stones which stood very close to the ancestral seat of the McNab clan and was a well-known landmark in the whole Breadalbane area. The standing stones fascinated him and, like many before him, he wondered about the prehistoric artists or priests who had assembled this near-perfect circle.

"All of this history, this intrigue, these remnants of a race of people long gone.... forgotten but for the stone relics they left behind. And my son, gone too. Gone to join them. How long before he is forgotten altogether? When his mother and I have passed on, who will remember Andrew? Not a soul; there is no one to remember him. Not even a gravestone. What has he left behind him for posterity? What has he done to be remembered by? What was it all for? What was the purpose of his sad, short existence? And why should it end in such uncertain circumstances?"

A flock of starlings clouded into view and swirled around the stone circle in a twittering fanfare of near religious excitement, before landing around the rocks to feed. Mackay marvelled silently at their un-conducted solidarity, their apparent one-mindedness, and the spontaneous cooperation of their flight and their feeding.

"Are not two sparrows sold for a farthing, and one of them shall not fall to the ground without your Father?" he quoted to himself. "What does that say about Andrew? 'Fear ye not therefore, ye are of more value than many sparrows'." Without warning he found himself begin to heave with emotion and for a full ten minutes he was singularly beside himself with an intensity of grief and loss and the desolation of hopelessness. The gnarled old Weeping Willow, under whose tears he stood, offered what privacy and solace it could; startled, the starlings blew away like the smoke of a gorse fire and the standing stones promised to maintain the silent vow of the confessional. He felt purged, on the other side of his emotion; drained but purged and readied for the reading of the journal which now must begin, once he had made his way back to his wondering wife.

He took off his hat and held it to his chest, ran his hand through his hair, tugged his ear and stepped out from the skirts of the tree. He lifted his eyes across the valley of Loch Tay to the slopes of the mighty Ben Lawers. He broke into his favourite psalm and sang with slightly quavering voice, "I to the hills will lift mine eyes, from whence doth come mine aid."

From the head of the glen behind him he heard the high-pitched shriek-hoot of the train and it cut short his singing. The Pug had begun its return journey from Killin Junction; he himself turned his steps back towards Killin Manse and his son's last testament.

The Dochart Viaduct

Chapter 10

<u>**Tuesday 1st June 1897**</u>
<u>**My thoughts before leaving for Ireland**</u>

I know I will sleep little this night. But I am experienced in this.
I will ponder the blank canvas that stretches before me.
What colours will rise to join the emerald and the blue?
What shapes will the lines bring forth?
What forms will grow from their convergences?
Will I understand these unknown designs?
Will I recognise the Hand of the Great Designer or will my scuffling hand make smudges of them all?

I wish to make my father proud.
I wish to make my mother happy.
To go from her is meant to make her happy.
Is meant to make him proud.
What is it meant to make me?

That will all unfold in the Grand Design, I am to believe.
And I do believe. I will believe. I believe I will.
But doubt will sleep beside me in my bed.
And walk beside me by the river.
And we will talk together.

How I will miss my dashing Dochart.
Loch Tay will call to me, I believe, from a distance.
It has a colour all of its own and never twice the same.
A hundred shades of green and blue and grey.
What could I ever see in Ireland to take its place?

My apprehensions are not of lonesomeness, for he has been my preferred companion.
Rather I fear the sea, the journey in the confines of some little ship.
The babble of fellow-travellers.
The meeting with my mother's uncle whom I do not know.
There was a meeting several years ago, I am told.
I do not remember, nor care to try.
Did he have a white beard I wonder?
If so, then yes, perhaps I do recall his white beard.
So he is a white beard of a man.
That is all.
Mr William Roberts, of Inverness, where I have been once, though why I do not know.
He is a righteous man, by all accounts, which I am glad of.
For his sake and for mine.
An expert, with vast experience.
And so his expertise is needed by the Irish to solve some problem of the route of a new railway line.
This I am led to believe by my parents.
My role as yet I am unsure of.
To draw imaginary tracks, embankments, bridges not yet built perhaps?
To position the Dochart Viaduct on some insoluble situation in an Irish bog?
It is just as well I have every detail of the construction firmly etched in my memory then. Every beautiful line, every precise angle, every sturdy block of stone, set in a perfect geometry, a

work of practical art precisely designed and assembled for its purpose.
Like creation itself.

I know not what to expect of Irish people.
I know little of the Catholic faith which, I am led to believe, the people of Ireland hold to.
On the whole.
The Holy Catholic Church.
I hope that I shall have few occasions to talk to such folk. I would not know what to say. I have had limited experience of those in Killin of that persuasion. Perhaps because I am a child of the manse. Of Killin manse at any rate.
From my classes in History I recall some problems with such people.
The bonny prince?
Wasn't he one?
Culloden and all that?
A Mary Queen of Scots perhaps?
But she is out of focus.
And may not mean a thing to the people of Ireland.
Perhaps I should have listened more attentively in History class.
But the Master's monotone drove me to think of something else, like railway tracks.
Otherwise I would have fallen asleep.

Tomorrow's journey I should find interesting, I am led to believe.
The train part anyhow.
The changes in Killin Junction, Callander, Stirling.
The size of Glasgow Station, with so many rows of tracks going who knows where. The journey to the docks.
The narrow gauge rail tracks there, shifting cargo from dock to dock, ship to train. But why am I preempting such excitements?
"Take therefore no thought for the morrow: for the morrow shall take thought for the things of itself. Sufficient unto the day is the evil thereof".
I believe this to be a more than useful Scriptural principle.

And so I will endeavour to sleep, yet I do believe I shall be disappointed in this, yet again.

<u>Wednesday 2nd June 1897</u>
<u>My thoughts on arrival in Glasgow</u>

Killin to Glasgow.
A journey of intense fascination.
For my father!
It was of-course thoughtful and considerate of him to accompany me to Glasgow, and I could not have done so without his guidance.
But!
Would that he had just looked from the window of the carriage without attempting to meet the apparent need to instruct me at every opportunity.
I know what villages are.
I need not know their names.
Not all of them.
Nor who is clergy there at present, and who preceded them.
Nor whether they are "sound" or not.
Nor who's daughter married whoever's cousin in that kirk by the loch-side.
Nor what height that mountain is supposed to be.

I wanted time.
Time to reflect on my mother's farewell tears, to try to comprehend them properly. It was a new experience for me.
I need time to think on what she said. And why.
But already her words were merging with the hypnotic rhythm of iron wheel on iron track, and the incessant preachers and grandmothers and marriages and in-laws and heresies and village missions of my father's catalogue.

What is wrong with being quiet?
I cannot absorb what he wanted me to take in.
And I cannot absorb what I wanted to take in.

And whatever it was my mother was trying to say is lost in the exasperation of that cluttered journey.
But one thing sticks in my mind from her goodbye. Something like, "Will you forgive us if this venture turns out to be a mistake?"
It is either a mistake from the outset or not, my poor uncertain mother.
Not "Turns out to be".
Is it in the Divine Design for me or not?
If it is not, then woe is me.
But despite my trepidation, I will believe it to be in the Plan.
The Plan laid out for me before time began.
So on with it.

When the train was at the height of its speed I enjoyed the view from the window. The flickering hedges and trees, gates and gable ends, flying past.
Like pictures blown in a breeze.
Reminded me of thumbing through the pages of a story-book at speed, like I used to love to do when I was younger. I would draw a series of pictures of a horse jumping a fence, or a train crossing a bridge. Then when I'd flick through the pages the images would run into each other and give the object an appearance of movement. This is what I remembered in the train and it made me happy to recall it.
A happier, flickering, childhood memory.

I do not, however, like this city, this street, these lodgings, this room, this gas light by which to try to write.
I saw nothing of beauty in this Glasgow.
Not that I had much chance to contemplate anything.
The station. The tall buildings. Warehouses and banks. Grand churches. The bridges across the Clyde.
Father whipped us through the environment as if in a chase with wild horses.
Wild horses there were too, in carts and cabs and carriages and drawing every form of transportation I could ever have imagined. By the dozen. It will be a relief to get aboard the ship in the early morning. The ship which will deliver me to Derry, or Londonderry, or whatever it is called.

In a place like this I am glad to be solitary.
Had I paid heed today, it seemed the city heaved with ant-like people.
There were people everywhere.
By the train-load, the street-load, the shop-load, the carriage-load.
Hurrying, scurrying, worrying, burrowing people.
Rushing in all directions.
Each caught in their own panic.
I was sorry for them, as I would be for a colony of wood lice when I upturn the protection of their chosen shelter, perhaps an old slate or stone in the back garden. I wanted to say to them, "Go and find a stream to sit by."
But I might have been punched.
The men were almost all grey, from cloth-cap to boots.
Many smoked cigarettes, newspapers under their arms, glints in their eyes.
Ladies I did not notice, though one approached my father near the Boarding House and seemed to incur his wrath very quickly. It may have been her painted lips which annoyed him. I know he finds that offensive. He said, "Jezebel! I knew I should have worn my clerical collar." How that would have helped I know not. So that is what a "Jezebel" looks like?
The inns and hostelries are much frequented here, more so than in Killin I believe. Begging children at every street corner. One begging mother with a thin child in her arms, skin and bones, the poorest of apparel.
My father fussily sought out a coin to give her.
She was thankful and said so, in a dialect I had not heard before.
Father said she was Irish.
What will happen if I cannot make head or tail of them over there?
I hope they will leave me in peace.
"Peace I leave with you, my peace I give unto you."

My father will take me to the ship very early in the morning.
It is to be an all day journey.
He has the ticket, a thin piece of yellowish paper.
Put me on board with my suitcase and my satchel of paper and my fiddle.

My fiddle is coming along to be inspired by the music of Donegal.
Which is good, because that music, I am led to believe, came originally from Scotland. (Or was it vice versa?) Perhaps my fiddle should therefore have simply remained in Scotland. For its own inspiration. But we shall see. Perhaps it will prove a useful ally for this wandering Scottish laddie. If only I could play it better. Perhaps a musical spell will fall upon me from a passing fiddler and I will be transformed into my father's image.
My father is a good man.
I owe him so much.
And I will make him proud, whether as an artist or as an engineer or as a theologian.
Probably not as a theologian.

<u>*Thursday 3rd June 1897*</u>
<u>*My thoughts on arrival in Ireland*</u>

I have reached the city of uncertain name.
"A city set on a hill which cannot be hidden."
It is no London, I should hope, even if it claims that prefix.

And I should hope I never live to suffer such a journey again.
I was led to believe many things about travel.
I have been wheeled, trained, coached, carted, bicycled, even sailed.
(If I may count a twelve foot dinghy under flapping sheets upon Loch Tay.)
Nothing and no one prepared me for the experience of a ship like this.
There is a fortune for the man who can smooth the seas, who can devise a way to lay rail track or a viaduct or any form of consistent levelness from one shore to another.

I was sick enough to die.
To die several times over.
I eventually hoped to die, as an alternative to those evil sensations.
A sickness of the belly.

A sickness of the brain.
And I was not alone.
I became part of the fellowship of the vomiters, a group I had not thought to join, not in free will, at any rate.
The ship rolled and lurched and groaned and heaved beneath me.
And I heaved above it.
Into buckets and basins and over the side into the ocean.
Which deserved all it got.
Several meals, it seemed.
Food which I do believe I had never eaten, to the best of my limited memory.
The ship was accompanied by a vast number of birds of the seagull variety.
Some sat on railings and ropes and watched for inadvertent food discharges.
Others swept down upon the waves to scavenge what they could on the surface.
Our discomfort was their opportunity, it seemed.

Oh to be able to follow the Master and walk upon the water.
Back to the shore.
I did pray.
I begged.
I commanded.
"Even the winds and the waves obey Him."
But not me, it seems.
I called out to my mother, foolishly.
Whether audibly or in my head I know not.
What have I done wrong to deserve such buffeting?
Or perhaps it was another among us?
Why should we all suffer for one man's transgression?
I raised this question with a passing sailor.
He looked at me strangely. In drink, I thought. (They have a reputation for rum, I am led to believe.) He denied that this was a storm. I have seen nothing yet, apparently.
"Are waves meant to go up and down and sideways all at the same time?" I asked. He walked on without an answer. A question he had not been asked before obviously.

Beyond the mouth of the Clyde estuary I saw nothing of the landscape.
The seascape I saw from several obtuse angles. It changed constantly and yet changed little.
One swell is very much like the next, it seems.
I could not stay below, such was the density of human collage.
I could not stay on deck either, so wandered between the two.
A lost soul in a watery inferno.
Up and down in sloughs of despondency, like Bunyan's Christian.
The hours passed too slowly, time apparently standing still so as to collaborate with the storm in the test of our faith.
I saw nothing of the famed beauty of the Irish coast. My father had instructed me to view it on the port side of the boat.
'Port' became to me less a direction and more a hopeless ambition.
Eventually, however, we did reach port, after a more pleasant, less turbulent passage through a narrow channel and a sea-loch protected by a tall land mass which I was informed is part of the county of Donegal. As the sun sank behind those welcome hills I thought that this was my first sight of the place which is to be my homeland for the following three or four months.
The ship slid gently towards the quay. How gently it can move, in contrast to its thrashing passage through that angry sea.
I saw with fascination the docking of the vessel.
The throwing of ropes.
The hauling of the dockers and seamen.
The shouting clamour and the orders issued.
The waving gesticulations, dim in the dusky brown evening light.
And then we were still.
I saw pale complexions begin to warm again, no doubt my own among them.

As I write I sit in a small bedroom of a poorly appointed hotel in the aptly named Shipquay Street. I found it with ease, having asked a pleasant gentleman for directions as we disembarked. It was a mere two hundred yards of a walk, past an impressively tall, red sandstone building with an elegant

clock tower. I presume it to be a city hall of some sort. Then through a robust-looking gate in the city walls and there it was, not much further up that steep street, on the right.
How nice to see such an ancient city wall, so well preserved. Reminded me of Stirling in its general profile, this Londonderry.
I wonder does the city have a castle? Perhaps it is a castle.
I may have time to explore the surrounding streets tomorrow, perhaps sketch the gate in the city's walls, before my contact arrives to transport me to where my uncle is currently engaged. The white-beard!
How will we take to each other?
What exactly will he expect of me?
What will be my role in this new place?
What have I to learn of life in this place beyond the sickening seas?
I am surprised that as yet I have not missed my mother or father.
Apart from when I called for her in that turmoil of a journey of-course.
I have the confidence of a man who as yet knows not what he is about to trip over.

Shipquay Gate

Chapter 11

Friday 4th June 1897
My observations concerning my first day on Irish soil

Sleep eluded me again last night.
Still a queasy feeling where my stomach used to live.
I believe that the smells of a new city disturb me.
The smells of the street, of the hotel bar, of the corridors, of the toilets, of this pokey room three floors above a sloping city.

I climbed the considerable incline of Shipquay Street after a porridge and bacon breakfast.
The horses on this thoroughfare strained at their loads, as drivers swore and cracked whips around their sweating rumps.
The welfare of the horse was not considered in the selection of this hill upon which to build a city, it would seem. Good for security and defence, and for trade and commerce but less so for Clydesdales and Cobs, ponies and donkeys.
Still, at least a wiry little hunchback of a man with shovel and wheelbarrow is there to clean up after them. And he is busy on a morning like this.
Stood in the central square which, I am led to believe, is called the Diamond.
Watched the city go to work.
Here it was the women I observed. Scuttling by in haste towards the honking sound of factory horns. A shadow of care on most countenances.
The factories make I know not what and are positioned by the river bank. A broad and sedate river, this Foyle. I looked down upon it from the height of the city's walls.
I discerned, with feelings devoid of any affection, my ship along the quayside. There were several others there, some large and ocean-bound, some small. This Derry is a bustling port.
On the other bank of the river, across an ageing bridge, is another settlement, streets running up the brae from the river at right angles.
Behind me is a squat, grey church, perhaps a cathedral, in a silent graveyard, as most graveyards are of course.

Awaiting heaven's factory horn.
Otherwise known as "The Last Trumpet".
I observed an inscription by the impressive door of this house of God which I found of puzzling interest. Imprinted in discoloured marble it begins by boldly proclaiming a date, presumably of the church's construction.
"ANO DO 1633   CAR REGIS 9"
(I am unsure about the meaning of the latter part; my father would probably know.)
Below is a pithy verse, as follows;
"IF STONES COVLD SPEAKE
THEN LONDONS PRAYSE
SHOVLD SOVNDE WHO
BVILT THIS CHVRCH AND
CITTIE FROM THE GROVNDE"
And then a name.
VAUGHAN.AED
(So they did know how to fashion the letter 'U'!)
I deduce therefore that London somehow was involved in the construction of this, a Protestant church or cathedral within the city walls.
St Columb's by name, Anglican by denomination.
I seem to recall a certain connection between him and our own Saint Fillan, back home in Killin.
Killin claims Fillan, but he was an Irishman I think. A missionary, from these parts to Scotland.
There, I thought of home, without too much of a pang of homesickness or similar emotion.

As I proceeded around those handsome walls in the direction opposite to the river I was drawn to look down upon the low-lying area between the city's edifice and the green hills rising beyond.
The picture here was quite different.
Houses are jammed together in a jumble of ungainly narrow lanes. Small houses, built of a range of materials and with little attention to design or beauty.
In contrast to the buildings I have seen behind me, within the walls.
Roofing of thatch, or tin, or wood, or slate, or even sacking it would seem.

Walls whose crooked faces look like they may never have had the benefit of plaster nor paint.
I seemed to discern the sounds of pigs and other animals.
Even from where I stood upon the battlements I could detect, by smell and general appearance, a sense of poverty and deprivation which stands in stark contrast to the elegance of the Diamond and the shops and businesses within the walls.
A city divided, it seems.
Divided by the existence of these historic walls.
Divided in wealth and fortune, if my observations are in order.
"A city divided against itself shall not stand".
This place should fear for itself.
As I walked around the walls I took some moments to sketch the Shipquay Gate.
Then I returned to the hotel to find a young man awaiting me.

A Mister John Diver, pleasant enough but of little wit I fear. He smiled droopily, ear to ear as they say, and almost without respite.
The journey to Letterkenny was by train, appropriately enough. We boarded at the station close beside the Foyle River, Diver having carried my cases the considerable distance along a street between walls and water. He also had my ticket in hand.
A useful fellow, despite his incessant grin.
Of little or no conversation, thankfully.
The journey was as uneventful as the countryside was unremarkable. No particular features of beauty as yet, and not unlike parts of landscape I had travelled through en route to Glasgow. Before long we had arrived in Letterkenny Station, not much over an hour I think. I had a sense of "The End of the Line" about this station.
Terminal indeed.
I was glad to be greeted from behind his white beard, and beyond some railings, by my uncle, William Roberts, who had taken the time to come to meet me. Nearing his three score years and ten, he still cut an impressive figure among the more bedraggled population of Port Road, Letterkenny, as he strode ahead of me towards his hotel and our mid-afternoon

meal. During which he studied me across the table in a way I have never been studied before.
His dark, hazel eyes strip me down to my very soul, it seems.
I begin to think of wrong thoughts I have recently had. I wonder if he is reading them.
He does not say a lot.
But then people like him do not need to.
He did ask questions regarding my health and well-being.
Then my interests and my studies.
This between fish and dessert.
Then my faith and convictions.
I hope I passed the test.
But time will tell.
How I should like to read what was written to him in my father's correspondence.

We will be based at this Gallagher's Hotel during our sojourn, I am given to believe. Following our repast my uncle told me of an important meeting tonight.
A public meeting, here in the Courthouse in Letterkenny.
I have arrived just in time, it seems, for the first significant episode in this mission. I was introduced to a Mr Joseph Tatlow, with whom my uncle is to work.
A smallish, fidgety sort of gentleman who has a predisposition to adjust his spectacles, or hair, or moustache, or necktie, or all four of these in sequence, at every opportunity.
At every occasion when he is not having a scratch at some other region of his little body.
Most interestingly, he has an accent with which I am unfamiliar. My concentration was severely challenged as I tried to establish in my head what he had just spoken to me.
I probably seemed dumb-struck.
My ears feel like they are drowning beneath foaming waves of unfamiliar vowels. He is, I am informed, from the city of Dublin.
That may explain it.
I have not heard this tongue before.
I am instructed that this Mr Tatlow and my uncle are appointed to conduct the Irish Railway Commission Enquiry into the proposed Letterkenny to Burtonport Railway. An important sounding job, I believe. I will learn more this

evening. And in the meantime examine some maps which my uncle has provided for my education.

This Donegal is an extensive county, the terrain of which I will, no doubt, become more accustomed to in time.
I shall also take time to study my allotted passage of Scripture which will, I pray, 'Be a lamp unto my feet and a light unto my path'.
After the sleeplessness of last night, indeed the past three nights, I must also try to take some rest before this meeting.

<u>Saturday 5th June 1897</u>
<u>My thoughts concerning the first railway consultation meeting</u>

Friday nights in a Main Street Letterkenny hotel are not conducive to sleep. I am feeling fatigued before we even begin this excursion into the unknown west.

As I write, we are travelling by coach and four to a town called Dunfanaghy, which, I am informed, is some considerable distance from Letterkenny.
The task of writing is not made easier by the tugging of our stout horses, nor by the jiggling of the coach wheels upon what looks and feels like a very rocky road.
Nor by the close presence at my elbow of the ubiquitous Joseph Tatlow, whose night's sleep does not seem to have done anything for his body's sense of well-being.
Indeed I suspect he may have exported on his person one or two additional companions of the tiny insect variety from his hotel bed.
Whilst I wish him luck in tracking them down, I wish he would do so elsewhere.
I have no great wish to be the recipient of any generosity in this matter.
He and Uncle Roberts are in constant debate and discussion today on the subject of last night's meeting, and I am taking this opportunity to record some of my own brief observations concerning its conduct.

Mr Tatlow in the chair.
Mr Roberts as secretary and note taker.

Both well-protected, should the need for that become a sudden consideration, behind a substantial oak desk.
And by the presence of two resplendent constables of the Royal Irish Constabulary.
A huge audience, which surprised me a great deal.
People of all shapes and sizes, of all social ranks and all manner of garment, crammed into every nook and cranny of the Courthouse, many more than it was intended for, I am sure, but no one objected or tried to control entry.
I got the impression that this issue of a railway to the western districts of the county was one which has had a long history, and one not without controversy.
Among the crowd, several clergy.
One of which, a Father Sweeney, presented a very detailed document to the assembly, reading it aloud, with much enthusiasm and extrapolation, to all assembled.
The railway would, it seems, go a long way to alleviating whatever the problems of the western half of this county are perceived to be. I noted in his "sermon" reference to many sea products.
Herring. Ling. Cod. Sole. Haddock. Cockles.
Something called Carrageen moss.
The export of these from the poor west to the richer east, and onwards to the cities of England and Scotland, would seem to be desirable.
No doubt the people of Liverpool and similar cities would appreciate fresher cockles.
Then there was reference to a host of other potential benefits.
The development of lime. Turf. Peat-moss litter. Hosiery. Stockings. Jerseys. Gloves. Shirts. Eggs.
And "sweet shore sheep", whatever they are. A tricky challenge to the tongue, at the very least. 'Other sheep have I which are not of this fold,' it seems to me. The people of Manchester surely cannot be doing without a constant supply of "sweet shore sheep". Not to mention even fresher eggs.
Several other clergy joined the debate, all out-doing each other to impress the two Commissioners, Tatlow and my uncle.
In the light of their persuasive wisdom, I began to wonder why on earth the railway was still only at the proposal stage and had not been brought into existence many years ago.

All spoke in English, albeit of peculiar accent and dialect, although, on occasions when the discussion became more intense, there were lapses into the Gaelic language.

I found with some interest that I could understand several of the words and phrases in that tongue. The general sense of what was being said, however, eluded me until Mr Tatlow would remind the speaker angrily to "Kindly refrain from use of native speech and return to the English, which is the language of this enquiry." I have formed the opinion that the Dubliner's grasp of his native tongue may not match that of the Donegal natives.

In similar vein, a priest called Dunleavey from _____, (I did not catch where), said that an area called the Rosses was the most congested district in all of Ireland, with currently 2806 persons and a rising population. (I noted that number carefully, lest I should ever be quizzed about the population of the Rosses!)

He spoke disparagingly about a pattern of seasonal migration of workers from his area to Scotland, every year.

Scotland is a fine destination, I thought to argue, but that was not his point of course.

No one asked him the obvious question which sprang to my simple mind. Might not this railway make the movement of such people out of his parish all the easier?

Mine is not to reason why.

Not at this early stage anyhow.

Father Dunleavey waxed warmly to his subject, a formidable character, I should imagine.

Shirt-making was his next theme, and the benefits of such an industry to his parish.

Are they short of shirts? I wondered. But no. For export and sale in other cities, it seems.

Other gentlemen made contributions, intelligent and well-thought-out speeches. One or two were more enamoured with the sound of their own accents, I suspected. Most seemed to be clergy, largely of the Roman Church, which is understandable.

So it all sounded very convincing, a fait accompli, I would have thought.

A good idea, this railway.

However, towards the end of the hearing I began to sense some disquiet and divisions of opinion among those assembled.
Murmurers among the multitude.
These objections I do not as yet understand.
They are to do with money, the root of all dissension, it would seem.
That and the proposed route of the railway.
But these issues I do not have a grasp of, not being in proper familiarity with the geography of the area, despite my uncle's maps. No doubt it shall become clear in time.
Mr Tatlow was at times under some pressure but I was impressed by how he handled the whole event, by his firmness and fairness, and, when he was struggling, my Uncle Roberts laid down his pen and was a colossus of conciliatory calm, in support of his colleague.

Now as we rumble westward, however, they are in argument, but, having been writing, I have not picked up the threads of their debate.

We have just exited from a narrow pass through rugged hills and are winding down a twisting road towards an extensive area of low-lying bogland.
The town of Creeslough is some way ahead, I am informed, where we shall eat luncheon before continuing in the direction of the seaside town named Dunfanaghy, in which we shall spend the night and the Sabbath tomorrow, I believe.
Looking ahead from the grimy window of this coach I can discern the top of a sizeable mountain.
At times I think its top is a flat plateau, while at other times it appears to be a zigzag of a summit, but I admit that these perceptions may have more to do with the uneven bounce of my current transportation, not to mention my heavy eyelids.

<u>Monday 7th June 1897</u>
<u>My reflections on a Sabbath in Dunfanaghy</u>

Yesterday was non-eventful.
Which is, after all, what Sunday is meant to be.

This town of Dunfanaghy is a neat, well-appointed little place, separated from the sea by an area of sand hills and a picturesque beach. Were it not the Sabbath I would have liked to attempt to sketch this town, this landscape.
I had the pleasure of accompanying Uncle Roberts on a very gentle stroll along this strand.
Gentle, to take account of his age and general corpulence.
A considerable distance from one end of this beach to the other, we discovered to our cost.
There is a stubbornness of character in the man.
I suggested at one juncture that we should give some thought to turning, but he would hear none of it. He had only reached the halfway point of his homily, it seemed.
So we continued to the bitter end of both sermon and strand, before turning to kill down the remainder of the day on the slow retrace of our footprints in the golden sand.
The tide obliged by keeping itself at a safe distance to the north.
To its disadvantage, it is, however, none the wiser regarding the passage of the Children of Israel from Egypt to the Promised Land.
Featuring another distant sea, and a miraculous safe passage.
This had been the theme of the sermon in the Presbyterian Kirk which we had attended at noon.
I recognised the Minister as having been at the Letterkenny meeting on Friday evening. A Reverend William Kane, I am informed, and he welcomed us publicly, and with some surprising warmth, to the service. Indeed he made passionate reference to the railway in one of his prayers. It would seem to me that he is putting a degree of pressure on both Our Heavenly Father and my esteemed uncle to ensure that the route of the railway take in his prosperous little town. Whether or not Uncle Roberts or, more importantly, the Lord above, was impressed by this prayer remains to be seen.
Uncle Roberts and I obviously did not discuss this matter on this Sabbath Day.
I soon understood, however, that he was not impressed by Rev Kane's handling of the significance of certain aspects of the story of the Passover and the Red Sea crossing in Exodus chapters 12 and 13.
Hence the "Sermon on the Sand".

Dunfanaghy does have an air of civilisation and ambition about it. The hotel has been the most comfortable I have experienced since I left home.
It would seem to be protected from the western winds by a large land mass which extends in peninsula form from just beyond the town.
On enquiry I am informed that this area of high ground is called Horn Head.
Well, despite it's abrupt title, it obviously does a grand job for the sheltered hamlet of Dunfanaghy.

The only disquiet I am beginning to be aware of within my self originated this morning as I further explored the town.
Tatlow and Diver were head to head in discussion in a corner of the hotel lounge. Logistical matters, I suspect, will be their subject matter, though they became quiet and looked strangely at me when I chanced to come within hearing distance of their conversation.
Diver seems to be our "fixer".
The man with the fixed grin.
The man who organises the travel arrangements, the horses, our accommodation and the like.
It may be they were planning something with regard to tonight's Public Meeting in the village hall.
Or perhaps the coach for our onward journey to our next port of call, another village further to the west with the comforting name of Burtonport.
Or perhaps soliciting advice on overcoming bedbugs.
Uncle Roberts was nowhere to be seen, presumably engaged in writing up the minutes of Friday night's meeting.
Having nothing else to do and being unable to amuse myself otherwise, I decided to walk through the streets of Dunfanaghy.
I say "streets", but really I mean "street" in the singular, for it seems there is but one thoroughfare running east to west through the town.
A street of small shops and businesses, homes and hostelries.
This street I followed until at the end of the village I reached a building which I ascertained to be a workhouse.

I stood outside for a short while, simply watching the building, admiring the functional simplicity of the architecture which struck me as very much fit for its purpose.
Clear lines and perfectly proportioned symmetry.
Dark grey in general colour, an edifice of foreboding import.
One knows where one stands with such a building.
By and by I had the distinct impression that I was being watched.
I am unsure by whom.
People from within the building?
Perhaps, though I saw no windows, nor did I notice anyone at the main gate.
The building itself had a whole aura of being what I can only describe as "on the look-out". I know not for what, except that I felt somehow implicated.
The feeling of being watched continued as I proceeded back through the Main Street, and towards the beach where I had enjoyed such a pleasant walk yesterday.
I did meet a considerable number of people on this walk. Local folk going about their daily toil. Several looked strangely at me and spoke in greeting. But as I continued I could feel their gaze upon me. I could sense their minds turning over. Their tongues beginning to wag within their mouths as they wondered who I was. What I was doing in their town. Who I was with.
These uncomfortable suspicions stayed with me all along the beach, even though I met not a soul upon the sand.
It was with relief that I returned to the hotel and sought the company of my wise uncle.
When I told him of my suspicions, he consoled me somewhat by saying that of course the local people were curious of all four of us within the town.
Of course!
He asked me if I had written home yet.
I replied that I had not.
He suggested that I do so today, as post would travel much more quickly from this town than from those further to the west.
So I resolved to write to my father and mother and will do so before the meeting tonight.

Because we leave early in the morning for our next stage of this pilgrimage.
This journey into the wilderness.
We, the Children of Israel, proceeding through this boggy desert of strange tribes, to whatever Promised Land lies ahead of us.

The mountain with the flat top lies just to the south and gives the impression of looking down upon this town. I am led to believe that its name, which is "Muckish", means "Pig!"
The poor, unfortunate mountain.
What has it done to deserve this title?
To me it looks quite a majestic structure, wonderfully architectured, beautifully constructed.
Strong masculine edges.
A bulwark of a mountain.
It could easily merit a name of Scriptural origin.
A Zion, or Hebron, or Carmel.
They say it looks like the back of a pig.
It looks every bit as similar to the back of a bull or a sheep.
Why not "Bull Mountain"?
Ah well, it has my sympathy.
This pig of a hill.

Chapter 12

My Dear Parents

Reverend Mackay placed the journal on the table beside him with a solemnity that resembled how he laid the Bible on his pulpit after reading the scripture lesson. His wife's gaze, fixed unseeingly on the rug at her feet until then, lifted to follow him as he shuffled to his mahogany writing desk in the corner. He opened the top drawer, with some difficulty. Where once the drawer slid easily, a combination of age and damp had caused some warping of the timber, so that now he had to struggle with it, to his instant annoyance. Taking a thin sheaf of papers from a folder, he returned to his chair.

"I think it might be a good idea to read his letters again, in the context of these diary notes, don't you agree?" he explained.

"Whatever you say, Gordon." A whimpered response.

He leafed through the pages, withdrew the one he was searching for, unfolded the letter and began to read aloud.

"Monday 7th June 1897

My Dear Parents,

It is at Uncle Roberts' request and on his wise and timely advice that I write to you this evening. Timely, because the postal service from this town, namely Dunfanaghy, is of a superior nature to that from other outposts which we will be visiting on the next stage of our journey. I am not at all sure of the names of these settlements as yet. No doubt I shall become familiar with them during the course of this summer. Anyhow, their names would probably mean nothing to you and you may never need to know of them, so it does not really matter. Dunfanaghy is a small town that has much to recommend it, although I am finding some of the local inhabitants overly curious. Uncle Roberts is a fine Christian gentleman and I have benefitted from his wisdom already. We walked together, discussing many things, some of which were of a theological nature.

I have found the countryside in this county of some interest, mainly because it has so many similarities with that of

Perthshire. There has been nothing as yet to compare with Loch Tay, nor indeed with Dochart Falls. But I will grant that my stay has been short and I have not had opportunity for extensive sight-seeing. To its credit, or more accurately, to its Creator's credit, Donegal can boast of an impressive coastline, if Dunfanaghy is anything by which to judge. The bogland seems to be endless and the mountains which have had the courage to rise above it, while not of the height of Ben Lawers, do at least have some intriguing names. My Gallic language is of some help in deciphering these names and understanding their origins.

As yet my fiddle remains in its case. Not unlike its tendency at home, I hear my father observe. Perhaps later I will have some occasion to exercise it. So far I have heard none of the famed music of the place, apart from a midnight songster in Letterkenny whose ribald singing owed much to the demon drink, I fear.

The business of my trip has begun and is most interesting. We have a second Public Meeting about the railway tonight in a local hall, within the hour, I have just realised.

This is really all my news and I must hurry to join Uncle Roberts and the others.

I trust that this correspondence finds you well, as I am.

Your son Andrew"

The letter rested briefly on the table before Mrs Mackay, who had been reading over her husband's shoulder, took it in her hands. She held it up to her face, as if to try to draw some final essence of her son, perhaps from his meticulous hand-writing, perhaps from his scent, still residual on the crumpled paper.

"Oh Andrew, dear, sweet Andrew," she moaned. "What has happened to you, my poor lost boy?"

Chapter 13

Tuesday 8th June 1897
Reflections on the Dunfanaghy public meeting and my continuing journey to the west.

Once again I am taking the opportunity to write as I travel. Not easily, I may add.
The carriage responds with regrettable violence to the provocations of the road surface. And the incessant bends.
I am told that the reason why Donegal roads twist and turn to such a degree is that the workmen around here always like to work with their backs to the wind. Which, I have deduced, must be extremely variable in direction.
It is to be hoped that the rail workers do not adopt the same principle when they eventually start work on laying the track.
Slept much better last night, the first occasion for some time that I can confess to that blessing.
'He giveth sleep to His beloved,' as I have often read.

As I look from the window, the scenery has become increasingly bleak. Bleak in a green, boggy sense.
We have left behind the sea-scapes and sand-dunes which entertained us between Dunfanaghy, Falcarragh and Gortahork, little villages whose names have obvious roots in the Gaelic language.
"The Field of Corn", for example.
The last one for a while, I imagine, because now we are surrounded by a sweeping cloak of bogland, generously spreading itself away on both sides of this track.
Protruding rakishly from the cloak are the elbows and knees of a more mountainous body of land.
Muckish is grunting away, several miles to the rear.

The particular hills I am studying at the present remind me of the Rider Haggard novel which I read in my final year in school. From this angle and distance, that mountain with the twin summits could be Sheba's Breasts, as described in the book. Sheba, who had such a hold over King Solomon in Scripture.

The wisest man who ever lived, we are led to believe. But he found himself enthralled by a beautiful woman? From a foreign country too, somewhere in the dark continent, if my recollection is correct.
How wise was that? I ask myself.
Was it her he wrote about in the "The Song of Solomon", chapter four?
Or one of the multitude of other strange women that he is reported in Scripture to have loved?
I have never understood his kind of "wisdom" I am afraid.
How could he bring himself to describe the breasts of his lover? 'Thy two breasts are like two young roes, that are twins, which feed among the lilies.'
Why such a fascination with these breasts anyhow? And why did Rider Haggard think to describe two well-shaped hills as the breasts of a woman, and why the Queen of Sheba?
Ah, yes! Her connection with the title...."King Solomon's Mines".

I do not as yet know what this local mountain with the twin peaks is called but I should like to find out.
Yes, and possibly climb it.
One of them, at least.
Put it under my heel.
I will be resisting the temptation to draw this mountain. Despite the gentle symmetry of its curves.
Such a course of action would inevitably have a detrimental effect upon my dreams. As did that image from the novel, as I recall. With unfortunate consequence in many succeeding nights.
I will content myself to think of flat-topped Muckish, as an antidote.
(The above is a private set of reflections of which I am none too proud.)

Last evening we witnessed some considerable ill feeling at the public meeting in the village hall in nearby Falcarragh. The degree of rancour took me by surprise. But not, it seemed, the brave Mr Tatlow. I am coming to admire his tenacity.
The chief protagonists? On one hand, the local clergyman, the same gentleman whose grasp of the Exodus story had failed to

impress my Uncle Roberts on Sunday, and, on the other, a Mr Robert Todd, solicitor to the Railway Company and the Board of Works.

Todd was formidable. He was all eyebrows; a prodigious red nose and a mouth heavy with authoritative utterances.

His main arguments were concerning the benefits of the railways to the very poor, congested districts of the west, and he listed these benefits again, in great detail and with many precise examples.

However, it was when he was quizzed about the exact route of the railway that the shouting began.

Troublesome natives.

According to Todd, the railway would not go through this village of Falcarragh, nor indeed the well-to-do town of Dunfanaghy. Instead it would be located several miles to the south.

This brought huge and uproarious protest from the assembled crowd, most of whom were local people. "Dunfanaghy has always been the hub of the North West," said several speakers. Rev Kane pleaded that the Board of Works reconsider this plan, calling it foolish and short-sighted, 'calamitous' for some towns.

Todd's counter-arguments were persuasive.

His finger-pointing and fist-waving equally so.

"Finance is limited," he said. "It can only pay for a certain amount of track and a certain number of stations."

To run the line through Dunfanaghy would cost a further £30,000, which the Board did not have.

And it would increase travel times between the two places by half an hour.

"Half an hour!" shouted the locals in derision.

"You don't want your lobster arriving in Liverpool half an hour late, do you now?" laughed one speaker.

In the end, argued Todd, the people of this area would just have to accept the decision. It was either that or scupper the chances of the railway being built at all, and no one wants to do that. This is the seventh attempt to develop this railway, and might be its last chance.

"Don't miss your chance now, because there are thirty one other applications for railways across the whole country at present under consideration."

This led to shouts of "Blackmail!"
Again, I began to feel myself the butt of some of these comments and the angry stares of the mob, compromised, as I am, by my association with the Enquiry.
"You are the government's lackeys," shouted the crowd.

Tatlow would have none of it and somehow brought the meeting to a relatively calm conclusion. There were a few jostling incidents afterwards, however, and we were glad of the assistance of the four constables of the Royal Irish Constabulary who helped us return to our hotel in Dunfanaghy intact. One travelled with us in our carriage as we returned, in case of any interruption from local militants.
I did notice that the affair seemed to take a lot out of my ageing uncle and was glad to see him retire quickly, after his cup of tea. He had apparently recovered this morning and is in fine fettle today, although dozing opposite me as I write, his beard cushioning his chin as it rocks back and forth on his chest.

Our horses have just resumed the journey, having halted for a long drink of water from a small mountain stream beside the road. We all alighted and stretched our legs and, as we did, my attention was drawn again to that most statuesque mountain standing at the end of the range of hills, just a little further south of the twin peaks which had so distracted me earlier. Diver informs me that this mountain is called Errigal, an appropriate name, given its general elegance. It is shaped like a near perfect cone, upturned of-course, very white in colour, perhaps because it is reflecting the mid-morning sun. Its surface consists entirely of a pale, glistening rock, devoid of vegetation, except for heather cover around the base. The middle slopes are covered in broken scree and the top rises to a magnificently pointed prism, sculptured in this iridescent rock. Above the peak, a thin curl of cloud hangs, like a halo in some nativity masterpiece.
Breathtaking indeed.
A credit to its Creator Architect.
Now this one I do pledge to myself to climb during the course of this summer, if the opportunity presents itself.

Alas, we have resumed our bone-shaking journey.

Some of these potholes have fish in them, I am convinced.
Onwards towards the port of Burton.
To another public meeting.

<u>*Wednesday 9th June 1897*</u>
<u>*My account of boredom in Burtonport*</u>

Rain of a most pervasive and annoying nature has hidden the day.
Fine drizzle driven in off the sea by a relentlessly gusting wind. I have watched this incessant smudge for several hours without once being able to detect a colour that is anything other than grey.
The town may exist beyond it but I could not argue this from the available evidence. Does Burtonport have colour?
Apparently we are again at the coast.
A picturesque coast, I am led to believe, with views of some local islands. I am told to "look out for Aranmore". A place of beauty across the channel, it seems. I will reserve comment till the wind dies and this mist decides to clear. But it currently seems that this may be a few days away.
No one, it seems, has broken the news to the local weather that this is actually the month of June.
Approximately summer.

If the weather is grey, the boarding house made every attempt to fit in with the general pallor. Successfully so.
I am surprised when anyone finds their way to enter, so well camouflaged is the place. Having said that, as only two fellow humans have actually entered, it may be that many others, if any there be, are still out there in the rain, looking for "O'Donnell's Boarding House" in the gloom. They may, in fact, be the fortunate ones and should consider staying where they are, such is the colourless fustiness of this house.

There have, of course, been many such days in Killin. My mother always finds such days depressing and tends to confine herself to her room.
I do not generally find this weather depressing.
Not any more than any other kind of day.

The journey so far has been a journey of discovery, of finding out about so many things outside my normal ken. I have been occupied. Exercised by many challenging new vistas. Intrigued by many new perspectives which I knew not of in my previous life.
But today throws me back inside myself.
Inside the grey caverns of my own thoughts.
Were I at home I should occupy myself in trying to improve some sketch or other.
I cannot do so here.
I did try to draw the Errigal mountain from memory but the end result reminded me so much of a limpet shell that I tore up the page, surrendered it to the turf fire and vowed not to sketch the majestic peak again until I am sitting in front of it. I then read several Psalms but they were all so joyful that I felt utterly rebuked and dejected within my soul. I would 'lift my eyes up to the hills, from whence cometh my aid', but the hills are so shrouded in Donegal mist that my spiritual vision strains to the point of hurt.
I know these are scriptural truths, allusions to spiritual realities rather than physical ones, but knowing this does not seem to help my mood. When I try to visualise the 'help which cometh from the Lord', I am mocked by the greyness which surrounds me today like a thick cloud, blocking out all rays of light.
'Where doth my help come from?' Yes of course I know the answer to the rhetorical question. I know the answer but do not experience the help.
Wretched man that I am!

But for the turf-fire, beside which I write, my dejection today would be complete. I wish I had been able to sleep beside its wondrous warmth last night, rather than having to spend the hours shivering beneath inadequate bedclothes in my top-floor bedroom, just under the rafters and the thatch.
I do not like to complain to Uncle Roberts.
He is a good and generous man, having enough worries of his own to contend with. I am but a guest, an imposition.

Within the hour I will accompany Mr Tatlow, Mr Diver, (whose smile has been noticeably less conspicuous in the slow, dank waiting hours of the day), and Uncle Roberts to the local Parochial Hall for the final meeting with the community. It is expected that this will be a more harmonious assembly, given that the people here will be of the opinion, shared by the Commissioners of course, that the railway from Letterkenny to Burtonport should in fact actually reach Burtonport, regardless of the claims of other worthy towns.

So, what controversy may await us remains a closely guarded secret.

Wrapped up in the fog, like everything else in Burtonport.

<u>*Thursday 10th June 1897*</u>
<u>*Reflections on a third meeting and the disgusting behaviour of Mr Diver*</u>

Another morning, another mist.
Or perhaps just the same fog blanket on extended time.
It all matches my dullness of spirit.
Would I were still asleep.
I endured a wet, cold night. The drizzle in which we walked home from the meeting pervaded every square inch of my clothing. And beyond, into my very skin I believe. I tried to dry myself off before retiring to bed but the towel provided by the boarding house was possibly even more damp than I was and had a sour smell which I associate with stale potatoes.
Why I am recording this degree of personal detail and despair, I no longer know. Save to say that I have nothing else to do this day.

Tatlow and Roberts are in conference together and my humble presence is not required.
John Diver has disappeared some hours ago in the direction of the nearest public house, presumably to rest his over-stretched lips in some tall glass of dark alcohol. I do not miss him overly.
A wag-at-the-wall clock is making no attempt to hasten the passing of the day and indeed seems to deliberately slow its clicking every time I chance to regard it. The faded flower-heads which sit in a cracked vase beside me should have been thrown out several days ago. There is a rough watercolour on the wall of this sitting room which, despite the stains of time

and mildew, does some justice to the mountain we saw on our journey here, the pointed Errigal. It only serves, however, to increase my restlessness to sketch it.

I close my eyes and think of Killin, of my well-remembered mountains.
The images are strong and comforting.
Until I think of how far away they are in both physical distance and in time.
I believe that I will not see them for several months.
I try to imagine my mother's voice call me from the kitchen below, but the tone is muffled and I cannot make her out.

Last night I learned further of the local resentments hereabouts; not so much against the railway proposal, nor indeed its potential to alleviate some of the economic sufferings of the people of this area.... more against the landlord class whose presence still seems to stir strong feelings in the more radical Irish folk. There is a suspicion, it seems, that the local landlord is in cahoots with the railway companies and the Board of Works so as to determine the route of the railway, and in a manner that brings advantage to his own business interests.
A Father Maguire argued vehemently that two coastal areas where there is huge deprivation and congestion were being completely ignored by the proposed route of the railways. (One of the areas was his own parish, of course.)
Instead, he claimed, the route will take the railway right past the door of the Gweedore Hotel, with a halt there for the rich tourists visiting the region and staying at the hotel.
And who owns the hotel? None other than the landlord, a Lord Hill by name.
This brought derisive laughter throughout the hall.
Uncle Roberts looked uncomfortable and Tatlow scratched furiously at an unwelcome resident of his armpit area.
Lord Hill was not among those present!

I have to say that all this makes sense to me, increasingly so. But if there is only a given amount of money, I can see that it should be used in a way that benefits the poorer areas. Except that some of the poorer areas are being ignored altogether, while the landlord gets his hotel serviced by the chosen route. Should I argue this with Uncle Roberts or might he think me an impertinent upstart? Tatlow would for certain. I will keep my mouth shut and wait until I can use my drawing skills to their benefit.

The latter part of this entry has been written in my cold bedroom, away from the glowing turf-fire of the sitting room. Not a choice I was keen to make.
The reason?
A chamber-maid, or at least I think she was of that occupation, who became overly friendly. Of a softly rounded variety, I observed absently.
I had made the mistake of looking at her as she stoked the fire. My thoughts were far away, and I was unaware that I was watching her. She misunderstood and began a babbling conversation in Gaelic, a one-sided conversation, if that be the term, because I did not reply. She could not take a fairly obvious hint, somehow mistaking my silence and my head-down return to writing for encouragement. In the end, I had no choice but to up and leave her to herself. She stopped abruptly, mouth open mid-sentence, and I could feel her beady eyes bore into my back as I fled.
However, as I exited by the sitting-room door, I was stumbled into by the mildly intoxicated figure of John Diver, his rested lips having apparently returned to the "grin-at-full-stretch" position. No sooner had he made entrance to the room than the chambermaid's sing-song began again, now directed at the helpless Diver instead of me.
I am almost sorry for him.
But at least he is warm.
One way or the other.

I have to confess a certain dread of such women.
Women, girls in general are fine as a species.
Just so long as they do not expect anything from me; do not attempt to talk to me or joke with me or act in that typically flirtatious manner or take an interest in me at all or molly-coddle me or patronise me. Grand if they leave me alone; I cannot bear inane conversation with the female of the race.

Nor the silly giggling such as that I *now* hear from Diver's room next door.
The couple have obviously relocated from the sitting room to the semi-privacy of Diver's bedroom.
Does the man have no self-respect in him at all?
And why must she make such a gratuitous exhibition of her sinful nature?
Such a celebration of man's fallen state makes me sick to the stomach.
Mostly.
Besides a certain curiosity and intrigue, I have to confess.
At the time, I could think of nothing better to do than to read aloud a relevant passage of scripture, loud enough for them to hear me through the wall. After all, were they not prepared to subject me to their depraved noises through the very same wall? I chose a passage from one of my favourite Bible characters, King David. Though it must be said that this passage finds him in what was not his finest hour. Still, a salutary lesson, I believe. I read 2nd Samuel chapter eleven, from verse two, as follows;

'And it came to pass in an eventide, that David arose from off his bed and walked upon the roof of the king's house: and from the roof he saw a woman washing herself; and the woman was very beautiful to look upon. And David sent and enquired after the woman. And one said, "Is this not Bathsheba, the daughter of Eliam, the wife of Uriah, the Hittite?" And David sent messengers and took her; and she came in unto him and she lay with him for she was purified from her uncleanness: and she returned unto her house. And the woman conceived and sent and told David and said, "I am with child."'

At this point there came a loud knocking on the wall and I heard the voice of Diver telling me to shut my mouth or he would come into me and do a severe damage to my person; (or words to that effect; some of the words I would not lower myself to recall or record.)
Mr Diver sounded very angry.
I desisted.

The one positive outcome of my reading was that the giggling stopped.
Only to be soon replaced by other unpleasant sounds.
Nothing for me to do but leave the premises altogether and walk in the rain until I judged it wise to return to the boarding house, some hours later.
At which point I resumed this entry to my journal.
The standard of handwriting is, I fear, testimony to the state of my health.
I am soaked; my teeth chatter and my hand shakes.
Obviously.

<u>Friday 11th June 1897</u>
<u>My reflections on a face of great beauty and a rock of sacred significance.</u>

The sun reappeared today.
In so many senses.
I awoke unusually early, at six o'clock, to be precise, to the sensation of yellow light pouring like egg-yolk into my elevated room below the thatch. Strong rays of dawning sunshine shone in through my poorly organised curtains.
From the landing window I saw a wonderful sight. The view out across the harbour and the bay beyond to what, I presume, is the island of Aranmore, so highly recommended to me earlier as a place of beauty. I should love to go there at some stage, should it become possible, never having been to an island.
Where has the mist and rain gone? And so suddenly? I can see Ireland again.
And this is a pretty village.
From my present vantage point I notice several small ships, (or large boats, I suppose) nestling snuggly against the quay with only a gentle bobbing up and down in the water. They ride high beside their moorings on what is obviously a full tide. I can see rows of what I take to be lobster-pots stacked neatly, end-on against the rock face behind the pier. They remind me of a honeycomb made by really large bees.
I will go to walk around the quayside now while I can because it seems that we are leaving before lunchtime to retrace our steps to Letterkenny. Uncle Roberts is doing the same. Diver

has not made an reappearance this morning since I saw him at breakfast. I had not been looking forward to his presence, given what he had shouted at me through the bedroom wall, but it was as if the incident had never happened. He was his usual affable self, even to the detail of dribbling buttermilk down his chin, a custom of his which I have observed on other mornings. (It may have something to do with a looseness of the lips and jaws, brought about by the constancy of his grin perhaps, but I am not a medical man and profess no great expertise in the realm of facial physiology.)
So to the pier.

An incident occurred on our journey today which has stayed in my mind ever since. We have now reached Gallagher's Hotel in Letterkenny once more, it is after nine o'clock in the evening and I am much fatigued from the journey .... but I cannot rest until I record my feelings about what was a most fortuitous encounter. I am excited now even to think of it afresh and I have been in a fervour about it throughout that otherwise tedious journey.
I believe I have encountered an angel in human form.
A beam of sunlight in the previous gloom of this dank Donegal. The morning's dawn sunshine which awoke me today was only but a dim foretaste of what awaited me.
It happened in the most unlikely of circumstances.
A coincidence which I cannot but feel was of Heavenly origin.
Our coach had departed from in front of O'Donnell's Boarding House around ten o'clock, only a few minutes after I had returned from my brief exploration of the Burtonport waterfront. There I had been quizzed by a friendly, if overly-curious, gentleman in a distinctive peaked cap; he turned out to be the Harbour-master and a fine job he seems to do there.
The conversation continued for such a lengthy period of time that Diver was sent to fetch me. I excused myself and returned with Mr Diver.
He took the opportunity to reproach me, in a jocular manner, it has to be said, about last night's "sermon", as he put it.
"I should have left you here, preaching to the Harbour-master, young sir," he grinned.
We travelled through the winding lanes of a region east of Burtonport, an area known as "The Rosses", according to

Diver. He seems to know this countryside quite well. The weather was hot, more so than any day I have so far experienced in this county.
An hour or so into the journey we had reached a picturesque little village which, upon later enquiry, I discovered to have the equally quaint name of Kincasslagh. Little more than a sharp bend in the road with a few small houses, a public house and a village shop. Given the rising morning temperature, Diver, bless him, made the suggestion to the driver that the horses should be allowed to take a drink from the water tank which stood outside the village public house; this was a customary practice, he said.
And so we stopped; I disembarked from the coach, simply to stretch my legs and take the air, escaping briefly from some of the less-than-welcome odours which had their origin in this morning's Irish breakfast, or last night's pork and cabbage dinner more likely, and which now emanated, I have reason to suspect, from some of my fellow passengers, I know not which. Fresh air was much appreciated.
As the horses drank, and as I stood by the rear of the coach, I heard music.
Faintly, in the distance.
I heard the strains of a melody.
Played on a flute, I surmised.
Or a whistle, a woodwind instrument of some kind, at any rate.
Perhaps a local variety of recorder, I thought.
A sweet, airy texture of tone.
I listened intently.
It was a such a tune. Wonderfully played, a Strathspey, I am almost sure. That distinctive quick leap between notes, so Scottish sounding, I always feel. A Strathspey, here in the west of Ireland? I remembered what my father had said about the musical relationships between my homeland and the county of Donegal, the closeness of the two traditions.
The tune came closer, I thought.
I moved to look around the village street, empty but for an ancient collie dog. There was still no sign of the origin of the tune but it seemed to be coming closer from the eastern side of the village. A pony and trap came into view, struggling up the brae towards us.

The tune was aboard the trap.

Or the player was.

There were three people in the primitive and ill-constructed little conveyance. A young man held the reins, brown of face, self-conscious eyes looking intently forward with barely a glance at our coach. He was perched far forward in his seat so as to make space for his passengers. Squeezed in on either side of him, two women. Well, one woman, to the driver's right; of middle age, a care-worn peasant-wife type of face.

And on the side next me?

A girl. A girl playing a whistle of dark wood.

I say, 'girl' but I mean something that I cannot as yet find any word in the English language to convey. Perhaps there is a more suitable expression in the Gaelic language which might come closer to doing her the justice she deserves but I am deficient in that tongue as yet. I will hope to learn such a term.

The pony and trap were past us in what seemed like a flash, and yet, in a most curious sense, their passage through the village, past our coach, around the bend, up the hill and out of sight seemed to be in slow motion, in a manner that I truly believe made some serious challenge to the normal pace and structure of the passage of time. It was as though the sun stood still in the sky, as it did for Joshua in the Scriptures. I can explain what happened in no other way.

The girl did not stop playing her whistle.

And how she played.

The most beautiful sound I have ever heard.

And a tune which, although unknown to me before, is now fixed in my memory, as much a part of my consciousness as my own name. I know that when I have opportunity I will take my fiddle from its case and that melody will flow from my fingers as though I had received it with my very first breath. I can barely wait until the morrow to take the bow in my hands and play tribute to that vision of loveliness.

Because she was lovely.

Lovely beyond my wildest dreams.

And beyond any words I may now use to try to describe her.

So I will not try too hard.

Her image is implanted in my very heart like a heavenly vision.

As I stared at her during the passage of her journey through Kincasslagh, her gaze met mine and she held my eyes in hers, I believe.
I know this.
Instinctively I believe this to be the case, that a bond from soul to soul was born at that very moment, between this girl and me, Andrew Mackay. A bond whose origin could only be in heaven. A connection so clear, so strong that it has to have been in the Divine Plan; perhaps the reason I have been brought to Ireland.
Her hair blew softly behind her, fair, fine and flowing, bouncing with the rhythm of the trap and the tugging of the pony. The breeze caught it as she rounded the corner, revealing the shape of her face as she looked back at me.
Oh heavenly thought! What beauty! What a face! What perfection!
I could not see whether she was tall or short, but I had the impression of a slim figure, in little more than a plain country garment. And yet her inner loveliness shone through in a way that, had King Solomon been watching instead of me he would have instantly forgotten about his Queen of Sheba, of that I am convinced. She did not smile, not with her face at least, but there was something deeper than a smile in her look which, should I never see her again, (and it is perfectly possible, indeed probable, that I may not), I will never forget, not to my dying day.
Oh, happy day!

The happy day was not complete however. No sooner had this blest interlude occurred than I was approached by Mister Diver, fresh from his conquest of a pint of dark porter in the tavern against whose exterior walls I had been leaning.
"I gather, Master Mackey," he began, "that you are a religious sort of a fellow. Am I right?"
I assented to this conclusion. After my 'sermon' of last evening I could do no other really, even if I had had the wish to.
"That being the case," he continued, "I have something to show you in this village which I think you should see. Will you come with me?"
In truth, all that I wanted to do was sit and remember that beautiful face. I assented reluctantly. He began to walk up the

hill and took me to a most interesting rock, situated behind a hillock and looking down over a most picturesque stretch of strand. The rock was substantial, flat-topped and table-like. A wreath of wild flowers grew around it. Even before I came to be informed as to what it was, I believe I sensed a mystical presence to the place.

Diver asked if I knew what I was looking at and I confessed that I did not.

"It's an old 'Carraig an Aifrinn'," he said, "a Mass Rock."

I further confessed that, as I am not a member of the Catholic persuasion, I was still somewhat in the dark as to the significance of the impressive stone. He took the opportunity to instruct me, for which I am grateful, even though my eyes continued to drift to the roadway in the hope of a return of the heavenly being in the pony-cart.

A Mass Rock, it transpires, is a rock from which a priest would serve the Eucharist to the local people of his parish at a time in history, not all that long ago, according to Diver, when to do so was against the law of the land.

This was news to me. I have been taught about the outlawing and the persecution of the Covenanters by the English establishment in my own homeland but knew nothing about what had happened in Ireland.

"The Penal Laws. Hard times for the Catholic people," Diver told me with no little passion. "Priests hunted down like game for simply giving Mass to the faithful. And this is one of the places where they did it. People came from miles around. Somebody always had to be on the lookout for the law."

I had no idea about such matters. It puts my own easy faith into something of an unfortunate perspective. I appreciate Diver taking the time and thinking me worth the effort to introduce me to this special and holy place, even though its holiness is of a different substance to that which I espouse.

We were not long underway again, however, until the mystique of the Mass Rock had faded in my mind and been replaced by the image of that beautiful maiden. As I dozed in the rocking motion of the carriage, I dreamt that she was sitting on such a rock, her whistle in her mouth, playing to crowds of people who had flocked from all over to see her and hear her play; indeed my own mother was somehow present. And my role was to stand on top of the hill to keep a lookout for the police who *were somehow trying to catch her and accuse her of disturbing the peace. A strange reverie. She has most certainly disturbed whatever little peace I had. And I fear she will be in my every prayer, my every waking thought, my every sleeping dream.*

It is now close to the eleventh hour and my fellow-travellers have all retired to their beds. And I must do the same. Whether to sleep or not I shall have to wait and see. Today my life changed for ever. The Divine Plan has, I believe, opened up a new chapter for me. A vista of beauty, of light, of hope. I am full of anticipation, and, should I never set eyes upon that face again, I know that the memory of it will inspire me from this day on and for ever. Thanks to an angel. 'My angel of the whistle', as I shall call her.

Chapter 14

Reactions in the Manse

Silence reigned within the dining room of Killen Manse.
The clergyman continued to stare morosely at the page of the journal he had just been reading aloud to his wife. She appeared reluctant to break the silence; head down, she fiddled with the damp napkin on her lap. It was deep into the afternoon but as yet neither husband nor wife had felt the need to interrupt this painful process to eat lunch.
"This is a significant entry, I cannot help but feel. This seems to me to mark the beginning of a descent for him," said Rev Mackay after a long, thoughtful pause.
"But he sounds so happy," came the quavering response.
"Yes but can't you see that therein lies the problem?" Irritation in his voice, he continued. "This is a false happiness, a boost of human .... joy, excitement, elation, call it what you will, which has its basis in nothing of substance, nothing of worth. In fact, it has its basis in the flesh. Not in the Spirit. Don't you see, Maureen?'
She said nothing. Just hung her head, a picture of utter dejection.
"Satan has got him through the oldest strategy in the book. The lust of the flesh. The desire of the eyes. He couldn't see it coming, the most obvious snare of all, the thing... or one of the things we warned him about, so often."
"But.... when did we warn him....about...?"
"What do you mean, 'When did we warn him?' Haven't we been warning him about the dangers of the flesh from the day and hour he could receive instruction? Isn't that why we taught him to read his Bible everyday? To warn him about the tricks of the Devil, the temptations that he puts in a young man's way? 'Wherewith shall a young man cleanse his way? By taking heed thereto according to thy word.' Didn't I drum that into him, almost daily? Didn't I hang that verse on his bedroom wall years ago? Don't frustrate me by asking foolish questions, woman."
Mackay banged the journal down on the dining table with a slap that made his wife shudder. He arose and strode around the room, his finger and thumb smoothing out his moustache in a

gesture symbolic of his inner need to smooth out his own ruffled emotions.

"It may be overly simple of me and I may be missing something which you are reading in the text, my dear," began the mother again, "but it seems to me that all Andrew is guilty of in this matter is recognising the beauty of a girl who passed him by on the road. Is it not the most natural thing in the world, for a young man to admire a pretty girl, Gordon? Nothing passed between them, no matter what he says. Nothing but a look, from what he says here. He sees her, she looks at him."

"But what was in that look? That's the point."

She shook her head. "You know how he misunderstands things so easily. He is such a simple lad, innocent as a child in such matters. You surely agree with that, my dear? Yes, he heard a lovely tune on a whistle. He recognised it as a Scottish tune, at least he thought so, and was pleased to hear it because it confirmed what you had told him about the music of that place. Shouldn't you be glad that he appreciated hearing such a tune? And he was simply astonished to hear it being played by a girl driving past on a donkey and cart. She looked at him because....well perhaps because he was standing too far out in the path of the...."

"Pony and trap!"

"I'm sorry?"

"It was a pony and trap, not a donkey, and I think you are simplifying the matter in your typically naive fashion, Maureen. Listen to how he expresses himself....and this is several hours after the event, I am guessing, when he has reached his lodgings in whatever the name of the place is." His forefinger tapped the cover of the journal vigourously.

"Letterkenny," she informed him.

"Doesn't matter where. Listen. He writes,

'She did not smile, not with her face at least, but there was something deeper than a smile in her look which, should I never see her again, (and it is perfectly possible, indeed probable, that I may not!), I will never forget, not to my dying day! Oh happy day!' And this part. *'And I fear she will be in my every prayer, my every waking thought, my every sleeping dream. Today my life changed forever. The Divine Plan has, I believe, opened up a new chapter for me. A vista of beauty, of light, of hope.'*

This is the language of infatuation, of unhealthy fantasy, my dear. It is the beginning of a road that leads to destruction....as we now know!"

"But he says that it is perfectly possible that he may never see her again, even probable that they may never meet again," countered the mother. "Surely you are exaggerating when you place such importance on such a fleeting.... interlude? Andrew would not be swayed by something so ...so ephemeral, not after his upbringing. Didn't we always try to ensure his protection from the world? Didn't we set him a good example from the day he was born? I cannot believe it."

Her husband looked at her with obvious disparagement. "You cannot believe it? You had better believe it. Andrew is our son and he is a good boy, always has been a good boy. Yes, he has his difficulties of .....well, of personality, but he has never shown any rebellion against us or the ways of God. But Maureen, and this is the vital point, he is still a fallen human soul, full of original sin like everyone else and is capable of as great wrong as anyone else. Or do you not believe in the fall? Do you not believe he is capable of sins of the flesh?'

"Of course I believe in the fall, my dear, but ...."

"But what?"

She continued. "But in this episode of his diary, for the first time since we started reading it, Andrew just seems so happy, doesn't he? I mean, there is even the change in the weather, the clouds lifting, the sunshine brightening his morning....and this girl driving past is just another little example of.... of a ray of sunshine brightening up his little life. Heaven knows he needs it, all the little glimmers of hope and light that he can get, considering the dark moods that seem to overtake him all too often, don't you agree?"

"Andrew does not need the complication of a relationship with a girl.... a girl in Ireland, a girl no doubt of the Roman Catholic persuasion. And all this reference to a Mass Rock..."

"Good gracious, dear, listen to yourself. He saw the girl! Once!" She emphasised the 'saw' and the 'once'. "He may never set eyes on her again. You are making it sound like he is contemplating marriage to her or something. They have no relationship. They most likely never will."

Rev Mackay returned to his seat at the table and picked up journal again. He flicked through the pages still to be read, almost as if to discover support for his argument. Then he held the document to his forehead, his eyes closed, before setting it down again. When he spoke again his tone was softer, patronising almost.

"Maureen, my dear, I understand that your instinct as a mother is to think the best of your son, our son, our dearly beloved son, and I applaud that instinct in you. And I understand that you are of the opinion that I am reading too much into what we have just been discussing. But let me remind you that, from the words, from the expressions that Andrew has been using in this entry, these are sentiments which place the girl at the centre of his happiness. He is attributing a spiritual significance to this chance meeting, that the encounter is part of a Divine Plan. You must see that this is highly dangerous, whether or not he ever sets eyes on the lass again. His faith has moved from the Master. His gaze has left the face of His Saviour and found a substitute loveliness in the face of a pretty girl. He has mistaken the creation for the Creator, the age-old failing of all mankind."

"Is it not possible that the girl's beauty is simply inspiring him to....?"

"I don't think you believe that yourself, do you Maureen?"

"But he just seems so content...for the first time since we began to read his account. I love to hear him happy. And, yes, I do understand what you are going to say.....that his happiness is not as important as his stability, and that it is perhaps misplaced but...." She tailed off in confusion and despair.

"Andrew's happiness at the moment is yet another example of his condition. He will be on cloud nine for a few days, but he will come back down to earth with a bump and then go under. Another example of this wave of emotional ups and downs which so characterise the boy. The last thing he needed at this point was something like this to cause him further imbalance. We shall see as we read on. I guarantee we will see a downwards trend in his mood."

Mrs Mackay stood up somewhat shakily and turned towards the door.

"I'm sorry, Gordon," she said. "We have entirely forgotten about lunch; my fault completely. Would you like me to go bring you something?"

"Please do. I am so engaged with this account that I haven't noticed the time slip by. It's as if I am a detective, trying to find clues as to why Andrew..... my own son, and I am only now getting to really know him better through his writings, now that he's gone forever."

There was a brokeness in him as he hunched over the table and his shoulders began to shudder, a condition in him which his wife had never seen before. She came to him and bent over him in an awkward embrace and they joined their tears for a long, solemn minute until he straightened up and said, "Yes dear, you go and prepare some food and I will continue.... just him and I, in a final father and son conversation."

She knew not to argue. She knew the importance of his attempt to understand and come to terms with what had happened to Andrew. She knew he would share with her whatever the boy said in the next chapters of his diary. She knew she would read them many times in the lonely future. She left the room and went to the soup vegetables.

~~~~~~~

Gordon Mackay's manners deserted him when his wife arrived at the table with lunch. The meal consisted of sandwiches, scones with her homemade rhubarb jam and freshly made soup but the minister barely noticed. He continued to read with intent focus, nibbling periodically at the bread and forgetting his soup until it had barely any warmth left in it. Mrs Mackay knew better than to challenge his behaviour or to urge him to eat. She finished her own meagre meal in a very short time. It was a further twenty minutes before her husband set the journal down and supped the last few spoonfuls without a word, before addressing the patient housewife.

"Well, I have read his entries for several more days taking me up to, let me see...." and he re-examined the text briefly. "Fourteenth of July. You can read them yourself, Maureen, but he seems to have entered a phase of boredom with the whole process. The commissioners are back in this Letterkenny place and there does not seem to be much doing. Perhaps that's not quite fair to them though. It seems that this Tatlow and your uncle are putting together their final report for a body called the Donegal Grand Jury who will make a final decision when they meet later.... I haven't read about their deliberation as yet."

"But how does Andrew seem?" asked Mrs Mackay.

"He seems very bored, as I say. One day is very much like the previous; there is not much he can do; he feels at times that he is getting in the way of uncle Roberts. He feels trapped in this Hotel. Letterkenny does not seem to hold much interest for him. He is not getting the opportunity to draw; in fact there does not seem to have been much for him to do at all during this past month. He seems to find the town drab and uninspiring, certainly from an architectural point of view, but he has been to church there on a few occasions, a Presbyterian kirk, which he found very like our own worship, he says. And his journal entries have become much more brief and much less informative, almost as though he cannot be bothered to write. As if his thoughts and activities are not worth recording."

"What about the girl? Has he mentioned her at all? I presume he hasn't seen her again?"

"Well yes, he has. Mentioned her, I mean, not seen her of course. I did expect continuing reference to her, and I wasn't wrong in that expectation."

Mackay paused and picked up the document again, leafing through it and stopping at particular pages to quote.

"There are early mentions of her beauty and so on, immediately following that first meeting. Listen to this.

'I lie down at night and her face reappears to me so easily, without me having to try to remember it; every feature, from those sad eyes to the little dimples on her cheeks as she blew so sensitively into her whistle, returns to my mind like a heavenly vision. A rapturous vision!'

And here he refers to the tune she was playing; evidently he is trying to remember it. He says,

*'Why oh why can I not find the path of that wondrous melody? I try and try, but each time I get as far as the middle of the second line and the tune slips through my fingers. That is not fair to my fingers. It is a fault of my musical memory, my capacity to lure back the melody from the deep pools of my stagnant brain. Would that I had listened to my father and worked much harder at perfecting the art of playing the fiddle. I am deficient in this matter and the deficiency is of my own neglectful making. It is not one I can lay at the door of my father this time.'"

"Ah bless him," was the mother's response. "He is regretting not listening to you, Gordon. He is wishing he had practised more, as you always...."

Mackay interrupted with a splutter of indignation. "But what does he mean, 'This time'? As though there are other things he can lay at my door, that I should take the blame for? Whatever could he mean by that?"

"I have no idea, my dear," soothed his wife. "It is just a meaningless phrase, I'm sure. Andrew was always utterly respectful and loving towards you. Don't begin to imagine otherwise...not now, not after he's gone from us."

"Perhaps you're right; I am being over-sensitive. But I wouldn't like to think he had anything but the highest regard for how he was raised. We did all we could for him; that is my belief and, at a time like this, we need to hold to that."

Mrs Mackay's eyes strayed back to the journal.

"This period of inactivity and boredom is most unfortunate, isn't it?" she said. "It's not what we envisaged at all. And is there no evidence of him drawing anything of note during that period?"

"Not very much, to be frank. There is one entry which I found of particular interest and which contains a sketch. Perhaps just a week or so back from where I left off reading. It concerns a visit to a castle, at a place called.... I forget its name, but from the drawing it looks like a beautiful location, the castle perched right on the shores of a loch."

"Can I see it please?"

"Yes, of course. Why don't I read you this particular entry. Actually, it is less of a diary entry and more an account of some historical affairs which he has become interested in. It's the only piece of writing of any real interest during this whole period. And it seems to have been one of his better days. He seems much more positive, more appreciative of the opportunities that this venture is affording him. Shall I read it to you?"

"That would be lovely, please do," responded Mrs Mackay, settling herself in a chair beside him at the table and slipping her hand into his.

Chapter 15

10th July 1897
My thoughts on Diver's Donegal

John Diver is a hero and climbs in my estimation after yesterday's experience.
Who would have thought that, deep behind that absurdly toothy grin, there was such knowledge of matters historical and geographical, as shown earlier by his discourse concerning the Mass Rock.
The man is no simple "fixer" of our circumstances, I have discovered. He has, among his other less creditable attributes, a wealth of local knowledge.
A passionately held resource. He shared a most interesting and distressing story of recent events at a place quite close to the village of his birth. And yesterday I was privileged to pay it a visit. Thankfully it was one of those days whose weather was in harmony with the activities Diver had planned for me. Sunshine and high clouds prevailed. The weather in this county does not always collaborate in this agreeable manner, as I have noticed over the past month.
It all began when Diver was telling me about his home village, a place called Gartan.
"Not far from where I was reared," he boasted, "is the birthplace of the greatest Irishman who ever lived."
I treated this claim with some disbelief, and, seeing traces of the scorn upon my face, Diver went on to inform me about the life of one, Saint Colmcille. I had previously learned a little concerning this saint and his connection with Killin's own St Fillan. The man is something more than a legend in these parts, I am led to believe, and from what Diver told me, his status is well deserved.
So the trip was arranged. We travelled to Gartan on horseback, leaving Letterkenny very early in the morning. I am not particularly accustomed to long journeys on horseback, but Diver made this sound like a mere morning jaunt. Little did I know what lay before me, nor how painful my posterior would be rendered by the late evening when we returned to Gallagher's Hotel.

As we jogged along, he told me the long story of Colmcille, a warrior turned Christian saint and missionary. A fascinating story indeed, not to mention deeply inspiring and humbling. My respect for celtic christianity, and indeed for the Catholic Church whose writ, at the end of the day, he was extending, has grown considerably by it. It and the Mass Rock.

So it was with a certain reverence that, a couple of hours after leaving our lodgings, we arrived at the inauspicious site where Colmcille was supposed to have been born; no more than a slab of Donegal granite by the side of a loch.

"You see this rock?" Diver said. "If you're homesick and you sit on this rock it will cure you. So they say anyway."

"I cannot confess to being particularly homesick, thank you John," said I, "so I do not feel the need to avail of its services."

I had the feeling that he looked at me strangely at this point.

We did not stay there long, long enough only to partake of the vittles we had brought; Diver wanted to show me a further site of historical interest.

"It's not far away," he said.

(I must learn to take his "not-fars" with a pinch of salty scepticism and add several miles in my mind's eye.)

"There is a fitting place for you to be drawing where I am taking you next, Master Mackay."

"And what is that?" I queried.

"I'll tell you on the way."

And he did. Yet another story of some historical import. This one concerned a place by the name of Glenveagh, a valley of unique beauty and unforgettable pain.

(Diver was waxing lyrical, yet another side to his character I had not seen before.)

There is a castle there, an impressive building beside a still loch, he told me. A castle lived in by one of the worst landlords that Donegal has ever seen, a man called Adair.

"The thing about him is that he was Irish himself, this Adair; not English, as most of them landlords were. He bought a whole big area of bogland and mountain around Glenveagh Loch, maybe as recently as forty years ago, some time after the famine," said my helpful guide.

I made the comment that my own country had had similar problems with landowners, especially up in the Highlands. To the best of my recollection these were Scottish lairds, the same nationality as the peasants they treated so badly.

"What's a laird?" he queried.

"Same as your landlord, I believe."

"And what was the problem with them?"

"Have you never heard of the Highland Clearances?" Now it was my turn to be the expert for a while.

He stared at me for a bit and said, "You are going to tell me, and I have a feeling that what you are going to say is not going to be very different to what happened here in Glenveagh!"

We had just rounded a high bend on the lane; the sun was high in the sky, it being around three o'clock in the afternoon; the scene before my eyes was breathtakingly beautiful and I reigned in my horse to stop to admire it. (The pause had the additional benefit of resting my suffering rear from the constancy of the horse's motion.)

Spread out before me for miles upon miles were waves of lush bogland. Barely a tree in sight to break the panorama. It was as if some heavenly painter had dipped his broad brush in a hundred different shades of green and smeared each liberally across the landscape. Deep greens, yellowy greens, bluish greens, grey greens, greens with a dusting of ash, greens sprinkled with scatterings of purple. Each layer had a life of its own and, while there was a total absence of order or symmetry to how they were laid down, each layer had a natural curve and depth and texture that spoke to me of a master artist at work.

I noticed, too, several dark gashes here and there in the ocean of green; like waves breaking in the distance, only appearing as thin brown splashes on the canvas. Turf-cutters had been at work earlier in the summer and these were the peat banks and the neat stacks of turf which had been the result of their hard labour.

As I took in this scene, there was something about the quality of the Donegal light across its various strands of landscape that transfixed me. The sunlight danced on the blue-grey rock faces beyond and reflected down on the verdant carpet beneath. I watched there for some time, uninterrupted, to be fair to Diver, (who was making his own contribution to the moisturising of the local bogland), and was uplifted in my *spirit again, just to be part of such wonderful creation and have the capacity to appreciate it. This was my first "renewal", my first recapture of vitality since that vision in Kincasslagh three weeks ago.*

Diver eventually brought me back to earth with a piercing comment. He said, "Wouldn't you think that a place as peaceful as this would bring out the best in people rather than the worst?"

I gathered that he was referring again to its sad history and whatever evil deed that the landlord had committed; so I asked him to continue his story as we rode on. And this is what he told me.

Adair wasn't long in the district until he was at loggerheads with the mountain people who were his tenants, over shooting rights first, then over bringing in black-faced sheep from Scotland. And, just like home, the tenants got evicted their homes to make way for the sheep. This I don't understand. Surely there should be room for both people and sheep.

Diver became quite angry as he described how forty seven families were thrown out on the roads by the police and troops. One of Adair's men was killed. The people had to go to a workhouse or wander the roads.

(This sounds as if I am back in Killin school, reading one of my school textbooks about Scotland.)

By the time he had completed the detail of his account I had begun to wonder what it was he had thought that I might like to draw in these parts. A memorial perhaps? Or a tumbled cottage, still standing as a reminder of the cruel injustice?

But I was wrong. We rode beside a beautiful stretch of water which reminded me of Loch Tay and, as we rounded a bend, there stood a quaint little castle.

"This is Glenveagh Castle," said Diver. "You would want to be drawing it."

Of-course I would. I had half an hour to make a quick sketch of the place. To be honest, what Diver had told me of its builder and current occupant made me less than enthusiastic about the project.

He was well pleased that I took some trouble in completing the drawing and obviously liked what he saw. I shall make him a proper copy and perhaps write some little appreciation to him for his kindness, not to mention his wealth of knowledge from which I benefitted so greatly on this memorable day.

As we journeyed home the July evening sun was like a glowing ember in a sky of ashes as is sank slowly behind us. Its beams were still warm on our backs until the last of them fell behind the horizon. Occasionally we rode past reminders of that terrible history, decaying carcasses of disused cottages, their gaunt stone walls protruding like the vertebrae of a skeleton through coverings of ivy and gorse bushes. We left the boglands and travelled through small fields and hedges in a more fertile area. The scent of the countryside rose around us, meadow-sweet and cow parsley and occasionally honeysuckle. The rhythmic screigh of the corn-crakes followed us from the oatfields beyond the stone ditches, their strangely haunting sound not unlike that of a door rasping back and forward on rusty hinges. And their dry, grating call echoed in my fitful sleep all night long, accompanying the unremitting sensation of jigging up and down on horseback, with all the attendant discomfort in an unmentionable part of my anatomy.

Nevertheless, yesterday stands out like a bright star in what has otherwise been a period of inner gloom. And at the moment I need such brightness as a monument to the possibility of joy and beauty.

The Castle at Glenveagh

Chapter 16

Light and Dark

Andrew's mother took the journal and studied the sketch. Her husband closed his tired eyes and rested his head heavily on his hands.

"He describes it all so beautifully, doesn't he. And it's a lovely drawing," she said. "Very typical of him. The shading. The contrast between light and dark."

"Yes," murmured Mackay. "Light and dark, light and dark. That sums him up very well. He flits between the two like a moth that can't make up its mind."

"I don't think that's fair Gordon. He can't help himself. Things get him down at times, that's all. You have to admit that this seems to have been a good day for him, indeed a great day."

"It would seem so but...."

"And this Diver fellow would appear to be a kindly sort, taking an interest in him; taking him around the sites of interest. He seems so at ease, so happy within himself after...." She faltered under her husband's glare.

"How can you be so foolish? So fickle? This is the same fellow who was engaging in immoral acts with a chambermaid just a few pages ago. A degenerate sinner he is. And now you are all enamoured with him because he took Andrew for a ride in the country. You are as bad as the chambermaid."

"Oh Gordon, that is a dreadful thing to say," she protested meekly.

"I'm sorry my dear, but you do think so naively at times. You clutch at the most ridiculous of straws. 'So happy within himself' indeed," he scoffed. "Were you to read on a few more pages you would find his mood very different."

"Why, what does he say?"

The clergyman took the diary from her and flicked through it. He paused to read silently from several pages before speaking again.

"Well, this 'happiness' you speak of didn't last, that's for sure," he said. "Boredom; long treks through the countryside along the proposed route of the thing; lack of sleep; constant tiredness; complaints about this one and that, especially some of the new engineer types who have joined their retinue. It doesn't make for pleasant reading. The entries get shorter and darker by the day."

"Does he mention the girl again?"

"He does. Unfortunately he has read too much into the encounter. He waxes on and on about it, how it must be all part of the 'Divine Plan' for him. He quotes Scripture, or misquotes Scripture I should say, to support this foolish notion. And the more he writes about her the more confused he seems to get. It's like a downward spiral. Listen to this passage.

'Can it be a full five weeks since I witnessed that heavenly vision, my angel of the whistle? I remember every line of her face as if it were happening before my eyes as I lie here in the stillness of my bed in Gallagher's Hotel.

I remember the look she gave me, the way her hair fell about her face, the curve of her figure as she bent into the whistle tune. And I ask myself, what was that all about? What was the Divine purpose in that meeting? I believe that, in God's Will, nothing happens by chance. There are so many Scriptures which underscore this Principle. I have been taught it since my childhood, at my father's knee, from my father's pulpit. It was the essential teaching of Knox and Calvin, the heroes of our reformed faith. The truth of the doctrine of predestination. That God 'ordains' the affairs of men. That he decides on the interactions of men, the timing of events, from the boundaries of nations to the fall of a sparrow.'"

The document slapped down on the table-top in his annoyance; his head rotated in rueful frustration. His wife could think of nothing worth saying. Picking up the journal again he continued. "Then he goes on to quote from Ephesians; listen to this; this is how he is manipulating Scripture to suit his own imaginings.

'Wherein He hath abounded toward us in all wisdom and prudence; Having made known unto us the mystery of His will, according to His good pleasure which He hath purposed in Himself: That in the dispensation of the fulness of times He might gather together in one all things in Christ, both which are in heaven and which are on earth; even in Him: In whom we have obtained an inheritance, being predestined according to the purpose of Him who worketh all things after the counsel of His own will.'"

Mackey read quickly, annoyance in his tone. "And this comment," he said.

"There! That's very clear to me! I note, 'That He might gather together in one all things....' This gives me great hope. Hope for a gathering together with my whistling angel.

'He worketh all things,' (including my encounter with her, here in an obscure corner of Ireland, of this barren Donegal), after the counsel of His own will.'

No question that it was God's will then. It is obviously part of His Divine will and purpose in me being here on this strange adventure in Ireland in the first place. If only I could discern what that purpose is.

What was the reason for me meeting that girl, in that coincidental circumstance, exactly when I did. Why? What will be the outcome? I cannot believe it was meant to be a 'once-in-a-lifetime' encounter which will lead to nothing.

What if I never see her again, as seems most likely? Am I to search her out? How would that lie with my present responsibilities? My role, such as it is, with Uncle Roberts and the commission? (My wandering-about, wondering-what-to-do, getting-under-people's-feet role?) What are the alternatives? I will sleep on that tonight. Or lie awake on that tonight, more likely."

The clergyman put the diary down on the table, stood and walked disconsolately to the window.

"So full of misunderstandings," he breathed. "So full of questions and so eager to grasp at the wrong answers."

"And we weren't there with him to help him find the right answers," said his wife.

"What a pity that he wasn't able to confide in your uncle about this.... this girl. That is what we had always hoped, isn't it?"

"I know. What I can't understand is why Uncle Roberts didn't write to us at this stage to tell us of his mood," said Mrs Mackey.

Her husband turned and looked hard at her. "But he did write Maureen. Have you forgotten? Let me find his first letter to us." He leafed through the file of papers. "Back in July, I believe. Yes...here we are. Why don't you read it while I go upstairs for a bit," he said, leaving the letter before her on the table as he passed.

"Thank you, I will do just that," she said eagerly.

Gallagher's Hotel
Main Street
Letterkenny
Co Donegal
Ireland
Saturday, 17th July 1897

My Dear Gordon and Maureen,
It is with regret and deep apologies that I write, in realisation that I have failed in my promise to correspond with you on a regular basis, to keep you informed of how matters are with my beloved nephew, your son Andrew. The commission in which I have been engaged has been one which perhaps on reflection I should not have undertaken. It has been much more onerous than I had anticipated, fraught with various tensions and irreconcilable issues which predate our involvement in the matter. As a regrettable result, I have been overly busy and have failed in my promise regarding writing to your good selves.

For the first number of weeks of his stay with us, I found Andrew to be a boy of unique qualities. He and I had some excellent conversation and, while not what one might call effusive in his queries, he did show a definite interest in the project in hand. He attended our various meetings with the local interested parties and quickly came to understand some of the complexities of the situation. On several occasions, he raised important questions to me, questions which, in the answering, I was able to clarify matters in my own head.

He engaged with me on one or two occasions in discussions of a more theological nature. You will be pleased to hear me say that I found his Bible knowledge and his grasp of many related questions to be far beyond what one might expect from a lad of his age. (But then he has had good tutorage from yourselves, there in Killin Manse.) At this stage there was an undoubted lightness in the boy's spirits and he was good company, for the most part. There were some worries that he was not always enjoying the normal pattern of sleep but I had felt that this had improved.

I noted as well that Andrew likes to write, as well as to sketch. He has spent many hours with his Bible and his journal and seems to have found this whole experience in Ireland one which has stimulated his thoughts. I have not, of course, read any of these writings, (they are his own private business, after all), but he has shown me some of his drawings and I have to say that his style and ability are unmistakeable, as you had assured me. Later in this mission I believe he will have profitable opportunity to exercise this talent. Let me explain.

Until now, the work of which I am joint commissioner, has been largely a 'finding-out' exercise. This was necessary in order to provide a report to the relevant authorities here in Ireland, so that an informed and carefully balanced decision could be made about the necessity, the viability and the route of the Letterkenny to Burtonport railway. That stage of the process, I am delighted and relieved to say, has now been completed. (Not to the delight of all interested parties, I might add, but then what decision ever is?) At a meeting of the Grand Jury of the County in Donegal town on Thursday last, our report was considered and approved and proposed railway has been approved. (Incidentally, I did not think it prudent that Andrew should journey with us to attend that Grand Jury as he was not in the best of form. He remained back at the hotel.)

Our next task as a commission, (which is the task I feel Andrew will be able to get his teeth into), is to survey the actual route and work out answers to the undoubted problems which will arise. This process could take several more weeks and it is to be hoped that my nephew will be able to stay with us for that duration.

In some ways I regret the fact that Andrew arrived with me here in Donegal as early as he did. I say this because there is no doubt that in the last few weeks he has found life here tedious and has displayed signs of frustration, introversion and boredom. Let me say straight away that I cannot fault him in this. I myself have been so busy with the work of the commission that I have not been able to give the time to him that you might have had every reason to expect. On those occasions when I did see him, at mealtimes and on the Sabbath, he was less than communicative and seems to have entered a closed little world of his own.

Please do not misunderstand me, dear brother and sister. I am not making a complaint. Rather this is an observation and an apology. I am fully aware that Andrew's present depression, for want of a better word, has arisen very much as a result of my neglect of him.

I am not alone in this observation. Mr Tatlow, my colleague, has raised concerns with me over what he referred to as 'Andrew's dark mood'. Even our assistant, Diver, has shown some awareness of it and, to his great credit, has tried to take Andrew under his wing, going out of his way to talk to him and taking him out around the countryside on horseback to try to alleviate his feelings of lonesomeness. His violin has lain in its case without disturbance for the last few weeks. Indeed I have really only heard him play on one or two occasions since his arrival, and one of those only seemed to bring him more distress and frustration. This I found disappointing as, like you Gordon, I am of the belief that music has the potential to really lift the spirit.

Believe me when I say that Andrew is in my constant prayers, as he is in yours, I am sure. And it is my intention, now that the enquiry stage of this mission is over and the practical stage about to commence, to endeavour to involve Andrew much more fully in our work, to see if meaningful activity can lift him back to the level of stability he was enjoying when he first arrived.

I will instruct him to write to you again soon.

I remain your humble friend and brother,

William Roberts esq.

A lonely tear dripped from Maureen Mackey's nose and splatted right onto the 'p' of 'prayers'; she watched the black ink dissolve into a blurry smudge and thought, "Oh dear, I've made a mess of his lovely handwriting."

Chapter 17

<u>Wednesday 21st July 1897</u>
<u>My unanswered questions</u>

I awoke to the realisation that no answers had struck me in the middle of the night. Despite my patience in the wee, small hours; despite my wakeful concentration.
I find a possible answer, only to realise that the answer leads me to even more complex questions.
And that reminds me of a key question for which I have no answer.
(One from my unwritten list of questions.)
The question of one thing and then the other.
Inactivity, then mad rush and bustle.
Strong lines, then soft curves.
Rocks, then sand-hills.
Light, then darkness.
Peace, then pain.
Purity, then vile thoughts.
Kindness, then sarcasm.
Errigal, then Sheba.
The reasons for, then the reasons against.
A sense of purpose, then a sense of despair.
The morning sunshine, then an evening of rain.
The straight road, the crooked path.
The broad gate, the narrow way.
The 'me', then the 'other me'.

I follow the men with the theodolites, the set squares, the protractors, the measuring tapes, the dirty language, the maps, the spades and shovels.
They wear me out.
I sit and draw a mountain, or a valley, a river or a rock.
And I wonder why?
I draw what I am told but no one talks to me.
So I talk to myself.
I say things like, "Peace be unto thee, Andrew!"
And "Nevertheless, not my will but thine be done!"

From Letterkenny, north west we walk. The contours are examined. The best possible route discussed. Local farmers have their say, about fields and rights and gradients and streams and cattle and rights-of-way and markets and I hear a cacophony of accents and raised voices echoing around my head, at variance with my own internal conversations.
"This way" or "That way"?
The perpetual question.
Yes, that is my second question.
This or that?
The third one which comes to mind is, "Is this how it is meant to be?"
Is there a master plan?
Is there a Grand Design?
For the railway route?
For how things are to be laid out for the future?
And, if so, where is it going to fit me into the scheme of things?
Sorry, that is three questions really.
Forgive me, I say to myself.
To the 'other' me.

Thursday 22nd July 1897

Kilmacrennan is to be our new base. A small hill of a village. I find myself carrying materials and tools for the surveyors and, while I appreciate the 'opportunity afforded to me to be learning the trade', I find much of the experience tedious and pointless.
There have been few controversies so far, few bridges or viaducts to test our technical experts. Indeed the progress has been faster than expected this week and Uncle Roberts and Tatlow are in good enough spirits.
I cannot say the same for myself. There is a lethargy upon me which I am finding difficulty in shaking off, a dullness of mind and spirit which deepens by the day, despite my prayers and, no doubt, those of Uncle, my parents back at home. This is not new to me, of-course.
Yet again, I find myself asking the big question, "Why? Why me? Why couldn't I have been created with a carefree spirit that takes everything in its stride and does not fall prey to the darknesses which stalk me like a pack of bristling grey

wolves?" I never really hear that question answered either, other than to reflect again on the whole Principle of predestination.
In other words, this is me!
This is how I was designed to be.
I believe this to be the only answer, though it is not one I rejoice greatly in!

<u>*Friday 23rd July 1897*</u>

A non-typical Donegal day today, in that the weather was exceptional for the entire day. I have just witnessed the most amazing red-skied sunset.
Today we made good progress beyond Kilmacrennan, reaching as far as the mountain range which I referred to earlier. There is, it seems to be accepted by the locally acquainted members of the survey team, only one readily accessible pass through these hills, so the railway inevitably has to head for that pass. Next week we will be up in the hills, trying to decide on the exact route and planning how best to design the various embankments and cuttings which will be necessary.
Tomorrow evening we are invited to attend a ceili in a local parochial hall. This may be an attempt to reward the commissioners for their decision not to bypass this village when planning the rail route. I hope that Uncle Roberts appreciates the gesture and that his aged joints hold up to the strain.

Chapter 18

Another letter home

Saturday 31st July 1897

My Dear Parents,

It is some time since I last wrote to you and I apologise for the delay. I have no excuse, certainly no meaningful reason for my tardiness, but I have been somewhat incapacitated during this past week. This unfortunate circumstance has made it necessary for me to spend several days recovering at the headquarters of Uncle Roberts' commission, the Letterkenny Hotel. I am almost seen as a permanent resident there by the staff and I have to say that the care they show me is very warm and much to their credit.

Things had been progressing moderately well in the period since you last heard from me. The commission was back on the road, surveying now, after all the uncertainty of the enquiry stage; it felt good to be of some practical use, although there were many times when I got the impression that I was being given tasks in an effort to amuse me, or occupy me, rather than doing anything of significant worth.

The reason for my present period of recuperation goes back a week or so to a most unfortunate incident at a ceili organised for the commission members in the village of Kilmacrennan. Towards the end of what had been an evening of music and fun and dancing, not unlike many we have had in Killin, a fight broke out.

It would be fair to say that there had been a growing sense of tension during the course of the evening, probably due to the copious amounts of alcohol which had been consumed by many of the local fellows and indeed by several of my colleagues. (Liquor seems to be an even bigger problem in these parts than it is in my native land, I have observed. The local supply of cheap illicit spirit would seem to be the main culprit.)

At one point during a dance which I think they called "Strip the Willow" my friend, John Diver, found himself partnering a tall, gangly, redhead lass. To be fair to John, she seemed to be enjoying the experience as much as he was; he spun her round like a flower in a whirlpool, her mane of red hair streaming out behind her like a scarf, and the whole crowd more or less stopped to watch; there was much shouted encouragement and whistling and the musicians were in full spate, so to speak. The next thing that happened was that a big lump of a country lad ran across the floor and launched himself at Diver, sending him flying and landing him in a heap at my feet, blood splattering from his nose. I could not believe what had just happened, and so quickly.

But the native hadn't finished yet. He stood and shouted at John in a horribly drunken voice, telling him to, "Stand up and fight like a man!" And that he would, "Bate the brains oota him!" John was in no fit state to get up and fight at that point, much less protect his brains, so the big fellow made another rush at him as he lay there. I could think of nothing else to do and, without really thinking at all, I just fell on top of John. It was in that position that I received some kicks to the back, and one to the head. This part of my tale is a hazy memory but what happened next was something of a riot, I believe.

Some of the railway team intervened to pull the local chap away to try to save Diver and myself from further kicking, but this led to more of the locals piling in to support their man. I have a vague memory of punches flying and a lot of yelling and swearing.

Somebody spat upon me on the floor and used two adjectives to describe me which annoyed and puzzled me and to which I took objection. The first was the term 'Scottish'. I have no problem owning up to my nationality but wondered briefly how my assailant could have known until I realised that my apparel, the kilt which I have always worn to such country dance occasions, may have been too obvious a clue! The second term I will not repeat, save to say that he had no possible right to doubt my parentage.

By the time that the more responsible folk got it all calmed down there were many cuts and bruises, with blood all over the dance floor. I'm not sure who they were, the people who managed to pull the protagonists apart and end the fight, but, whoever they were, they were brave and did a fine job. There were girls among them too, courageously trying to pull their *men away.* On the other hand, the redhead who had caused the thing simply stood to the side and laughed. She went neither to Diver nor to her would-be protector; indeed, when the thing was settled, she turned her back on the big local fellow, blew Diver a rather cheeky kiss and was gone into the night, her scarf flaffing behind her. (This final episode reminded me of my long held belief that women, as a species, are less to be understood and more to be avoided..... on the whole, I hasten to add. I still have hopes of proving my own observation to be in error.)

Diver, (whose surprising propensity to attract the most unlikely of women still astounds me....is it the generosity of his smile, I wonder? It cannot be his build. I have seen more robust looking clothes-horses), was most profuse in his thanks to me for what he called, "My heroic action!" He shook me warmly by the hand. Unfortunately this movement caused me a further near black-out; the pain was intense. When he saw my reaction, he took me to Uncle Roberts who examined the hand. It seems that the madman had stamped upon it in his efforts to get to Diver. To try to move the fingers hurt a great deal, but I did feel that I could move them by some small degree, so it seemed that the hand was not broken, merely bruised. My ribs and forearms also hurt and there was a substantial bump in the region of my left eye. The blood about my person, however, seemed to have emanated from poor John Diver's nose, a nose which appeared now to have a slight bend in its trajectory that I had not previously discerned.

It was decided that I should return to Letterkenny in the morning to have these injuries examined by a doctor in the local hospital. Which is what I did, under the caring accompaniment of the faithful Diver whose nose also required attention.

My examination showed that in fact nothing was broken, although the discolouration and bruising on various parts of my anatomy led the Doctor to suggest that I take a week of bed-rest. The hand would be no good to me for drawing, nor indeed for carrying, for several days so a short stay in Gallagher's Hotel seemed a wise prescription.

Diver was good enough to procure me one or two books to read, to "shorten the evenings," as he put it. As I could neither write or draw until today, reading seemed to be a sound past-time. *(This letter has taken a considerable time to pen, such is still the degree of discomfort in my hand.) One of the books, which I have made some progress in reading, has the intriguing title, 'The Vicar of Wakefield'. Do not concern yourself, father; I detect no similarities with the Minister of Killin, you will be happy to know.*

The main disadvantage of my current absence from the survey is that, for the first time since the commissioners left Letterkenny, my skills in drawing might have been of some use to the team. This week, I imagine, the surveyors will have been working in the pass through a rocky tract of land known as Barnes Gap. They will be deciding on where cuttings will have to be blasted through the rock, and where embankments will have to be raised to support the railway track on as level a gradient as possible. There may even be the need to construct bridges and viaducts in that section of the course. Of all the times to be missing from the venture, this may be the most unfortunate.

I hope to rejoin the team very soon, really as soon as Diver reappears to escort me back. In the meantime, I am reasonably content to read Mr Goldsmith's account of the descent of Wakefield's Vicar and learn whatever lessons ensue from those pages. Please do not worry about me. I have learned, with Saint Paul, "in whatsoever state I am, therewith to be content." For the most part. Although I would not try to deceive you, my parents, by saying that I live in a state of perpetual happiness. There have been days of intense misery of spirit, but I have learned that these pass and that some bright stars arrive to illuminate my distant horizon.

I trust that you are both well and that things at home are satisfactory.

Your loving son,
Andrew

~~~~~~~

"How good to know that, even in those trying circumstances, he was able to be of help to someone else. He was a good boy at heart, wasn't he?" said Rev Mackay, still holding the letter in his hands. The couple had resumed their painful perusal of their son's writings. Time seemed to have become an irrelevant concept in the manse. Parishioners had decided among themselves to give the place a wide berth and allow their clergyman and his wife to grieve in peace.

"But look at what cost to himself. My poor wee boy, getting hammered and kicked by some drunken ruffian....and so far away. Oh I feel terrible about this Gordon. I felt at the time that we should have been going to see him. Or writing to have him sent home. He was far too vulnerable for this experience. We should never have sent him in the first place."

Mackay had a wry expression on his face as he placed the letter back into the folder of correspondence on the table. He shook his head slowly and sadly. "I'm sorry, Maureen. You are correct of-course. Now. But at the time.... yes, in hindsight, you were correct then as well....obviously so, in view of what transpired. But hindsight is a wonderful thing. It's a pity we didn't have hindsight at the time....it might all have been so different, mightn't it? At the time, when we received this letter, on the heels of Roberts' letter, if you remember....we tried to balance it all out. Your uncle was concerned about him but he blamed himself; he blamed his absence from Andrew. We felt that his mental state was no different from the usual; up and down as always. The journal for that following week proves that, doesn't it? Some good days, some not so good."

"I just wish he had been at home. Then we could have kept an eye on him," she said into her handkerchief.

"Of-course you do. So do I. But even at the time we received this letter, despite the fact that he had been injured, didn't we feel proud of how he had handled the situation? Proud of his self-sacrifice, and his instinct to protect his friend? Such a Godly response, to put himself in the way of punishment which was intended for someone else. 'Greater love hath no man than this, that a man lay down his life for his friends.'"

"He didn't lay down his life, Gordon. He just lay down! Maybe fell down in shock, the poor lad," countered the mother. "I wanted him home. And you wouldn't do anything about it."

Mackay's head went down and he looked stung to the core. He sat in this manner of dejection for a considerable period, the silence punctuated irregularly by his wife's snifflings, before taking up the open journal again.

"It's all very well," he said in defeat, "but, as I say, hindsight is a wonderful gift. Shall I read on in the diary?"

"I don't know if I can bear it anymore, Gordon," she whimpered. "What is there to hear but more fears and worries, more examples of the terrible things he was going through? It only brings me grief in the extreme to listen to his inner thoughts...all this pain he was going through....all on his own among strangers. I'm not sure that I want to hear it anymore. It only makes me grieve for him all the more. I just so regret that we did nothing about it, while we still could."

"He was not entirely on his own, among strangers, as you put it. He had your good Uncle to look after him. And this fellow Diver who had become such a friend."

"Diver! Diver in the place his mother should have been, taking care of him! Diver who is such a degenerate character....you said so yourself, did you not?"

Again Mackay nodded his head in some degree of submission. "I did say that, yes. He doesn't seem to have been the best example for Andrew, morally speaking, but you have to give him credit that he seems to have been kind...he went out of his way to try to lift Andrew's spirits, didn't he?"

Maureen persisted, "When we should have been the ones to be doing that. And Uncle Roberts? He seems to have been so preoccupied with his business that he barely noticed what Andrew was going through."

"Now that is unfair, Maureen. The man was engaged in a professionally challenging task and he did not have time...."

"Exactly!" Mrs Mackay's interruption was more forceful than her husband had ever seen before. "He did not have time... time to be the parents that should have been there for a son."

"Andrew is nineteen, Maureen. He needs to be learning to...."

Mrs Mackay howled like a sudden gale at the window. "Is nineteen? Is nineteen? Don't you mean 'Was nineteen'? Or have you forgotten?"

Gordon Mackay was shocked at her vehemence and sat quietly for a little, listening to the sobs. Then he went to his wife and, hand upon her shoulders, spoke in what he hoped was his most comforting voice.

"Now that wasn't fair, Maureen. Of-course I mean, 'Was nineteen'. And I am sorry that how I said it offended you so deeply. Nineteen is what he was, and, in a sense my dear, nineteen is what he will always stay. Now, if you do not want me to continue to read his journal aloud, so you can hear the detail of it, I will read on alone....and then I can summarise things, or bring any relevant writings to your notice as I see fit. You can read it at a later stage when you feel inclined and able to do so. Would that be what you wish, my dear?"

"I would like to read what happened to Andrew at the end. What was it that pushed him over the edge...I don't mean literally, of-course, but what drove him to such a low place that he felt the only thing was to ...to do what he did? Do you understand that, Gordon? I do not need to hear what he was doing at every turn of the page, every little up and down of his moods. What evil entered him to make him destroy himself?"

"I understand, and I'm sorry," returned the minister, "but I feel I need to trace every sign of his descent, every activity and every thought he had in those last few weeks. I know it won't help now, but if Andrew took the trouble to write it all down, then I feel I owe it to him to read it, to ponder it all and try to understand my son, even for this the final time. Don't you see that?"

"I do see that, and I may do the same at some less painful stage, but in the meantime, why don't you read on as you suggest, and then bring me in on the relevant events towards the end? Would you do that please, and let me leave you to walk along the loch shore for an hour? I feel that a bit of fresh air wouldn't go amiss."

She left him trying to find the place where he had stopped reading and, pulling on a full-length tweed coat, put the sombre, grey manse to her back.

`` `` `` ``

The following morning, after a night broken by bleak thoughts and tormenting dreams, she brought a breakfast of porridge, tea and toast to the dining room. Her husband, having risen some three hours earlier, barely raised his eyes from Andrew's diary, so engrossed was he in his quest to uncover the reasons for his son's demise. Maureen stood, her back to the crackling hearth fire, as freshly-cut logs spat in spasmodic protest at their fate. She waited patiently for him to lift his head and engage with her, nervous after her emotional outburst of yesterday and tentative about asking any question. The wait went on and the porridge cooled, its steam adding to the density of the condensation on the window-pane. She began to suspect that there was an element of sanction in this silence, that she was being punished for her tantrum of the previous evening; she would just have to wait until he was good and ready to share anything of note from her son's writing. He might have been reading a Gallic guide to river fishing in the Highlands, for all that showed in his face as she studied it for signs of reaction, good or bad. Eventually she gathered the courage to draw attention to the cooling breakfast.

"Will you not eat, Gordon? It's going to be completely cold."

"I will in a minute, but listen to this bit. This is most interesting. This will make you proud of him." He lifted the porridge and shovelled a spoonful mouth-ward, reading between sups.

"It's from, let's see, the sixth of August, a Friday.

'The little Owencarrow River meanders northward towards the sea, a lazy, innocuous looking stream. The water is peaty dark and flows so slowly that you would think it in two minds as to whether to continue or turn back for the hills. But, for such an innocent waterway, the Owencarrow is keeper of a deep, dark secret. The bog through which it flows, right in the path of our railway, is less of a bog and more of a pure swamp.

There is a difference, I am led to believe, between 'bog' and 'swamp'. While a bog has a bottom of rock or of clay some feet below the deposits of peat, the Owencarrow swamp has seen an accumulation of slimy peat coming off the hills for centuries and, crucially, does not seem to have a bottom. At least, the surveyors are struggling to find an actual bedrock below the sludge upon which to lay the foundations for the necessary viaduct across this valley.

I have been present and watched the digging process and it is a frightening endeavour. A squad of big strong mountain men men have to dig with ropes around them, so they can be pulled back up to the surface. The peat gets hauled up in large buckets as well. Every time they excavate down into the swamp, the liquid, peaty mess flows in almost as quickly and fills up the hole behind them. They have, on occasion, reached a depth of fifty feet, only to return the following morning to find the space filled again with a dark, porridgy sludge.

My interest in this particular area is partly to do with a fascination with how the surveyors and engineers are going to solve this problem. I have been asked to sketch what the eventual viaduct might look like.

I made a rather simple suggestion to Uncle Roberts, based on something I read about regarding the construction of a viaduct in a similar Scottish situation. Its builders devised a system of sunken walls made of bales of sheep's wool to prevent the liquid peat from refilling the space, thus enabling the excavators to reach the bedrock and begin to lay a firm foundation.

Uncle Roberts was pleased with my suggestion and told me so, (although I do suspect that such solutions were already in his mind, from his vast experience of designing railways in my homeland.)'"

Mackay stopped to pour himself a fresh cup of tea and his wife took the chance to ask what to her was an obvious question.

"And why, Gordon, do you find this 'interesting'? I thought you may have come upon some clue as to his state of mind, something to explain.... this is just a.... a technical detail."

"It is," defended the clergyman, "but in the details there are such indications of his attitude; I mean, doesn't this passage confirm our motivations for sending him over there? He is in his element, looking at logistical problems and using his mind to solve them. And, when I turn over the page, you will see his wonderful ability to sketch. In this case, to sketch what he does not see. A possible picture of how this viaduct will look, when it gets built eventually."

"But what is the point of all that when he will never get to see it? Don't you see? He is lost to us forever. No amount of pride in him, no amount of imaginings, none of this journal of his is ever going to bring him back to us, is it?"

Gordon Mackay's complexion flushed with sudden frustration and anger and his moustache bristled darkly. He thumped the table as if it was the pulpit in his kirk.

"What is it you want then, woman? What can I do? Every time you open your mouth what I hear is that it's my fault!"

"I have never said that it is your fault. That is unfair of you. It is our fault, though. Both our faults. There's no getting away from that, is there? We reared him. We protected him. Then we sent him to that God-forsaken place. Alone. It is our fault!"

Mackay's fists clenched and unclenched on the linen table-cloth and he opened his mouth to speak, but thought better of it. His wife hadn't finished.

"And you are reading his diary as if you were some sort of master detective, sifting through the remains of some unsolved crime, spinning it all out as if you were getting paid by the hour. As if this was a theological conundrum you were having to trying to solve for your Sabbath homily."

He stood up abruptly, enraged, and, in a moment of extreme cruelty, picked up his son's journal and threw it into the open fire.

"Is that what you want then?" he yelled at her.

There was a moment of terrified silence as she stared at him, the image of his irate face distorted and ugly through her teary eyes, as if seen through the thick glass of a jam jar.

"What are you doing?" she screamed and leapt forward to the hearth. Ignoring the orange flames licking up from the pine logs, she whipped the precious journal up from their attentions and, holding it to her chest, fled from his anger to her bedroom above.

"What am I doing indeed?" he echoed and slumped down into his chair, his elbow knocking over a half-drunk cup of tea. The stain spread across the white linen cloth like brown bog-water; he thought of the Owencarrow swamp.

Later he went up to her. He opened the door softly and found her curled in foetal comfort on the bed, apparently asleep, with her son's final words still clasped to her chest, as if suckling an infant. His hand on her shoulder brought her back slowly but her eyes bounced away from him instantly.

"I'm so sorry, Maureen. That was a terrible thing to do."

She did not speak. Stared unseeingly at the four-paned window. His hand traced the curve of her shoulder, up the side of her face to her forehead and he stroked back the grey, lifeless straggles of hair that had fallen unchecked across her dull, brown eyes.

He tried again.

"Will you forgive me please? We have to try to be patient with each other at a time like this, forgiving of each other, understanding each other. We are all we have. We must stay close, my dear; avoid dissension, cleave to one another. 'Bear each others burden'. Don't you agree?"

She turned away, face to the wall now, leaving the diary behind her, its cover showing only a small hint of scorching from the flames. "Thank you for the sermon," she said dryly.

The wind coming up through the village off Loch Tay had increased in strength and now soughed through the conifers around Killin Manse and moaned at the window panes, as if in harmonic resonance with the pain in the bedroom. Otherwise silence reigned between husband and wife, a seemingly impenetrable curtain, like the acrid smoke of a gorse fire on the mountainside. A full ten minutes of desolation passed before the clergyman reached to lift the diary and went around the bed to sit facing his wife.

"Here," he said, offering the book to her with outstretched hand, "you take it, Maureen. You read it to me as you wish. Proceed to the end if you like, if it helps you to understand what happened to him. I will... I will just listen to you read. Come on, my dear; do not let this silence become any more sullen between you and I."

She pushed the journal gently back at him, at the same time taking his hand in hers and looking him in the eye for the first time since she left the dining room.

"I am sorry," she said softly. "I am just so low, and I have been so lonely without him over the whole period of the summer and..... to think I will never see him again. But you are right, we shouldn't try to hurt each other with blame ....and we do need to be strong for each other."

She sat up on the pillow and made room for her husband to sit beside her. "Here," she said. "Sit beside me and read whatever bits you think will help."

He joined her on the bed. Opening the journal again at the page showing Andrew's drawing of the anticipated Owencarrow Viaduct he held the sketch for his wife to examine.

"Yes," she said, "it is a lovely drawing. He was good, wasn't he? Is this the last sketch he did? Are there any more?"

"There is a very good one of a mountain further on; I saw it earlier. Let's move on to that and see what it's about," he suggested, flicking forward several pages. "Here we are; let's see, Saturday 21st August is the date. What does he say about it? Do you want to read it, Maureen?"

"You go ahead; I'll listen. Then we can read his last letter again," she said and she closed her eyes.

A suggested viaduct over the Owencarrow

Chapter 19

<u>Saturday 21st August 1897</u>
<u>My thoughts on a wonderful mountain</u>

It is almost midnight, nevertheless I cannot but write of today's adventures.
This was one of those unforgettable days when all the world seems to be a better place than I had ever imagined heretofore.
Today I climbed to the top of the most marvellous mountain. Errigal!
Not so tall as many of the Trossachs which I have scaled back at home. But what it may lack in height it makes up for in sheer, stark beauty.
It is an uncomplicated mountain.
It seems to consist of a rocky material which Tatlow, (who did not climb, needless to say!) calls 'quartzite'. He tells me it is a sedimentary rock, laid down in thin layers under the sea millions of years ago, then metamorphosed by the heat of some volcano in a more recent age into this shinny, mineral-

ladened rock which gleams out across the bogland of Donegal, like a giant jewel-encrusted pyramid.

(This is a challenge to me, this explanation. There I was thinking that God had created it with a simple wave of his mighty hand. Why have I never learned of such processes before?)

The climbing of it was quite a challenge as well.

The weather was most agreeable, the clouds high above the peak of the mountain, which is of-course important when planning a climb. It was neither too warm nor too cold, although I did as I was instructed and tied a light coat around my waist so as to have it available for the cooler upper reaches. I had been led to believe that it can become penetratingly cold up there, should the breeze get up, and I proved it to be so.

Several of my surveyor colleagues joined John Diver and myself for the climb, leaving our Gweedore Hotel just after a substantial Irish breakfast to make the journey. The horses trotted gently along the side of a very Scottish looking loch, at the head of which Mount Errigal waited welcomingly for us.

(Diver made a great joke of asking me repeatedly how my posterior was feeling, except that he did not use the word 'posterior'. I understood though. My understanding of general vocabulary has been greatly enhanced during this trip.)

Leaving the horses at a village inn we began our ascent, the first section of which was circuitous and across a sloping bog. What else? This is Donegal. My legs were nearly pulled out of their sockets by some of the gluey holes that my feet strayed into. A slough of despondency to be avoided by any decent Christian. Not this innocent one, it seemed. I had to be pulled out by my friends on two occasions, such was the strength of 'the miry clay' in this most 'horrible pit.'

Then, after the gunge, a rising slope of scree, acre upon acre of broken, slate-like stone. Each upward step upon such glistening, brittle rock shifted the underfoot stones in a downward direction, so that it felt like two steps up and three back down. Again, tiring in the extreme, especially on the calf muscles.

Above the scree slope, the climb seemed to steepen. We were clambering up over a jagged rock-face, once or twice on all fours. We rested at intervals, just for a few minutes to rediscover our breath. I appreciated these pauses as they gave me opportunity to look below at the spreading countryside, the bleak mountains to the east of us, a long slash of the freshwater Loch shining below us and the headlands and bays of the coastline, visible further to the west. On such a rest I chanced to spy a huge bird of prey swooping around above the lower slopes, at the same altitude as ourselves, just about a few hundred yards away. Riding majestically on the upward currents of air, with barely a flutter of its feathers. A magnificent creature, probably a local eagle deciding on what to eat for its lunch. Does it realise how fortunate it is, to be able to soar effortlessly above its surroundings like this? What a great feeling it must be, 'to mount up with wings as eagles,' as the prophet put it.

I eventually arrived at the summit, made up of two separate points joined by a narrow path. We were all delighted with the view, a wide panorama of hills, lochs, rivers, bogs, fields, forests and islands. The furthest island in our view, away to the north, is Tory Island, I was informed. And to the west, the long, low bulk of Aranmore Island. We remained there for an hour or so.

While standing on the narrow little path at the very peak of this mountain, I had the strangest sensation; perhaps it was due to the atmosphere, the coldness of the wind currents around my bare head; I know not. It was as if some instinct, some voice deep within me, beneath the level of my consciousness, was telling me, urging me even, to jump off. It was a strong compulsion and I had to actually sit down quickly on a flat rock and talk sense to myself. It was the clearest example yet of the 'me' and the 'other me'. The 'other me' has a gloomy element in its character, a bent towards self-abasement, self-destruction almost. I can talk to it, to 'myself', I suppose and it listens....which is good, obviously. That such a conversation should have occurred at this point, when I had just fulfilled one of the objects of my dreams in climbing Errigal, when I was enjoying the elation of being 'on top of the world', so to speak, is very unsettling for me. I found myself reminded of the passage about Our Lord's temptations, when he was taken up to a pinnacle by Satan and told to throw himself off; the idea was to test the Scripture that says that God would send His angels to bear him up, incase he would dash his foot against a stone. Thankfully both of us were wise enough to resist that temptation and stay on our feet, (or in my case on my bottom.)

The return journey was almost as difficult as the ascent. I found my knees protesting at almost every downward jolt. No one was injured, which was quite a miracle, especially as the idiotic Diver took off on a leaping run at one stage. He whooped like a madman and bounded like a deer over the scree until we were all sure he would come to a terrible grievous end over the edge. He survived intact, much to his credit and our relief. What a strange fellow he is, so exuberant yet so self-effacing, so humble and kindly of nature; despite my early impressions of him. We have become firm friends and I am glad to have him looking after me. (As events later this night have confirmed!)

To cut a long story short, we made it safely down the mountain and rejoined our horses for the trek back to the hotel. An excellent day. I stopped a mile or two from our destination so as to try to sketch Errigal, from along the loch-side. (I did not want to leave it until later because, with tomorrow being the Sabbath, and with the likelihood of our moving on to Crolly and beyond next week, I may not get the chance to attempt this drawing again.) I am pleased with the result and will treasure it as a memory of this day.

But the day was not over yet.

When we arrived back at the Gweedore Hotel, in good time for the evening dinner, I was told that a renowned fiddler was in the vicinity and that he would be playing with a few local musicians in a ceili house only a few miles away in a village called Bunbeg this night. My Uncle was keen that I avail of this opportunity to sample the delights of the local music tradition. (I have confess to mixed feelings about the matter. My legs were sore beyond anything I've ever felt, with the possible exception of the night after the kicking I received in Kilmacrennan; but I did want to hear the music, not least for my father's sake. So I feigned intense enthusiasm for the venture and rested before dinner accordingly.)

So, following another wonderful meal, we made the trip to Bunbeg. Uncle Roberts came too, the disadvantage of his presence being that he insisted that I bring my violin along. (It has not been out of its snug little case for a month, I'm sure, so perhaps it deserves to hear some decent Irish tunes for its patience.)

We were directed to the home of some people called O'Gallagher, arriving around nine o'clock, the brassy sun hitting us in the eyes as we had journeyed west. A few local lads were around the door and, while our host was most welcoming, I did not like how these rough-clad fellows looked at me. There were a few words, all in grumbled Irish, so I did not really catch the meaning. In fact, the whole night was conducted in the Gaelic language and, I am pleased to say, I did understand quite a lot of what was being said, especially if the speaker was taking his time and speaking clearly to the whole company. I tried one or two expressions myself, in Scots Gallic of-course, and most of these efforts were well received. One or two of my phrases, however, were met with blank looks of bewilderment and occasional smiles of amusement. (I hope that it was the phrases which brought such smiles.)

There were several folk already in the parlour of the house, a few with fiddles and flutes. A piper hid away in a tight corner, his Irish pipes, (played with a bellows under the right elbow, I discovered later), making a most plaintive sound, quite different in effect from our own Highland pipes. Listening to its doleful tone, especially in one of the slow airs played later in the evening, brought me near to tears, such was its emotional effect. A most spiritual instrument, I feel, and one that it might not be good for me to be around for very long.

People sat around the walls of the room on stools or upturned boxes. Visibility in the room was poor, due to the clouds of tobacco smoke wafting up from numerous pipes and mingling with that from the turf fire in the open hearth. Little glasses of local poteen were being offered around but I did not partake. Neither did Uncle Roberts of-course. It was interesting to see so many of the local men sidle up to him and Tatlow and engage in conversation, no doubt trying to secure themselves some hope of employment when the railway construction begins. Tatlow and my uncle did much shaking of hands and almost as much shaking of heads.

I learned that the guest musicians were two brothers from another part of the county, McConnell by name. They are apparently widely known as travelling fiddlers and tinsmiths. During the course of the next two hours or so they made their way through a veritable feast of tunes. Everything from barn-dances to jigs, strathspeys to waltzes, reels to slow-airs and laments.

People danced at times, sometimes in a style I have never seen before, their hands swinging loosely by their sides and their feet clattering on the clay floor in the most exhilarating rhythms.

An old story-teller began to recount a tale from local folklore. A strange sensation, listening to his lilting Gaelic accent. I understood the gist of it. It concerned the ancient Colmcille who had apparently been given to making prophesies. Among his fore-tellings, there was a vision that a large black pig would race all the way from Derry Bay to Burtonport across the bogs. The Seanchai left a pregnant pause at the end of his tale, obviously waiting for some intelligent person to make what to him was the obvious explanation. No one did, and so he was forced to say, "Don't you see? The prophesy is nearly fulfilled! It's the train that's coming! That's the black pig that will be racing over the bog to the Port!" Suddenly the people saw the point and he received an enthusiastic round of applause, the people nodding their heads and slapping their knees and confirming the thing to each other.

My uncle embarrassed me by suggesting that I play a tune; well, what made it much worse was that all my colleagues joined in until it became a virtual chant. Reluctantly I took the fiddle from its case and twanged the strings...they needed a little tuning after their prolonged vacation. I did not want to start anything too fast but I struggled to think of anything at all which I could play with some degree of assurance. In the end I went for Neil Gow's 'Lament for his Second Wife', a slow atmospheric tune, and to my surprise and delight, the tune was picked up by the McConnell brothers who played right through to the end with me. This brought a round of applause and, inevitably calls for "More!" Now I was in a fix. I made a calculated decision, a risky one.

I began to play the first line of the tune I had heard played in Kincasslagh by the girl with the whistle. I played it slowly, aware that, should no one else join in, I would be left high and dry half-way through the second line. To my immense relief I was joined by several of the other players and I was able to ease back and try to figure out the melody as they were playing; I was surprised, again, by how easily the tune came to me. When it was finished, I asked the company what it was called. They all looked at one another blankly and I realised at once that these people play a whole repertoire of tunes that they do not know the names of. If names they have.

By eleven o'clock I was fatigued to the extent that I was almost falling over. John Diver noticed this and suggested, very honourably as usual, that he and I excuse ourselves and make for the hotel. My uncle was in agreement so, having shaken hands with the host and thanked the musicians, I went out into the night, followed by John. Within a matter of seconds and before we had reached the horses we realised that this was a mistake. The fellows who had been hanging around the doorway at our arrival began to pelt us with all sorts of rubbish, bits of turf, pebbles, lumps of cow dung and so on. I was unsure of what to do, whether to return to the house or not but Diver, to his eternal credit, picked up a long stick that someone had left at the door on entrance and, shouting at me to mount the horse, he completely surprised the assailants by rushing straight at them where they stood behind some low bushes, waving this stick and shouting obscenities which will have to be seriously recalled the next time he goes to his confession. The brazenness of his trick worked, initially at any rate. The boys took to their heels for a bit, giving Diver and I the chance to untie the horses and mount. We spurred the beasts on and as we galloped down the road we were chased by the local heroes, throwing after us whatever materials they had left in their limited armoury. None did any damage, however, although the horses did not like it and whinnied nervously for the next few miles. Half an hour later we were entering the yard at the Gweedore Hotel and called on the groom to take care of our valiant beasts.

My trouble is that, despite the tiredness in my bones, my legs, my feet, my head, all over in fact... I still remain unable to sleep. This day needed to be recorded immediately and so I have done so. The adrenaline induced by the chase, indeed by all the excitement of the day, does not easily disappear and I am its victim tonight.

Errigal Mountain

"Seems to have been a very good day for him, doesn't it?" said his father studying the drawing. "And another fine sketch. A very handsome mountain."

"Oh Andrew," breathed his wife, succumbing again to the wave of emotion rising in her chest, "what happened to you, my poor darling boy?"

Mackey's head shook from side to side as he stared at the page. "There's no answer to that question Maureen."

"How did he fall so low so quickly, after the enjoyment of a day like this one?" she asked. "I just cannot understand. It was only a matter of two weeks after this that he...." She fell into silence.

Her husband spoke. "Shall we read his final letter again? I don't think it will help to answer your question but I think I would like to read it anyhow, brief and all as it was."

"Yes, read it," she said in resigned despair.

Gweedore Hotel
Gweedore
Co. Donegal
Ireland
23rd August 1897

My Dear Parents,
I apologise that I have not written for a while. Almost a month it must be. I am sorry. I hope you have not been overly worried about me. I do enough of that for all of us.
I do not have much news to tell you. It is the late afternoon here in the western reaches of this vast county. I am tired after the exertions of the last few days. And because I sleep little. As usual.
The scene before me as I write is one of wild beauty, of a loch not unlike Loch Tay, stretching away before me to the mountains beyond. I miss my own mountains, and rivers, and lochs. Does the Dochart still flow, I wonder.
On Saturday past I enjoyed an energetic day, climbing a local mountain called Errigal. You will be pleased to hear, father, that I have been persuaded, at long last, to produce my fiddle in public and play with a few local musicians. Yes, you were correct; the tunes around here owe much to the close connections between Scotland and the west of Donegal; a blending of traditions.
Uncle Roberts is in good health.
My general health is fine. My injury has recovered fully.
The work drags on. One day follows another, very slowly, it seems to me. While I continue to learn a certain amount about this planning process, I have to confess that there are times when its tedious and painstaking progress are challenging to my patience and sense of purpose. I long for it to be over and to find out what, if anything notable, awaits me afterwards.
I look forward to seeing you both in the not too distant future.
Your loving son,
Andrew

Chapter 20

His darkness grows

Having read what turned out to be Andrew's final letter, Reverend Mackay had set aside Andrew's journal for the remainder of the day. He had needed time to prepare himself for the unwelcome task of chairing a monthly meeting of the Kirk Session down in the church.

Normally this was a task he did not mind at all, so long as he could hold some of his more argumentative elders to the subject under discussion. But tonight was difficult in the extreme. For the obvious reason that he did not welcome their questions about his son, sympathetic and all as they were. His decision prior to the gathering had been to stonewall and deflect, saying that there was no news as yet of Andrew's whereabouts, no news of a body being found and no definitive news as to what might have happened to him. This decision was tested to the full by the subtle inquisition to which he was subjected at the start of his session meeting. In the end, he had just about held his emotion in place and somehow moved his elders beyond the theme of his own trials to the more mundane business before them. But then, during the course of that business he had found his mind wandering and had had to really struggle with his internal imaginings to stay with the discussion himself. His mental state was noticed by the Clerk of Session who moved to have the meeting adjourned until a later date, in respect to the 'unfortunate difficulties that our minister is having to handle at present.' Mackay had not objected and returned to the Manse before nine o'clock, an unheard of occurrence.

When he re-entered his kitchen he was doubly glad of his chance to return early. The sight that greeted his strained eyes was that of his wife curled up on a sofa, crying in outright, heart-wrenching despair. He went to her, knelt down in front of her and took her in his arms. The journal slipped from under her and flopped down beside him on the stone tiles.

"You have been reading on," he said, the slightest hint of rebuke in his tone. "You shouldn't have, Maureen, you shouldn't have. I asked you not to before I left. I made you promise. What have you done?"

"I didn't read on, not at the start anyhow. I was catching up on some of the bits you had told me about. Then I just couldn't resist ....going on to the end to see.... Oh, Gordon, it's terrible. I can't begin to tell you. You will be so.... so angry, Gordon. Please don't be angry with him, Gordon. Please. It won't bring him back. He's gone for ever and it won't bring him back."

Her sobbing became something of a demented howl, something from another kind of creature, not something he could ever have imagined being uttered by his placid wife, his lovely, pleasant, good-natured Maureen. Not such an otherworldly scream of anguish. He pulled her close and, amid soothing noises, lifted her from the couch and held her like he would have done a child. Like he did Andrew when he had fallen and cut his knee on the rough stones behind the shed outside. And as he held her, and as he soothed her with cooing gentleness, his eyes fell to the journal on the floor where it had come to rest. And how it had come to rest brought a sigh of emotion from his own mouth.

The journal had fallen open at a page showing a drawing. A drawing of a girl. Her emotionless eyes stared up at him from the floor. A fair-haired girl. A pretty girl. And she was playing a whistle.

He carried his wife upstairs to her bed and returned five minutes later, doubly eager to read to the end of his son's story. To the end of his son's life, really.

25th August I think

Oh my mother, I wish I was with you in my home.
The waters rise around me.
And they are heavy with sediment, evil smelling sludge, the washings of the bog. These days are so hard.
I survive but I know not how.
There is an external world which goes on around me, the survey people continue to work.
But I do not care, I do not connect.
This is the deepest trough I have been in, that I can recall.
I do not see a reason.
Roberts tries to force me to sleep, telling me I am exhausted.

He will call a doctor, perhaps obtain a sleeping draught for me. Or a warm blanket of darkness to wrap me in, one from which I need not arise again.
What is the point of these meaningless words? Who will ever read them, or take note of my anguish?
I walked through the mushy bog today and examined long pools of Bible-black water.

26th August; A Thursday in 1897

I write propped up in my bed.
Between the sheets, between the days.
Propped up by the promise that they will see about getting me home soon.
These cool white sheets which mock my hot purpleness. Deep, dark purples in the high alcoves and recesses of my mind.
Since I climbed that mountain I have rejected myself.
I do not get a reply when I talk to myself, the other voice is strangely silent.
It is like a wall of grey silence, not even an echo of peace coming back at me. And the faces stare, and stare, and stare, like I am a freak show.
The tongues wag continuously. I hear them from a distance. Those men should be working along the route, but I can hear them from my bed, no matter how far away they are. Their language does them no credit either.
These feelings are so difficult to describe, even to myself, and I am the one in the middle of them.
All is distorted!
Food is questionable!
No one can be trusted!
I am in a cocoon of shadows and they seem determined to torture me with uncertainty. This feeling of enclosure, of entrapment, is as tangible as my bed.
What is to become of me?
I am making myself write again tonight but I know it is of no help.
What can I say?
I read the previous pages of this journal and many of the lines twist into a scowl before my eyes.

Friday 27th August 1897
My concern about time

Diver has deserted me.
He has given up on me, I believe. And I do not blame him. I would give up on me too.
They take me for walks, along the loch which, a few days ago, I found to be so idyllic. The might of Errigal frowns down at me from the head of the valley. I believe I can see that mountain shaking its head at me, as if in despair of me.
At night I am terrified of the visions I see.
I am told that they are mere hallucinations but that does not make them any easier to survive when I am in the flow of them.
I have been in dark forests of the mind before and somehow I have found my way out. But this path is a longer one than I have walked previously.
I am struggling with the idea of time.
What actually is it? No one has ever tried to explain it to me, I believe.
Is it outside the possibilities for humans to define?
How would I define time, if I had to do it to save my life?
I cannot think of words which sum it up, which get to the essence of it.
All I can say is that 'it passes'; that is its main characteristic, but that does not tell me anything about it, does it? What a characteristic to be defined by, that 'it passes'. It passes all understanding.
The wind 'passes'. The clouds 'pass'.
Time 'passes', but not in the same way.
I am caught in it, like a fly in a spider's web. And, like the fly, I am waiting for the spider. I am waiting for the end. The end of time.

Saturday 28th August 1897
My reflections concerning Gola Island

Another special expedition today.
Very considerate of Diver to plan this 'diver'-sion for I have not been good company this week. And I have not been of any

use to anyone, in terms of the mission. I have been marooned on a desert island of my own making, I realise.
No one can be blamed except myself. I am aware of this.
So, a boat-trip to an island. (Appropriately, and fulfilling my wish.)
Offshore from Gweedore. A place called Gola.

Uncle Roberts tells me that he is writing home regarding my health.
The work here in this area is almost complete. A further week of walking, measuring, sighting, sketching, climbing, scrambling, planning and so on should take them to Burtonport.
The end of the line.
And he intends to secure me passage from there back to Glasgow and home.
Which I suppose makes sense.
Rather than trekking all the way back to Letterkenny and then Derry, to get passage on a ferry. Fishing boats and cargo boats sail all the time from Burtonport to Glasgow, I am led to believe. One even calls at this Gola.

A lovely island which was intended to lift my spirits.
It did not do so, but I have become a master of pretence.
We rowed there in just over an hour. With a fisherman, Duggan by name. A quaint and strangely shapen little individual. Muscular of arm. Dark as an Arab and with a head which looked as if it had been attached to his shoulders at an entirely wrong angle in childhood and never readjusted.
As I walked around the little lanes and looked at the tiny thatched cottages, I had the feeling that we had rowed back in time to a different era.
Times and eras are a matter of continuing intrigue for me.
This picturesque place stands in defiance against all that the ocean can throw at it.
And has done for how many years?
Arches and sea caverns, sculptured out of the tall cliff-faces by the endless power of the waves.
Its men are the hardiest of breeds. Barely a word of any sort from them, and then only in very hurried and softly spoken Gaelic.

Sometimes I think that they speak as if they were singing. I close my eyes and it sounds like a lullaby.
Its women are every bit as tough and boney. Weather-beaten like tree-bark. Many scrawny wee bairns peeking out from behind their tattered skirts.
There is obvious poverty here on the island. I have been aware of sub-standard housing and over-crowding in many of the parishes we have travelled through but what I have seen on Gola is a level of impoverishment which has shocked me. Many cottages seem in a state of partial ruin. Clothes are thread-bare and the people wearing them appear to lack nourishment and vitality. It is a hand-to-mouth existence here and, it seems, more often than not there is very little in the hand.

As we said our goodbyes to these bravely content islanders and returned their shy farewell waves, I could not help but feel an inner voice bring me a measure of chastisement.
I suffer my own mental turbulence and dwell upon the shadows of my mind. It is simply who I am and I cannot seem to help it. Today was meant to bring me pleasure, a distraction from myself. Instead I feel rebuked in my spirit.
These islanders live a life of real hardship, without any sense of deprivation showing on their faces, it seems to me. And I said a prayer for them, with the setting sun shining orangely from over our shoulders and glinting on the abundant white cottages which are strewn like a handful of thrown shells along the coastline. The sea was mill-pond like, appearing almost oily on the surface and the boat glided beautifully over it.
Behind us, a fiery, red phantom hovered in the evening sky as the sun infused the clouds with vibrantly warm colours; Diver saw a butterfly, whereas I could clearly discern an angry dragon. We conducted a jocular argument about this, foolishly and without agreement in the end.
I had the strange sensation that, were I to step out over the side, I could possibly walk on top of this calm veneer without sinking.

Chapter 21

A Further Letter from Roberts

Tuesday 31st August 1897

My Dear Gordon and Maureen,
I hope you are both in good health.
Our work here in Donegal is rapidly coming to an end and it is with a deep sense of relief that I can say that the various aspects of our mission have been a qualified success. I am also relieved that Andrew has made it safely to this juncture and will soon be returning to your good selves.
I feel it my duty to make you aware that of late there has been some deterioration in his mental state, or at least some severe fluctuations in how he has presented to myself and his fellow-workers. From one week to the next I never quite know what sort of mood he is going to be in. This is, of-course, something which is not news to you; it has been difficult for the less patient members of my team to accommodate this inconsistency.
The past week has been a period of morose isolation; Andrew has barely appeared out from his room and certainly has been in no fit state to be working with us along the route of the railway. I am not sure myself what he did to pass the time, but he does spend many hours alone in deep contemplation. In such circumstances I have found it impossible to engage with him at any level other than the most basic of pleasantries.
We are but a few miles now from our destination. I anticipate that we will have completed the survey by the end of the current week. The team will then be dispersed and, by this day week, my colleague, Joseph Tatlow, and myself will be making our way to Dublin to meet with some members of the Privy Council and the Board of Works. Today we will re-locate our lodgings to Burtonport.
I mention this because it will be necessary for me to make arrangements for Andrew to travel back to you in Killin at this time. It would seem unwise to me to contemplate taking him with me on our journey to Dublin. I would be unable to afford him the time and care which his condition may merit, indeed it would seem unwise to consider any other course of action than

his return to you. I hope you will feel that he has benefited in some small way from the venture. He is a fine lad and does indeed possess many grand qualities.

To this end, I shall be in communication with the harbour master at Burtonport to ascertain the most suitable vessel which will be sailing to Scotland in the near future, probably at the start of next week. I will be in touch by telegram to appraise you of the details of Andrew's travel and so inform you of his arrival in Glasgow, where I believe you should meet him to accompany him home.

It goes without saying that I will continue to remember Andrew, as yourselves, in my prayers. It has been a wonderful experience to meet him and get to know him during these past few months and to begin to share some of your burden for him. He has so much potential as a young man and, who knows, one of these days he may receive healing from his unfortunate condition and go on to make you both very proud.

I remain your humble friend and brother,

William Roberts Esquire

Chapter 22

Saturday 4th September 1897
My thoughts on the end of the line

And so the end of the line; the railway reaches Burtonport. Hooray!
(Except that it has not, of-course; merely the planners have reached this terminal.)
I should like to return to this area when the track is eventually laid.
I should love to travel on this train, this 'Black Pig' of Colmcille's prophesy.
Travel through the cuttings in the Barnes Gap, and across the Owencarrow Viaduct, probably wondering if the foundations way down there below the slime are actually secure.
Journey around behind Muckish, peering out of the window to see if I can spy Dunfanaghy in the distance. I can visualise some residents of those by-passed settlements, vainly waving their fists at the smoke and rumble of the far-off train.
Ignoring these towns may prove to be a short-sighted mistake; even I as a total novice can see that.
How Tatlow and my uncle can argue for this particular route as the 'most economically sound' is beyond me.
A railway through a wilderness, it seems to me.
I should love to be whisked along through the peace and quiet of the bogland, skirting lochs and rocky crags, watching the peat-cutters wave and laugh in disbelief from their peat-banks as we pass.
Stop at Cashelnagore, where a station is planned in the dead centre of nowhere; get out, stretch my legs, salute Mount Errigal and wonder at the barren isolation of this most randomly located station where, surely, only black-faced sheep will be standing to await the arrival of the steaming 'black pig'. Chug along the side of Dunlewy loch to the Gweedore Hotel Halt and see Lord Hill smile contentedly through his window, from between piles of new silver coins.

I rejoice that I have made it thus far on my journey, my real journey as opposed to this imagined one.

With St Paul, "I have fought a good fight, I have finished my course, I have kept the faith."
This past week I did my best to regain interest in the project. I sketched occasionally when asked to do so and submitted my efforts.
I did, however, get the feeling that these drawings would end up in the back section of some file, never to be seen again. (Tatlow seemed dismissive of them, at any rate.)

Not many people tried to talk to me this week, I noticed. Perhaps too busy in the completion of the task before the deadline of yesterday. Perhaps because I have been unwell during the previous week. Perhaps because I suspect that they would rather talk about me than to me.
And I know they talk about me, even strangers who meet me in the corridors of this boarding house. If they could all mind their own business I would be most grateful. It cannot be in anyone's interest that I am the subject of their suspicions and illicit jokes.

Today several of the surveyors and labourers took their leave, their task being over. They return east to Letterkenny by coach, having received their salary from Tatlow. John Diver remains here until next week, as general helper for the two commissioners. He has been a great personal support to me at many times during the past three months and I shall miss him. Unexpectedly!

My Uncle Roberts informs me that he will depart for Dublin on Tuesday next, leaving me here until Sunday 12th, when I shall be able to board a ship called 'The Mary Ellen', a cargo boat, transporting produce of the sea to Glasgow. I have been assured that a cabin has been secured for myself. I am distressed inside when I contemplate the actual journey. I pray for good weather, a calm sea and a smooth journey to my homeland.

So I shall have some days of freedom in this port before I sail. From Tuesday until Sunday I am to be trusted to survive on my own here. This will be a strange experience for me and I must resist the immediate instinct to panic. Usually I prefer good strong boundaries and fixed expectations but I shall have to see how I manage in the uncertainties of these next few days. Already I have the feeling of a cloud of twittering starlings swirl around my inner self, a darkening shadow of perplexity across my horizon. I hope these birds do not decide to roost there... I cannot wish for another week like the one I suffered recently.

Tomorrow and Monday, then, are my last opportunities to socialise with my uncle before he departs. I wonder what will transpire for him in Dublin. Will his plans be slapped down as short-sighted, as I feel they should be? But who am I to have such an opinion? I must concentrate on my own agenda and survive until I reach the Falls of Dochart again.

<u>Tuesday 7th September 1897</u>
<u>My response to Uncle's sermon</u>

I have made my farewells to Uncle Roberts and Mr Tatlow and offered them my sincere gratitude for their generosity to me during the past three months. They left by coach this morning, travelling southward toward Dublin, a very long and twisting journey, I am led to believe. I wish them safety and good speed.
Before he left, my uncle introduced me to the Harbour-master, a Mr Hughes, the same gentleman I encountered here in June. I am to report to him at six o'clock on Sunday evening, to be taken aboard the vessel bound for Glasgow.
As a consequence of my conversations with my uncle over the past two days, he has allowed John to stay with me here in Burtonport until Sunday. This is very kind and I shall appreciate his company. The gesture may have come about in response to some intense questioning of me by Uncle Roberts. We engaged in what I can only describe as a very deep discussion, largely about faith, perception, personality and character, and the inter-play between these in shaping a man. I am not sure what the outcome will be.
While he and I share our religious convictions and a love of the Scriptures, I am not sure that he was able to identify with how I frequently see things, how I perceive the world. In the

end, it felt more like a personalised sermon, well intentioned of-course, but it was seed landing on soil not quite disposed to receive it. Stoney ground, I fear!

In the end, I basically shut down my inner ear and deflected the 'bolts of wisdom'. I continued to nod assent of-course, as manners required, but I could not help the conviction that he was preaching from a different place to the one I inhabit. My mind is my own domain and, if someone cannot see my perspective as valid, then they become as a 'sounding brass or a tinkling symbol'. This is not to be critical of my most kind and Godly uncle whose acceptance of me, up to this point, has been most warm and supportive.

So John Diver will stay with me for the next few days, I am informed. I am unsure as to how or why this decision was made but I welcome it.

<u>Wednesday 8th September 1897</u>
<u>My innermost thoughts on feeling 'lost'</u>

Not unlike my last sojourn in this little port, the weather closed in and curtailed any desires to explore the area surrounding Burtonport.

Frustrating in the extreme.

For me, at least.

Less so for John, who has resumed acquaintance with our plump little chamber-maid and has already spent much time inducing her to join him in what sounds from my room next door like a giggling competition. (I try to imagine that it is all as innocent as that. I try not to imagine other things.)

So no opportunity to sketch today.

I had hoped to see Aranmore Island from a local vantage point, so as to make a drawing of the place but this must wait until tomorrow, at least.

I took the fiddle from its case and made some screeching attempts to play but with painful results, I am ashamed to admit. Either my fingers have stiffened up through the manual labour of this mission or, more likely, I have just not practiced as much as I had intended, certainly not enough to please my father.

I wonder will he be angry at my lack of progress.

One thing which I accomplished today and which will please him is that I managed to locate a barber in this small village and had a tidy-up of a haircut, removing those unruly dark locks which had developed over the summer and which tend to annoy my father so.

Later, at our evening meal in fact, (a "feast" of greasy Irish Stew,) John made some fun of my musical efforts. He said that he had heard a sound during the afternoon which, he suspected, had come from the throat of a dying donkey nearby. Either that or from a pig having its manhood tampered with! (He did not, I have to confess, express the latter idea so delicately!) I promised him that I would play no more, especially if it interfered with his amorous intent. He assured me that my music was 'the food of love' and had had no such detrimental effect. I seem to detect a kind exaggeration in these well-intentioned words!

Tonight the preoccupations which normally fill up my mind for so many of my waking hours seem to have abandoned me. I am left with the feeling of a dull void. Almost like an absence of thought, a sense of desolation, the source of which I cannot trace.
Such dark, empty mental spaces are painful to me and I dread their unheralded arrival like I dread my worst nightmare.
There is, of-course, no logic to it; no perceptible order or symmetry; no answer in terms of underlying meaning.
I cannot right myself, nor can I write myself out of this lostness. Not when I do not know from which 'foundness' I have strayed, or even if I have strayed. Not when I do not know what it is to be found. The difference between me and the Lost Sheep of the Gospels is that it was lost and did not know it was lost. I know!.... at least I feel I am being lost, and it is a sooty tunnel to be walking in. Yes I know that there is always a light at the end of the tunnel. I know and believe that, theologically, I cannot be lost. I have been found and my soul is eternally secure. I know all that in my mind.....the same mind that darkens with the doubt of insecurity, the same mind that drags me inexorably down this shadowy tunnel of lostness to God knows where.
He must know where!

Chapter 23

__Thursday 9th September 1897__
__A Dream Fulfilled__

My Angel of the Whistle
Today my dreams have come to pass!
I have seen her again!
The Divine Plan takes shape!
Here is how it happened.

Following lunch at the boarding house, John and I parted company, he to continue his flirtations with his friendly maid and I to try to find a spot from which to draw the island across the channel.
I walked around the headland, past several houses in sheltered bays, until I came to an appropriate location which afforded an excellent prospect of Aranmore. I was positioned on top of a sand hill, amid tall shore grass. Below me lay an idyllic little beach, white virgin sand untouched by footprint of any kind, running down to where it met the gentle waves of a translucent, blue-green sea. The weather had cleared up and the afternoon was fine, cloudy but warm and clammy for the time of year, with occasional bursts of sunlight playing upon the foreboding brows of Aranmore.
The light, as I have noticed before in this part of Donegal, is of a most tantalising quality and is generally an extremely obliging ally to the artist. I was concentrating on the drawing pad upon my knees and making good progress with the sketch when I began to discern the sound of sweet music.
From a distance.
The sound of an Irish tune, beautifully played.
On a whistle!
My heart skipped and stuttered for a moment.
It surely couldn't be her?
My eyes followed my ears to discern the direction from which it came and, after a short time which seemed like an age, I saw a girl appear from behind another sand hill, not a hundred yards away, and make her way down across some flat rocks onto the beach before me.

A small, black and white collie dog scurried along behind her as she walked.
I could hardly believe my eyes.
It was my angel.
Was it a dream? Another hallucination? Was I imagining it? But no! Here she was! In the flesh! And even more startlingly beautiful than I remembered her. Tall, taller than I imagined, having only witnessed her sitting down in that cart.

I hid down into the tall grass instinctively, to avoid detection, and watched her walk to the water's edge, whistle in her mouth, the reel joyfully dancing up across the sand to my worshipping ears. And her form to my worshipping eyes.
She wore a simple country dress, a dull, well-worn, brownish affair, full of length. No shoes on her feet, which now played with the shallowest of the breaking waves.
The dog scurried back and forward along the sand, picking up the occasional stalk of dried-out seaweed and shaking it. I was dreading the animal finding me but thankfully the slight breeze was coming off the sea into my face and my scent was therefore blowing away from it.
The tune soared up through its final stanza.
How she can play!
How did she learn to play like that, with such natural, effortless flow? With such subtle phrasing and tone?
The echo died away quickly in the sound of the small waves.
The girl stood still at the water's edge.
Then a surprise, a shock...and something I never expected to see.
She hitched up her dress around her knees and waded slowly into the water!
It must have been very cold, but she gave no sign of noticing it.
I formed the impression that this was a complete joy to her, a joy that was being shared by the dog which swam out around her, yelping and splashing.
And it was, of-course, a joy to me to behold it!
She shuffled gradually forward, further out into the water.
Slowly it rose around her legs.
The dress rose higher up to her thighs and beyond.

*I watched transfixed as she stood there, in that cool, crystal-clear water, the waves breaking around the very top-most part of her legs, her beautifully slim and elegant legs; I know not what to compare them to. I continued to watch, fascinated......
Until "David and Bathsheba!" came a small voice, echoing in my head like a gong.*
In disgust at myself, I realised what I was doing and hid myself again below the rise of spiky grass.
Not for long though.
My curiosity too quickly overcame my sense of shame and I raised my head again and watched her return slowly to the sand, her dress once more covering her flesh.
She played with the collie for a while, throwing a stalk of seaweed for it to recover from the sea.
Then, tiring of that game, she put the whistle to her lips again and started up a very different kind of melody, I know not how to describe it, a haunting, soaring air of supreme beauty.
Like the musician herself.
It suddenly occurred to me to try to capture this moment.
That I may never experience the like again was my thought and, using the background which I had already drawn, the beach and the headland and the island beyond, I began to sketch the whistle-player as she stood on the sand below me. The dog scampered around and so I included its frolics.
(I am less than delighted with the results of my effort, I have to say. The shading is too dark and, try as I might, I failed to realise on paper the perfection of that moment and of her sublime human form. She was distanced too far below me. The landscape which I had captured to my initial pleasement now tended to minimise and detract from my angel who should have been the highlight of the composition.)
I was so intent on getting her form correct, my eyes flicking up and down between page and subject, that I did not realise that the collie had somehow sensed my presence and was climbing the sand hill towards me. As soon as it saw me it began to bark with some aggression and, inevitably her gaze followed the sound, up to the summit of the hill where my attempts at remaining hidden had been thwarted.
The dog continued its protest, a short distance from me.

I could think of nothing better to do than to stand sheepishly to my feet and wave down at her in a friendly fashion, meanwhile trying to pacify the dog with soothing phrases.
The collie gave no appearance of understanding my Scottish accent.
She did not move for a considerable period, just stared up at me and her yapping dog.
Then she moved, towards me.
Slowly she climbed the bank of sand, hitching her dress to her knees again, her feet sliding down in the softest areas between the grass.
"What am I to do?" I thought frantically, out of my depth here in this circumstance.
"What would John Diver do?" I considered, then immediately dismissed the idea.
When she reached me she stood quite a distance from me and just looked.
Her eyes flitted between me and the dog, and then she noticed the drawing pad in my hand and her gaze stayed there.
I could discern no emotion in her look.
She did not speak.
Neither did I, my tongue as transfixed as I was, ten, fifteen feet from her.
Eventually I did the mannerly thing and stuck out my hand.
As if she could somehow shake it from that distance.
She didn't move.
My arm subsided.
I tried speech next.
Indicating the sketch, I said, "I beg your pardon, Miss. I was drawing you. I hope you don't mind."
Not a word from her.
We stood looking at each other.
Across ten feet of time, ten feet of an eternal destiny that I could not think how to span.
I tried again.
"I saw you before. You were in a.... a... " (I could not bring myself to say the word 'trap', for some reason, perhaps in case she thought that this was, in fact, exactly that. A 'trap'!) "You were playing a tune on your whistle. You were travelling through a village, I think its name was Kincasslagh. With a young man and an older lady. A tune that sounded like this."

At this point I embarrassed myself even further by attempting to whistle the tune she had been playing.
She did not respond, as I thought manners should have required. She did not put the whistle to her lips and help me out, as I had hoped she might. She did not do anything. Just stood there and looked at me, through two of the most beautiful clear-blue eyes I could ever have imagined.
But she did not speak.
"I am Andrew," I announced into the void between us.
She did not tell me her name.
But at least she moved this time, towards me.
Her eyes falling to the drawing pad in my left hand.
I clumsily stuck out my right hand again, thinking she might want to introduced herself, shake my hand, recommence the interlude with some of the normal human graces, now that her shock at being spied upon had diminished. But she didn't take my hand. Instead she looked at the drawing and then at me, without a word.
"Ah!" I said, "You want to see my sketch."
And I showed it to her and looked at her eyes to gauge her response, a smile, a laugh, a frown, anything.
"It's not very good," I clarified, "because I didn't have much time. You had just come out.... out of the....."
But there was nothing. No response! Not a smile! Not a rebuke! Nothing!
"What do you think?" I tried again.
She looked away to the west, to Aranmore and the sea beyond, and simply stared into the horizon.
I was dumb-founded and puzzled beyond words.
So I shut up and waited.
What was going on here?
What was this creature of beauty, this silent angel?
And why was she not talking to me?
In fact, not communicating in any way, by even the most subtle of gestures.
Then she gave me yet another surprise. Her gaze returned from the blue beyond and she turned towards me, quite close to me, actually, and she sat down. Sat down right at my feet, right on the sand between clumps of marram grass.
The dog chased around after whatever scents it was picking up.

What could I do but sit as well, opposite her, my well-worn boots rough against her sand-covered feet. I wanted to remove them, so my feet could touch hers, but it felt awkward to start to fiddle with the long laces, so I stopped half way through, conscious of her watching me. My boots stayed unwillingly where they were.
She seemed happy, relaxed, so far as I could tell.
And she played again.
Yet another tune from what seemed to be a sizeable repertoire.
I had now heard four of her tunes, each one different from the last.
When she finished, (and she played it through three times, my eyes feasting shamelessly upon her face as though I had never seen a girl in my life until this moment,) I applauded slowly and noiselessly.
Her music seemed to seep into my very soul.
This time I did not speak.
And I felt that I detected just the tiniest hint of a smile at the sides of her mouth, perhaps just dimples, her eyes now looking into mine as though trying to search out approval.
Needlessly to say, I smiled back. Briefly! Because, at that point and much to my embarrassment and to my own consternation, my smile turned inside out and I cried.
Not a lot, not a sobbing kind of breakdown.
Just some tears forced their way out of my eyes and down onto my cheeks.
It was sheer joy of-course.
And I wondered how she would respond.
Laugh at me? Rebuke me? Run away?
Perhaps this spontaneous emotional 'outburst' would prompt her to speak.
Instead, with the most gentle, the slightest of movements, her hand came up to my cheeks she touched the tear, running it delicately onto her own finger, then putting it to her lips to taste it.
It was a magically intimate gesture.
I had a sudden realisation. This was no normal girl!
I had already known that, of-course.
But I mean something more, something far more significant.
She was not a normal human being, as other girls are.

I began to understand that she did not speak as normal humans do.
Perhaps she might be a mute, perhaps incapable of speech, of normal communication.
But she had reached right inside me as a fellow human being; she had touched something deep within my very spirit, something entirely liberating and healing.
And she had tasted my tears.
I did not need to say anything more.
She did not need to speak. She did not need words. She had spoken!
We sat in that speechless heaven for a considerable period of time.
Although there was no time aspect to it.
We were beyond time. It was a meaningless concept now.
Except that, when she stood up suddenly, I realised that she might leave and that might be the last time.... Time was back on the agenda as an issue.
So I said, "Will you come again tomorrow, to the same place, at the same time? I will bring my fiddle," (here I foolishly improvised the movement of playing a violin, as if she was deaf and could not hear me), "and we can play your tune together. Please?"
She did not reply, of-course. Just turned away and skeltered down the sand hill without much attempt at grace, the dog following her. The grace came when she was halfway across the beach. She turned back and looked up, even walking backwards for a couple of steps, her upturned gaze meeting mine.
So now, back in my room I wonder how will I sleep tonight.
And I so wish that I had taken my boots off.

Girl on a beach

Chapter 24

<u>Friday 10th September 1897</u>
<u>My hopes for today.</u>

This morning I feel like I am back on the summit of Errigal, the twin summits, to be exact.
One of the peaks represents a height of elation which I cannot begin to describe in words of the English or any other language, short of that of Heaven itself.
The other, though, is a peak of some trepidation, disorientation, guilt.

A wakeful night. But for once the reason was not the usual dark tide of ugly thoughts rising around me.
The opposite, in fact.
I am totally infused by her!
By the vision of her eyes, her serene quietness and beauty, those lips tasting my uninvited, my untimely, my unfortunate tear.
(My fortunate tear.)

Her finger, inquisitive and intimate upon my cheek. The only time we touched.
The wafting of her hair in the breeze.
Her feet touching my boots in a most natural and innocent manner. How I wish I had removed them, just to feel the softness of her skin against mine.
And, yes, her legs in the water, shapely as deer's on the hillside. (Not a bad simile, but then I think I may have borrowed it from the Song of Solomon. Him again!)
I revelled in this waking dream for every minute of the night hours. My imaginings took me to places I have been before, to Bathsheba's roof top, to Adam and his Eve, to Diver's room next door, to that occasion high in Glenogle last summer when I chanced upon a courting couple and spied in secret on their intimacy.
But my desires for my angel are all holiness and purity.

I joyed to recall her stare back up at me from the beach, as if to remember, or to prove to herself that I really existed, that this had actually happened.
(As I have wondered several times myself.)
Chiefly, though, my thoughts are forward thoughts, to today.
Wondering if she will return.
Afraid that what I had experienced yesterday was a sophisticated hallucination. Terrified that today will be an anti-climax.

The hint of shadow in this picture? Just the suspicion that this is all a false mirage of happiness.
In all my past philosophising I have held firm to the principles of Scripture; the principle that God is not merely in control, in a kind of "fix-it-if-it-goes-wrong" manner, but that He ordains the affairs of men, that He predestines my life down to the smallest detail. This being the bedrock of my faith, I have no doubt that He has brought me together with this girl, that this life-changing experience has been in His Divine Plan for me from the beginning of time.
What have I done to deserve such a blessed surge of joy?
Nothing that I can think of, but then I remember that this is a similar principle which runs through all of God's dealings with man, including the mystery of Salvation itself. It is all

about Grace, undeserved favour handed out by Him to whoever He pleases.
So my meeting with her is of that order, a Divine gift to me. Not one I deserve, but one I am given to luxuriate in, to enjoy to the full.
I tremble to think that the logical end result of this circumstance is that she and I are to be man and wife. I can think of no other alternative. Never have I experienced happiness and fulfilment such as this in all my life.
But the shadow darkens!
It is an unthinkable realisation, that I only have three more days on this visit during which I can be with her.
Three more days of bliss, of silent joy in each other.
Three more days to bring her to a shared understanding of what God has planned for us.
Which, given her inability to communicate in the normal way, may prove difficult.
I am confident, however, that, with God's help, I can show her all this.

~~~~~~~

So night is falling upon a day which has been no anti-climax.
I organised myself after a hasty and largely uneaten lunch, leaving Diver to gorge himself on my left-overs. (Needless to say, I did not appraise him of my encounter with the girl. He might have insisted upon coming along.)
I brought my pencils and drawing book again, but I also took my fiddle under my arm, in its case of-course. I walked much too hurriedly to the same beach and climbed the same sand hill, totally out of breath as a result, my heart pounding in both expectation and exhaustion.
I waited.
I kept listening for the whistle.
In vain!
My eyes bored into the horizon from which she had appeared yesterday. Surely her collie would soon appear from between the rocks or from the tall grass.
No sign of a dog!

No sound other than the wind off the sea, sighing sadly through the vegetation. That and the constant rhythm of wave after wave washing up upon the sand in the bay below.
And the sound of my heart thumping in my chest!

Then, above the brow of a bank, I saw her hair, her head, her shoulders....appearing as though in slow motion.
Her slender form, but not in the brown garb of yesterday. No! She was wearing a much more attractive dress, lighter in colour and texture, setting off her hair, her whole form really, to best advantage as she wandered, almost aimlessly, lethargically, across the white sand.
No shoes on her feet again.
No sign of a dog with her, I suddenly realised.
Just the whistle, in her left hand, by her side.
Her eyes seemed to be cast downwards and strands of hair fell and wafted before her face, obscuring her features.
Then she stopped and stood quite still for a few seconds, as if studying the sand. She had come across my earlier footprints, the only ones on the beach. Her foot arched forward in a delicate motion and her toes traced the shape of the print.
She followed the route of my footfall with her eyes, along almost the whole length of the short strand and up to where I stood in the sand hills, and then she began walking towards me with that same fluid stride.
My excitement as she climbed up to me was palpable; I barely breathed.
She repeated yesterday's performance of standing some feet away from me. Still, with that same stare, devoid of any expression other than innocence, I thought.
But not such a long 'introduction' as yesterday.
This time I moved towards her and smiled and held out my hand.
Less in a 'hand-shaking' way, more of a 'let-me-take-your-hand' kind of gesture. More of a "Come-and-join-me" welcome.
And she did, after the briefest of hesitations, and I led her to a secluded little dip in the curve of the sand hills.

"I would like you to sit here," I said, indicating a position which I had researched earlier, "so that the sea and the island *are behind you. Would it be alright if I sketch you while you play your whistle, with Aranmore in the background?"*

I had planned this as a strategy because I desperately wanted to make a proper picture of her face and I thought that she might not want to sit and do nothing for that length of time. Whereas if she was playing a few tunes she might be more inclined to remain in the same spot. I am not sure if she understood, because for several minutes she just stood and looked at me, stared me in the eyes in a manner which, had I not begun to feel that I was bound in some sort of heaven-ordained contract with her, I would have found most disconcerting.

Then she sat, exactly as I had hoped.

Exactly as I had imagined it.

No expression on her face that I could decipher, but I had come to love the constancy of those amazing, sky-filled eyes. Into them I could paint any message I wished and she would not disagree.

She slowly brought the whistle to her mouth. Watching that engagement of the instrument, a simple, inanimate piece of wood, with the opening lips of this gorgeous musician transfixed me and I was again deeply aware of the ancientness of this simple partnership, the inextricable twist of humankind with the tools of their music. I marvelled at the Divine inspiration which brought such creative processes of craftsmanship and musicianship into being and which so reward the human spirit. Almost to the extent that I forgot to organise myself to begin drawing her.

As I sketched, half-closed eyes shuttling between pencil and whistle, she continued to produce some of the most startling music I have ever heard, or will ever hear. Several melodies flew from her lips, I did not count them. Reels, hornpipes, polkas, jigs and some whose meter I could not rightly decipher. And then she stopped and looked away from me, towards Aranmore.

Almost as she had done yesterday.

For a moment I was afraid that she might just walk away. To preempt such a disaster, I took my fiddle case from behind me and, opening it rapidly, twanged the strings, all four in quick succession. It was in tune I thought, roughly so anyhow.

She turned to look at me again.

I said, somewhat clumsily, "Do you remember when we first saw each other, when you were driving by on that pony and trap? You were playing a particular tune. I think that it sounded a bit like this." And I scraped out the first few notes of the melody in a manner that would have embarrassed me to the core had I not been confident of the mutuality of our connection, my affection for her and her acceptance of me.
Acceptance, at the very least.
I had barely reached the end of the first line when, in one of the most rapid gestures I had yet seen her make, the whistle came to her lips and she began to play along. I say 'play along', but in fact what really happened was that she took over the tune and gave it a fair old rollicking ride, up and down over many hills and valleys, twisting around many impossible twirls and trills, long after I had put the fiddle down and listened, open-mouthed and open-eared.
When she finished she did a remarkable thing. She lifted my fiddle from where I had laid it on the sand, sniffed closely at the woody smell from inside the hollow body of the thing and then, turning it round in her hand placed it back on my chest, under my chin, holding it there until my hand came up to take the neck.
The gesture said, "Play again please!"
And I could not refuse.
I scratched my way through the Neil Gow "Lament" again. I know it well, if not play it well.
While I played she lay back in the sand, in a most restful position.
I watched her with every note.
As she watched me.
And when I finished she did not move.
She waited there for me, I thought, stretched out on the sand. Between clumps of shore grass. The colour of her dress matching that of the yellowing stalks. The lightness of her hair, falling over her face as she turned towards me. I leaned forward to stroke it from her eyes, awkwardly, my heart pounding. Her hand reached up to my face again, as if searching for another tear, and I, losing my balance as my hand slid in the sand, fell clumsily upon her, my head coming to rest on the softness of her breasts. I thought to rise at once,

to apologise. Instead I stayed where I was, in the comfort of my Sheba, her fingers playing in my hair as I lay by her.
Our intimacy grew over the succeeding minutes.
We kissed as I lay by her!
I don't know how it happened but....
I lay with her!
In the Biblical sense.
It was not an experience which I had intended.
It just happened, very naturally.
In a sort of 'meant-to-be' fashion.
In a sort of 'what-I-was-born-for' fashion.
It is not an experience which I will put words upon.
Words, unlike musical notes, are mere meaningless pencil-marks on a page.
There are no words.

Afterwards I fell into a happy, hazy sleep. As if in a silent capsule, separated from the hiss of whatever little wind was playing through the grass, from the incessant waves echoing each other endlessly as they broke below on the shell-sand, from the sound of her breathing, from the warmth of her nestling beside me. A hypnotic slumber of peace and well-being enfolded me like the softest of blankets. I have no idea how long I slept. I know that I was much fatigued from lack of rest last night. At some point I thought I heard the sound of someone calling, a man's voice shouting a name. As I dozed, this became part of a dream. I dreamt that I was beside the rushing noise of the Dochart River and the voice I heard above the noise was that of my father calling me to come home. When I awoke I had no idea where I was. It was as if I had wakened in another life, as another person, someone that I must introduce myself to.
Something was missing, possibly that was what had wakened me.
The warmth of her was missing.
She was gone!
Whistle and all!

I was struck by a sudden dread that this had all been some kind of dream, something like a prolonged, out-of-body experience which was only real in my own perceptions. That I

had gone over some hither-to unknown boundary and entered an imaginary world of happy madness. This feeling of panic stayed with me for quite a time, until I convinced myself that her footprints, leading into and then out of this little nook, were tangible and real. And, with feelings of intense disorientation, bordering on despair, I began to follow the prints which were leaving me. Down the slope of the sand hill again, onto the flat of the beach. But further confusion awaited me.
I could only follow these prints so far.
Because the tide had turned, had swept up the beach and had washed away the marks of her feet.
All was so fleeting, so temporal, I realised, not for the first time.
Time had returned with its own form of vengeance and had obliterated every trace of her.
And the tide colluded cruelly.
I ran to the end of the beach and searched for her footprints.
I found them above the tide line.

Both coming and going. Perhaps it had happened in the last few minutes; perhaps she was not far away, I thought to myself. So I ran after them, up to the top of the hill from beside which she had emerged earlier.
No sign of her!
I descended, searching the landscape with strained eyes, wondering where she was. I saw some cottages in the vicinity. She must have disappeared into one of them, I thought, so I ran in that direction.
I stopped short of these poor dwellings, unsure of what course of action to pursue, too embarrassed to approach, to knock a door and ask....what would I ask?
"Is there a nameless whistle player within?" sounded a bit of a strange question from a complete stranger with a Perthshire accent.
I did not dare such risk.
I did not have the courage.
So, I waited and watched these houses from a distance for a period of time. Pointlessly!
I saw nothing, no sign nor sound of her.

I gave up and returned to the sand hill to collect my fiddle and drawings. I walked slowly back to Burtonport in despair. And thought long about the events of the day. Did she leave because of what we did?
Because of her shame?
Her anger at me?
Had I misunderstood everything?
Why, why, why had I fallen asleep?
That was a really stupid thing to have done.
"Where are you? Where are you?" I repeated to myself, like a magical mantra which might be answered miraculously from somewhere.
From somewhere there came a voice, as if in echo, a remembrance of the text from Genesis where God comes to walk in the Garden of Eden. Adam had eaten the forbidden fruit with his Eve and God was angry, and was searching for him. "Adam, where art thou?"

My thoughts have begun to crowd into my mind like wave after wave of dark, bat-like creatures.
Tormenting me with confusion and guilt.
What have I done?
"Adam, where art thou?"
Was it all a huge mistake? Was it not all in the Divine Plan? Surely God had been ordering my steps? Surely the finding of my Eve had been predestined to happen in His eternal plan? Yes, of that I am convinced! And it was all too beautiful not to have been ordered by God.
But was it not a sin, a sin of fornication?
I did not mean it to happen.
I had not intended to commit that action with her.
I did not plan it.
It just happened, as in the natural course of events.
Wasn't it all in the Divine scheme of things as well?
Maybe I am over-reacting. Maybe she didn't leave because of anything I had done. I will return to the same spot tomorrow and she will come again and this will all be alright. I will apologise to her for my impetuous action and ask her forgiveness, if I had offended her and brought shame on her. She is my angel, my Eve, and she will understand and forgive

me and all will be fine. I pray so anyhow, as I lay myself down to try to sleep tonight.

My Angel of the Whistle

Chapter 25

<u>Saturday 11th September 1897</u>
<u>My thoughts on today's wretchedness</u>

Oh wretched man that I am!
I have sought for her but have not found her.
She has vanished from the face of the earth.
Was this an angelic visitation, as happened so often in the Scriptures? Was it a test for me, Divinely ordained? Led by the Spirit out into the wilderness to be tested? But, unlike the Master, I have failed the test.
At the first hurdle.
He was 'tested in all points like as we are, yet without sin.'
When did he face the test of a beautiful woman?
It is not recorded, is it?
Unless his relationship with Mary of Magdala was such a test perhaps?
A woman of bad reputation.
A sinner!
But my angel was not a sinner!
She was pure as the driven snow.
As the morning shore-sand, more like, newly washed by a high tide.
The music which flowed from her lips was pure, her eyes were pure, her mind was pure, her body was pure.
Was pure!
Oh wretched man that I am!
(It would have been helpful to have had some clarity on how Jesus handled that temptation. I might have benefitted.)

I am not sure whether what I am feeling is loss, or regret, or guilt, or grief, or self-loathing.
Or a mixture of these perhaps.
I feel so alone in this place, in this world.
There is no consolation in anything, not even in the memory of her.
The two sketches mock me tonight. I feel like tearing them into small pieces.
As my heart is torn.

I went to the beach soon after breakfast this morning.
Diver had gone to speak with the Harbour-master. He seems unaware of my mood and spoke nothing to me of my prolonged absence yesterday. Nor of my lack of appetite in that dreary dining room. Nor of my early retirement to bed.
I walked back and forward on the sand until my footprints looked as though an army on exercises had passed that way.
I sat again by the dip in the sand hills where we had loved each other and I watched the shadows come and go on the cliffs of Aranmore.
My eyes became sore from scanning the surrounding horizons to try to catch a glimpse of her.
All to no avail!
I walked among the scattered cottages of this strip of coastline.
I walked as if in a funeral procession.
I studied every house for clues.
I peered at every window and through the open space of every half-door.
I examined the faces of any local folk I met and tried to discover a family resemblance.
I whistled frequently to try to attract a dog from any hidden hearth.
I looked on other beaches, other areas of sand hills, other lanes and villages which lie, scattered like blown straw, between the crags and lochs of this area.
I prayed for some guidance from above, some miraculous sign which would lead me to her.
Someone astride an ass, a woman carrying water, a burning bush, a still small voice, a star in the sky which I might follow.
No such sign became apparent.
The day turned cold and I regretted not having brought a coat.
But I knew that, as soon as I would return to the boarding house, she would reappear here and I would miss her, so I resisted such a temptation.
I had spent the morning and afternoon in my search and became chilled, shivery and shaking.
Without food, and after my sleepless night, I began to weaken.
I walked in a daze, and I realise that some of the things I thought I saw may not actually have been there in reality. Such

hallucinations are not unknown to me. That does not make them seem any less real when they appear.
Rocks, for example, began to have faces. Some benign, familiar. Others twisted in demonic snarls. Some sneering at me in a most humiliating and mocking manner.
I felt chased away from that place which, only four and twenty hours ago, had been the most hallowed spot in the whole wide world, even more hallowed to me than that other special place which I hope to see soon, beside the Dochart Falls.

Thoughts and emotions tumble through me like the river in full spate.
My chest area hurts as though some vital organ has been removed.
The blood pounds in my ears when I think of what I have done.
Regret and remorse compete with loss and desolation. They swirl together in my very soul and I am struggling to stay afloat this night.
Would that it had all been a dream and that I could look forward to awaking to some sleep-washed innocence in the morning.
But I fear I shall not! Neither the wakening nor the sleeping!
Shall I try again to seek for her on the Sabbath, before the dreaded ship sets sail?
Eve, where art thou?

Chapter 26

<u>Sabbath Day 12th September 1897</u>
<u>Hard Pressed</u>

I am confined this night in the tightness of a cabin which, in other circumstances, would be hard pressed to be considered as a cupboard.
As it is, it is I who am hard pressed.
In every sense.
Physically, emotionally, mentally, spatially, creatively, spiritually.
Hard, hard pressed.
In the tightest of prisons.
A bondage of the body to echo that of the mind.

A stench rises to my nostrils which I should have expected, this being a fishing and cargo vessel. Nothing, however, could have prepared me for the sickening and all-pervasive smell in which I feel I am drowning. It seems to enter my body through every pore, every opening; even when I pinch my nose for a moment of respite, I still taste it in my mouth, repulsively. And I wretch repeatedly. All this before we put out to sea.
('The Mary Ellen' remains in the harbour tonight because of some unforeseen circumstance which necessitates a journey to another port early tomorrow; the purpose was explained to me by the captain, a Mr Brownlow, but my mind was in such a fuddle that I did not take it in properly.)

She did not come again today.
I have lost her.
Have I lost her forever?
I know not.
And it is this 'not knowing' which troubles me so deeply.
I sought for her again today. All day, from early morning.
I left before Diver was awake.
This was because of his anger. He shouted at me yesterday. John, my friend, shouted at me! Abusively! And using sailor's language. Shouted that he was supposed to look after me for Uncle Roberts, but how could he do that if I disappeared all

day without "having the decency at me to be telling where I was going or why?"
He has a point.
He would not let me out of his sight today, he threatened. I would be "un'er his notice, like a cat with a mouse," as he put it.
For this reason, I sneaked away from the place before he had stopped snoring.
I have betrayed his generosity to me, I have rejected his friendship and I hate the truth of his anger.
What is happening to me?
I sought for her, so long. I sought through my tears and, in the distortion of my vision, I saw again things I should not have seen. I heard voices I should not have heard. Mocking, sarcastic figures, shadowy in the gloom of today's Donegal drizzle. Horrible faces, peering, leering through between the reeds that line the little pools and lochs in these parts.
Mouthing disdain at me. Soundless words.
"You will not find her! We have her!"

I thought all day of Esau. He sold his birthright to his brother. His inheritance gone, for the price of a moment of fulfilment, a fleeting pleasure. (Albeit a good meal, in his case). When he tried to retrieve it, he could not, 'though he sought it with bitter tears.'
I share those tears, that bitterness.
The bitterness of guilt against the elation of that pleasure.
The contrast of her beauty against the ugliness of my corruption.
The scent of the sea on her hair against the stench of my sin.
Wild-rose against rotting fish guts!

And I think I will never see her again.
What has happened the Divine Master Plan? Where has it all gone wrong? Was it on course, running along as it was pre-ordained to do, until I somehow interrupted and derailed it?
Was I the boulder on the track?
At what stage did this occur?
Was it simply my fornication with her?
Was that the fruit of knowledge?
The apple falling from the tree?

My Eve did tempt me and I did eat.
But she did not.
There was no sense of her seducing me. It did not happen like that. She was not to blame, anymore than I. It just happened.
But I was to blame, of course I was. Even though I feel I was only acting on some deep and inexplicable impulse. As though this was something I was born for, something that I instinctively knew was my destiny, was designed for me before the beginning of time itself.
A creative impulse. An urge to love, and give in love.
But it was wrong, so wrong.
And I hurt her so much that she left me, and did not return.
Left me forever!

There was not a trace of her there today. I even struggled to find our nest in the sand hills. I staggered around the rocks. I waded out into the sea at the same place where she had done. As if to lure her from the water. I kept my clothing on and my trousers and boots filled with sea-water.
Her naked legs in the tide haunt me. Their perfection!
I have an understanding of King David's mistake. That look. From his rooftop. From my sand hill.
What a disastrous look that was.
And what cruel consequences it had.
Will have?
I know not what those consequences will be, what judgement will fall upon me. How will I be purged of this guilt?
I am in the throes of its torment tonight.

Oh the smell of decay crawls up my nostrils, through every passage, along every sinew, to the very kernel of my soul. Worms and maggots twist there in the slime and I loath who I have become. Wood lice and earwigs defecate upon my face as I lie here.
A sailor sings raucously and swears at me from beyond this filthy curtain.
A filthy, purple spew of putrid language.
To match the colour of my soul.
My sin is ever before me!

And I would sacrifice everything to see those eyes again. To feel her hair blow across my face. To hear her music, the melody of her breathing by my ear. To share the rhythm of her heartbeat next to mine. To have her finger trace the tear upon my cheek just one more time.

Chapter 27

Monday 13th September 1897
My thoughts; my darkest thoughts.

There is no way out.
Darkness rises up at me.
In me!
Traps me, as in a tomb.
Has its arms around my rib cage; it is pressing me, face downward, onto this rotten bed. I see no way out.
My wretchedness is complete.

My pen moves like heavy rock upon this page. And words squeeze, painfully, slow and wormlike from the blackness of my ink pot.
Vile substances have flowed from my body, from every seared orifice.
My stomach is empty of food. Of everything. I have no more left to spew or excrete. I roll in my own stink.

I know not where this ship is. Nor care any longer.
Other than at sea. At raging, heaving sea.
Now I understand the sailor of my earlier voyage.
Since we sailed from that other port there has been no respite for me. I cannot leave this vomit-covered bunk. I feel the substance encrusted in my hair. I wear it like a mask upon my face.
No one has looked in at me, despite the groans and shouts I utter. Perhaps they do not hear me above the howling of this wind as it screams like a banshee through the grills and crevasses of this benighted vessel. And whistles across its taut ropes and wires. Screams like an out-of-tune violin. Or as a flute being blown through the rotting teeth of a master-demon. It is a sharp arrow to my heart, to remember the seemingly innocent role that music played in my fall from grace.
It was the tainted food of love that led to my entrapment.

When docked within the shelter of that earlier harbour, (I know not its name, I know not how long ago, having lost the sense of time,) I turned again to read the Scriptures. I read the

passage from Exodus Chapter 15 which I have just now scribbled on a page of paper and placed within my violin case, by way of explanation to whoever wants to read it. The meaning of the passage is as clear to me as the midday sun. The peril of bitter waters! The solution? To do as Moses did and cast a piece of wood into these waters. For their healing. For my own healing.
Bitter waters have engulfed me since I have been expelled from the garden forever. I know this. I accept it. There is no return to the garden.
I am anathema.
I am lost!
There is no doubt in my mind about this.
They are the same bitter waters which threaten this ship. Threaten it and everyone in it. There is only one thing I can do. To heal this bitter water which is suffocating me! I have the power. The final say! I have the wood. I am the clay. The wood must be thrown to the water, for its healing.
The fiddle to the deep.
And the whistle would go as well, if I had it.
It was the death of me.
That instrument of seduction. Of destruction. Destruction from her lips.
That, and the fiddle my father gave me.
Which she then placed into my hand.
And laid herself down.
Laid a trap for me.
And listened. And looked. It was a plot. A scheme to thwart the Divine Plan. But it shall not.
It shall be accomplished.
Whatever it is.
I go to cast the wood upon the bitter waters.

~~~~~~~

The heaving bitterness has not stopped. It has increased!
The storm rages out there and swept me off my feet.
I slid around on the slimy timber until I grabbed a railing.
I cried out in terror but there was no one to hear me.
The deck is desolate, abandoned.
The ship is in danger of perishing.
I can feel it, hear it in the voices. Fear for their lives.

I hear the sailor's voices but I saw no man up there.
They are there, all around me, voices swirling round my ears.
The sound of phantoms, howling dread and torment.
The writhing of condemned souls, awaiting destruction and judgement.
The storm at sea will take them. As it has so many others.
The disciples feared for their lives. How much more these crude, heathen sailors? There is no master aboard the vessel this time. No Creator to calm the waves which He threw up. No Paul to give advice and make the right decision. No Jonah to placate the water-gods. We are doomed and it is my fault.
This is a judgement on my indiscretion.
My fornication. (How that word convulses and writhes upon the page, fighting against its incarnation. Fornication.....the word becomes my stinking flesh.)
Oh wretched man that I am. Who shall deliver me from the bondage of this death? With my mind I served the law of the spirit but with my body... the law of the flesh. The flesh! Corruptible! I know. I was corrupted.
But a still, small scream reminds me that I corrupted her.
I am responsible.
For her disappearance, out of my very arms.
For her absence thereafter.
I am to blame.
I am the Jonah here.
And I am bringing this vessel to the bottom of the sea, with all on board.
If they only knew they would throw me overboard.
There is no other way to end this pain. I have lived with it too long, all my life, it seems. I must do it.
And, should He prepare a sea-monster for my salvation.....? I have mixed feelings about survival. There is nothing left to live for. I see no end to my continuing torture. My failure to live satisfactorily in the world. My inadequacy as a human being, as a child of God.

Have I not read in the Gospels.....
"It is impossible but that offences will come: But woe unto him through whom they come. It were better for him that a millstone were hanged about his neck, and he cast into the sea, than that he should offend one of these little ones."

I will go out of this world as I came in, as I have always been led to believe, taking nothing with me. I will leave as I came, in the nakedness of Adam before.... before it all fell apart.
With my last breath I will thank God for my mother. I will cry to her. And to my father, who has been my rock. And to her, my little one, my offended one, my fallen angel whom I shall never see again.
By my own hand were these errors fashioned.
By my own hand are they appeased.
If my courage holds!

Chapter 28

An exchange of letters

The Manse
Main St.
Killin
Perthshire
Scotland
19th October 1897

Dear Mr Diver,

Please forgive the liberty I take in writing to you at this time. I obtained your address from your former employer, Mr William Roberts, who is a relative of my wife. By way of introduction, let me explain that I am the father of Andrew Mackay, the young man with whom you worked during the recent railway investigation.

I hesitate to be the bearer of the solemn and tragic news that my son Andrew has been lost at sea, feared drowned. You may already have had these sad tidings communicated to you and, if so, please excuse the repetition. You will understand that the inquiries which follow are irregular and of a particularly sensitive nature, but are nonetheless necessary and of great importance to my wife and myself in our present distress.

The circumstances of Andrew's death are unclear. There were no witnesses that we know of; there is, as yet, no body. You may be aware that our son was in the habit of keeping a diary, a journal in which he recorded not only the events of his visit to your county but also details of how he was thinking and feeling about these experiences. We are in fortunate possession of this journal and, while some of the content makes extremely difficult reading for his mother and myself, at least the account gives us some pointers as to how the boy was reacting to his adventures there.

May I take this opportunity to thank you, Mr Diver, in the most sincere terms at my disposal, for your compassionate and considerate care of Andrew during his trip. In his diary he refers frequently to your many acts of kindness and to the oft occasions when you went beyond the call of duty to engage him in diversion, to try to lift him from his frequent periods of loneliness and depression of spirit. I hope I shall have opportunity to meet you soon and to express this gratitude in a more tangible manner; more of that to follow.

Sadly, however, it would seem from the final entries in my son's account that he had entered a slough of despondency from which he could not be rescued. We can only deduce that this led him to take his own life by jumping off the vessel which was supposed to bring him home to the safety of his family. Oh horrible, lamentable thought! Forgive me, Mr Diver, but the pain of loss is matched only by the dread of our imaginings of his last few hours, his final few moments of consciousness in that cold, stormy sea. Where his body is now we do not know and we have no way of discovering. Given the raging storm which was running at the time of his disappearance, his remains are, I am led to believe, as likely to decay at the bottom of the Atlantic Ocean as they are to be washed up on some distant shore, in the Americas or in Scandinavia or on some uninhibited island in Ireland or off our own Scottish coast.

Now to the reason for my present correspondence. As someone who was perhaps closer to Andrew than anyone else during those last few weeks of his life I should very much like to speak with you to see if you can shed any further light on the reasons for his demise. There are a number of questions which I should welcome the opportunity to ask you. These concern matters to which he alluded in his diary and upon which you might be able to elaborate, so as to clarify details and to help our understanding of events. You are probably the only person who could so do. Mr Roberts has been to see us here in Perthshire but, while he tried to be of comfort to us, there were many questions which he was unable to answer. This is, of-course, understandable, given that his relationship with Andrew was rather more distant than your own and in view of the fact that he had left the party before those final, few, fateful days when you were acting as guardian of Andrew as he awaited passage back to Scotland.

One of the many issues about which we would desire some clarification concerns a certain young lady with whom Andrew appears to have had an unfortunate assignation during the final few days of his trip. In his diary he writes in lurid detail of his encounters with a local girl, one of ill repute it would seem. He even included a drawing of the said person; in his sketch she sits upon a grassy sandbank, a headland in the background across a stretch of sea. She is apparently playing a musical instrument, which is ironic in itself as the lassie, according to Andrew, is a mute. Whatever about her handicap, she seems to have bewitched our son entirely, to the extent that he developed an emotional and, to his shame, a physical fixation with her. He calls her his 'angel', which illustrates the depth of his deception. 'She-devil' more like, in that she seduced him and initiated a downward spiral of thought and action which led to his death by his own hand.

I am resolved to travel to Ireland in the near future, certainly before the winter storms commence, in order to retrace some of Andrew's steps and to meet and talk with some of his acquaintances during his sojourn there. You, Mr Diver, would be the key person in this proposed venture. I should very much like to spend some time conversing with you. I propose to employ you for a short period of time, to accompany me on this visit to the west of your county. I am prepared to remunerate you as you require for your services, should you be available and of a mind to join me at a mutually agreeable time. We might together endeavour to ascertain if there are any rumours of a body having been washed ashore around that coastline. Furthermore, and this may seem to be an irrational quest, not to say impossible, but I should like to trace the whereabouts of the lassie I have mentioned, although my wife doubts the wisdom of this and counsels me that such a discovery could only prove to be non-productive. Be that as it may, I do believe that this is a pilgrimage which I must make and one which may better enable me to come to terms with my loss and so move forward in the ministry to which I have been called.

I await, with eager anticipation, your reply and trust that you find my request not unreasonable.

Yours sincerely,

Rev Gordon Mackay DD

56 St Columb's Terrace
Letterkenny
County Donegal
29th October 1897

Dear Rev Mackay,
                     I am right sorry to be hearing about your loss. I did not know. You see after I bade farewell to Andrew I left Burtonport. I travelled back to Letterkenny. So I heard nothing from nobody. That is terrible sad news indeed. I am more than sorry for you and your missus. God rest him, wherever he is. He was a nice chap and I wouldn't have a bad word said about him. For all his shyness at the start me and him got on like a house on fire. Aye, he did get himself into a terrible state of worry be times but he always came up out of it. I am just sorry I was not with him on the boat. I had no idea he was so bad. I went on home, the same as him. He never mentioned no woman. Well, except that he preached a bit of a sermon at me whenever I had one. He never looked next nor near a girl the whole time he was in Donegal, that I could swear to. He was too shy of himself and, from the way he lectured he, he didn't hold with it. No, there never was no woman, mute nor talking, for if there was I would have noticed her first and he would have had to line up behind me. I know he kept a diary but what he wrote in it I couldn't say. He never did much so there was never much for him to say. Except for the times we went up mountains and the like. And the time he tried to protect me at a dance and finished up injured himself. That was the kind of him. So what I think, your reverence, is this. Because he was so shy and never did much, he had to imagine a lot. I think the girl he writes about was just in his mind. Maybe because he saw me with a woman quite often. He made one up in his mind for him to be with. His mind was a strange one you know. Especially toward the end. He would tell me about things he saw that he could never have seen. Voices he heard that were never there. Things that happened that he just imagined. Or pretended, without knowing the difference. So there never was no woman, you can be rest assured of that. I was with him near enough all the time. I am shocked to hear he has gone. And you and your missus will likely never know where he finished up. I am afraid I am not able to help you. You are asking about me taking you to

some of the places Andrew worked. But I am leaving Ireland. That is why I am no help to you. You see, I took the job with the railway people to raise enough money to pay for my passage to New Zealand. I hope to get work there in a place called Auckland where I have an uncle who went down. I have my ticket bought and my brother's too. He is only sixteen and a good worker. We sail from Derry on the fourth of November, next week. So you are lucky I was even still here to get your letter. And that is why it is impossible to help you as I would like to. Anyways you will not find any friends of Andrew to talk to. He was only friends with me. You will not find a railway because it will take years to build. You will not find a dumb girl because she only lived in his imagination, of that I am sure. You will not find Andrew because his body could be anywhere. I am very sorry for you. He was a good fellow, your Andrew.
Yours sincerely,
John Diver

~~~~~~

Reverend Mackey held Diver's letter to his moustache, sniffing the staleness of the paper, struggling against the finality that it carried. His wife broke the silence.
"I cannot believe you would go ahead and write that letter and send it without telling me, Gordon. Did you have no consideration for my feelings at all?"
"O-course I had considerations...."
"When were you going to tell me about it? Maybe you wouldn't have told me; maybe you would have just disappeared off on a wild goose chase if I hadn't been the one to get the post today and find this...this strange looking letter from Ireland."
"We have been over this ground already Maureen. Of-course I was going to tell you. I just didn't want to have you worrying about it without cause. And you see the way it has turned out; there was no point in you having to even think about it. Diver will not be able to help me with my plan, so...."
"My plan! Yes, your plan! So that's an end to it then? There is no point in you even thinking about going."
Mackey waited, not looking at her.
"I wouldn't say that yet. I still would like to go, at some stage, just to see where he spent his last days on earth. To see if it

would help me to better understand what happened to him. To see if I could find this girl he....."

"But there was no girl. She doesn't exist. This Diver person is sure of that. You cannot find an imaginary girl."

"I'm not so sure she was imaginary. Look at the sketches he made of her. Read all the detail he wrote about her, the tunes she played, the dress she wore, the dog that was with her the first day but not the second. These details seem very convincing to me, don't you think so?" he said.

"But if it was all a self-delusion then the details are part of that delusion too, don't you see? I think Diver is right. He seems to be the sort of fellow who would never have missed noticing a pretty girl, as he says himself. And he was looking after Andrew during that final week."

"He was supposed to be looking after Andrew during that final week! That's a different thing from actually looking after him. Doesn't Andrew write about giving Diver the slip? Not telling him about the girl? And Diver being cross with him for disappearing? No, Diver wasn't with him all the time; and the more I think about it, the more convinced I am that this was a real flesh and blood girl, not some figment of his imagination like you want to believe, Maureen."

"And I think you are wrong. This is our son we are talking about here. This is Andrew who could barely raise his head along the street to say 'Good morning' to his friends, let alone a girl, let alone a complete stranger. This is Andrew who preferred to sit all day by himself along the river rather than play with the other boys and girls of his own age in the village, children that he knew. Andrew was shy, remember? Shy with everyone. Couldn't say a word, even to us at times....and you want me to believe that he was capable of talking to a mute lassie, a total stranger in a foreign land, capable of spying on her in her nakedness, capable of touching her, let alone committing the immoral actions that you suspect him of? Is that what you believe about our son? Is it? How could he have changed to that degree, in so short a time?" The hurt and anger in her voice silenced the minister for a time.

"I don't know how you could begin to think such evil of him," she began again. "You who are always preaching about God's goodness and His grace and how he protects His children, those He has chosen to be His. His Divine Plan? How does all your sermonising fit into this, Gordon? How does it help me to understand what has happened to our son?"

Mackey stood abruptly, looked hard at her, then shuffled to the window to stare unseeingly at the blue hills rising behind Loch Tay. She watched his back, noting the stoop of defeat around his shoulders which aged him by several years she thought. When he spoke it was with a desperate brittleness.

"I do not know all the answers. I have tried to minister to.... to the people of this village; I have tried to minister to you, and to Andrew. I have tried to bring the comfort of the resurrection to families who have lost children. I have talked glibly in my homilies about being led through the valley of the shadow of death, beside still waters, and so on. How often have I not read from John fourteen about a place prepared in heaven. 'Let not your heart be troubled.' But now, when it comes to answering these questions, these troubling questions about my own son.... I feel lost. Where is he now? What happened to him? Where is his soul? I don't know," he quavered.

"Gordon," she protested, "Andrew was a good boy, a good Christian boy. He is in Heaven surely? He could not have done this."

"You're forgetting about the Fall. If Adam fell from grace then...."

"Oh don't give me the Fall!" she snapped. "Can't you see how you have become a prisoner of your own theology? Why can't you just grieve for our son? Grieve the way that ordinary people do. Believe for the best in him like I want to do. Forget about trying to solve these big divine riddles for once."

"I wish that I could. How I wish that I could," he whispered. "Sometimes I wish I was in the cold sea with him, just to talk to him and hold him, one last time. But it's too late. It's all too late now, Maureen."

Section 3

Chapter 29

'Home from the Wars'

A flour-like dusting of December snow coated the whin bushes and lay thinly on the twisting lane between Crolly and Annagry. The sun, wreathed in thin, horizontal feathers of saffron-coloured cloud, was sinking quickly in the south-west, resigning itself to disappearing beneath the horizon for the longest night of the year. The air chilled noticeably as the greyness of twilight overcame the last of those wintery rays. Stars were beginning to be visible in the wide arc of the greying sky. Smoke from the chimneys of a cluster of white-washed cottages rose more or less perpendicularly into the thin air.

Hardly a sound in the deep stillness of this winter solstice in the Rosses.

Apart from a curious noise, barely audible; a gentle, slow, repetitive kind of scrape coming steadily closer along the rutted path; a light crunch followed by a sort of dragging sound and all the while accompanied by a constant, unpleasant wheezing, like the rasp of a blunt saw on knotted timber.

Around a tight bend in the lane there emerged a pathetic figure; that of a man, a skinny youth really, but with the limping gait of a much older man. Over his shoulder he carried a small, tattered bundle, his few possessions tied up in a hessian bag. His clothes were of the poorest, filthiest kind; he was unshaven, a stubbly scrawn of a ginger beard jutting out over a dirty-looking scarf which he had fixed tightly around his neck; his unkempt hair protruded in wild, untameable bunches of rust-coloured wire from beneath a battered brown cap which seemed far too small for his head; his eyes appeared to stick out bulbously from the stretched tension of his face and they had about them a glassy wildness. His nose had the appearance of having been recently knocked sideways from its original course by some heavy blow. There was a purple-red scar, an inch and a half long, above his left eye. The eye itself was surrounded by a wide area of mottled bruising, blackish-blue mixed with sickly yellow. But, for all these disfigurements in his general appearance, it was the lameness of the fellow that drew the keenest attention. One foot, his left, was obviously of little use to him and was being dragged along behind him, leaving a weird track in the snow. Under his left arm a crude crutch, fashioned out of a Y-shaped branch cut from an ash tree, to support his weight.

Johnny O'Donnell was coming home for Christmas, and he was a changed young fellow.

As he shuffled his way towards Annagry, his steaming breath puffing out in front of him and hanging wraith-like in the freezing air, his mind wandered again over the unlucky sequence of events of the past six months as a hired labourer. These recent memories had haunted him with incessant regularity on his long journey home; a journey which normally would have taken the most of a day but which, on this occasion, had taken three full days.

He had begun his journey by train, had then taken rides on a variety of carts and wagons but had had to tramp for far too many miles through the cold winter air. He cursed his lameness for the umpteenth time. Nights he had spent hiding like a fugitive, firstly in the comforting straw of a prosperous-looking barn; then, out of sheer necessity and exhaustion, he had lain in the corner of a draughty, derelict shed, somewhere in the Derryveagh Mountains.

~~~~~~~

Seven months ago, back in May, on the twelfth of that month, to be precise, he had attended a hiring fair in the town of Limavady. Known as "The Gallop Fair", he had heard that this event was a major highlight for the people of the Roe Valley, attracting folk from all parts of that fertile farming area. Listening to the general conversation of some others among his fellow travelling labourers while waiting to be hired in the Strabane fair last year, he had learned of the Gallop Fair.

His third year in the Strabane and Omagh area had been a reasonably successful one. The money had been alright but the farmer he had been attached to was a mean sort of a character, his wife even meaner, soured, he guessed, by the absence of children in the marriage. This can happen, he had observed. The farm was a quiet place, far too quiet. Apart from the actual constrictions of the homestead, situated several miles east of Donemana in a bleak, god-forsaken Sperrin valley, there had been next to no social life around the locality. No dances, hardly another young person to be seen, even at Mass which he attended sporadically. And the fact of these deficiencies sat so badly with the gregarious Johnny O'Donnell that wild horses would not have drawn him back to within twenty miles of the place. So this year he had decided, just in case of a repeat, to give Strabane hiring fair a wide berth, head north to Derry and then a further fifteen miles east to the prosperous little town of Limavady, to its renowned fair.

On reflection, given the choice again he had no doubt that he would choose differently, even if it meant burying himself in the back-end of some Sperrin glen for the six months.

The Gallop Fair had been a revelation to him. Such a sense of excitement. A quite chaotic occasion, he recalled; bustling activity everywhere; always something to look at, something to do. Hawkers shouting well-worn cliches to advertise their wares, their unfamiliar dice of vowels and consonants stirring the simplest of phrases into a soupy gibberish to his Gaelic-tuned ears. A fiddler and a whistle player providing a steam of lively tunes at the door of an inn where a couple of drunks had been ejected and now supported the lamppost outside. He had listened there for a while to see if he recognised any of the tunes from his sister's repertoire; "Annie would love this!" he had thought. Across the street a dexterous juggler, a tiny, hunchbacked fellow with three or four duck eggs in the air at any given time. A colourfully bedecked character holding out a black bowler hat for pennies from the marvelling onlookers as his talented collie dog jumped through hoops, rolled over, walked on its two hind legs and did everything short of whistling 'The Londonderry Air'.

There were cattle, horses and donkeys by the dozen, their manure splattered randomly in every square yard of the main thoroughfares. From the entrance of a bank, a dandy-looking gentleman with a black-thorn walking-stick, tip-toed hesitantly through the mess of turds and skitter with the gait of a swamp-feeding crane, his foot poised in mid-air while searching for an uncontaminated landing place. Potato-faced farmers were haggling with potential hirelings, shouting, swearing, frequently spitting on their hands and slapping palms together. Riotous children dashed around between the lot of them, begging a copper here and pick-pocketing another there. And, to top it all, the girls! Loveliest creatures he ever saw. And the way they looked at you! Smiles that would lighten the dreariest of labouring jobs. Of-course, this was just the fair, the town, the thrill of the day....there would be no guarantee that whatever farm he got work upon would have any such feminine attractions to provide levity and diversion. He had crossed his fingers never-the-less and kept his eyes open for a farmer with a couple of lassies in tow, whether daughters or hired girls he didn't really mind.

The man who hired him had no such attractions with him but the genuine manner in which his eyes had held Johnny's and the fact that he offered a wage that was well in excess of anything Johnny had heard of, let alone received, in Strabane proved too strong an incentive. Remembering his mother's saying, "Never look a gift horse in the mouth", Johnny had spat in his hand and grasped that of the farmer in a firm handshake to seal the arrangement.

The farmer's name had turned out to be Robinson, Ezekiel Robinson in fact; a christian name which Johnny had never come across before but one which, given the nature of the relationship between most farmers and their hired hands, he was unlikely to have to try to get his Irish tongue around. His grasp of English was sufficient to make him capable of understanding most simple commands and of engaging in straight-forward small-talk, especially if the sentences were short and spoken reasonably slowly. Words like 'Ezekiel' he was content to leave on the outer rim of his consciousness.

Robinson's farm was several miles north of the town of Limavady, on the wonderfully arable flat-lands of an area called Magilligan. Johnny was to find the soil of Magilligan warmly light in texture and colour, a very sandy constitution and a joy to work with compared to the clabbery clay he had been stuck in during previous stints of labouring in the Strabane area.

He understood instinctively something of the nature and history of the places he found himself working in simply because the place names were almost all from the Irish language. Limavady, for example, he recognised as an English version of the Irish, 'Leim an mhadaidh", 'the leap of the dog'. He reckoned that the name 'Magilligan', on the other hand, had probably a connection to someone by the Irish name of Mhic Giollagain. To his surprise, he had even found out that there were still one or two of the older folk in the Magilligan area who spoke fluent Irish and he spent a couple of evenings in their company, taking great delight in their conversation in Gaelic, especially in their different dialect pronunciations and their local stories.

Even more enjoyable had been the various ceili dances at which he had found himself, dances which attracted young people, indeed all ages of people, to be fair, from both sides of the community. Catholics and Protestants seemed to be able to dance together with no great bother in these parts, unlike what he had been led to expect from his experiences in west Tyrone. Dances in this area were held in all sorts of venues, from farm barns to local halls. There was even the chance of a dance in the open air, at the crossroads in the town-land, during a good spell of weather in August. Stranger still, he found himself dancing familiar ceili sets, to well-known Irish tunes, in a local Orange Hall during the early part of September. He had wondered at the time if Sean Ban and the other fellows in the Rosses would believe him if he told them that he had spent a great night dancing with with a crowd of Protestant girls in an Orange Hall. Dancing below a huge Lambeg drum which had been retired after the summer marching season and now hung precariously above the proceedings, roped up to the the rafters. Dancing under a framed picture of King Billy on his grand white horse, his steely gaze seeming to follow Johnny wherever he danced around the room; every time Johnny had glanced up at the picture he had the strongest feeling that William the Third had him under scrutiny and would expose him as a treacherous Donegal Catholic if he so much as had a bad thought about one of those sweet-looking Protestant lassies. "Out, you Fenian rebel!" he could imagine him thundering down from his warhorse. Mind you, he looked like a fairly mild-mannered sort, up there on his white charger. Ah, but you have to watch that type too.

King Billy or not, Johnny connected that night. Right under the warhorse's nose. And then outside, directly on the other side of the wall from the beast.

Kathleen was her name. "And love was her game", as Johnny had said to himself on the way back to Robinson's afterwards. Kathleen Millar, a tall, dark-haired beauty with a smile as wide as the mouth of the River Roe and a laugh that sounded like the bubbling water of the Curly Burn. Everybody noticed her, all the fellows watched her; the girls too, jealousy oozing from their pores along with the dance-induced sweat. The fiddler and the melodeon player played to her, joked with her, flirted with her, while the comical little drummer, stuck away in the corner behind his snare-drum and cymbal, half stood up as he strained to get a look at her, frequently losing the beat of the tune entirely. A line of partners waited on her for the next dance. She spun around the floor like a demented spinning-top, her slim figure in perfect balance with her nimble feet, her skirt flying up around her during the turns and twirls in a way that drew every eye that wasn't half-blind to what lay beneath and to those gorgeously long legs. A temptress of the highest and shapeliest order.

"And yet," thought Johnny as he headed painfully up the last hill towards Annagry, "And yet, she picked me? Why the hell did she have to pick me? Out of all the innocent craters at that ceili, why did she have to pick me?"

He reflected on that night with bitter-sweet memories. The dance itself which drew him in, like a moth to the flame, the mesmerising locking of the eyes, hers to his and vice versa, the fleetingly sweet promise of that first kiss, the tangle behind the hall afterwards and the promise to meet again at the next dance the following Saturday night, this time in a public house near Downhill.

He knew nothing about her, other than her name and that she lived in Myroe. He didn't know then, although he became aware of the facts subsequently, that she was a farmer's daughter, that her father was the strictest of old-style Presbyterians, an Orangeman, an elder in the local church and a man who would whip his dog within an inch of its life if it made a mistake in driving his cattle or sheep. He didn't know that her mother was a weak minded woman who had caused much grief to her husband and to the family circle through ill-advised and foolish liaisons. Worst of all, he didn't know that there were no less than four Millar brothers who were, in varying degrees, mirror images of their intolerant father. All this useful information he was to learn later, to his cost.

Johnny saw Kathleen again at the Downhill dance. She was as winsome as before and she danced almost non-stop with Johnny that night, unlike the previous week when he had had to wait for his turn with her, along with most of the other fellows. This time he could hardly believe his luck. She was returning his attention and with interest. Johnny thought to himself as he kissed her goodnight at the end, "Johnny O'Donnell, you have fallen in love!" As he was thinking this, as he was disentangling his tongue from her mouth and his hands from her clothes, he was entirely unaware that a burly, dark-haired chap of about twenty, whose features bore an uncanny resemblance to those of Kathleen herself, had drawn up in a pony and trap and had fixed his gaze upon the kissing couple, a cloud of disapproval forming on his brow. As Johnny had been saying, "I'll come over to Myroe next Saturday night. I'll wait for you at the old schoolhouse, about nine o'clock, alright?"

Kathleen had been looking over his shoulder at the sight of her brother disembarking from the trap.

"Go Johnny!" she had said, "Go now!" And she pulled herself away from him and ran to her approaching brother, throwing herself into his arms like a long-lost loved one returning from America.

"What about Satur...?" Johnny had begun but then he had looked after her and a penny of some kind had dropped in his love-befuddled brain and he thought, "Maybe I'd be better to be disappearing here." Which he had done, around the back of the public house, hiding behind some old wooden barrels, the smell of which, mingled with his own self-disgust at his cowardice, was enough to make him nearly vomit.

Looking back on the whole saga now, Johnny wished he had been cautious enough not to risk going to Myroe schoolhouse that next Saturday night. He'd had a great week, partly of anticipation but largely because he was really enjoying the work on the farm. Robinson was the best of a man to work for, quietly spoken, mannerly and not too demanding. He was also the first employer Johnny had ever come across who was able to say "Thank-you" to a hired man. This had astounded Johnny the first time he heard it... he had looked around to see if someone else had come into the barn without him noticing it; he'd stood in disbelief for a few seconds, Robinson looking at him curiously, stroking his greying brush of a beard with a gnarled hand before turning on his heel with the ghost of a smile on his sallow face and leaving Johnny to finish whatever the task was. He found himself working harder for Robinson than he had ever worked for any of his previous employers, almost in spite of himself and certainly unconsciously. It wasn't that there was any great chat between them; little was said and, in fact, Johnny found himself taking on things that he hadn't exactly been told to do. When he showed initiative like this he watched to see how Robinson responded, and he was not disappointed. Just a quietly spoken, "Good for you" or "Well done".

The weather had been great that week and the harvest was actually ahead of itself, unusually so. And Johnny had put in hours well above what he was supposed to work, gathering those lovely purple-coloured Aran Victor potatoes from the sandy soil, with the fresh, earthy smell as powerful as a perfume in his nose, until it became so dark that he was grappling around in the gloom to feel for the spuds, rather than see them. Then unhitching the mare from the chains with which it drew the mechanical potato spinner; leading it along the lane back to the farmyard through the smell of ripened grasses and mint in the hedgerows; waiting while it filled its belly with long draughts of cool water from the glimmering stream which crossed the lane at the foot of the yard; rubbing down its chestnut coat in its stable for the night.

Once or twice, when he'd still had the energy, Johnny recalled that he had run the half-mile to the shoreline, to Magilligan's beach, a wonderful stretch of the finest sand you could find anywhere, even rivalling that of the strands of the Rosses back in Donegal. He had stripped off his farming clothes and dashed into the shallow waters at the ocean's edge, just to cool down and relax his tired muscles at the end of a day. This is something he would never have done at home, despite the abundance of nearby beaches, but here? Here was different. Here was great altogether. Here there was good money, good food, a sound master to work for. Here there was no oul mother to nag at you, no daft sister to be worrying about. Here there was this beach and this beautiful healing water with no-one but himself enjoying it. And here there was Kathleen, beautiful, exciting Kathleen. A dream of a girl. Life could not get any better, he had thought.

True, but it could get a whole lot worse.

He had waited patiently for Saturday night to come around, the anticipation of how good this was going to get with Kathleen setting his heart pounding at times. Nothing in his mind, not a hint in his spirit warned him that there might be anything other than delight at the end of the evening.

The end of the evening had never come. The beginning of the evening had never come, not as he imagined it anyhow, and he had done a lot of imagining. He had walked all the way to the old schoolhouse and sat on the wall behind it, watching the colours of the autumnal sunset over Inishowen on the other side of Lough Foyle. There was no sign of Kathleen so he just sat waiting. The seagulls from the lough-shore spun around high overhead, catching the up-current of air around the walls of the mighty Benevenagh Mountain which stood as guardian protection above Myroe. He watched them spiral to incredible heights, becoming mere specs above the cliffs. Time was not important to Johnny. Everything in life was lovely. He was not impatient. He was not worried about why Kathleen did not appear. She would come in her own time. He was barely conscious of time passing.

As the darkness began to gather, he had also been unaware of the shadowy figure creeping up behind him from the side of the school yard, and of the sturdy ash-plant swinging viciously and without warning at the back of his head. The blow had knocked him temporarily unconscious and he had fallen heavily, face first onto the rough stones on the outside of the wall. As the mist of confusion cleared spasmodically from his head he became aware that he was being held up on either side, held by the shoulders, his back against the wall on which he had been sitting, held by several men, or at least by several faces which faded in and out of focus before his dazed eyes. A face in front of him had been speaking but he couldn't make out a word of what was being said. It sounded like a foreign language; a shouted, very angry, foul-sounding foreign language. It took some time for him to realise that it was English....but that did not make it any easier for him to understand what was being said.

"Do you hear me? Do you hear me?" This expression echoed around his brain, each echo bouncing off the back of his head like a hammer blow. Johnny had made no attempt to defend himself. It had all been too sudden. Too late he realised that he had been set up. Too late he heard one of the attackers say something about Kathleen being "a dirty hoor". Kathleen!

Where was she? That's what this is about? "Kathleen," he thought. "Kathleen?" he must have breathed because the result was an explosion of expletives spat close into his face, followed by an unmerciful punch right onto the middle of his nose which, even now, all these weeks later, he could remember the accompanying sound, a crunching noise like you had stepped on a crab-shell on the rocks around Mullaghdearg. He had tasted blood running down the back of his throat and gargled and spat and spewed it down over his chin. He heard the words "Never again" and, amid several oaths and curses, the promise to "Kill" if he should ever look anywhere near her again. Then, he recalled, there was a punch to the stomach which doubled him up, at which point he was dropped back down onto the stones. "Surely it's finished now?" he had thought; wrongly, as it turned out. The last thing he could remember before passing out was the kicks that began to land upon his body, continuously, powerfully. He had covered his head instinctively with one arm and his groin area with the other and had passed into oblivion soon after.

Johnny had lain in the same spot all night and only came to his senses around mid-day on the Sunday morning. With much will-power and through terrible pain, pain all over his body but most severe in his mutilated face, he had managed to get himself upright and, using the wall as a support, had stumbled his way back out onto the road. He knew he had to somehow make his way back along this road to Robinson's, if for no other reason than to explain to the man why he hadn't been around to do the cattle feeding and milking that morning. It was a three mile walk and Johnny felt barely able to put one foot past the other. He began but after thirty paces or so he fell over in exhaustion and had just continued to lie by the roadside, tears of despair spilling from his bloody eyes.

Unbelievably, of all the people to come past in a pony and trap, it was Ezekiel Robinson and his wife who were on their way to the twelve noon service in the Presbyterian Church. Johnny had dim memories of being helped up onto the trap, of the spasms of pain which accompanied every jolt of the journey back to the farm, of the questions which Robinson was putting to him and, most surprisingly of all, of the fact that Mrs Robinson, with whom he'd had little or no contact during his stay, held his hand and sobbed all the way home. She had taken him into the farmhouse and bathed his wounds, his broken nose, a gash on his forehead and bruises to his back. The good man and his wife had then set up a huge copper bath-tub on the kitchen floor and filled it with steaming hot water for him. He soaked himself in it while he heard the couple talk in the parlour next door. Mr Robinson had then reappeared and produced a bottle of whiskey, poured a generous amount of it into a tumbler of hot water and told him to drink it. Johnny had obliged. At that point he had gone to sleep beside the hearth and had slept right through until the Monday morning. Johnny had then been taken up the narrow stairs and put in a bed which had previously been that of the Robinson's oldest son; he was to learn that this son was practicing as a solicitor in Belfast. No farming life for him, it appeared.

Two days he spent in the comfort of that bed, all his food carried to him by the farmer's wife; he had a visit on each day from Robinson himself, not a long visit, just a "How are you doing?" kind of visit. But on the evening of the Wednesday Robinson had said to him, "I want you to tell me the truth about what happened. Who did this to you and why?"

There was no point in telling lies about it, so Johnny told him everything, including the fact that he did not really know who had committed the assault. When he had mentioned the name, Kathleen Millar, however, he had noticed an almost imperceptible shift in Robinson's posture, just the slightest intake of breath. When he finished, the farmer said very little; he didn't accuse anyone, didn't say anything immediately about Kathleen or the Millars; he just stood in silence for a minute, thinking.

Then he said, "How are you feeling now, Johnny? Do you think you can help me with bringing the corn into the stack-yard tomorrow?"

Johnny had smiled painfully and said, "As long as you don't think the horse will take a scare at the face on me."

"Good," smiled Ezekiel Robinson, "Sleep here tonight and then tomorrow we will try to get back to normal."

Johnny had stuttered a bit in his attempt to thank his boss, emotion and appreciation getting the better of him, but Robinson had just said, "That's alright, Johnny. I just wish it had never happened. I just wish you had said to me that you were seeing the Millar girl, but then, why should you have? And you likely wouldn't have listened to me anyway, would you?"

"Likely not," Johnny had said.

Robinson had given a small shake of the head as he paused at the bedroom door. "There's four brothers of them, big sturdy fellows they are. You wouldn't be the first to enjoy their form of hospitality." And he had shut the door behind him, leaving Johnny trying to puzzle out the meaning of this phrase which was new to him, "Enjoy their form of hospitality?"

\\\\\\\

By this stage the sun was well set behind the hills beyond Annagry and Johnny had dragged himself through the frosty air as far as Sullivan's pub, just opposite the white church in the centre of the one-street village. There was no choice to be made; money or no money, he had to have a hot toddy before setting out to reach home; he turned right into Sullivan's. He entered and stood squinting in the dim, fuggy light of the battered oil-lamps above the bar. There were three or four drinkers present and, to a man, they turned in unison to stare at the newcomer. Johnny knew them all as local men and old acquaintances. There was a silence; a silence either of lack of recognition or, alternatively, of incredulity.....Johnny couldn't decipher which. In the end he spoke first.

"Can a man get a drink anywhere around here?" he asked, the frost affecting his vocal chords and taking his tone down several notes, this alteration in his voice not helping those trying to figure out how they knew him, why he seemed familiar, who the divil he was. In the end Jim, the barman, broke the ice.

"By all that's Holy!" he said, "If it isn't Johnny O'Donnell home from the wars!"

The ice was well and truly broken now and the men gathered around, somewhat gingerly, to shake his hand and welcome him home. There were a few "Happy Christmases" and "Welcome backs" and, from old Tom Rogers in the corner, "Yer mother will be glad to have you home, son."

"I'd heard you'd had a bit of an accident," said big Paddy Cassidy, his arm paternally on Johnny's shoulder, "but I didn't think it would have affected you as badly as this Johnny."

"Is it the foot, Johnny?" asked Seamus O'Donnell, nodding his round, bald head towards Johnny's leg.
"And what happened the eye? And the nose, for God's sake? You're only half the man you were when you left here," chirped John Joe Roarty with his usual degree of tact.
Johnny half-turned from the bar and made as if to head towards the door again. Paddy caught him by the arm and guided him firmly back to a stool. "Here Johnny. He didn't mean anything. It's just John Joe talking. Sit yourself down a minute and tell us whatever you want to tell us. You're in no condition to be trying to make it up to Maggie Dan's the night."
"Naw, he's not; he's definitely not. He looks like....." John Joe's high-pitched quaver spluttered to a sudden end as an elbow in the ribs from Seamus silenced him.
"And you shut up for once, John Joe," commanded Paddy, "Unless you're buying him a drink. You hear me now?" And he winked at John Joe. "Buy the man a drink."
"A drink it is then. What'll ye have Johnny, for you look like you need...." John Joe was again brought up short by the same elbow as before.
"A hot whiskey, if you please," croaked Johnny, his head down and the wheeze nearly deafening him.
"Whiskey it is; hot and handsome," said Jim, going to retrieve the kettle from the hearth in the kitchen behind the bar.
"Make it a big one Jim," called John Joe, fishing in his waistcoat pocket for his last remaining coins. Then in a whisper as he counted his hoard, "Maybe not too big though."
Johnny was still the centre of attention at the bar. They crowded around him, waiting on whatever words would fall from his tired, frost-bitten lips. A bit more thoughtful, but still as curious as ever. There had been no word from Maggie Dan about any injuries to his face, just about the rusty nail in his foot. Still they waited, John Joe almost bursting with unspoken questions and observations. Until he could wait no longer.
"So was it a long nail, this rusty nail? There's nothing worse than standing on a long, rusty nail," he intoned, keeping himself well out of reach of any editorial elbows.
"To be honest, John Joe," began Johnny slowly, "I never saw the damned nail. I slid down off the top of a corn-stack and there it was, sitting waiting for me, pointing straight up at me out of an old bit of wood. There might as well have been a sign on it

saying, 'Half-blind, thick Donegal labourer by the name of Johnny O'Donnell, jump here and stick your big, unlucky foot unto this here nail.' 'Cause that's exactly what I did."

"Was it sore?" pestered John Joe.

"It was that," replied Johnny, "Just what you would know. The worst thing about it was that I was just getting over another set of injuries I had got for not minding my own business when this happened. I had been in bed for a few days and the farmer, to be fair to him and his missus, looked after me really well. Got me back on my feet in no time. Back on my feet!" He laughed at his own irony. "The stupidity of it. If I hadn't been working a bit of overtime by myself, to try to make it up to him sort of, this wouldn't have happened. I was on my own and there was nobody about to shift the ladder over for me to climb down, so, like the hero I am, I jumped....right on top of the bloody nail. It must have gone in near enough an inch....agony!"

"That must have been a killer for you," sympathised John Joe. "And you with the broken nose and all."

A dark stare from Johnny before he turned away; Paddy took John Joe by the arm and led him away from the bar. "Would you ever run over to the Parochial House and tell Father Dunleavey that Johnny is home and that we're going to need the mule and his wee cart to get him up home to Maggie Dan? Would you do that John Joe, like a good man?"

"I would surely. I'm your man there, Paddy. I'm your man there," was the enthusiastic response, and John Joe made for the door, his loping stride producing a characteristically bouncy walk which looked not unlike that of a hare and drew wry smiles from some of the bar-stool observers.

"And take your time, there's no rush. We don't want you slipping on the snow and damaging yourself into the bargain," advised Paddy to his departing back.

When he rejoined the others at the bar he just picked up the tail-end of Johnny's account. "What were you saying about blood poisoning?" he asked.

"The thing turned septic on him before he knew it. Seems rust and blood don't mix well," Seamus filled in. "What did the doctor do for it Johnny?"

Johnny was getting very tired and the hot whiskey was further dulling his senses but he tried to answer, slowly and softly by this stage. "He gave me some sort of medicine to cure it, the fever, I mean. And he had the woman of the house putting on hot bread poultices four times a day to try to draw the poison out. The foot was swollen up to twice the size, and as red as a rose; it's not so bad now though....." and his head went down on the counter beside his empty glass. He had downed the whiskey with an enthusiasm that surprised his companions at the bar, never having been a noted drinker in the past.

"Walking on it all this way can't have helped it much," observed Jim. "The fellow's exhausted. Will I let him sleep here tonight, do you think? And we'll get him home in the morning?"

"That's maybe a good idea," said Paddy. "I sent John Joe for Father Dunleavey but it was more to get him out of the way for a bit, before Johnny hit him one. I'll take a wander over myself and tell him to leave it until the morning. It's far too cold to be sending this fellow out again tonight. If you'd let him sleep by your fire, that would be the best plan."

And they lifted a semi-sleeping Johnny and carried him through into the back room of the public house, laying him full length on a wooden bench by Jim Sullivan's hearth. They spread a sheep's-wool rug over him, put a cushion under his head and stoked up the fire in the hearth, throwing some more turf unto it, before Paddy and Seamus left to bring the news to Father Dunleavey and relieve him of the urgency of his pastoral duties, until the morning, at least. Jim stood and watched the pathetic sleeping figure for a while until he found that the sound of Johnny's pig-like snoring through his rearranged nasal passages was beginning to overcome his sympathy for the fellow. A wry shake of his head and he left him, to wash a few dirty glasses.

"You'd wonder what poor oul Maggie Dan did to deserve another bit o' bad luck like this," he thought to himself. "She could've done with a fit and healthy son coming back to her with a pocketful o' money for the winter, instead o' this poor cripple."

Chapter 30

Johnny Goes Down-Hill

Johnny O'Donnell lay around his mother's cottage all the way through Christmas and the New Year and for the best part of three weeks. He stretched himself out on the settle bed, his foot raised up over the side of the kitchen table; this on the advice of Bridie Boyle who walked two or three miles every other day to tend to him. There was no money to pay a doctor, so nobody even bothered to suggest sending for one. Bridie was the next best thing, a fussy but very caring being who was well known and respected in the neighbourhood as the person you sent for if there was a corpse to be laid out or a baby to deliver, an illness to cure or an injury to be ministered to. She had been fetched almost as soon as Johnny had been deposited at his mother's hearth by a very concerned Father Dunleavey.

"Do what you can for him, Bridie," he had told her, "for the fellow has nearly ruined himself altogether by walking so far on that foot of his. If they'd only sent for me I would have travelled over with the trap and brought him back. They had no mercy on him at all, and no sense either, sending him out to walk on a foot like that in the depths of winter. What sort of people are they that they would do that to the boy, and him as lame as a three-legged dog?"

What the clergyman did not know, and what Johnny was not about to tell him, was that his employer had driven Johnny to the railway halt in Magilligan, bought him a ticket to Derry and had given him sufficient money to pay his fare to Strabane and on to Glenties in west Donegal; this would have left him with a journey of less than twenty miles up to his home in Ranahuel. Robinson had shaken hands with Johnny as he boarded the train and had promised to hire him should he be fit enough to be back at the Gallop Fair the following May.

Much in awe of the generosity of the man and moved by his offer of work in the future, Johnny had reached Derry just as the bars were opening. Having developed a taste for good whiskey during his misadventures in Magilligan he thought the thing to do would be to sample whatever of the spirit was on offer in the public house across the road from the station. Good whiskey it was, he discovered, and with a good name, guaranteed to attract the eye of a Donegal man. It was called "Tyrconnell Whiskey" and was the proud product of a Derry distillery. Great tasting liquor and the more of it he drank the more certain he was that the pain in his foot wasn't as bad as it had been and that it would not prevent him walking from Derry to Letterkenny and on home to the Rosses if need be. After several glasses of this "Tyrconnell" which, he was starting to believe, was the finest spirit in the whole of God's good world, he no longer had the wherewithal to pay the train fare anyhow, so walking was all that was for it.

His stomach empty of all but the juice of the barley, he had set out along the road west which seemed to rise and fall and swing one way and then the other in a manner which he had never noticed a road doing before. He was lucky in that, staggering down the middle of the highway a mile out of Derry, he was overtaken by a wagon that was drawing bales of cotton material. The driver, who could not get safely past Johnny on the road, had stopped and bundled the limping labourer unto the back of the cart where he slept like a baby until he was robustly shaken and awakened in the yard of a warehouse in Letterkenny town. From there Johnny had dragged himself slowly westward through the Donegal hills, his foot becoming increasingly more painful. He had two further rides, one for a short distance on a farmer's cart and the other the following day, a longer journey on a smelly, fish-carrying flat-cart returning empty to Bunbeg.

But now he was back in his own home and for much of the time Johnny's face was to the wall. He seldom spoke to Maggie Dan; there wasn't much point in speaking to Annie and, apart from a few occasions when she had come closer to him as if to study him in an effort to understand why he was stretched out in this fashion, she tended to ignore him. His mother was concerned for him; initially her worry was that his foot might never heal up properly and what effect that outcome would have on his prospects for earning for the household. But this worry was only part of it. She waited for his dark mood to change, for him to turn and face the kitchen, for some sign of his old carefree self to reappear. She waited in vain. He was a seriously changed boy, she began to realise after a week or two of patient care of him. When had her Johnny not finished a plate of potatoes and white fish, the latter a gift from the neighbouring Cavanaghs? When had he ever sworn at his sister and told her to take her whistle up the mountain if she wanted to play it?

Sean Ban Sweeney noticed the change too, probably before anybody else had. He was a frequent caller in the O'Donnell's kitchen in those days before and after Christmas and had been very disconcerted by Johnny's lack of response to him. He had been so looking forward to his friend's return, to hearing stories from the Lagan and to telling Johnny the various things that had been happening around Ranahuel in the six or seven months since he left. But he found Johnny's lack of interest every bit as perplexing as his apparent injury. Not even the story of the body washed up on the beach had stirred him. Sean had recounted those events to the back of Johnny's head on Christmas Eve but the patient had said nothing, hadn't even asked a question. The only time he'd spoken a full sentence to his mate was to ask him to refill his tin mug from the jar of rough-tasting poteen that Maggie Dan had obtained for the seasonal celebrations. It didn't take him long to down it either, Sean had noticed. He was so annoyed and bewildered by what he saw of the change in Johnny that he had uncharacteristically talked to his mother and father about it.

Sean's father had even risen from his bed and hobbled heroically down the lane through the thawing slush to O'Donnell's on New Year's morning, 'first-footing' as the local tradition required, a lump of turf in his twisted hand. Frank had never been the most effusive of characters but when he spoke he was generally listened to, all the more so on account of his stoic response to his own illness. And after Sean had mentioned his worry about Johnny to his father, Frank had responded by venturing out into the cold, damp, morning air for the first time in weeks and making his way slowly to his neighbours. He was chilled to the bone marrow as he arrived in the kitchen.

"Go mbeannai Dia an teach seo," he blessed the house through chattering teeth. Maggie Dan, he discovered, was nowhere to be seen, having gone 'first-footing' herself to the Cavanagh cottage along the lane.

Johnny had turned from the wall, sat himself up on his elbow, shaken Frank's offered hand and returned the season's best wishes with good grace. Frank sat down stiffly on a poorly-fashioned chair, between settle bed and hearth. At fifty seven he still had a youthful look about his face, in spite of the past few years of his intermittent battle with rheumatic pain. He had the same fair hair as Sean, still full on his narrow head, and the same physical shape about him as his second son. But, while Sean could be described as lithe and loose-limbed, Frank was a shadow of a man, his frailty and the general greyness of countenance in marked contrast to the light that he still had in his warmly blue eyes.

"So how's the foot progressing? Have you been able to do much walking at all?" he began.

"Aye, it's improving, I think. I can put a bit of weight on it if I try; there's just not much to be getting up for," was Johnny's response, his voice nasal and different, a niggling reminder to him of his broken nose and that night of terror. "What about yourself, Frank?"

"I can't complain," came Frank's standard reply, and silence ruled for a time until the creak of the bedroom door.

Annie is coming through from the coldness of her bedroom; she sits down at the hearth, her back to both men, ignoring them. There is even more of a listlessness about her than is normal. Her face hides behind the unruly drape of her hair which looks as if it could do with a good wash in the soft water of the Ranahuel burn. She is wearing an old knitted cardigan of her mother's over a long shapeless garment that did not deserve the compliment of being called a dress. She sits awkwardly on a three-legged stool beside the meagre fire on the grate. Her bare feet play with the cold ashes that have spilled onto the clay floor in front of the hearth and her hands clasp and unclasp irritatingly in her lap.

"Throw a bit more turf on that fire, Annie," said her brother and she did, roughly, the resulting sparks flying out in all directions.

"You're thin of yourself, Johnny. Are you eating right?"

"I'm alright."

"You need to look after yourself, put on a bit o' weight and build yourself up for the spring," advised Frank.

"I haven't much appetite, at the minute..... and look at her. She eats for the two of us." This with a nod of his head towards his sister's back.

Frank glanced at Annie. "Aye, well....she's just right too. A healthy, growing girl she is. If you could get yourself up off that bed and start walking again, just a wee dander every day, you'd soon get an appetite again. If you lie too long in the one place the strength in your legs starts to go. Believe me, I should know. While you have the chance, while you have youth on your side, you should try and get yourself up and out again."

"Youth on my side, is it?" Sourness in his voice; anger and hurt etched on his distorted countenance. "Youth's not a lot of use to me now. A face like this. And lame into the bargain. I curse the day I ever went near Magilligan." He spat on the floor and struggled round to stare at the wall again.

Frank didn't respond. He just sat there and waited. The thin heat from the hearth was slow about warming him. He looked at Annie from behind and thought what a sadly lovely child she was. Well, no longer a child of-course; a fine lump of a girl, so completely dependant on Maggie Dan, so much in need of her brother to be taking the initiative and earning a living for the three of them. And here the brother was, in danger of descending into a bog-hole of disillusionment and self-pity. And him only twenty something, a young man with is whole life stretching out in front of him. What could he say to the lad to try and rescue him from this descent? Maybe nothing; but maybe if he could get Johnny to talk, to tell the stories of what had happened to him over there, to open up about his feelings.... just maybe that would help him begin to come to be reconciled with himself. But three-quarters of an hour later they were still sitting in silence, just the two of them as Annie had retreated to her bedroom. The sound of a softly played waltz had slipped through under the door and, for whatever reason, Johnny hadn't objected this time. Such music had become as integral to the peculiar ambience of Maggie Dan's house as the aromatic smell of the turf smoke. Frank enjoyed the gentle beauty of the melody and gave it his full attention, echoing the notes of the familiar old tune silently in his head, hoping, praying that in some way it would maybe help Johnny to unlock his emotions.

As if making a sudden decision Johnny turned from the wall again and looked at Frank.

"Are you still here Frank?" he said, although they both knew that he knew that Frank hadn't left.

"I'm still here. Enjoying the heat," he lied.

The tune continued in the background. Johnny lay and looked at the rafters and the discoloured thatch beyond, one arm behind his head, the other hand gingerly manipulating his broken nose as if to ascertain if its shape had improved any.

"It's a mess, isn't it? This nose of mine."

"Sure you only need it for smelling through," returned Frank. "It's not in a bother whether it's straight or not."

"Aye, but I'm in a bother about it. Who's going to look at me now? I look like some sort of ugly freak that you'd have to pay to see at a fair."

"Now you're talking nonsense, Johnny. You were always a handsome fellow and you'll have no bother in that regard. Especially if you let the story get up that you got the nose in a fight with a crowd of ruffians and you were defending an innocent wee lassie in the matter."

Johnny looked at him for a bit. "But that's not how it happened," he said.

"Will the folk around here know how it happened? If you sit in here, hiding away from everybody, people are bound to think you are ashamed of how you got damaged. Instead you should be turning it to your advantage. You should be acting as if you have nothing to be ashamed of, maybe that you're actually proud of your war-wound."

Johnny was silent, contemplating this notion. The waltz tune from the bedroom continued, being played for the fifth or sixth time and now beginning to grate on the patient ears of the two listeners.

"How did you get your injuries, Johnny?"

It took him a while but Johnny started to talk; slowly and hesitatingly. He had always had an unspoken trust in this well-meaning neighbour. The story of life at Robinson's was gradually laid out, the beginnings of his courtship with the capricious Kathleen Millar, the hiding he had taken from her brothers and then the unfortunate event that had put a hat on the whole summer when he had been dealt such a blow by the unlucky positioning and sharpness of a rusty nail. Frank listened as he explained how he had been too embarrassed to admit straight away to the benevolent Robinson what had happened; how he had tried to hide the injury and how it was only when he was at the end of his tether and totally incapacitated by the swollen foot that the farmer had discovered what was wrong and had taken control of matters. He had sent for the doctor and put Johnny to bed in the farmhouse yet again, to be nursed through his fever by his kindly wife.

One aspect of the story which Frank found very strange was that, when Johnny had recovered well enough to begin doing some of the lighter jobs on the farm again, he discovered, to his amazement and consternation, that Robinson had found another labourer to cover his work while he was recovering. And the new worker was none other than the youngest of the Millar boys, Hector, the stout twenty year old. Robinson had spoken about the matter to Johnny on the first morning that he had reappeared in the yard to resume work. He had told Johnny that he had been to speak to young Millar's father and that, as a result of what had been discussed, Millar had volunteered to send Hector over to the Robinson farm to help out until the damage suffered by his hired hand had cleared up; this by way of restitution for the hammering that the Millars had given Johnny, it seemed. Hector was going to stay on and do the heaviest of the tasks, working alongside Johnny for a week or two until he was properly recovered. Naturally enough Johnny had been very nervous about this arrangement. The thought of working beside one of those Millars had scared him and his anxiety showed to his employer.

"Don't you worry about it Johnny," Ezekiel Robinson had said. "Hector Millar will be far more nervous about it than you. One false move from him, one word out of place, one smile of mockery and he and his father know that they'll be dealing with the Royal Irish Constabulary."

Johnny found this very strange but had taken his boss's word for it and had worked away in the farmyard as best he could for the few remaining weeks of the season, quite often alongside Millar and without any issue between him and the younger man. Millar had hardly looked at him, barely said a word to him. When he had occasion to speak he had always been polite, even showing at times, Johnny thought, civility bordering on the contrite. Curious though Johnny was about her, the subject of Kathleen was never mentioned, nor was the beating behind the schoolhouse. There was much about it all that Johnny did not understand; some serious talking had happened behind the scenes between Robinson and the Millars and his admiration for the quiet strength of character of his employer had grown even more. Unfortunately, despite the care of the doctor and of Mrs Robinson, Johnny's foot had never really recovered from the poisonous injury and he dragged it painfully behind him as he went from job to job around the yard. Millar did all the heavier work and showed no sign of resentment that he was having to undertake much of Johnny's share of the labour, as well as his own. Millar had actually come and muttered a head-down "Good-bye" when he was leaving just before Christmas. Altogether it had been a frustrating and confusing experience for Johnny.

"So you were able to do a few weeks work for the farmer after you recovered?" quizzed Frank gently. "That was good; gave you a chance to save up a bit of money to bring home to your mother, after all."

Johnny did not reply to this observation. He wasn't ready yet to confess to his own recklessness in pouring so much of what he had earned down his throat in the form of alcohol. And this Frank was able to guess, based on the shadow of guilt which passed over the young man's eyes and turned him away from Frank's gaze and from the transparency with which he had recounted his story up until now.

"Seems to me that you have a lot to be thankful for. You met a very decent man in that farmer, that man Robinson and, as you said yourself, he must have been able to pull some strings with the other family behind the scenes to have one of them come and actually do your work for you. There's manys a tale of fellows being put out of a situation and left to suffer on their own, to make their own way home, no medical help or anything else. As I say Johnny, don't be letting this thing keep you down. There's no shame in how you got your face damaged, or your foot. Don't let the thing become a mountain for you, because it's not. You could have been a lot worse. You could have lost the foot. Try and get up and get both feet below you and take a step toward the rest of your life. That's what your father would be telling you to do, God rest him. Now, I've said my piece to you Johnny so I'll be going on home."

There was no response from Johnny but, as he watched Frank shuffle towards the door, his eyes travelled beyond him to the top shelf of the dresser across the kitchen and to the green bottle behind the jug of buttermilk.

~~~~~~~

A few days later Sean called at O'Donnell's to see if Johnny's foot and his general health were showing any signs of improving. He was surprised to find that Johnny was not in his usual place. Annie was there, bent over the table washing clothes in a tub. She and Sean looked at each other for the first time in a while. And as they were weighing each other up and as Sean was trying to understand the tentative nature of that look, Maggie Dan was talking, saying that Johnny had been up yesterday and had walked a bit around the yard and that today he'd felt well enough to take a walk down to Annagry. "Likely going to see Father Dunleavey," she thought aloud.

Her eyes soak into him. There is a bleak sadness there. She needs him to be as he has always been to her, the brother who talked to her, listened to her tunes, heard her heart. Especially now, now that her real brother is back and is showing the same cold absence of thought for her, of time for her, that he had always shown. But as she looks at Sean she sees something she doesn't understand, some stifling reserve in him, some holding back, something that makes her doubt..... And her eyes sink away from his. They side-slip like a clam-shell dropping back to the depths of a rock-pool, and they take their refuge in the swirl of the dirty suds she is working in. And her thoughts and memories swirl together in the basin of her mind. The vague image of the stranger's face; the feel of his short hair between her fingers; the sound of Sean's shouting across the strand, bringing her back to reality.

"Was he walking alright?" Sean asked.
"Aye, he seemed to be doing alright," the mother replied. "The foot was taking his weight."
"I'll maybe take a walk down there and see if he's alright," Sean said.
"That'll do," Maggie Dan sighed.
Sean waited for Annie to lift her head again to acknowledge his leaving but she didn't seem to notice. She rubbed clothes together half-heartedly in the tub but she seemed to be miles away from the mundanity of the action. As he left he thought of how complex and unsettling this relationship with her had become, of how, despite the long years he had known her, he could never predict how she was going to act or react at any

given time. The blankness of her expressions, the frequent dullness of her lovely eyes, were as painful to him as her lack of words. And he knew her and had studied those eyes and those expressions more than anyone, apart from Maggie Dan. Maybe even more than her mother, he thought.

"And if I'm lost," he said aloud to himself, "what chance has anybody else?"

In twenty minutes he reached the Parochial House and knocked. The Gallagher woman appeared in a bit and told him that the Priest was away somewhere; maybe Kincasslagh, she thought. And 'no', she hadn't set eyes on Johnny O'Donnell, he hadn't come to the house today. Sean thanked her and left, wondering where his friend might have gone. He drifted on, past the solemn presence of the church, towards the bridge in the centre of the village and sat on the wall, the granite stones chill against his hips. Within five minutes John Joe Roarty appeared from the front door of Sullivan's public house further up the street. Sean watched him disinterestedly as he came sauntering towards the bridge, his stride far too long for his little body, giving him his strangely bouncing walk. As he approached he spoke.

"Ah, Seanie Ban, you'll be looking for your friend Johnny. Well he's in there trying to drink Jim Sullivan out of stock, so he is." This in his usual flutey voice. "You'd be doing both him and Jim a favour if you were to go in there and rescue him, for, unless he discovers gold in Ranahuel Mountain, I have no idea how he's going to pay."

Sean didn't waste a second. He half-ran up the street to Sullivan's and entered the gloomy light of the bar to the sound of raised voices. Jim Sullivan, behind the counter, had his two hands raised to his head, elbows sticking out, looking as he would have been pulling his hair out except that he didn't have any to pull. He was taking some shouted abuse from a well-fuelled Johnny O'Donnell.

"You'll get your money, I swear it on my mother's life. Now just set me up another drink and it'll be the last one I ask you for."

"I won't do it Johnny. You've had more than enough already, and everybody knows you can't be affording to pay for it. Now, here's your old mate Sean, so just go away on home with him and no more nonsense out of you."

"You baldy bastard you! I'll remember you for this. Here, Sean. You have money on you I'm sure. Pay the oul bugger for a drink for me. Go on, with you Sean. Get your hand in your pocket for me, oul friend." He slurred his words badly as he spoke and turned from the bar stool to embrace Sean.
"Take him outa here, Sean," said Jim quietly but firmly.
"I'll get you a drink, surely Johnny. Come on with me here," said Sean, his arm around Johnny's shoulders, guiding him towards the door. "I know where I can get you a drink."
"Where Sean?" queried Johnny coming fairly submissively to the road outside.
"Up home in Ranahuel," replied his friend.
"There's no drink left in Ranahuel, not a drop," argued Johnny pulling away from Sean, his arms flapping around aggressively.
"There's plenty of drink in Ranahuel," said Sean. "I have just the drink for you up in our place."
"What sorta drink have you?" Johnny began walking again as Sean humoured him; his foot seemed to be well mended for, although he staggered plenty and had to have a bit of help from Sean, he was marking it to the ground quite confidently.
"There's a whole can of buttermilk. Just the very thing you need, my friend," said Sean, taking an even firmer grip on Johnny's jacket and pulling him along the road towards the hills. The journey home took much longer than it should have, for the simple reason that every so often Johnny would stop to protest. What business of Sean's was it what he did in his own time, he argued. He wasn't a child, he wasn't sick any longer, he should be able to come and go as he pleased. He should be able to drink as much as he wanted, whenever he wanted. He was a free-born Irishman and he knew his rights, Home Rule or no Home Rule. Sean was called all sorts of names, sometimes under Johnny's breath, sometimes screamed into his face in a rage he had never seen any previous hint of in his friend's character. When Sean drew attention to the lack of money as a good reason for not buying any more drink, Johnny really lost his temper and went into a fist-swinging tantrum which shocked him to the core. He had to duck and dive to avoid the assault and, at the same time, try to hold unto his intoxicated mate so as to prevent him trying to run off again towards the village.

"You call yourself a friend of mine?" Johnny raged. "It's not my fault there is no money. I worked my guts out over there and I would've had plenty of money if those black Protestant bastards hadn't ganged up on me. A whole gang of them there was. One or two of them I could have handled, even three. But a whole host of them, creeping up on me from behind. Cowards and blackguards, the lot of them! If I was back over there now I would take them on and beat them to pulp, so I would." And he tried to pull away from his captor again. "Let me go, Sweeney," he screamed, throwing his fists around him in Sean's general direction. "You're no friend of mine. If you were you would be coming with me to take them on, instead of holding unto me. Let me go; why are you still holding me back? Let me go or I swear to God I'll swing for you."

Sean held on like grim death although it did cross his mind to let the fellow go and watch him crash into a ditch.

"We are nearly home, Johnny. What you need is a good rest, sleep it off. Your mother will make you a cup of tea to settle you," Sean consoled.

Consolation was not on Johnny's agenda. As Sean held him loosely, his fist came up violently in an unexpected uppercut and connected with Sean's face, producing a spurt of blood from his lower lip. Sean's hand instinctively let go of Johnny and went to his mouth. Johnny pulled away with vicious determination and broke free. He laughed mockingly at his friend.

"You see? You see what I could do to those Millars? One punch and you're bate, Sweeney, and I'm away back to Sullivan's. I have me pride. You? You're nothing but a Mammy's boy. Go on home to your Mammy, son."

All this in tones of slurred vitriol, his eyes standing in his gargoyle-like face, his body swaying above his widely planted feet, his fists raised in the stereotypical pose of an old-fashioned prize boxer. He turned himself deliberately and awkwardly around in the lane and began a drunken march back down the hill.

Sean watched for a while, very much in two minds; let him go or try again to bring him home. In the end his decision was more or less made for him. At a particularly steep section of the path thirty yards further along, Johnny's body started to travel more quickly than his brain could communicate to his legs and he pitched forward clumsily and painfully unto the rough stones. He tried to get up at once but only succeeded in rolling over on the slope at the lane-side and ending up entangled in the needle-sharp entrapments of a whin bush. Sean made his way towards him, the pain in his own lip an effective antidote to the temptation to smile at Johnny's prickly resting place. He grabbed him roughly by the collar and coat sleeve and pulled him without ceremony back onto the path, helping him to his feet. Johnny was holding his nose, blood and swear words oozing through his fingers. He had thrown himself right onto his face, his reflexes so dulled by the alcohol that his arms had not reacted quickly enough to break the fall.

"Agh!" he gasped, "that's bloody sore, so it is!"

"It's definitely bloody, that's for sure. I can't tell how sore it is but it's definitely bloody," smiled Sean in spite of himself. "Come on, let's get you home to your Mammy and see if she'll wash that face of yours for you."

The 'Mammy' reference found its mark and Johnny glowered angrily like a cornered, black-faced ram but said nothing. He shrugged off Sean's arm of support again but at least he was moving towards home, albeit at the pace of a slow stagger. Sean walked beside him and observed the fight drain out of him, being replaced by a sullen, reflective sadness. They covered the remaining half-mile in silence until, just at the end of the O'Donnell lane, Johnny stopped and looked at Sean and said in a voice more reminiscent of his old self, "You should have seen her, Sean. Best looking woman I ever set eyes on." His voice faltered, in self-pity, Sean thought. "She was nearly worth getting a hiding for, the bitch," he finished through a typical Johnny grin that matched the crookedness of his nose and they made their way towards Maggie Dan's door.

Later Sean sat in the stillness of her kitchen and watched him sleep on the settle bed beside the hearth. "How he is changed," he thought. "How everything is changed. Is this the way things were always going to turn out? Will this changed state of affairs continue? Will Johnny and I ever be the friends we were before whatever altered him so drastically this past summer? And what is this change that has happened between me and Annie?"

Johnny snored and the fire crackled. Maggie Dan poked the back of her head with her knitting needle, scratching at some invisible irritation. Annie sat like a statue at the end of the table, her arms folded across her stomach. Sean sipped his tea from the battered enamel mug.

For the life of him he couldn't puzzle out if the change in Johnny was because of the beating he had taken, a life-changing, confidence-sapping occurrence for sure. Or because of the stupidity of the action in which he had injured his foot, especially coming on top of the beating. Or had he experienced a bizarre over-reaction to the generosity of spirit of the good people he had been working to, a sort of rejection of what he had come to see as their sickeningly righteous care of him as a stranger and a mere hired hand?

"At least you knew where you were with those normal bastards of farmers," Johnny had said at one point.

Or was this all the result of some weakness in him with regard to drink, some latent tendency which had hither-to lain under the smooth surface of his friend? He and Johnny had shared many a drink in the past, usually porter, to be fair, and had found themselves in happy intoxication on several occasions, if never drunk out of their heads. Was whiskey the secret? Did it have some mystical power over him, some primeval fascination which produced this apparent addiction? And if so, was he already moving beyond redemption and recovery? Sean had an instinctive dread of the consequences of the answer to that question if, as he suspected, the demon spirit had already taken a deep-seated hold over his friend. He had not yet had time to reflect on the things Johnny had said to him on the way up from Sullivan's; yes, he knew it was the drink talking, but he feared that some of Johnny's real opinions and attitudes might have been revealed in those raging outbursts. Were those utterances evidence of his true feelings about the fellow he had been running around with since they were both children?

All these confusing thoughts were forming in Sean's head as questions to be puzzled over in the coming days. They were intensely troubling questions, a truth that he knew in his head and his heart, but he had the presence of mind to be able to leave them for today and not make the situation in the little cottage any more tense than it needed to be. He turned to Annie behind him.

"Go and get your whistle and play me a tune, Annie," he said.

She reacts very slowly, apathetically, rising clumsily from the table and hesitating. She looks at Johnny, his mouth open like a cave, fog-horn snores blaring from his ugly, disfigured snout.

Sean looked at him too. "It's alright. He's fast asleep; he'll never hear a thing. Go on, where's your whistle?"

Annie ambles to the bedroom; she turns to look at him briefly and pushes open the door with her rear end. She backs through the door and disappears inside. The door scrapes on the uneven floor and then eases shut behind her.

Sean waited.

She does not come back.

He left Maggie Dan's and headed up the mountain into the cool January air.

Chapter 31

A Nameless Hornpipe

January flipped over into February, the new page just like the old, wet and windy on Ranahuel mountain. Day after day of driving, crow-coloured clouds whirling in off the Atlantic, persistent sheeting rain and then the monotony of bleak, lightless drizzle for a period of a week or more. Dark brown water filled the landscape and ran off hills and into the burns, turning them the colour of weak stout as they rushed to feed Mullaghdearg Lough. The saturated bog was a sponge that had reached its limits and could take no more. Murky bog-holes and ditches overflowed. Trees drooped and dripped precipitation unto the heather, soaking the deep carpet of sphagnum mosses underneath.

In the worst of the storms it was difficult at times to walk upright in the powerful wind. Bodies angled down into it, mirror images of the bushes blowing in the other direction; hands grappled with stone walls for steadying security against it; as farmers crept to feed cattle, bundles of hard-saved hay were whipped away into the whining air from beneath their armpits and were strewn randomly over far-away acres of black moorland. Backs were damp and sore from the incessant struggle with the elements and lumbago, influenza, chest infections and worse afflicted most cottages. Sniffing, sneezing and raucous coughing punctuated every conversation. The voice of the priest could barely be heard above the mounting clamour of it in Mass and Father Dunleavey was unamused and crotchety, until, that is, he took a dose of it himself and lost his voice and credibility all in one Saturday evening service. And the faithful smiled to themselves behind their wet sleeves.

The atmosphere in the O'Donnell house matched the melancholy of the weather. Donegal at its depressing worst.

Sean Ban continued to attempt to be sociable, trying to lift Johnny's spirits. He was generally met with indifference, occasionally with something closer to hostility, depending on Johnny's mood. It wore him down and his visits became less frequent. He missed Johnny's craic but there's only so much silence a person can take. Only so many negative comments that even a friend can survive. Sorry and all as he was for Annie, he left them to it. There was plenty to be done around his own yard, especially now that his father was making an effort to be up and about the place again, in brave defiance of both weather and pain. And Father Dunleavey was never any more than a few hours away from croaking a request for help with this or that.

Maggie Dan herself wasn't in the best of form. She had lost another tooth and was now down to three brown stumps at the front and a couple of molars behind. And she had the winter cold in her head which had eventually settled on her chest, so that she found it very difficult to sleep at night. It didn't help that she was back in the same bed as Annie, in the cottage's one bedroom, now that Johnny was home and sleeping on the bench in the kitchen.

She has always been a sound sleeper, Annie; but of late this habit has deserted her; she lies awake half the night; the other half, she tosses and turns in the bed, pulls the bedclothes around her, sometimes removing them from her mother's side of the bed until the older woman scolds her and tears them back to protect herself from the dank coldness of the night. Her feet drum on the bed-end in time to whatever reel is in her head. Her fingers carry the melody and dance on the tightening skin of her belly, underneath her nightdress. She turns again when the tune stops and lies on her back, her eyes wide open, staring into the blackness of the underside of the thatch above. And her hands remain on her stomach, sensitive to the tiniest of movements from inside her. There is no fear apparent in her eyes, no want of understanding, no panic, no curiosity, no joy, no sorrow, nothing! Her fingers tap back to whatever rhythmic sensations she is feeling from the child growing within.

She alone knows of this. No-one else. Nobody has looked at her long enough to recognise that she is changing. No-one has said anything. It is her secret. It is alright. This is as natural to her womanliness as breathing.

She knows a bit about where calves come from. She has watched the event, and she has seen piglets being born too, at Cavanagh's farm. So many of those baby pigs at a time. Calves generally squeeze out in ones, sometimes ones and twos. Sweeney's cow had had twins once, she remembers. She wonders, in her innocent silence, how many will come from her.

She feels a gentle kick against the inside wall of her stomach and turns again, turns from her mother; a protective, maternal instinct runs through her, natural as blood-flow.

Maggie Dan lay awake and silent as well. Wheezing but deeply thoughtful. Thinking about Annie. These past eighteen years had been tough, trying to rear a daughter who couldn't talk to you; a girl whose world was so different, so secret; a child who was so restricted that the master at the National School had told Maggie Dan in frustration not to send her back. "She's not capable of learning," he had said. "She just sits there and stares. She's wasting her time and mine." It did not stop him sending for her whenever there was Christmas music to put on, or when there was a visitor whose ears needed tickling with an Irish air, thought Maggie Dan. The one gift she had, God love her. Apart from her prettiness. But, if you were going to be given a special talent to compensate for being dumb, surely it could have been a more useful one than playing that damned whistle.
"What will ever become of her? She needs to be married," the mother told herself silently. "Especially with me getting older; I am not going to last for ever, not like my mother in Cloughglas, who seems to be eternal. What will happen to her when I'm below the sod?"
And what were these unaccountable changes in her of late? She was not herself, not since last summer, since she came back. Even with Sean Ban. There was a cooling in that relationship, she had noticed. They had been so close, so devoted to each other, and now? What had happened to sour their closeness?
Annie turned in the bed, yet again. A sudden dread stuck Maggie Dan. A sudden question whose answer she began to realise in the damp, chilly blackness of the bedroom. "When was the last time she bled?"
Suddenly she was thinking of the difference she had noticed in Annie's face, a fullness that girls get when they are pregnant. But it couldn't be that. Annie was not pregnant. How could she be, for goodness sake? So no, it couldn't be that. She must be just at that stage when her girlish figure and features were deserting her and she was putting on a bit of weight as a woman naturally would. The more she had observed, silently and with her motherly instinct sharpened, the more she was sure it was all alright. And her denial and self-deception

protected her from the panic of anything else until that particular night in bed beside the tossing daughter, and diverted her from that particular, if obvious, question.

"When was the last time? Could she be overdue? God above, she's not bled this weeks, this months."

It was all Maggie Dan could do to stay in the bed beside her and not create a fuss in the middle of the night.

What she did do, as soon as she felt sure Annie was definitely asleep again, was place her hand gently on her daughter's stomach, as if she was just hugging her unconsciously. And then she was sure. Just the tiniest stirring from an infant forming in the womb.

"Who's infant?" she thought, dread arising in her like indigestion, fear and horror for her poor daughter. "Sean Ban Sweeney's, for certain. She has never been near anybody else. Sean Sweeney...well, would you have thought that of him? Such a good-hearted, kind, decent fellow; more like a brother to her than anything else! More like a brother than her own flesh and blood is, that's for sure. Maybe that explains why he hasn't been coming in as much of late. Oh Annie, how could you have shamed us all like this? How could you have let him touch you? What came over you? But you're not responsible, you poor darling daughter. You poor, simple, innocent crater. It's not your fault. It's his! He should know better. I thought more of him than that. Well, he'll have to marry you now, so he will. Nothing else for it. But he will, he's a good enough fellow and always has been, up till this, and he'll do the right thing by her, of that there is no doubt."

Maggie Dan's bigger panic was when she thought, "What'll happen when Johnny finds out? He will hit the roof altogether, so he will." And there and then she made up her mind that she wouldn't be telling him any time soon; he could find out in his own time, in his own way. She spluttered and coughed again and turned away on her feather-filled pillow as tears trickled down her face unto its surface.

By Saint Valentine's Day, as would be typical of Donegal weather, there was a complete turn around. The skies cleared to a wonderfully rain-washed blue; there were days of weak, lemony sunshine, albeit not the warmest, given the low angle of the sun in the sky above the Rosses; the wind reined itself back beyond the western horizon to wait its turn and peat smoke pencilled straight into the air from the cottages below in Mullaghduff; the watery muck on the lanes and tracks dried up and crusted over in places, and people started to see each other out of doors for the first time in a while. Spring was thinking of springing around Ranahuel.

The supply of turf was starting to run low in the stack at the end of O'Donnell's cottage. There were still a few more heaps patiently lying in the bog further along the hillside, turf that Maggie Dan had not managed to bring back to the yard. She had relied on Sean and Annie to help her with the donkey in October when the peats were reasonably dried out and when the ground was firm enough, but the weather had beaten them to it and turned to rain back then, drenching the turf and rendering the bog-lane a quagmire. Now, she thought, there was a good chance for Johnny, now that his foot seemed to have mended itself, to saddle up the ass with the two pannier baskets and see if he could fetch down a few more loads.

Johnny protested and turned her down at first. "It's still far too wet up there," he argued. "Leave it to see if this good spell of weather dries up the rodden. Sure there's no rush. It's not as if I'm going anywhere."

But a week later, as the turf dwindled and the kitchen heat dissipated in the face of a colder easterly breeze that had arisen, Johnny stirred himself into action and saddled up the old donkey for the trip up the hill to their turf bank. He told Annie to come as well to help load up the baskets and they set off in the late afternoon for what was to be a traumatically eye-opening event for Johnny.

The bog-rodden which led up into their plot had indeed dried out remarkably well and neither donkey nor Johnny had any problem staying above ground. Annie found it more difficult though; at one juncture she found both her feet stuck in a hidden hole, just off the main track, a deep wound in the bog's surface which was filled with a gluttonous, sucking slime of black peat-muck. The older brother had to go and help her out, which he did by putting his arms around her from behind, under her armpits, and half-lifting, half-dragging her out of the hazard. He swore mildly at her, semi-jovially.

"You could do with loosing a stone or two!"

And whatever nerve he had managed to touch in her by this comment, Annie took off along the track, head jutting forward like a disturbed moorhen, and left him shouting after her.

She by-passes the O'Donnell plot and the three or four lonely stacks of their turf which sit there, awaiting retrieval. She scrambles on up the hill, unto its rocky summit, a further thirty yards or so above where Johnny would stop. Here she stands and surveys the landscape of the Rosses; the lifeless torso of the bogland, scarred by the black slashes of innumerable lakes; the brown breadth of it, stretching away to the rocky Derryveagh Mountains, a wavy, charcoal line in the east; in the north the land folded itself down like a crumpled blanket, descending to the still greenness of Mullaghdearg Lough with its scattering of quaint little humps of islands and its necklace of corn-coloured reeds.

She pulls her whistle from the pocket of her buttonless old cardigan. There's a peace in her; almost a joy to be out of doors; away from the heaviness of the home; up above it all in the freedom of the hill tops. She swoops, swallow-like, into one of the best tunes she knows, a hornpipe of some name that she couldn't remember....and would it matter anyway what it was called, for her in her silence? A dance tune she is recalling from having been at a wedding with her mother in Loughanure.

She is so far away in the elation of the tune that she doesn't even hear Johnny's angry shouting to come and help him. She sees his mouth move. She sees him start to come towards her, in temper. She cares not. Her head held high into the freshness of the air. The breeze cold on her face, lifting her hair out like a streamer behind her, joining in the ecstasy of the tune. The melody twists itself into the breeze, whistling and singing through the natural reeds of bog-cotton and rushes; the same breeze that catches her unsuitably thin dress, bending it back against the curves of her body. The new curves of her body where there hadn't been curves before.

Which Johnny sees in stark, shocking silhouette against the brightness of the February evening sky as he climbs angrily up the hillside towards her. The dress driven back against her legs, against her breasts and against the pronounced bulge of her pregnant stomach. He stopped and stood stock still, initially thinking how fat her swollen belly looked, and then as the realisation and the shock battered into his senses. "In the name of God," he said aloud, "Annie is having a baby!"

She stops playing, midway through a stanza. She stops and looks down at him where he has stopped. Where the world has stopped. She stares at him. And he up at her. Then she looks out over towards the sea and slips the whistle into her pocket, sadness and resignation in her gesture. She comes down the hill towards him. He waits, a fury building in him, but building behind a wall of silence. She passes through his stare and out the other side of it, like it is a magnetic field that has no power over her. And she bends to begin lifting the peats to fill the panniers on the donkey's back.

Johnny stood in stunned silence for an age before joining her. Then, as he worked, he mumbled constantly; she ignored him, until, unable to hold back any longer, he caught her roughly by the arm and squared her round to look at him.
"You're not so dumb as you let on then, Annie amadan. You've kept your mouth shut all these years but you couldn't keep your legs shut when you needed to. Could you, now, ye wee scut? You've gone and shamed your mother and me, and your dead father. What do you think of yourself? Go on, speak up for yourself, ye stupid wee hoor!" And he slapped her hard on the face, his labourer's hand leaving an immediate red welt on her cheek.

She is down on her knees in the dirt, holding her face, surprise and terror in her eyes. Her eyes up at him, with wonderment, incomprehension on her face. Her other hand, arm, instinctively drawn across the area of her womb. She tries to get up but her feet skitter away from her in the loose peat dust. She feels his boot connect with her bottom as she slithers to the ground. She hears the ranting of his voice, high-pitched, furious, out-of-control. She gathers herself, foetal-like against the turf-stack. There she remains, cuddling herself, rocking back and forward on the stibbled surface of the peats.

Johnny lurched around her, his language as foul as his temper. He threw a few peats into the baskets, before turning back to her with another mouthful of shouted abuse, sometimes aiming another slap at her head. Suddenly there was a shout from further along the lane, beyond the spindly sally bushes which they had passed earlier. The figure of Maggie Dan appeared in the evening gloom, her ash-plant stick waving furiously above her.

"You leave her be, Johnny O'Donnell. You leave her alone, you hear me!" she shouted. "You have no call to be taking it out on her, the poor girl. You scoundrel you! Look at the state you have her in, and her in this....." She stopped and bent to hold Annie.

"So you knew? You knew about her? When were you going to tell me? She's nothing but a cheap wee tart, that's all she is. As bad as any of them street-girls in Derry. A dirty wee hoor. And she's a sister of mine." Johnny took to thumping the donkey instead and the poor beast, startled out of its wits, took off and hobbled in panic up the lane ahead of them.

Maggie looked up from Annie. "And I suppose you think she did this all by herself, do you? You think it's all her fault? And her the way she is. You haven't much mercy about you. Nor much sense either. The girl is hardly to blame for her condition, is she now?"

"Well who is then?" shouted Johnny irrationally but suddenly coming to realise what his mother was driving at. Why hadn't this thought entered his mind until now? "Who did this to her? Do you know who the father is?"

"Ah, now you're starting to think more like a human being and less like a man," she said. "Who did it to her? I don't know who did it to her. Why don't you ask her yourself, see what she says."

He turned to Annie, still down on the ground. "Annie, for once in your life, can you tell me.....agh, what's the point? Sure she'll never be able to tell us."

"Exactly," said Maggie Dan.

"But who would....ah Jesus, not Sean Ban? Surely not Sean? Who else has been with her, mother? Has anybody else been talking to her, or shown any interest in her? Has she ever gone out walking with anybody else, or gone out walking by herself even?"

Maggie Dan shook her head. "Not a soul but Sean Ban," she confirmed.

"Annie," said Johnny getting down on his knees again beside her, "do you understand what I'm asking you here? Was it Sean Ban who....who did this to you, this baby? Did he, did he do anything dirty with you?" Then looking up to his mother, "Agh, this is a waste of time. Annie, if it was Sean Ban will you do me a favour; just look at me and do this; nod your head, like this." And he demonstrated; he held her face up to his and looked into her eyes. He nodded his head solemnly, just once. "Annie, was it Sean Ban Sweeney? Just nod if it was, like I showed you! If it wasn't, don't nod."

Her eyes looking into his, the ice-blue terror still deeply in them, her chin resting on the black dirt of his open hand. He grasps her chin lightly between his fingers and thumb, then tighter, now hurting her jaw beneath. She hears "Was it Sean? Was it Sean Ban Sweeney who did this to you? Nod for me Annie! Go on, there's a good girl." Maggie Dan watching closely over his shoulder, her eyes boring into Annie's. The grip on her lower jaw is hurting more. There is pressure there, she resists until she can hold out no longer and she dips her head and diverts her eyes away from the despising bile in Johnny's gaze.

"There, you see," Johnny shouted in triumph. "She was able to tell us. She nodded alright, you saw it too, mother, didn't you? Sean Sweeney it was. Had to be him. Sure he's always been round her like a dog on heat. Why could you not have kept a tighter eye on them?"
"Who would ever have thought you would need to keep a tighter eye on her and Sean, for goodness sake? Sure he's been like one of the family, like a brother to her, and to you too. Years, he's been with her. I can't believe it of him. Sure he always looked after her, even when they were children." And she bent to help Annie slowly rise to her feet.
Johnny set off up the hill to find the startled donkey. Over his shoulder he shouted, "Like a brother to her? One of the family, is he? Well he will be now! He'll have to marry her, and quick too. But not until after his face heals up from the battering I'm going to give it. She'll maybe not even recognise him at the altar when I've finished with him."

~~~~~~~

On the way back down from the bog, as they approached Sweeney's, Johnny grabbed Annie by the arm and turned off the lane into the entrance to the neighbour's small farm-yard. Taken by surprise, Maggie Dan shouted after them.
"Where are you going Johnny? What are you going to do? Where are you taking Annie?"

"Where do you think I'm going? I'm going to see Sweeney, where else would I be going?"

"Not yet, Johnny. Leave it a while. Don't go in when your temper is raised. It would be better to wait until...."

"Until what? What is there to wait for?" he interrupted and started down the patchy gravel of the lane towards the Sweeney home, Annie being dragged along unwillingly behind him. "Come on Annie. Come with me. Go you on, mother. I'll be down in a minute."

"Just you stop there, Johnny O'Donnell. This isn't the way to do it. Leave it to me to talk to Sean's mother first. Come back out of there this minute."

Maggie Dan, surprised at her own strength, stood back on the lane, the donkey pulling on towards the comfort of its stall and she trying to hold it back. In her head she prayed, "Oh Bartley. What am I to do with these two? I wish to God you were here with me now. Look down on us and help us, if there's such a thing as you able to help us."

"I can handle this myself. Me and her. Take the peats home... we'll be there in a bit," argued her petulant first-born.

"You're not going to be handling nothing yourself. Get yourself back up here this instant and come home with me now. You don't have to go in there shouting as if it is something that has never happened before in the history of the world." And she stood her ground until Johnny released Annie and wandered reluctantly back to the main lane, a resentful, hang-dog look about him. He slouched after his mother along the path and into their own place, a couple of hundred yards further down the hill.

Maggie Dan went inside straight away, leaving the two young ones to empty the panniers of their load. They were still stacking the peats against the gable wall of the house in such a way that the rain water would run off them easily when Maggie Dan reappeared around the corner. Johnny looked up and saw that she had pulled on the coat that she would usually only wear to Mass or on special occasions and she had a head scarf tied on her head.

"I'm away down to Annagry," she said. "It's time I saw Father Dunleavey. He'll know what to do, for I am lost between the two of you. Now you leave her alone when I'm away, you hear me Johnny. She has enough to be contending with without you making it worse for her." And she turned her back on them and stomped off towards the lane.

Johnny's anger continued to simmer as he worked and his festering desire to confront Sean Ban did not diminish; indeed, his emotions had churned around inside him now to that point that, if he didn't act, he would be physically sick. He knew that he would not be able to settle to sleep tonight unless he could do something. Now that his mother had left him, he saw his chance to take the matter into his own hands. He knew he was going completely against the way she wanted to handle it but he was a man now; he had handled difficult issues on his own when he was far away from her in the Lagan and he would handle this... his way! He tied the donkey to the fence.

"Come on, Annie," he said. "We're going back up to Sweeney's." And he pulled his sister along with him and headed back towards the neighbour's cottage.

She is as passive as ever. Today she is being dragged this way and that, up the hill, down the hill, back up the hill. She is very tired now and starting to feel sick in her stomach. She looks over her shoulder at times to see if her mother is coming to her. There is no sign of anyone who could help her. Johnny is hurting her arm and her feet and legs are sore as they reach Sean's house. She would like Sean to be there and yet she hopes he is not there.

He pushed open the door and stepped straight unto the clay floor of the kitchen, Annie in tow. In his aggression, he didn't bother with the usual "Bless the house" type of greeting. Frank and Brid looked up in surprise from their evening potatoes and buttermilk. They recognised immediately the expression of Johnny's face, the anger in his body language and the awkwardness of Annie hanging back by the door.

"Where's Sean?" demanded Johnny, standing legs apart in the middle of the room, tension drying up his mouth.

"What's the matter, Johnny? Come in and sit down here..." Frank half rose as if to make room but was interrupted almost at once.

"I said, 'Where's Sean?'" repeated Johnny, aggression reddening his pallor and twisting his features even further than before.

"He's not here; he's at the Point, as far as I know. Why, what's wrong?" said Brid, getting up and going to Annie by the door.

"What's the matter with Annie? Come up to the hearth, Annie. You look foundered and there's dirt all down your back, you poor thing. What on earth were you doing?"

"Never mind that. If that was all that was wrong with her we could fix it. But we can't fix this," shouted Johnny, going to Annie grabbing her garment from behind in such a way that it tightened around her, clearly displaying the unmistakeable bulge of her pregnancy. "Look at her," he shouted. "Look at this! We can't fix this, can we, Granda and Granny Sweeney. Look at the shape of my sister!" His voice screamed into the shocked faces of the older couple.

Annie stands weakly in their gaze. Six eyes boring into her, making holes into her stomach to see this child inside who is making this bump on her. She clutches at the front of her dress, protectively, modestly. She pulls the material forward from Johnny's harsh grasp and wraps the open cardigan tightly around her at the waist.

Her eyes dart around the room, animal-like, as if searching for sources of danger; they come to rest on the dust-covered 'Virgin and Child' icon above the sofa. She advances slowly into the room from the door and moves to stand in front of little statue, staring at Mary and the Christ child, and she remains there as if in trance. She hears in her head the singing of the choir at Mass on Sunday morning last and she is soothed in herself. In the echoing caverns of her mind she joins in the old Irish ecclesiastical music; the modal harmonies reassuring; the lilt of the Gaelic comforting. A tune of the baby and his mother.

Frank was speechless in his shock. His thin, oyster-shell lips opened and closed a couple of times but he couldn't get beyond a hoarse gasp; his pained eyes skipping between visitors and wife, desperate for understanding. Brid was still beside Annie, arm around her waist, feeling the increased girth of the young mother-to-be. Neither spoke. Brid sat down suddenly on the sofa and started to cry.

"Well may you cry, Brid Sweeney. Well may you cry. My sister is ruined. My poor simple sister that your son has been sniffing around for years. How could he do this to her and her like a sister to him? What sort of a son have you reared that he could disgrace my sister like this? What sort of morals did you teach him that he couldn't keep his trousers shut? Wait till Father Dunleavey hears about this. Wait till the folk around here find out. Sean Sweeney will not be able to hold his head up ever again around here. He's finished!"

Frank managed to get his voice to work and his tongue in edgeways, such was his young neighbour's ongoing rant. "Johnny, this is a terrible shock to us, as you can see by..."

"Not half as big a shock as it was to me and her mother. Yous don't have to live with the shame of it like we will."

"Poor Annie. Oh you poor girl," sobbed Brid quietly, her arms now around Annie's impassive body, still standing before the image. The older woman's hand stroked the girl's swelling stomach, the tears still running down her face. "Poor wee Annie, you poor girl."

"Poor Annie is right," echoed her brother. "But what about Sean? What are you going to do with him? He's going to have to marry her right away of-course, but what are yous going to do with him?"

"She must be four or five months gone," Brid sighed, her hand resting on the bump. "Does your mother know, Johnny?"

"Aye, she knows. She's away to see Father Dunleavey," he said. "What are yous going to do with Sean Ban?"

Frank spoke softly. "I don't know what we'll do with him, Johnny. He's only a young fellow like yourself. He makes mistakes, like everybody else, yourself included. If you're right in your accusation....it looks as if he's made a big mistake with poor Annie and I will make no excuses for him. But as for what to do with him....I don't know. What do you suggest yourself?"

"Well, you're hardly fit for it but he needs a damned good hiding, so he does. He needs taught a lesson that he'll not forget in a hurry. He needs his neck broke for what he did to Annie."

"And from your experience of life, Johnny, you think a damned good hiding is the answer, do you? A good neck-breaking?" said Frank quietly without a discernible trace of sarcasm.

Johnny was about to answer and then he paused, bristling under his flame of red hair and seeming to catch the hidden implication of Frank's question. "Now wait a minute," he said, rising to the bait like a salmon to a fly on the Crolly river. "Wait a minute here Frank. You're not going to compare what happened to me to this, are you? You're not saying, I hope you're not saying that there's any similarity, because if you are, you need to think again. I got a hiding for nothing, nothing at all. I never touched nobody. And I got beaten senseless for no reason. This here is not in the same field, so it's not. Sean has done the dirty with my sister. There's a mile of a difference between the two situations."

Frank paused, as if thinking. His head swayed side to side slightly, considering what Johnny had said. "Do you not think, Johnny, that we're missing the point here a bit? Firstly, it's your poor sister that has the biggest problem. She had problems before and now she has an even bigger one. You don't have a problem at all, compared to what she is facing. Secondly, you're talking about giving Sean a hiding. All I was trying to ask you was to reflect on your own situation. Did the violence you experienced have any good outcome? For you? For anybody else? I don't think it really achieved anything, do you? Maybe made the brothers of the girl that you were thinking about feel a bit happier that they had stopped you before you could get to do what you were thinking about doing? Do you see what I mean? As Our Lord said, 'Let him who is without sin cast the first stone'."

Johnny swore at Frank and continued to rage. "I can't believe you are taking his side in this. You oul hypocrite. Defending your son in a situation like this. Can you hear yourself, Frank Sweeney? Your son gets my sister in the family way and all you can do is think of clever ways to get him off the hook. Well, this I did not expect. My good God, what is the world coming to?"

"I don't think you were hearing me right, Johnny. I wasn't defending him; I was asking you if you thought violence was the solution. Like, if you think about it, what will it achieve now? Have you an answer to that? If you have an answer to that, then great, I'll be all in favour of you getting a crowd of fellows from Sullivan's to join you and giving Sean a beating. So what's your answer? What will it achieve?"

"I don't know what it will achieve but it will make me feel a whole lot better," argued Johnny.

"And if it makes you feel a whole lot better that's a good enough reason, is it? What if it was to leave him with a broken arm, or a hole in his skull that left him not fit to work for the rest of his life? Would that please you?"

"It would be no more than he deserves," was Johnny's answer.

"And if he's not fit to work, not fit to earn a pound or two to look after Annie and her new baby, are you going to take on that responsibility yourself then Johnny? Have you thought of it that way?"

"Agh, you're far too clever with your arguments. I'll deal with that side of things whenever I meet him and none of your smooth chat will get him out of it, you oul windbag you."

Johnny took Annie by the arm again, preparing to leave. Frank stood up from his chair at the table for the first time, wincing with the difficulty of straightening up. He spoke again, moving towards Annie by the door.

"Annie, I am right sorry for this. You are the best of a girl and you'll be a grand mother to your wee baby, but I am so annoyed for you, to find yourself in this situation and you the way you are....not married and not able to tell us who your baby's father is."

Johnny poked the older man in the chest with his forefinger. "Here, hold on Frank. She has told us. It's Sean, so it is. Who the hell else could it be, for God's sake? Sean is the father."

Frank waited for Johnny's shouting to subside again before speaking softly, to Annie as much as to him. His eyebrows came together in a question mark, a query in his eyes as he said, "She told you, Johnny? How did she do that, God love her? Sure she's never said a word in her life."

Johnny's voice honked nasally again in his exasperation; he sounded like a swan chasing a rival off the lough. "She told Maggie Dan and me up on the mountain there now. I asked her if it was him. I told her to nod her head is it was Sean was the father. And she nodded her head. I swear to God she did, you can ask my mother yourself. She nodded, like this." And he demonstrated, with a few movements of his head. "Anyway Frank. Who else could it have been? Sean's been with her morning, noon and night at times. They're always together, always have been. Sure the talk in Annagry is that Father Dunleavey has him all lined up to marry her. You yourselves must have thought that they would marry, if you're being honest with me. No, it's Sean's baby, there's no doubt about that. And don't you go thinking anything else."

"That's alright Johnny," replied Frank. "I'm not disagreeing with you. You may very well be right and, if so, all I can do is apologise from the bottom of my heart for my son's actions; and of-course we will insist that he marries Annie as soon as we can arrange it. The only thing I would add is that it's only fair that Sean gets a chance to admit it was him. Do you not agree that that would be a fair thing to ask? Let him speak for himself."

Sean's mother joined in. "Johnny, you and him go back a long way as friends, back to when you were children. It would be a terrible shame to be destroying that friendship now over the head of something like this, would it not?"

"I'm not destroying any friendship, Brid. Your son has done that already." And he grabbed Annie again and stormed from the dismayed house into the dusk of the evening, kicking out wildly at the waddling ducks and speckled hens which crowded around him in the yard, expecting feeding.

Chapter 32

Expectations

Johnny hurried to Sullivan's public house immediately after leaving Annie back home and after searching around the house for any loose change he could find. Two shillings was all that he could come up with; no doubt his mother had secreted away the few remaining notes somewhere that he couldn't find them. "And me the one that earned them," he thought resentfully. He needed a drink; he was desperate for the invigorating lift that he got from the fruit of the barley to help clarify his befuddled thinking; and he needed someone to pour out his family troubles to, someone who might be ready to join him in taking on the boul Sean Ban Sweeney. Tonight was as good a time as any other; he was aware of the urge to strike while the passion in the iron of his soul was still red-hot. Sweeney would feel the same kind of feelings, the same kind of pain, that he had felt after the Millars ambushed him. He arrived in the sanctuary of Sullivan's and called an order to big Jim behind the 'altar' for a shot of the life-giving spirit.

He peered around the bar-room. His blood-shot eyes took a moment to adjust to the dull, sepia light which struggled out from the three hanging oil-lamps above the counter and diffused itself slowly into submission. The clouds of smoke in the room always tended to be victorious in their battle with the light, be it from the candles and lamps or from the two semi-blinded windows, windows which seemed to snoop on the street outside and on the church across the road. Turf reek belched in lazy clouds from the ill-drawing fireplace, mingled with fumes from the lamps and with the tobacco smoke furling up from several cigarettes and a few pipes. One or two of the regulars who had a lifetime habit of spending hours on end in Sullivan's had the appearance and smell about them of having been cured like a leg of ham. The place possessed that all-pervasive odour that, had a decaying fish been hidden for a month behind the beer barrels in the back corner, not a soul would have discerned the stink of it. And such a circumstance could easily have occurred; Jim Sullivan ran the bar in a most grubbily haphazard manner. This was in marked contrast to his sharp little wife who was in charge of the grocery part of the business which operated on the other side of a thin wooden partition at the eastern end of the bar. While her shop was always spick and span, the rough planked floor of Jim's domain would be littered with cigarette ash, lumps of dirt off the punter's boots, sticky brown pools of spilled drink and dusty caps or coats that had fallen off the ineffective cloak-pegs on the wall. In the corner by the door, a lazy-looking broom would always be leaning indolently against the wall, its sparse stubble resting on a heap of last week's sweepings.

Jim himself rolled around on his high stool behind the counter, seldom raising his barrel of a figure from this strategic vantage point. Bald, bull-necked and with a beer-belly which seemed to begin immediately below his double chin, Jim could remember fitter, slimmer days when he was the star full-forward on the village Gaelic football team; he still held the club record, he claimed, for points scored in a single match, though the figure had tended to rise with inflation over the intervening years. A nostalgic character, as many men of his particular vocation seem to be, his attachment to things past was in his stories alone. The bar-room itself was uncluttered by any memorabilia from earlier times, save for a long, lonely looking pike strung up high above the door. This was a revered weapon which, Jim claimed, had been handed down in his family for many generations and which, according to him, had seen action against the forces of the Crown on several, long-past outings. "You can still see the blood on the blade if you look close enough," he was known to claim, much to the derision of the locals. John Joe Roarty's stock response had always been, "Agh, sure you likely cut yourself shaving with it."

Johnny surveyed the regiments of bottles and vessels ranged up on the shelving behind Jim's stool.

"Why does there have to be so many different shapes and sizes and colours of liquor bottles," he was wondering; from clear glass to blues, browns and, of-course, bottle-green; and then the various earthen-ware jars and jugs, the different sizes of kegs... "I would get lost in here," he thought. "Yes, I definitely would get lost in here with that amount of drink!"

He stared long at the glass of locally-made poteen in his fist, downed it in a single gulp and rapped on the oak-topped counter for a refill. Then, sufficiently fortified, he turned to the waiting assembly of fellow-drinkers and made his pitch. He spilled out his angry story of Annie's pregnancy and of what he believed to be Sean's culpability. As he lectured, the spiky halo of his carrot-coloured hair, backlit by the flickering lamp just above his head, added a certain dramatic ire to his performance. After their initial shock and their sympathetic consolations, the fellows around him at the bar were in a mood to encourage his spirit of justice and retribution. Most of the chat was the bravado talk of fellows who, on one hand, had had their sense of decency offended by one of their own and who, on the other hand, could always be relied upon to find some dark humour in a neighbour's unfortunate situation.

"See what happens when you go away," said Jim from his perch behind the counter. "A sister like yours needs you around to be looking after her, with the way she is."

"But who would ever have thought it of Sean Ban?" was a general response from several.

"And there I was thinking she was slow of herself. Not a bit slow at all, by the sound o' it," smirked John Joe to his table-mates behind his raised pint and getting a quiet kick below the table for his flippancy.

"There will have to be a wedding. Sean'll have to do the right thing by her," said Paddy Cassidy, "and he's a decent enough sort. He'll not let her down."

"Sure he's Dunleavey's right hand man. You'd think some of the priest's abstinence would have rubbed off on him," added Seamus O'Donnell, a second cousin of Johnny's. "It's a terrible shame on him, more on him than on our Annie, for she has little or no wit about her, dear love her."

"Mind you, she's turned into a good looking lass in the last while," observed Paddy.

"And she never said 'No'?" said John Joe Roarty, half in innocence and half in another attempt at humour. The comment was greeted by an icy silence, until what John Joe had meant penetrated Johnny's fuddle of thought. He turned quickly and lashed out at the small fellow. "What did you say, you wee turd?" he breathed through clenched teeth, his neighbours restraining him quickly.

"He meant nothing Johnny. It's just his way, trying to be funny and putting his foot in it," said Paddy, calming the troubled waters.

"I'll put my foot in your mouth, Roarty, if you ever say another word about my sister, you hear me, you wee...grasshopper."

"What did Frank say when you told him? Was he not mortified altogether?" asked Seamus.

"Aye, he was shocked," answered Johnny. "Couldn't believe what he was hearing at the start. But I had Annie with me and Brid was looking at .....you know, examining the size of her belly and that. Ah, she's well and truly gone, according to Brid. But Frank? Frank's a bag o' hot air, so he is. Sean Ban needs a good hammering from him but the oul boy is not fit to give it to him. Aye, he'll insist on a wedding to make things right but he's all smooth talk and no action. That part of it I'll have to see to myself."

"What do you mean there, Johnny?" asked Seamus. "You're not thinking of teaching him a lesson, are you?"

"That I am! There's no other way for it. Any man who abuses my sister, whether she has all her wits about her or not, is going to have to answer to me. Just because he used to think he was my best mate doesn't get him off the hook. He has to look into my eyes and get down on his knees and apologise."

"God Johnny; you'd think it was you he put up the skite," said John Joe grinning.

Johnny gave the little fellow a long stare but decided to ignore this remark. Instead he said, "John Joe, I hope you are ready to come with me to back me up, 'cause you can always think of something to say....let's see how good you are in action."

"What do you mean, 'Go with you'?" John Joe looked nervously around the faces of the others.

"I mean that I'm going to give Sean Sweeney a damned good hiding before this night is out, so you will be coming with me, along with all these other mates of mine, right?" said Johnny, his fist banging on the counter so that the dirty glasses quivered and rattled.

"Wait a minute now Johnny," said Seamus. "Would you not be better waiting to see if Sean owns up to the thing? If he holds his hands up and agrees to marry her, there'll be no need for any fighting, will there?"

"Aye, Seamus is right, Johnny," agreed Paddy. "You don't want to be getting into a fist-fight with him, not at this stage anyway. If he doesn't admit the thing, then you'd have every right to get stuck into him, and we would be behind you if it comes to that, but not yet. Give it time to settle."

Jim joined in from his languid pint pouring. "You don't want to be landing in on him tonight when your gander is up, Johnny. What is it they say about revenge? 'Revenge is a dish best served cold.' Isn't that it? His folks will be talking to him tonight about it. Give them all time to work on him. Keep your powder dry till the time is right."

"Life's too short to be.... to be... to be beating people up all the time," philosophised John Joe nodding his head sagely. "Sure you, of all people Johnny, should know that."

"You're all a great help, so yous are," exclaimed Johnny, turning from his drink to stare at each of his advisors. "Will none of you have the guts to come with me this night to confront him, is that what I'm gathering here?"

The company looked from one to the other, as did some of those dishevelled characters who were watching and listening in from their chairs and tables around the room. There were a few guilty looking grins and a few eyes took a sudden interest in the labels on the various bottles lining Jim's shelves. Nobody met Johnny's wide-eyed challenge and Seamus said simply, "I think you're gathering right, Johnny. Leave it till you see what way the wind blows later on."

Johnny picked up his battered cap from the bar top and pulled it angrily on his head, bunching the hair out at the sides in a comical looking fashion. He gave an ironic shrug of his shoulders as he scanned the blank expressions on the faces of the company, no eyes meeting his. "You're a great crowd of supporters, you boys," he said and stormed out into the street.

John Joe smiled a watery smile and jerked his thumb towards the swinging door. "He's a rare bull of a boy when he's in a temper, our Johnny, but Sean Ban will be able for him all the same."

"You think?" said Paddy.

"Well," answered John Joe, "seems like he was able for the sister anyways."

``````
``````

Sean Ban entered the courtroom of his mother's kitchen at around six o'clock and sensed immediately something different, something wrong in the atmosphere of his home. For a start there was no evening meal on the table, which would usually have been the case; there wasn't even the smell of anything cooking, not a sign of food or preparation of food. What he did see was the strangely sobering tableau of two motionless backs, those of his mother and father, turned from him and somehow drooped and aged since he had left in the morning to go out to Carrickfinn. Like his parents had been turned into wood carvings of themselves.

He had worked hard with the Stewart family all day, helping in the heavy, difficult work of putting roof timbers on the stone-built structure of a new barn, much of the wood having been salvaged from debris which the tide had washed up on the beaches around the Point over the last year or so. The experience of working with others was something Sean had always enjoyed; it was a lovely contrast to the lonely labour around the Sweeney's own small-holding on the mainland. There was always a sense of fulfilment in working with another family in the practice known as 'morrowing' whereby labour became a social commodity exchanged between families. No money changed hands; a task which required more labour than was available within a family-farming unit would be completed with the help of a few neighbours. The obligation would be paid back in kind at a later time; 'I work to you today; you work to me tomorrow'; this was the general principle, common in Donegal and in most rural parts of Ireland. In the case of the Sweeneys and the Stewarts, Sean's support was called in by Robert Stewart in recompense for the services of the Stewart bull with Frank's three or four heifers and cows over the course of the past year. The exactness of currency of such exchanges was not a matter than anyone worried about. In Sean's case, he would willingly have given Robert John Stewart a day's labour simply for the diversion it offered. The general chat, the stories shared and the foolery and devilment of the younger Stewarts was reward enough and today had been no exception.

Sean had wandered back over the sand flats in a happy state of mind, wandered too slowly, as it turned out. He had thought when he started his home-bound journey, as dusk fell, that the incoming tide was still well out in the channel. Lost in his thoughts about the subtle differences he was always aware of when working with the Stewarts, he hadn't heeded the speed at which the estuary had filled up and how quickly the water was cutting off his route back to the mainland. Halfway across the flat, open expanse he had had to break into a jog as the grey, metallic-looking liquid had appeared to speed up in the murk of twilight. It covered the muddy sand so quickly that his last twenty paces, before he reached the rising ground of the mainland, were through seawater already a couple of inches deep. The icy water had seeped through the holes in his battered boots as if desperate to find any source of heat; his feet had felt the chill immediately and he had laughed at his own stupidity. Apart from this experience, and apart from the sharp pain of a few skelfs of driftwood in his hands, received inevitably as he had been manoeuvring the heavy spar of a long-dead tree into position at the pitch of the roof, Sean felt in great form. And in that form he had arrived into the silent solemnity of the home kitchen. Neither father nor mother moved. Neither spoke.

He had to crack open the brittle shell of silence himself.
"What's wrong?"
There was no reply, not a flicker of movement in the two hunched bodies at the hearth.
"Has something happened?" he tried again and approached his parents. He looked down at their dejection, his eyes searching for some clue which might explain this changed atmosphere, this presence which had darkened his home. Neither father nor mother looked up to meet his eye; indeed he discerned a further dropping of the head on his mother's part. He balanced on one leg and began to drag off his wet boots, setting them by the fire to dry out, all the time watching his mother, probing.
"What's the matter? What has happened? Is it news from America? Is Dermot alright?"
"Dermot's alright," his father said, sullenly thought Sean.
"Is it Mary then? Or one of the wains?" asked Sean, his imagination taking him to a kitchen in Scotland where his sister Mary was married to Pat Quinn and had two children. Could something have happened to steal one of these grandchildren away before they had ever had the chance to see their grandparents?

"No, Mary's alright. The wains too, I hope to God," said Frank, bringing his eyes up to look at Sean for the first time since he had entered the house.

"Well, what is it then? Don't just sit there; if there's something wrong tell me what it is."

Frank spoke slowly in little more than a rustle of sound. "Have you no idea yourself, Sean?"

"Not a notion. I have not the slightest idea. Do I look like I have the gift of second sight?"

His father stared back at him in silence and Sean detected in his gaze just the slightest hint of disappointment, perhaps even more than that....perhaps hurt of some kind.

"The way you are looking at me makes me think it might have something to do with me, but I haven't got a notion what. Unless Father Dunleavey is annoyed at me going to the Point instead of helping him with something. Is that it?"

His father sighed deeply. "If only it was as simple as that. No Sean, Father Dunleavey hasn't been here yet, but just you look out for him when he does come, for come he will."

Sean shook his head and held out his hands, upturned in a gesture of hopelessness, of innocent question. "How have I annoyed him now?"

Frank's eyes went to his wife's feet, then to her down-turned face. "You tell him," he said simply.

Brid's countenance shocked Sean. She was a mother who seldom showed her feelings, seldom cried. He couldn't remember the last time he had seen his mother cry, maybe when Dermot, the oldest of the three Sweeney children, had left to go to Boston, and that was years ago, maybe eight or nine years. But now the evidence of an evening's tears stained the dustiness of her cheeks. She wiped her eyes and then held Sean's worried stare.

"Annie is expecting a baby."

Sean didn't understand. "What?" he breathed, his mother's words making as much sense to him as if she'd spoken in Russian or Greek or some other obscure language.

"Annie," repeated his mother.

"What about Annie?"

"She is having a baby. She is pregnant," his mother said.

He stood in an uncomprehending silence, the mind-stunning shock of the words slowly dripping into his consciousness.

Seconds later the sound of breathed invocation from his dry mouth.

"God and Mary to her!"

Then a strangulated quietness took over the kitchen in which nothing moved, turf and logs burned without a sound, no-one seemed to breathe, not an eye connected to any other, and Sean suffered a tearing sensation of pain, of fear and deep anguish, somewhere in the region of his chest. He gave a small gasp and struck himself around the ribcage, as if to challenge or disperse the piercing shock of the pain, of the news.

"Annie?" he said, grief and disbelief in his voice. "Dear God, Annie, what has happened to you?"

"That part of it is easier to answer," said Frank. "The thing her mother wants to know is, are you the father?"

"Me the father?" Sean was again struggling for understanding. This question completely puzzled him for a second. 'What does he mean, am I the father?' The thought rattled around in his head like a crab in a tin bucket.

"Me?" he said. "I'm not the father."

Brid sobbed quietly into a cloth at her face. Frank looked at Sean with an expression of angst in the watery blue of his eyes that Sean had never seen before, not even in the worst of his physical pain. "You're not?" he queried doubtfully.

"No, I'm not." Sean's reply was brief but stated with underlined certainty.

"Johnny and Maggie Dan say you are."

"Well, they are wrong. I am not. I have never touched her. Why would they say that? How would they know anyway?"

"They see what everybody sees, that you and she are always together. There's nobody else it could be. She's never out anywhere. She's never with anybody else. You and her are like.... it's like you're married already, though there's never been a wedding."

Sean shook his head firmly, a look of dismay on his face. "Well, she must have been with somebody else, God love her, for I didn't do this, father. I have never touched her....like that. I... I might have held her hand a time or two but....dear God. It's Annie we're talking about here. How could I have done that to her? How could anybody do that to her, and her the simple, lovely wee... her, the way she is? Are they sure she has a child coming? How do they know for sure? They could be wrong, surely? It has to be a mistake."

"I saw her, Sean. I felt the baby kicking in her. She sat here, beside me on this chair, earlier on today. And I felt the baby moving in her belly. She is pregnant, son," said Brid. "She's going to need you now Sean, more than ever before. The poor girl."

Sean thought quietly for a bit. "She's going to need us all," he said.

Frank spoke again. "You are going to have trouble convincing Maggie Dan and Johnny that it wasn't you."

"Well, they'll just have to believe me."

"They say that Annie told them it was your baby," continued Frank.

Brid joined in, reaching up to take Sean's hand. "She told them you're the father Sean."

"And how did she tell them that? Has she had a miracle cure and now she can talk and blame me for something I never did? Listen to what you're saying mother," he argued, ignoring her hand. She withdrew it to her lap again and twisted the cloth she held there.

"They asked her to nod if it was you. And they say she nodded. They both saw her nod her head," said Brid.

"Sure they saw her nod her head. In Annie's mind they could have been asking her if I brought her a shell from the beach, or if she saw me going down past this morning. They could have been saying anything to her and she would have nodded....especially if Johnny was pushing her head up and down like she was a puppet. That means nothing. I did not do anything to Annie. I never have and I never will. She would not have told a lie against me, I know that as well. We know each other well enough for that. Annie is.... Annie, dear love the girl. What is she going to do now?" Sean's posture was now resembling that of his parents, the crushing distress of Annie's situation invading his senses.

"But Annie has never been with anybody else, Sean. To the whole community it will look like it's your baby. Nobody will think anything else," his mother came back at him. "Will you not stand by her now at her time of need?"

"You mean, you think I should take the blame for something I am not guilty of? Are you serious mother?" Sean was shocked by his mother's question. "Or do you think I did it, after all I have said? Do you not believe me? What about you, father?" he said, turning to Frank.

"It's not a question of believing you or not," his father replied. "Look Sean, these things happen. You don't mean them to happen; maybe you don't even know what happened or how it happened. Maybe things went a wee bit further than you intended, a wee accident. Now what we're saying is that, for the sake of Annie, for the sake of your own reputation and the standing of this family in the neighbourhood, you need to think this out and make a wise decision. We want you to stand by her."

Sean exploded like he had never done in his home before, his face becoming the colour of liver.

"Stand by her, is it? How about you standing by me? I have told you the truth. It...was...not...me! I have never 'gone too far' with Annie. There has never been 'a wee accident', as you put it. For the simple reason that I have never touched Annie. Never! You hear me? Never! It is not my baby. It is some other bastard's. And if I knew who, I would be joining Johnny in taking a horsewhip to him. That's how I would stand by Annie."

"So you won't marry her?"

"Oh mother, can you not understand? I won't marry her. I won't be blackmailed into something that will change my life for ever. Surely you can see that?"

"Well, we will just have to wait and see what Father Dunleavey says about it all," Brid responded, drying the remaining wetness off her face with the cloth.

"And he will likely gang up with the rest of you against me," said Sean ruefully. "He won't believe me either. He'll have me damned to hell forever, on suspicion alone."

Frank tried to rise from the chair and reached for Sean's hand to get some help. Sean hesitated and kept his father waiting for a second before offering. As he did he said, "I need to hear from you two that you believe me."

Frank grasped his outstretched hand and, as he was about to haul himself up, felt the tension needed for the lift recede from his son's grasp. He looked up at him.

"Do you believe me?" asked Sean again.

His father said nothing and Sean left him still sitting in the chair, while keeping his grip on the twisted hand.

Frank looked up and said, "Pull me up Sean!"

Sean did so, slowly, still engaging the older man's eyes. "I need to know that you believe what I've told you. I swear it on my mother's death. I am not responsible for Annie's baby. Do you believe me? I need to hear it! Both of you."

Frank looked at Brid across the kitchen; she had risen to get some soda-bread and tea ready for supper. Sean still held his father's hand. Brid murmured, "I want to," and came back from the table to put her arms around him.

"Alright, I believe you son," came Frank's response, "and your mother does too. It's just....it's all been so much of a shock, you understand. And the sure way that Johnny and his mother put it to us earlier....well, you can see why they would be blaming you. You and Annie have always been so close. In their minds it could only have been you."

"Aye, I can see that," replied Sean, "but why do people always jump to wrong conclusions? It's not as if I'm the only young fellow about here."

"Aye, but you have to admit that you are the most likely candidate. People will always put two and two together," said his father.

Brid joined in again, sitting down with husband and son at the table. "And when they do they'll all think it's you Sean. Would you not be better marrying her like everybody will expect you to?"

"If I was to marry Annie now, they will all have the confirmation they need. Can you not see that? I can't marry her now, even if I wanted to."

"So you had thought about marrying her....before, like?" asked Brid, pouring tea for her men.

Sean winced. "Annie is.... she is my friend. But she's... no, I couldn't have married Annie. It wouldn't be fair. Not to her, not to me. It's an impossible thing, that's how I feel about it."

"And it has just become a lot more impossible," said his father.

"That it has," agreed Sean Ban. "Should I not go down to O'Donnell's before bedtime and explain to Maggie Dan that it wasn't me?"

"You could do that," answered Frank, "but it won't be her you'll have the problem with. It will be Johnny. And if he's as angry tonight as he was when he was here, then my advice would be to leave him to simmer down a bit. Go and see him and Maggie

Dan in the morning. He is less likely to have drink taken in the morning and he might be easier talked to. There's no point in going down tonight and antagonising him. Let them sleep on it."

"And Father Dunleavey will want to have a chat with you too," chipped in Brid through a full mouth. You'll have to take account of what he says. It won't be the first time he has mentioned you and Annie to me, you know that, don't you?"

"Oh aye! It wouldn't be like him to be missing an opportunity to be telling me what to be doing," said Sean. "No doubt he will believe Maggie Dan as well. I am going to have my work cut out for me in this parish from now on I can see."

Later, as he lay on his straw-filled mattress, he could think of nothing which would have contradicted this assessment. Life had changed for him in Ranahuel, in the whole area. From now on, no matter how he acted, no matter what he decided to do, he would be talked about behind his back as the fellow who got poor, simple Annie O'Donnell pregnant. And no matter how much he denied it, with Annie's inability to speak and with Johnny's aggressive character traits, recently boosted by his love of liquor and the confidence that gave him, Sean was going to be the subject of rumour and ridicule and even of threat. Past reputation would count for nothing. The fact that he had been a decent, helpful member of the community would be quickly overlooked and forgotten, swept over and submerged by a dirty tide of distrust and distaste, of speculation and innuendo. This he knew in his bones; it was how people were. And, he thought regretfully, they were the same in the Rosses as any other place. They could barely wait for someone to fall from whatever grace they were supposed to have had in order to enjoy the destructive gossip. Like a flock of hungry carrion crows they would descend on the victim and join in the feeding frenzy. No matter who the victim was, any little weakness in its defences would be pounced upon and it would be incapable of protecting itself. Sean was already starting to identify with this feeling of helplessness as he stared into the dim light of the kitchen, that light emanating from the smouldering remains of the fire in the hearth. Already he knew that this was a night during which he would not get much sleep. What to do, how to handle this unwelcome circumstance? These tangled thoughts dragged him down towards despair.

He thought of Annie and immediately started to feel less sorry for himself and more anxious for her plight. What was she thinking about all this? Was she aware of her condition? Was she conscious of the baby inside? How did she feel about it? Was she terrified? Frightened of what was ahead? And not just the birth of the infant, the way she would be thought of in the neighbourhood after this. 'No, that is silly,' he thought. 'If she hasn't been able to feel anything about how people have regarded her up to this point in her innocent existence, the sorts of unkind and unfeeling things that people have said about her up until now, she's hardly likely to start feeling bad about it now.'

Inevitably Sean's mind began to wonder who the father of the baby actually was and, in his quest for answers to that particular dilemma, he drew a total blank. In his imagination he went over the faces of the various young men, and some older men, in the area. Not a single person could he remember ever having shown any interest in Annie. Not one had ever tried to talk to her, in his memory. She was never really with other people, apart from Sean himself and, of-course, the folk in her family circle. No-one came to mind as a possible suspect, no matter how much he racked his brain, no matter how wide he cast his net of suspicion. He himself had always been her company, her protector, her best and only friend....and, he realised, he had guarded this position with a degree of jealous pride. And now he began to see just how difficult it was for his old friend Johnny to imagine anyone other than himself having had such a relationship with Annie. Johnny who had observed their closeness for years; Johnny who had gone away each summer to work in the Lagan, leaving Annie in his care; Johnny who had had his own huge disappointments in the recent past regarding matters of the heart. His disillusionment over love and courtship, over the affair with the girl in County Derry and the hiding he had taken from her brothers....all this, Sean realised so clearly now, would be playing into Johnny's reaction to his own perceived transgression. The situation wasn't getting any easier, the more he lay and thought about it. Eventually, in the early hours of the morning, he fell into a dream-filled sleep; and he held Annie in his arms there, protecting her from the distorted face of her fury-ridden brother.

Chapter 33

Confrontation

In all his experience of life, Sean Ban had never felt the way he did walking down the familiar lane to O'Donnell's house the next morning. Everything was the same as always around him. Along the lane-side the usual gorse bushes; underneath these, the first blooms of primroses breaking out into striking creamy-lemon coloured flower; pussy willows, just beginning to assent to the arrival of spring in a show of little, greyish, furry catkins; scrawny mountain heathers waiting for some regenerative warmth. Further back from the path, on the more exposed crags jutting up from the bog, stunted rowan trees showed their resilience in surviving another winter with the appearance of a first hint of fresh leaf shoots. Around the shores of the lough below, however, there was still no sign of new growth from the roots below the dried-out stalks of last season's reeds. He watched disinterestedly as a majestic heron glided in towards the lough-shore and then, folding its wings, drop and swirl like a falling leaf to land on a low rocky outcrop, welcomed by its own reflection in the still, oily-green water.

The birdsong of sparrows and finches around him was interrupted by the discordant noise of a braying donkey. Either Maggie Dan's animal had just wakened up or something had disturbed it. Sean paused at the end of the lane, hesitant about this visit, wondering just how he would be received, half-hoping that Johnny was still asleep and that Maggie Dan would send him away with no further argument. Confrontation was not something that came easily to Sean; it was something best avoided, if at all possible. Indeed he had little experience of argument or of rows of any kind. Life was fairly quiet and predictable around these parts. Yes, he could remember raised voices in his own cottage when Dermot had been at home, before he emigrated to the United States of America, like so many from west Donegal. Sean had always suspected that it was probably the fact that Frank and his oldest son found it hard to get on and had manys a shouting match that had made Dermot's mind up for him and had driven him to the Derry boat. But as for Sean himself, he found it hard to think of any rows he had been involved in; ironically, he recalled, most of his arguments, if you could even call them that, were with his priest, Father Dunleavey. And of-course, in recent weeks there had been the various tensions with Johnny since he had returned from the Lagan with such a different attitude; the friendship between the two neighbours, which he had always imagined would be solid and unchanged throughout his life, had altered quite drastically. He wondered if it would be changed irrevocably by this current poisonous climate of suspicion. Well, he was about to find out; there was no point in postponing this any longer; he headed towards Maggie Dan's door and, when he reached it, he found himself knocking on the flaking paint before slowly taking the latch in his hand and opening the door, something he could not recall having done before.

He entered the gloom of Maggie Dan's kitchen and his eyes flicked around the room, taking in at once that Annie was sitting at the table facing him, eating her breakfast of porridge and buttermilk, Maggie Dan was on her knees at the fire and Johnny was still stretched out on his settle bed in the bed-outshot, face to the wall, possibly still asleep. It may have been this fact, or it may simply have been the new sensation of nervous tension in his throat, that influenced the pitch of Sean's voice as he whispered a morning greeting to the two women. "Bless the house," he breathed.

Maggie Dan seemed to freeze at her task before she turned round slowly to look at him; her eyes then glanced at Johnny's prostrate form on the bed. Annie ate away without change of expression, as would have been usual for her.

"That's one normal reaction," Sean comforted himself straight away. Any crumb of comfort; any early passing straw to be clutched at. Maggie Dan's expression, however, was not so encouraging. There was a ferment of hurt and anger deep behind her bloodshot eyes; another querying look between Sean and the sleeping Johnny. She still had not returned his greeting, had not spoken. Then she seemed to make up her mind.

"Sean Ban Sweeney," she said loudly. "You have a cheek on you marching in here as if today was the same as yesterday."

The timbre of her voice had the intended effect upon Johnny who sat up slowly, face still pointed away from the kitchen, emerging from the depth of a sleepy stupor. Suddenly he seemed to come to his senses in a flash of understanding of his mother's meaning. His body jerked around in the bed and his eyes locked to those of Sean, still by the door. Johnny jumped from his bed, still wearing his clothes from the previous day but bare-footed. His scream reverberated in Sean's brain and produced a shocked reaction in Annie.

"You bastard, Sweeney! You bloody bastard!"

The insult spat like venom against him, searching for cracks on the facade of his resolve, smarting in the raw flesh of his vulnerability.

The flurry of a flailing body across the room as Johnny dived towards Sean; his arms whirling as he threw punch after punch at the figure of his former friend; Annie's hands at her head in an unusual posture of fear, of panic; Maggie Dan, arms akimbo, her wrinkled old face in animated assent to her son's attack.

Sean defended himself, initially with raised arms simply to fend off the blows. He sensed that Johnny wasn't quite as fit as he had been, or perhaps that he was disadvantaged by the simple fact that one minute he had been sleeping, while the next he was engaged in a furious fight; the suddenness of this transition put him at a disadvantage compared to Sean who had his wits about him and was in good physical shape, even if a bit smaller than his adversary. As Johnny's thrashing limbs began to weaken, Sean managed to grab on to one arm and pull Johnny around a bit, disorientating him and rendering his attack largely ineffective. Then, as a blow caught him on the side of the neck, he got a grip on Johnny's right arm as well and he found he had the strength to hold him at bay and to throw some words into the confrontation.

"Johnny, for God's sake will you listen to me," he began, above the noise of Johnny's animalistic roar. "I did not do this!"

Johnny's answer was a further stream of verbal foulness but, with his hands secured and being pressed to his sides, he was making no physical impact upon Sean. He tried to butt Sean with his head, bucking forward like an angry goat, but these attempts were easily avoided. A spittle splatted against Sean's cheek and then Johnny's bare feet went into action. Perhaps it was the spittle, perhaps the ugliness of what was being shouted, or perhaps just the incongruity of the situation, but Sean saw his chance to put the other fellow at a more serious disadvantage. As Johnny's right foot came arcing up in a vicious kick towards his groin, Sean swayed slightly sideways and, seizing the opportunity, stamped firmly upon Johnny's other foot, the vulnerable one which had been so damaged in the autumn. The shock of hard leather boot on bare skin and bone made the attacker howl with pain and hop into the air, instinctively trying to grab his foot with his hands. Before he knew it, Sean had him on his back in the centre of the floor, a crushing thump of a fall, his own weight landing on top of Johnny. The fight went out of him, as well as the breath.

Sean relaxed. Too soon! Maggie Dan's motherly instinct sprang into life as she watched her son being knocked back by the same fellow who had knocked up her daughter. She had a long, hard wedge of black turf in her hand and now she swung it at Sean Ban, catching him full on the back of his unprotected head. Little pin-points of light accompanied the searing pain as he sank down, spread-eagled on top of Johnny's defeated body.

"God and Mary look to me! What have I done?" she said, terrified.

God or Mary did look to her, for at that moment the door of her cottage was pushed open and the tall, dark, duck-bellied figure of the parish priest stood in the frame of it, looking at the scene and trying to decipher what was happening.

"What under heaven is going on, Maggie Dan?" he said and then made strides towards the two bodies on the floor. "Water, Maggie Dan! Get me water quick!"

Johnny was struggling to get up off the cold clay floor from under the prone figure of Sean Ban and not making much headway.

"Sit still a minute Johnny!" commanded the priest, one hand under Sean's head, the other trying to gently turn over his semi-conscious body. The water arrived and he took it from the shaking hand of the woman of the house and doused it over Sean's head. The coldness of the burn-water did the trick and Sean came back to his senses, albeit a little bit at a time. As he came around the first thing he saw was Father Dunleavey's face and, trying to focus on it and to remember what had just happened he made one of those comments which he would not be allowed to forget in a hurry.

"Father Dunleavey?" he said, slowly looking around him to make sense of everything. "I thought I had died and gone to heaven. Then I saw you and..."

Dunleavey smiled for once and said, "I hope you weren't about to say what I think you were about to say, young Sweeney. No, it's not heaven, and it's not the other place either, thanks be to God."

"What happened?" asked Sean getting up slowly and being helped into the chair by the fire, allowing Johnny to make a retreat to his bed.

"I don't know what happened. I have just arrived in on it, whatever it was," answered the clergyman. "Can you tell us, Maggie Dan?"

She was still standing in shock and turmoil at what had taken place in her own peaceful kitchen, and at her part in it. She answered softly, "I am sorry, Father. It was all my fault. These two were at it, at the fighting on account of what has happened to her. And then I hit him on the head with a peat. God have mercy, what'll I do now?"

"Just sit down a minute and give yourself peace, Maggie Dan. This isn't the confessional you know. And it's not your fault that these two rascals were fighting. That's their responsibility. Now, my dear people, this is as good a time as any to let everybody have their say about....about the situation we find ourselves in. And when everybody has had their say we can work out what's the best thing to do. Sean is here, and it's very good of him to have the courage to come down to you this morning and face up to his responsibilities. Very good and courageous indeed and I admire you for it Sean, but then I've always known you were a sound chap, even if you have made a serious mistake. And poor Annie is here, and we all want the best for her, now that she finds herself in this plight. It is a shame and it is a disgrace and it goes against the laws of God, but there we are. We are all sinners! We have to beg for the mercy of God and try our best to do what's right. And what's right in this situation is for there to be a quick wedding within the next week or two, a simple affair; no need for any big fuss, just Sean and Annie and your immediate families. I'll do the ceremony and the community will be satisfied. All will be grand. People make mistakes....not Annie, now. I don't mean Annie. I think, with the way she is, she has little or no blame in the matter at all. But it's a mistake all the same, and mistakes like that....well, there's only the one way to fix them. To go to the altar and, in the sight of God, to enter marriage through the blessed sacrament and go on in your lives as man and wife." He paused and looked at Maggie Dan. "Maybe you would take that boiling kettle off the crook and make a wee cup of tea, Maggie Dan, and then we can talk and make plans."

The woman of the house seemed calmed by the priest's words and rose obediently to do his bidding. Annie still sat on the same chair, her hands clasped around her stomach. Johnny hadn't stirred from the bed and lay back on his elbow in defeat, his face diverted from the priest and from the centre of the room.

Sean's expression was one of stoic bewilderment. His head was still ringing from the blow and he was struggling to bring any coherent thinking to the situation. He had heard the priest out to the end of his homily, patient but despairing.

'I have to take my stand,' he thought, 'and I have to take it now. My life is being snatched away from me like a gaffed salmon, before my very eyes, this very hour, unless I take my stand. I have to speak now or my chance has gone for ever. I will speak the truth. I have to. I have no friend here but the truth.'

"Father," he began hoarsely, as the sound of water hissing into the hot teapot came from beyond Maggie Dan's bent figure.

"What do you want to say son? Now remember it's Maggie Dan and Annie and Johnny you need to be saying your apologies to, not to me. I'll hear your confession at another time, whenever you are ready. But it's the good folk of this house you need to be speaking to first and foremost."

"I am not the father!"

The words tripped awkwardly over his teeth; they stumbled out and splattered on to the clay floor like a spilled basketful of eggs. All eyes looked at him in varying degrees of shock, Johnny turning sharply from the wall.

"What did you say?" he rasped.

"I am not the father!" Sean repeated. "I have never .....Annie and I have never done anything."

There was silence, the priest and Maggie Dan looking quickly at each other, Johnny staring at Sean and slowly starting to rise from the bed, Annie looking blankly from one to the other, aware of the tension in the room but not really comprehending it. Father Dunleavey stood up, the action being intended to add gravitas and authority to what he was about to say.

"Now look Sean, we know this is very difficult for you; I understand that. So does Maggie Dan. But there is nothing to be gained by such a hasty denial. You need time to think this over...it has come as a huge shock to you that something so....so impetuous, so simple, could lead to these serious consequences! I know all that....."

Sean interrupted him. "Father Dunleavey, you are not listening to me. I said, 'I am not the father.' That's what I meant. This is nothing to do with me. That is the truth."

"You are not the father?" shouted Johnny. "Of-course you are the father. You have to be. It's always been you and her together. Always! Since she was a wain. You and her. You couldn't have slid a blade of grass between yous. Nobody else ever came near her, 'cause everybody knew it was you and her. You did it, you lying bastard, and you'll never convince me of anything else."

"Johnny, I swear on my mother's life that I have never touched Annie. I love her like a sister. I would never do this to her. You have to believe me."

"No I don't have to believe you," shouted Johnny, taking an aggressive pose in the centre of the floor, his fists clenching and unclenching, his broken beak of a nose jutting forward like the jib of a ship in a storm.

Maggie Dan and the clergyman moved closer, instinctively getting between the two young men in case violence should erupt again. Dunleavey backed Johnny towards the bed.

"Sit yourself down Johnny and let me handle this," he said "I'll get it out of him without any more rough stuff."

Maggie Dan turned to Sean and took his two hands in hers in a simple maternal gesture.

"Please Sean," she pleaded, "if you think anything of my Annie, please pity me, and pity her, and have a bit of mercy on us. It was just a wee mistake; nobody's going to hold it against you. The chat will die down in no time at all; people will forget about it and you and Annie can rear the child just like I reared these two."

"Maggie Dan, you know me, as well as anybody else alive. You have been like a second mother to me. Surely you know me well enough to believe me when I say that I did not do this to Annie? Nor would I ever.... you should know I would never do anything to hurt Annie. Do you not believe me?" he begged in return.

Maggie Dan turned away from him, tears of confused despair brimming in her eyes. She held out her hands to Father Dunleavey in a gesture which said, 'I am defeated. What are we going to do now?'

The priest resumed his appeal in conciliatory tones. "Maybe Sean.....maybe... perhaps you don't know what it was you did, I mean...."

Sean's interruption was quick and vigourous. "I know what I did. I know what I didn't do. You should know that Father. I've seen enough of your ram with the ewes, for goodness sake. I've taken heifers out to Stewart's bull at the Point enough times. I know what you're meaning but, believe me, I know about these things. Annie and I have never....we have never been that close. You asked me about this before Father and can I tell you the truth? It disgusted me to think that you would imagine that Annie and me were...were.... you know, at it. I have never touched her. I am sorry that she is having a baby. I am truly sorry. And I am as shocked as you all are. More than that, if I knew who was responsible....I told my parents this....I would be joining up with Johnny to make him do the decent thing."

"You are the greatest liar in Ireland!" shouted Johnny. "Look at her! Look at my sister! She is ruined! As if she wasn't ruined enough already. You dirty, lying dog!"

Sean shook his head but did not see any sense in replying to Johnny in this state. Father Dunleavey turned around a couple of times in the centre of the room, his eyes studying his sturdy brown boots. Maggie Dan leaned her hips on the table beside where Annie sat and took her by the hand, stroking the back of it soothingly. Then she said, "Annie told us you were the father, Sean."

"Maggie Dan, with all respect to you, that can not have happened. We all know that. How is she supposed to have told you?" asked Sean painfully.

Johnny spoke up again. "She did tell us, as sure as I am sitting on this bed."

"How Johnny?" asked Sean.

"Johnny said to her to nod her head if you were the father," continued Maggie Dan, "and she did; she nodded her head. I saw it myself. I wouldn't lie about that either, Sean. She did it!"

Sean appealed to the clergyman. "Father Dunleavey, you can't believe this. When has Annie ever been able to understand such a thing? She wouldn't even know what you were asking her to do, Johnny; she probably doesn't even know what happened to her, or that she has a baby growing in her. How could Annie understand enough about this to nod? It's daft."

"I don't know," responded the priest. "I think Annie knows that she is expecting a baby. I think, by how she sits and holds her tummy there....like she is doing now, look. I think she realises there is a wee life in there. Do you not think so, Sean?"

"Maybe she does, maybe she doesn't," said Sean. "But it's a different thing asking her who the father is. She likely doesn't even know how it happened, that's what I think. And dear love her, she can't tell us."

"And that makes you very happy, that she can't tell us. This is one of the times you are delighted that she is the way she is; she isn't able to speak so she can't tell us that it was you who... who was meddling with her." Johnny's voice rose and fell in bursts of sarcasm and rage. "But she did tell us, like my mother said. We both saw it. She nodded. She didn't have to, but she nodded when we asked her if Sean Ban was the baby's father. That's good enough for me. And what's more, everybody from Annagry to Kincasslagh knows you're the father, 'cause I have told them so myself."

Sean looked at him with a mixture of resignation and disgust.

"Yes, you would! You would do that, whether it's true or not. The truth of it wouldn't matter to you, Johnny O'Donnell, just so long as you can put the pressure on me to stand by your sister. Let me ask you this, and you too Maggie Dan. When you asked Annie if it was me, were you standing well back from her or were you holding on to her? Did you have her by the neck, or by the head?"

"She nodded her head of her own accord, if that's what you're wanting to know," argued Johnny.

"You didn't answer my question. Were you.... was he holding unto Annie at that the time?"

"What are you trying to make out? That I am a cheat? That I tried to....you have a right cheek on you, Sweeney. You are the blaggard here, not me," cried Johnny, his face contorted and purple with anger.

"You had her by the neck You made her head nod. Maggie Dan, answer me this. 'Yes' or 'No'? Was he holding unto Annie at the time?" Sean rose and appealed right into the mother's eyes. Maggie Dan's gaze went to Johnny as she answered.

"He was angry, Sean. Yes he had the hold of her, but that doesn't mean she didn't nod her head of her own accord. Johnny wouldn't be doing that."

Sean had the hint of a smile about him as he turned to his priest.

"Father Dunleavey, if she nodded her head to say I was the father then, she will be able to do it again, do you not agree? This time though, you be the one to ask her. We will all stay well back and we'll watch her nod her head just to be sure. And when she nods her head, then I'll agree that it was me. Alright? Can I be fairer than that? Johnny, what do you say?"

"I say you are a dirty, squirming rat, trying any road to get out of your duty to my sister," replied Johnny, still sat on his bed.

"And," continued Sean with growing confidence, "if she doesn't nod, then you'll have to agree that this bit of the story is nonsense? Are we agreed on that, at least? What do you think, Father?"

The priest had been very pensive for a long time, his left arm across his chest, the finger of his right hand across his upper lip, his weight shifting from one foot to the other as he listened to the argument. When he spoke now, he did so very quietly.

"I think that you have made your point very well, Sean. And if you insist on it, I see no objection to following your suggestion. I will say that whatever Annie does or does not do won't prove anything one way or the other though."

He turned to Annie and hunkered down beside her chair, so that his gaze was more or less level with hers. He looked hard into her eyes and, although his hand went out automatically as if to take hers, he did not touch the girl. "Annie," he said softly, "I am going to ask you a question. I am going to ask you who is the father of the baby inside you, do you understand? If Sean Ban here is the father of the baby, if it was Sean who did this to you, then I want you to nod your head, like this, up and down, alright? Do you understand, Annie?"

She is looking back at the priest. There is something in her head but it is nothing to do with him, nor with his question, nor with the here and now.

In her head she is hearing a tune. A tune from months ago. A tune she played in the sand hills when she was staying with her grandmother at her cottage near the sea, far away along the roads. It was a great tune, that one. She had her granny's dog with her then. That wonderful tune. The notes of it in her ears, mingling with the sound of the waves breaking on the sand. Strong as the ocean smells in her nostrils, the salt on the breeze and the odour of decaying seaweed. And she remembered the boy. And he was drawing pictures. She was in the sea waves. The water was up around her. She raised up her dress around her waist. It was so cold on her skin. So clear to look into. It tickled her. She loved it, gasped in it, was excited by it, like the brightest, most thrilling tune you could ever hear. And the dog ran up to the boy on the hill. He stood up for her and talked nice to her. She never met a boy like him before. His hair was very short. Tight to his head and brown like a cow. He was strange, strange and gentle. His way of speaking sounded very different to Sean Ban, different to the sound of Johnny's voice, not the way her people sounded when they talked.
And now this strange, old voice of the black priest speaking to her. The droning sound of him trying to fight with the sounds already in her head. Trying to beat down the tune and stifle it and shut it up. This tune of vivid memories.

"So, Annie," Father Dunleavey continued, "Was it Sean did this to you? Is he the father of your baby?"

"Baby," she is thinking. "Baby! That is what it is. My baby. Not Maggie Dan's baby. I was a baby. I remember that. I know they took my daddy away when I was a baby. Do they want to take my baby from me? My baby is crying in me. I hear the tune of it. It's sad. They want to own my baby but it isn't theirs. It's not Sean's, it's not Johnny's, it's not mammy's, it's not this priest's. It's mine. It's staying inside me! Oh, the tune is so strange in me. Will they not stop their looking at me? What are they talking about?"

"Do you hear me Annie? Do you understand? Nod your head like this if it's Sean's baby."
No response.
Silence and a statuesque stare into nothingness. Annie looked away from him and held her stomach more tightly. Then, after a bit, she got up, ungainly, accidentally kicking the table leg with her foot. She pushed back the chair with the backs of her legs and walked slowly towards her bedroom.

As she went Johnny stirred off the bed to follow her, annoyance in his movement and his voice.

"Annie, come back here and tell them. Nod your head the way you did before. Sean did this to you, didn't he? Annie?"

The others watched as she opened the door and went inside the small room. Johnny stopped at the door in exasperation and then turned.

"She did nod the last time," he insisted. "We both saw her. She said it was Sean's child, I don't care what you say. It's a sad look out when I have to come home from the Lagan to find that somebody who was supposed to be my friend has been messing with my sister behind my back when I was away. Could hardly wait until my back was turned to be at her, like a dog with a bitch. Father, don't let him sweet-talk you. He has to marry her. There's no other way out of this. And if he refuses, I swear to God I will swing for him."

"Johnny," said Sean, "I will swear also. I will swear that I did not do this. It has nothing to do with you being away and not being here to protect her. I would have protected her too, with my life. Always have done."

The priest spoke again. "I am more confused by this whole thing than I ever remember being about anything, in my whole experience. Maggie Dan, Johnny, if Sean is swearing on his mother's life that it wasn't him, are we not bound to give him the benefit of the doubt?"

"The benefit of the doubt, is it?" roared Johnny. "Alright, if it wasn't him, let him answer this. Who does he blame? Who was it then Sean, if you have always been her protector? You were with her all the time, near enough, weren't you? So who else was around her? Who did you ever see her with, or even hear of her being with? Answer me that, if she was never out of your sight.'

Sean shook his head. "I can't think of anybody who even looked near her," he confessed.

"See what I mean? There stands the guilty man, if ever I saw one!" said Johnny, and with that he opened the cottage door and was gone.

Maggie Dan broke the short silence. "Sean Ban has always been very good to her, always looked after her. He even took me over to see my mother and to bring Annie back from Cloughglas," she said. And then she and Sean Ban looked at each other as a different suspicion entered both their heads, and neither could bring themselves to voice the notion that something had happened to the unfortunate girl when she was away from home for the summer, away from the influence of both of them. Sean's head went down into his hands where he sat. Maggie Dan began to cry softly. The priest said, "Holy Mary, Mother of God, Pray for us sinners now and at the hour of our death."

Chapter 34

Decisions in the Night

It was two nights later that the matter became a life-changing crisis for Sean Ban.

Over the twenty four hours since his difficult visit to O'Donnell's cottage and his altercation with Johnny he had tried to keep a low profile, staying around his own place and avoiding any chance meeting with his former friend. His mind had been on little else, so engaged was he by thoughts of Annie and her heart-wrenching situation. There had been some further chat with his mother about the matter after he had been to Maggie Dan's, and then with both his parents when they returned from an evening visit to see the stricken old neighbour. Johnny had not been present during the latter visit; presumably he was down in the village again. As a result, the conversation had been sorrowful but supportive and completely neighbourly. Annie had sat with them, in her own little world as usual. Maggie Dan and Brid had cried together, the first time they had done so since Bartley's drowning all those years ago. Frank had sat quiet most of the time, obviously in some physical discomfort, but he had assured the older woman of the Sweeney's sympathy and assistance. "Anything we can do, just ask," he had said. Brid told Sean that at one point Maggie Dan had said something along the lines that she found herself wishing that Sean himself actually was the father. "He would make a great daddy for the child," she had cried to Brid. "Would he not just.....could he not just say that it's his baby? That way, he would marry Annie and everything would be alright."

As Brid told this detail to Sean, he got the feeling that his mother was gently making the same case to her son.

"Would it be such a bad thing if you did?" she had asked him. His response had been that he didn't feel cut out to be a sacrificial lamb at this point in his life.

"No doubt," he had said, "it would please Father Dunleavey; it would help poor old Maggie Dan and Johnny; the folk around here would think I had done the right thing; and, of-course, Annie would have a father for her child. But what about me? What about the life I might want to live?"

"What sort of a life is that son?" she had asked. "What plans do you have that you've been keeping to yourself? Are you not intending to marry and live out the rest of your days around Ranahuel, the way your father and I have done? What would be so wrong with that? It's not as if you have ever wanted to go anywhere else to work, like your brother and your sister did. We don't want to be losing you to some foreign place, as well as them."

"I don't know, mother."

Sean's reply had been full of uncertainty, but equally brimming with resentment at the notion that there was something of a preordained path which he was meant to follow. Again he felt the pressure to fulfil an implicit set of parental expectations.

"But surely you can see that if I was to marry Annie all the other possibilities would be closed down to me straight away. This baby thing makes that all the more obvious. She would need my constant attention. Look, I like Annie....everybody knows that. But it's not that kind of liking. I told Father Dunleavey that already. You can't make a man do something that goes completely against his very instincts, against his rights, just to make everything alright for the community. Or to make everything seem alright for his blessed church."

"What about for Annie, though? Somebody needs to make this alright for her, don't you think?" his mother pushed further.

"For Annie?" He had stood back against the dresser, rattling the rows of kitchen crockery, head down in deep thought for a minute. "I can't do it, even for Annie," he had confessed and had left the house to walk up over the mountain, just to clear his head.

The walk hadn't done the trick though. His conscience churned at the options before him. The fresh air did nothing but sharpen the issues even more intensely. And a further unusual little incident had occurred which annoyed him deeply.

He had wandered aimlessly along the mucky bog roddens until he eventually arrived back on the main lane from Ranahuel to Kerrytown. He had turned towards home along the narrow, twisting path and had noticed a horse and cart coming in his direction. As it came gradually closer he saw that it was that of Seamus O'Donnell, a local small-holding farmer that he knew well. He stood to the side among the heathers and waited for the cart to stop by him, as would have been customary....any

chance meeting like this normally involved a ten or fifteen minute neighbourly chat about whatever was current news in the parish. The horse, however, showed no sign of slowing up. Sean had lifted his head in greeting to the occupant of the cart as it lumbered past him but Seamus had averted his eyes to look in the other direction. Thinking that his neighbour had perhaps not actually seen him he called after the receding vehicle.
"Hello Seamus! Did you not notice me there?"
The other man had ignored him at first but further along the lane had turned and shouted back, none too pleasantly, "I will notice you again when you do the right thing by Annie."
Sean was stunned. He had stood on the bank for a while, looking after the cart, initially wondering if he had heard O'Donnell correctly. The impact of the comments beat around in his consciousness and continued to depress him all evening. As with the previous night, it had been almost impossible to get over to sleep. Sean had tossed around on his lumpy straw mattress through the small hours, unable to dispel the slowly dawning certainty that life for him in this community had changed for ever.
Not alone had he lost the fellow that had been his best friend through childhood and their juvenile years. He worried that Johnny was himself on a path that would alienate him from the normal healthy relationships that most folk enjoyed around here. His devotion to alcohol was already souring his interaction with family and neighbours....and this was early days in what he feared might well become a life-time addiction.
Sean felt that the last grains of the innocence of adolescence were slipping through his fingers like the fine, white sand of Mullaghdearg strand. And how deeply he resented it.
Above all, Sean Ban resented the rising tide of circumstance which seemed determined to overwhelm him; "This is like social drowning," he thought as he lay staring into the darkness. It came down to a very stark choice.
He could, on the one hand, volunteer to marry Annie to save her from her shame and so confirm what most people in the parish already believed, that he was the guilty man who had put Annie in this lamentable condition; in doing so he would be sacrificing all of his rights and his secret, if unformulated, ambitions.

On the other hand he could basically sit it out; refuse all the pressure from family and church and community and try to maintain his innocence and his freedom; except that, after the earlier incident with Seamus O'Donnell, he had begun to realise that this was not going to be as simple nor as painless as he had imagined. There would be ongoing speculation and pressure; if Seamus' attitude was anything to go by, he could envisage a regime of alienation whereby he would be ostracised throughout his own neighbourhood. How would he be able to survive in Ranahuel and the wider area in the face of this perpetual suspicion, he wondered.

Either way he was trapped. There were no answers in the gloom of the kitchen, no solutions in the soughing of the wind through the gaps in the door and the ill-fitting windowpanes.

He began to re-evaluate his attitude to Annie herself. Did he still feel the same way about her as he had before this revelation? Had the events of the past couple of days affected his inner, secret obsession with the girl? Was there any hint in his subconsciousness that Annie was now damaged goods and that, as such, had ceased to hold the same fascination for him as she had done when she was in her virgin state?

In his memory, he retraced the steps of the last few months; he went back to that day when he had gone out along the sand hills of Cloughglas to find her, to bring her back to her granny's and then on home with Maggie Dan. That had been a day of deep realisation for him. He had seen Annie in a different light that day. He remembered how he had been struck and smitten as he never had been before by her physicality; the shape of her in that dress, wherever she had found it in her grandmother's cottage, as the wind blew the flimsy material back on her, accentuating her figure; the movement of her hips as she had walked ahead of him up the slope towards the lane; the way her hair was caught by the breeze, blown back from the lines of her face, speaking to him of freedom and desire and sensuality. And he realised that he was not immune from the temptations to which she herself had yielded; the temptations which had also, he presumed, overcome whatever local fellow she had become friendly with during the summer months along that tainted seashore. He wondered would it ever come to light who that fellow was. What possibility of success was there, he wondered, that if he went to Cloughglas and spent time among the local fellows he could uncover the identity of the person who had fallen for Annie's charms. How would he go about it? You couldn't very well go up to any of the men of the area and pose such a delicate question. "Excuse me, but I was wondering if you have ever been intimate with a girl who couldn't speak?" It didn't sound like a good plan, he thought, but there might be a way of finding out.

How would Father Dunleavey react if Sean were to ask him to make inquiries of the parish priest over in that locality if there had been any men making confessions about this sort of thing? He suspected that he would be reminded in no uncertain terms about the secrecy of the confessional.

"But," he reasoned, "I wouldn't be wanting details of the thing, not even the name of any suspects; just confirmation that someone over there had fallen into such a sin with a young, unknown girl. I could try him with that suggestion."

It was a long shot but he could think of little else to try. To ask any questions of Annie's ancient grandmother, particularly in her state of health, would hardly be productive. Annie was out along the bays and beaches on her own; the granny would have had no idea of who she had been with, he considered. And he knew of nobody else in that neighbourhood who might be able to help.

With the helplessness of these troubled thoughts depressing his mind, Sean eventually began to succumb to sleep. But, as he did, he was aware of a vague realisation swimming around somewhere in his deep, suppressed consciousness, the unquestionable truth that, above anything else in the world, he, Sean Ban Sweeney wished that he had been Annie's lover and the father of her unborn infant. How he would love to have her with him now, here by his bed, simply to tell her that.

"And yet," he realised guiltily, "I haven't spoken a word to her in so many days."

~~~~~~~

The following evening Sean did not even make it to bed. And, as things turned out, that was something for which he would be forever grateful.

The course of the day had been a relatively normal one, the usual round of tending to the small number of livestock which he kept and which were still in winter housing around the farmyard. He cleaned out the byre and threw hay to the three heifers; the pig needed moving to a new pen further along the yard so her bedding could be changed; he swept up around the midden and cleared a drain at the bottom of the yard that had become blocked, creating a pool of dirty brown water there after the earlier rain. Again, as yesterday, he had tended to stay close to home; he had had no further contact with Johnny O'Donnell. There had been no more conversation with his mother either. And Annie had not made any appearance along his lane as she often did in past, more innocent times.

By nightfall Sean and his parents gathered as usual at the kitchen table and ate their simple meal together. Not a lot was said, conversation having tended to dry up quickly since the revelations of two days ago. What could be said about it had been said; there was little more to say, and saying anything didn't seem to help much. All three were content to hold their conversations internally.

The silences did not help the atmosphere of tension in the house, a tension which Sean felt in his bones to be bordering on dread. He couldn't put a finger on why but he did have a sense of foreboding. Was it because there had been no further word from Johnny? Not a sign of him anywhere, not a sound of his anger, not a clue as to his intention. Had he somehow come to understand that Sean was not to blame for Annie's baby, that he had been accusing an innocent man in the matter? Sean doubted this, given Johnny's obsessive tendencies. More likely, he suspected, Johnny has taken his sorrows to Sullivan's and tried to dull the shame of it all in his recently adopted habit. He was sorry about that, if it was the case, but he did not think he was the person to try to do anything about it.

The evening dragged on towards bedtime. The oil lamp spluttered and hissed above the kitchen table and the flame of the candle high on the mantlepiece wavered unsteadily, giving variable amounts of light to the room. Brid tried to sew in the half-light and sighed as the lamp faltered. Frank had gone stiffly to his bed after the supper with barely a 'Goodnight'. Sean sat forward on the low chair by the hearth, aimlessly prodding bits of half-burned turf around in the last embers of the fire. Not a word had been spoken in the kitchen for most of an hour.

"You're only hurting your eyes, trying to do that in this light," he chastised his mother. "Would you not be better going to bed and letting me get to my bed too?"

"I'm not stopping you going to bed. Let me finish this hem and then I'll go," she mumbled, head down to her exacting task.

Sean stood up and stretched and, as he did, something caught his eye at the window, a flicker of light of some kind. He moved closer to the pane in curiosity, squinting out through the uneven glass to try to see the source of this glimmer.

"There's somebody out there, mother," he said, just a hint of apprehension in his tone.

"Out where? Who's out there?" she asked, not looking up.

"Whoever it is, they have some sort of flaming torch in their hand," he said. "All I can see is a...."

The sound of breaking glass! A fist-sized stone crashing through the window that Sean was looking through. Splinters of glass flying at his face. The stone missed him and bounced across the floor. He recoiled from the window, his hand going to his face where something had embedded itself. A shard of thick glass hanging out of the skin of his cheek from just below his right eye. The shock of it made him instantly nauseous. He wretched, leaning back against the shelter of the wall beside the shattered window.

His mother came to him, white shock fixed in her normally placid features, eyes wide open in terror. His father's voice from the bedroom.

"What are you doing? What was that noise?"

"Come quick Frank!" she shouted. "Somebody is outside. Sean's hurt!"

She tended to her son, the garment she had been working at still in her hand. "I'm going to pull this glass out. You hold this to your cheek to stop the blood," she said and a splinter the size of a half crown came out in her hand. He felt blood trickle down his face and drip to the floor even before he had the garment against the wound. The feel of it roused an anger in him. The anger took over from the nausea. He heard Frank struggle from the bedroom. He saw his father's thin little body and his pale, worried face appear in the doorway. For the first time in his life he saw his father as an old man, gaunt and bony as a famine victim, translucent like a pencil drawing. He sidled along the wall to the cottage door; his hand to the latch; he stood listening at the door as his father watched, the older man trying to make sense of what was before his eyes. There wasn't a sound from outside.

"What in God's name has happened? What ails you son?"

Sean took down a stout cattle stick which hung behind the door.

"There's somebody outside," he said. "They threw a stone through the window. It didn't hit me. I'm alright. I'm going out to them, whoever it is."

"Are you sure you should son?" And, as Sean ignored him, "Be careful, for God's sake."

Sean discarded the garment. The blood flowed and dropped from his chin. He opened the door slowly. There was a half-moon in the sky to the south but it was having to contend with a bank of cloud and coincidently disappeared as he stood there in the doorway. He stepped out into the darkened yard, fear and bravado churning together in him. The stick was out in front of him like a bayonet. He was ready to use it, to whack whoever was out there, whoever threw the stone. He was ready for action, his body tensed like a wire coil, the cudgel beating firmly into the palm of his free hand. His eyes scanned the street.

There was something of a flickering gleam of light being cast across the cobblestone from around the corner of the house. Somebody was there at the gable-end, where the peat-stack was. The dry turf, stored there, ready to burn in Sweeney's hearth. Someone with a blazing torch was by the turf.

Sean stepped further out into the yard.

"Who is there?" he shouted. "Show your self?"

The track of light cast by the torch shifted and Johnny O'Donnell stepped from behind the corner. In his hand he held a flaming bundle of tightly-tied and well-dried sticks, about three feet in length. By the vigour of its blaze, Sean judged that it had probably been doused in lamp-oil. Before he could take a step forward, O'Donnell, in a slow, deliberate action, raised his torch above his head towards the overhang of thatch which protruded at the corner of the homestead. The flames leapt up hungrily towards the dry straw. The Sweeney cottage which had stood there for over a hundred years was seconds away, inches away, from being consumed in a fiery inferno.

"Stop Johnny! Don't do it!" screamed Sean. Immediate realisation of Johnny's cruel intention. Instant appreciation of his family's vulnerability. He stepped back towards the door, towards his mother. He dropped his stick. Brid dropped to her knees, partly in panic, partly in supplication. Frank stood shivering in his night garment, his grey face frozen in dread and he spluttered half-formed words which made no sense and little impact on the insolent indifference on Johnny O'Donnell's countenance. Johnny who still hadn't spoken a word. Johnny who was enjoying this new and sudden feeling of authority. Johnny who was surprised at his own audacity. Johnny who was marvelling at the sudden surge of power he possessed, a new experience for him.

He moved the torch up and down towards the thatch as if to emphasise this power. He watched their faces, careless of how close the naked flame was to the fraying strands of straw, enjoying the differing degrees of tension which he could see rising and falling in their expressions. He didn't need to speak. He was in total control here. Total control, for the first time in his life. He recalled having had the idea of arson back in Magilligan, as a way of getting back at the Millars; he had chickened out, but now he almost wished he had torched one of their corn-stacks. It would have been worth it just to see their faces.

"Johnny, don't do this! You are our neighbour! You are my friend! I will do whatever you want me to....just put that flame down will you," pleaded Sean. He would go on his knees too, like his poor, terrified mother, if only it would save their home.

"Please Johnny," came Brid's voice. "Please think of Maggie Dan and how she's going to feel about this if you set the house on fire."

Johnny grinned back inanely, drunkenly, anarchically. The light breeze changed momentarily and blew the smoke of his torch towards his own face. He coughed some and spat against the wall, the taste of stale stout in the spittle, some of which dribbled down his stubbly chin.

"What do you want of us, Johnny?" croaked Frank. "Just tell us what you want. Whatever it is, we'll try and do it for you son."

Johnny lowered the flame a bit, as much because his arms were getting sore holding the thing up at that angle; he started talking for the first time.

"You know what I want. I want that bastard of a son of yours to admit that he he interfered with our Annie. That's simple enough, isn't it?"

The Sweeney's looked at each other; Sean turned his back on Johnny briefly and whispered, "Keep him talking. The torch will go out in a while. Keep him talking."

Frank realised the wisdom of his son's advice. He took a step towards the aggressor.

"Aye, that seems simple enough Johnny. If you put that torch down now, we can go inside and have a chat about it. Will you do that son? What do you say? We'll have a cup of tea and a bit of a chat."

"I say this. I say if you don't stand back and shut your mouth, this here is going up on top of your roof." And he made as if to throw the torch unto the sloping roof. "You are a great oul talker, Frank, but you wont be able to talk your way out of this. You'll just have to try and talk a new roof over your head, so you will. A cup of tea and a chat, you oul fool. This isn't about you. This is about me and Sean Ban. Is he listening to me? What are you going to do Sean?"

"I'm not going to do anything for it wasn't me, Johnny," replied Sean firmly. "Don't do it, Johnny!" he screamed as the torch was raised again to the thatch in quick response to his denial.

"What did you say? You didn't do it? We'll see about that, you bastard!" yelled Johnny.

The flame licked around the wall just below the overhang. A couple of sparks were dislodged from the fire and floated upwards to the straw and the three Sweeneys watched in horror as they landed. But the dampness on the outer surface of the old thatch roof was such that they failed to ignite and almost at once lost their glow. Frank spoke quietly and urgently to Sean.

He said, "You don't argue with somebody who has a torch to your roof son. Just agree to everything he asks for. Go along with whatever he wants. It's our only chance of saving the house. Don't antagonise him."

"You did it, Sean Ban. You did it and the whole place knows you did it. There won't be a person round here that'll ever speak to you again if you don't own up to it. You're nothing but a cheatin', lyin' coward and you know it. Everybody knows it! You try showing your face in Sullivan's again and see what you get.

Not a soul will speak to you. They all know now, the whole place."

"Go on, keep talking," whispered Sean through his teeth, watching the flame as it began to die down. Johnny hadn't seemed to be aware that he only had a minute or two left before it burned out just above where he was holding it, but, drunk and all as he was, he followed Sean's eyes and he looked at the flame himself.

"Don't you be worrying about this here torch, Sean. I'm in charge here and before you get any idea of rushing me just watch this," he laughed. And with that he stooped to behind the corner again and lifted another similar bundle, even larger, if anything, than the first, certainly not so well tied together. In a split second he had lit this new torch from the dying flame of the old one, its sticks blazing up instantly.

"This one should do the trick," he said and held it up to the thatch.

"Jesus, don't do it," breathed Sean, stiff with horror.

"Now Sean," he said with a deeply chilly threat in his tone, "you have one more chance. I am going to count to ten. You are going to agree to marry my sister. Your mother and father are witnesses. You are going to keep your word. And when I get to ten, if you haven't said 'Yes, I will marry Annie', this here is going up into this dry thatch. That is how it is going to be. Do you understand me?"

"You can't do this, Johnny. You'll finish up in court, so you will. Think of your mother," argued Sean in anguish.

"You think of your mother, Sean. I may finish up in court but at least I will have a roof over my head. Your mother won't! Do you understand me? Yes or no? It's your choice." Johnny's voice had an evil edge to it that Sean found perverse and utterly chilling. There would be no reasoning with it, he thought.

"I understand," he whispered.

"One. Two. Three. Four. Five. Six. Seven. Eight....."

"Alright! Alright!" screamed Sean, sinking to his knees by Brid. "I will marry her."

The torch stayed where it was, the flame a mere foot from the thatch. "Frank, Brid. Did you hear that? What did he say?"

Brid spoke tremulously. "I heard him. He said he would marry Annie."

"Frank?"

"I heard him too Johnny," replied Frank. "I heard him say he would marry Annie."

"And you'll hold him to it? You'll not let him try and squirm his way out of it?"

"We'll hold him to it," whispered Frank, his body visibly wilting in the flickering light cast by the torch, now lowered to shoulder height.

"Let me here you again, Sean," came Johnny's taunt. "I want to hear you admit it. What did you say?"

"I said I would marry Annie."

"Do I have that on your oath? Swear it on your mother's death, Sean."

Sean Ban looked long at his mother; he took a deep breath.

"I swear it on my mother's death. Now go away Johnny and let us get to sleep. My father isn't well. You got what you came for. Now just go!"

The defeat in his voice was painful to his father's ears.

"Aye, away you go, Johnny," he said soothingly. "It'll all work out for the best, I'm sure. Go on home and get a good night's rest."

"Ah, there's time enough," he said, sarcasm now replacing the terror in his tone. "How about that wee cup o' tea now Frank? The heat of this thing is making me thirsty."

Frank looked at Brid uncertainly. Sean stepped forward.

"Go on home with you, Johnny," he said firmly. "My mother's making no more tea tonight. Your mother will make you a cup if you need it. You've done enough here for one night, do you not think? Go on and let us get to bed."

Johnny leered back drunkenly at him.

"I wouldn't drink your rotten tea anyway," he laughed. "Tastes like Frank's piss."

He turned on his heel with an element of triumphal arrogance in his movement. Showily he held the flaming torch aloft and waved it from side to side, like a Roman warrior in victorious procession, and then began a somewhat meandering march out along the path towards his own home. As he neared the main lane he turned and shouted, "Don't you forget now. Go and see the priest tomorrow. Get this wedding done quick, before you change your mind. I don't want to be having to come back up here with another torch for yous!" And he disappeared down the hill leaving the shattered family looking after him.

~~~~~~~

Sean spent the next day in a state of turmoil and nervous exhaustion. His face hurt, but at least the blood had more or less stopped oozing from the cut overnight. His mother had insisted on washing the wound with lukewarm salt-water and pouring some honey over it. She had then taken the lamp and gone out to the barn to collect as much cobweb as she could and smeared that over the wound as a primitive, binding film to speed the healing process; she had seen her own mother do this many years ago. He would have a scar of about an inch long underneath his right eye but, although it was a deep wound, he realised that he had had a fortunate escape....an eye could easily have been lost had the glass hit him just a fraction higher.

The realisation did little for his mood, however, and he found himself disorientated and unsettled. He sat by the hearth when he would normally have been working. He rose and paced about on the floor until his father turned from the broken quarter-pane of glass which he was replacing with a thin piece of wood and said, "Either sit down or go outside and wear out the yard."

He went outside and sat listlessly on an upturned barrel at the far end of the house, breaking twigs off a long-dead branch of mountain ash. He walked up into the bog again, although this time he avoided returning by the lane, just in case he should run into Seamus or any like-minded neighbours. When, in the slow breakfast hour, his mother had asked him what time he was planning to go down to see Father Dunleavey he had baulked at the idea entirely.

"I don't want to be going down there," he had said.

Brid had been perceptive about his sensitivities and had volunteered to go down herself and ask the priest to come up to talk to Sean; "to make arrangements for this wedding," as she had put it. And indeed she had done so, but only after she had hand-washed the blood out of Sean's clothes and hung them by the hearth to dry.

At the meal table later on, Frank had broken the silence to enquire of him how he felt about the events of the previous night. Sean found the question well nigh impossible to answer. The trauma of the whole thing. The threat to the house, to the whole family. Initially he had tried to answer his father in as glib a manner as possible, so as to not give the older man further cause for worry. He knew he had made a sensible decision in making the promise he did, given the menacing circumstances at the time. Indeed, when they had re-entered the house last night, after Johnny's departure, there had been a period of almost unprecedented physical closeness as first his mother and then Frank himself had hugged him emotionally and thanked him for the way he had handled the situation. While Brid had cried quietly and Sean himself shook with the delayed shock of it all, Frank had put his arms awkwardly around both of them and consoled them.

"Thanks be to God that ended the way it did! You made a difficult decision, son," his father had said, "but it was the right one and we are proud of you for it. You saved the home and we will always be grateful. It could have been a disaster for us all, including Johnny himself. He would have finished up in Letterkenny gaol."

"Should we not be reporting him to the police....or to somebody? Should we not be telling Father Dunleavey about this? Would you not go over and tell the RIC sergeant in Kincasslagh?" Sean had asked his father. "He's becoming a danger to the whole neighbourhood."

Frank's reply had been as immediate as it was firm. "And if we go to the police they'll arrest him and he'll be in a cell for a while until there's a trial....if it ever went to trial. Maggie Dan doesn't need that on top of everything else. And what happens when he gets out of the cell? He will come straight back here and the next time it won't stop at threats. He will burn us out of house and home."

"But should we not tell the priest?" Sean had persisted.

His father had thought about this for a bit and shook his head. "Telling him would have the same effect. Maggie Dan would have to be told. Johnny would be madder than ever. I am starting to think that fellow's head is away with it altogether; he's capable of anything. He might not even stop at burning us out."

"So we just have to pretend that last night never happened? How are we going to explain my face? What about the broken window?"

"Aye that's a problem alright. We'll just have to say that somebody put a stone through it, which isn't a lie. But we don't know who it was. That's all I can think of at the minute son."

Brid returned from her trip to the Parochial House out of breath from her exertion but tight-lipped about the conversation. When Sean enquired what happened she simply responded that Father Dunleavey would be here soon. She avoided Sean's eyes and tried, without much success, to camouflage the sadness she had about her by burying herself in housework, brushing the floor and dusting the dresser and the mantlepiece. He left her to her silent fussing and returned to the lonely peace of the outdoors.

From the bottom of the yard he watched the arrival of the priest; imposing and yet comical, Sean thought, with that strangely-shaped hat perched on his head. As he dismounted he called from a distance to Sean Ban to get a bucket of water for the animal. Sean did so as the cleric entered the cottage.

Ten minutes later he stood and observed the slow procession of Maggie Dan and Annie who were making their way up along the lane. They turned in towards him. Maggie Dan shuffling, her head down in concentration or in shame...he could not decide which. Annie plodding and meandering carelessly back and forwards across the lane, apparently oblivious to the ramifications of their current mission. Gone the seductive gait she had had when he saw her in Cloughglas, he observed. More of a sad waddle now. There was a weightiness about her bearing, a fullness around her face, that he hadn't detected before. Why hadn't he noticed it in the previous weeks, he was asking himself. Looking at her now, the old dress tight to her stomach, he could tell fairly easily that the girl was pregnant.

"Surely," he thought, "I should have seen this before now? Why on earth did I not notice? She must be more than half way, God love her. Why, why did she have to leave me and go to Cloughglas last summer? That's where it all went wrong."

The two women failed to see him at the end of the yard and entered the Sweeney cottage to join the priest and his parents. He stood pensively between the mule and the byre. And, for the first time he thought he could see the only possible solution to the crisis that he found himself in. But he walked slowly to the door.

The priest was holding court. Not that he expected anything different. He occupied the centre of the kitchen, standing with his back to the heat of the hearth and absorbing most of its warmth.

"No change there either," thought Sean.

"Come in Sean" invited the priest. "Come in and sit beside your bride-to- be. Annie make a space on that seat for Sean." Then, noticing the fresh cut on his cheek, "What on earth happened your face? That's a bad looking cut."

Sean's eyes flicked to the window and then to his father. His glance took in the fact that his mother had hidden the damage to the quarter pane behind an old black pot which usually sat by the hearth. Incongruous as it looked, it was doing its job and helping to keep up the appearance of normality. His father's eyes met his and gave an almost imperceptible nod of the head. Sean mumbled an answer to the priest's question.

"It's just a scratch. I wasn't watching where I was going and walked into a sharp branch of a tree up on the mountain." And he sidled across the floor to sit beside 'his bride-to-be' on the settle-bed.

She sits still. This is Sean's own bed she is sitting on. Where he will lie tonight. She looks up at him and she would smile if she could. If the impediments in her brain would allow her face to express what she is inside. Inside the dullness of this entrapment. She stares long at the redness of the gash below his eye and the smile in her head turns slowly to concern.

'He is hurt! He has blood on him! What happened to his face?' But her emotional demeanour does not change. The same passive look in her eyes. That same blank face. She hears the low sounds of the priest's words. Low and rumbling, without any joy in their pitch, heavy in their tone like the drone of a badly tuned set of uilleann pipes.

She likes it that Sean has sat down with her. She likes it that his strong legs are against hers, pressing against her thigh, as he squeezes onto the bench beside her, into the narrowness of the space, because she had not moved along to give him room.

She does not like the tune of the priest's voice. The monotony of it; the beat of his consonants fighting against the drawling vowels. The toneless cant of this crow of a man. And she wishes she could hear Sean speaking. It wouldn't matter what he would say...just any old thing, just to hear the sound of him again. She hasn't heard the sound of him for a long time. She likes his sound, she realises. And she misses it. And how it used to be before..... before the soft tune of the baby in her. She hears the tired voice of her mother. There's a hot cup of tea being pushed into her hand. It's too hot but she holds it in both hands and the pain is spread around. Sean has it now, putting sweet milk into it for her. And sugar. She drinks now. The sweetness of it a joy to her taste. The muscles of his thigh against her. The rawness of the bright, blood-red cut running up to his eye. Two sides to it. Like a mouth, a small mouth put on his face in the wrong place, at the wrong angle.

But the purple mouth on the priest's face was still working, chewing its way through some sort of over-cooked steak of a sermon, dripping with chastisement, eyes focused mainly on Sean, sometimes on her.

Why is he looking at me like this? Why is he still talking?

~~~~~~~

When they all left, and the house returned to its own honesty, Sean Ban seemed to awaken in his mind from the self-induced coma he had been in during the discussion. He had said very little, just a grunt here and there, generally by way of approval of whatever someone was suggesting. Now he could barely recall the details of the arrangements; he smiled inwardly at the absurdity of it all; his wedding, and he was finding it difficult to remember the plans that these good folk had made for it. In some strange way he felt that he had entered Annie's world of silent isolation, a kind of bubble where people talked around you, about you, for you, at you. Never really to you. And yet a world where, despite its intense relevance to you, there is no sense of you having a say in it, of having control over it. The world of the fly in the spider's web.

The torpor of mind he had allowed himself to be overcome by was partly real and partly a mask. Real in the sense that he was in denial; he was not assenting to the whole idea of a shot-gun wedding, never mind the details of it. The date of it, in four weeks time, some date towards the end of March, was as irrelevant to him as any imaginary date between now and eternity. 'The reading of the banns', which the priest had mentioned but had quickly glossed over as 'something that has to be done at Mass for the next three weeks', struck him as an ironic feature of the whole thing. He wondered if, in the history of marriages in the Catholic Church, there had ever been a situation where the bridegroom had spoken up against his own bride, against his own nuptials.

"Yes Father Dunleavey, I do have an objection to marrying this woman. There is just cause and impediment to this marriage. You see, Father, she is pregnant and the baby is the bastard of some other bastard, not me at all. And more than that, Father Dunleavey, I am only marrying this woman because, if I don't, her brother will burn us out of house and home. How's that for an objection, your reverence?"

That would go down well in the annals of Annagry chapel.

But you couldn't do it!

You wouldn't do it to Annie. You wouldn't do it to Maggie Dan. You wouldn't do it to Frank and Brid.

Would you?

The clergyman had talked to him quietly when Sean was helping him unto his unwilling mount.

"What made you change your mind Sean? Your mother wouldn't tell me earlier." This with one of his head-tilted, eyes-narrowed, kind of stare, the penetrative kind more usually employed in the confessional.

As he tried to think of an appropriate answer, Sean had realised that, while he was still wearing a sullen mask of resignation, even of downright recalcitrance, he was actually smiling inwardly. He had mumbled something about 'things changing,' but Dunleavey wasn't satisfied.

"You know that you have to come to confession and tell me the whole truth, don't you? You haven't been in a while, whatever is wrong with you. And it's not just the truth about what you did with Annie. You have tell me what possessed you to make this all so hard for Maggie Dan and everybody. Why did you keep up the pretence so long? Why did you lie in the first place? Could you not have confessed to the thing and got it over with, instead of this whole charade?"

The man of the dark cloth was darkly angry as he stared down the length of his nose from the height of the saddle on Saint Vincent's sagging back at this confused, shabby, young sinner. Sean ignored the look and the questions. He slapped the animal hard on its rump and it almost unseated its rider as it sprang forward unexpectedly.

And Sean thought to himself, "Little do you know, you old fool! You may think you are high and mighty, your reverence, but I am above you at the minute. You believe a lie because it suits you but I am living the truth. Or at least I will be tonight. I am taking the moral high road this night."

Before they went to bed his parents tried to raise the subject of the wedding with him a couple of times. To no avail. Sean had closed down all communication about the matter. Apart from a few indistinct, monosyllabic sounds he did not stir himself from the reverie into which he had fallen. He was miles away. Planning. But as they rose after supper and gave signs of retiring for the night, Sean did something uncharacteristic. He went to each parent in turn and gave them a quick hug, not an emotional one, just a sort of appreciative hug. They interpreted it as such, as an affirmative gesture regarding the decisions of the day, an assent to the wedding process which had now begun. He even responded to their muttered, 'Goodnights'.

But an hour after they had left him he listened by their door and judged, by the pattern of snoring from them, that both were fast asleep. He moved to the mantlepiece and, lighting the candle there, began to rummage along its length to find a number of items. One was a round tin which had once contained boiled barley sugar sweets. From this tin he took three pound notes and a ten shilling note and stuffed them in his trouser pocket. Another item he brought down was a pencil. Yet another was a sheet of blank paper. Finally there was a bundle of letters tied up with a length of wool. Having found what he was looking for in the pile of correspondence, he tore the blank page in half and on one piece copied an address from his sister's last letter. He folded this and put it in his pocket. Then he sat down at the kitchen table and wrote on the other half.

Father, Mother,
I am sorry to do this to you. You have always been good parents to me and I love you dearly. You have always told me to be true to myself. Tonight I am trying to follow that advice. I cannot marry Annie, you will understand why. If I was doing it out of my own free choice that would be a different thing. But I am being blackmailed into it by the threat of Johnny's violence. I will not give in to that. If you say to me that I made a promise, I will say that I made that promise under duress. I believe that this leaves the promise as invalid. The oath was

made simply to save our home. But the home will be safe now, now that I am going away. If I stay and marry her I will always be laughed at around here. If I stay and don't marry her I will be thought of as an immoral and unreliable rascal who did the dirty thing and then failed to keep his promise. So there is only one thing to do. I must leave this place.

Please do not worry about me. You have taught me well enough to be able to take care of myself. I know not where I am going or what I will do. But when I get there I will write to you. I am sorry to be leaving you two to do the work around the place that was mine but maybe Johnny will help. It would perhaps give him something to do and keep him out of Sullivan's. I will try to earn money and send you as much as I can, but if there is any left over please give it to Maggie Dan for Annie and the baby.

Goodbye for now. You will see me again. Pray for me as I will for you.

Your son

Sean

PS. I have taken 3 pounds 10 shillings from the tin to help me on my way. Please forgive me for this. I will repay it as soon as I can.

He placed the letter on the table, propped against the milk jug and put the pencil in his pocket.

He took an old sheet off his bed, doubled it over and spread it on the floor. Then he gathered up whatever of his clothes he could find under the settle bed and placed these, along with the semi-dry clothes his mother had washed earlier, in the centre of the sheet. His decent shoes went on top of the small pile. He wrapped the whole thing up into a bundle and, taking a length of hemp rope from a drawer, tied it around the neck of the thing, so he could carry it with ease over his shoulder. He pulled on his well-worn coat and stuck his cloth cap on top of his head. Picking up the improvised bag he stood in front of the statue of The Blessed Virgin and Her Child. He looked her in those sadly intriguing eyes and prayed. "Hail Mary, full of grace. Blessed art thou among women and blessed is the fruit of thy womb, Jesus. Will you take care of my mother and father when I'm gone. And will you look to me now as I take the road to God knows where. In the name of the Father and of the Son and of the Holy Spirit, Amen". He blessed himself three times and bowed his head, eyes closed against the stinging of the first sign of tears. Then he tiptoed silently to the door, opened it so slowly that the creak of it blended with the sighing of the wind in the chimney and stepped out into the faint light of a low half-moon. Into an unknown and uncertain future.

Chapter 35

Flight

A semi-naked Jacob Stewart cupped his two hands in the trough of rain water outside the cottage door, lifted them dripping and threw the icily-cold liquid at his face. He rubbed his tightly-closed eyes, then behind and inside his ears and finally under his armpits before stretching around to the window-sill to find a towel. The vigour and joy of youth was on him and, at seventeen, he looked a fine figure of a fellow, his chest and stomach muscles ribbed and tensed against the chill of the morning air. Before his breakfast he intended to have the three milch cows milked as usual. He dried his face, gave his body a rough rub with the towel and pulled on his shirt and waistcoat. As he crossed the yard he whistled a tune through his teeth, struggled into his working coat and made his way to the barn.
The whistling continued as he squatted down on a three-legged stool, pail clasped securely between his knees and his forehead resting against the warm flank of the cow, in the hollow between haunch and stomach. He talked to the animal like she was a relation. His hands grasped the teats and began a firm chugging motion, the milk flow starting slowly but soon zinging musically against the bucket's metal side. He had finished milking the roan, which always liked to be first, and was halfway through milking the more difficult Kerry Blue when he began to have a vague feeling that he was not alone in the old stone-built outhouse, that he was being watched. His regular tugging action slowed down and he peered around suspiciously into the dark corners. Nothing there except a couple of geese which had followed him in, hoping for a treat morsel of spilled corn. He resumed his rhythmic action and the strones of fresh, sweet-smelling, creamy milk began again. Then, from a few feet above his head, he heard a hoarse whisper.
"Jacob, it's me, Sean Ban."
To his credit Jacob didn't utter the oath of surprise that entered his head but he did jump on his stool to such an extent that the bucket slipped from between his knees and jibbled half of its contents onto the floor before. Looking up he saw the dishevelled face of his friend peering over the side of the

hayloft which formed a low internal ceiling in this half of the building, covering the byre area above the cows.

"What on earth are you doing up there?"

Sean's finger went to his lips to hush the clamour of Jacob's voice. "Sssh Jacob. I don't want anybody else knowing that I'm here. Please."

"Alright," said the younger man looking out through the open barn door to see if his father or any of the other members of the family were nearby. "Wait, I'll pull this door closed." And he did. "What happened to your face Sean?" he asked. "Have you been fighting or what?"

"No, not fighting but I am in a bit of trouble all the same. That's why I came out here, in the middle of the night, last night," he explained. "I could think of nowhere else to go. I thought you were the best person to help me."

Jacob put his hand against the cow's shoulder as it became restless and impatient. "Steady girl," he said. "Help you how? What can I do for you? What has happened anyway? You look in a bit of a mess, if you don't mind me saying it."

"I know I do. And keep your voice down. I don't want your father or anybody else seeing me here. It has to be you, just you, Jacob. I couldn't trust anybody else. They would have to go and tell my father where I was and where I was going. Do you see what I mean?"

"Goodness Sean! Are you running away or what?" Jacob sounded as mystified as he looked. "You're leaving home without them knowing? Are you mad or what has come over you at all? What has happened at home? Sean, for goodness sake, you can't just be leaving like that."

"I left them a letter. They'll understand when they read it."

"But....why? What on earth has made you do this? Do they know you have come out here to us? They'll have the police on us, so they will."

"Keep your voice down Jacob. That's the reason it has to be you and you alone, do you see? Then nobody else can be blamed. If anybody asks your father or mother if they have seen me then they can say 'No' and they won't be lying."

"What if they ask me?" stuttered Jacob. "What'll I say?"

"Say you haven't seen a hair of me...because you haven't, yet. I still have this cap on." And he smiled down from his perch in the softness of the hay.

"Hide, Sean! There's my da coming."
Sean pulled back from the edge of the loft quickly as Robert John's heavy footsteps stopped outside; he pushed the door open and put his head around it.
"How are you on? Have you the other two done? Your mother is calling you to eat," he said.
"Aye, I'll be there in a minute. The cow kicked the bucket," he lied, indicating the spill of milk seeping into the straw and manure on the floor.
"I see that," said his father. "Not like her. Hurry in for we need to be saddling up."
Jacob resumed milking as his father departed leaving the door open behind him.
"Sean, can you hear me?" he whispered. "We are supposed to be going to Loughanure today for a load of hay. I am supposed to go but I'll see if I can get Bobby to take my place, maybe Richard as well. When I get them away I'll come back and hear your story and we can work out what to do. You sit tight up there and keep your head down till I come back, alright? I'll hurry through this one and the black one will not take me long; she's nearly dry."
"That'll do; and thanks," whispered Sean.
Jacob quickly completed his task and hurried off to his breakfast. Sean lay back in the hay and tried to suppress a cough as he inhaled the dustiness that rose around him, the tiny particles floating and dancing in a shaft of morning sunlight. This was a chance to put some definite structure on the vague idea of a plan he had been forming before he left home. His decision had been heart-wrenching but now that he had made the move and stepped over the proverbial cliff-edge he was impatient to be moving on. He wanted to put distance between himself and Ranahuel, distance in both the physical and the proverbial sense. He could allow himself no emotional retreat, no looking back. Indeed his escape had almost been derailed minutes after leaving his own home last night. On his moonlit trek down the lane past O'Donnell's he had yielded to the powerful temptation to be near her again, one last time. He had made the mistake of allowing himself to be drawn to Annie's window. There he had stood for a few seconds, the palm of his hand placed against the wavy surface of the glass. Then, in a moment of weakness which bordered on reversal, he had

knocked on the pane, gently with his knuckles. He rationalised this action; it wasn't so much contrition for his abandonment of her; it was more that this might be the last occasion for a very long time that he would see her face. The face of the girl whose enigmatic presence had haunted him for so long, the girl who had been, in so many senses, a shadow to him, albeit a darkened shadow in recent times. The untainted Eve to his innocent Adam. Until whatever serpent had poisoned her garden.

He had waited at the window, had almost given up, thinking that she was probably deeply asleep, and was turning to continue his flight. Suddenly the raggedy curtain moved beyond and her face appeared at the window, slightly distorted behind the variable thickness of the old glass.

She is peering into the gloom of the night. Whose is this silhouette outside, dark against the moon-bright sky? She recognises the shape of him but cannot see his features. The baby moves for him inside of her. It twists and kicks in an excitement she cannot replicate herself. If only he could see it. Feel it. She holds her stomach as if to say, "It's alright. He is here." She moves closer and presses her face to the glass. Cold on her forehead and her nose. She is looking for the cut on his face, her eyes searching for it against the shadow that is his face. She sees him lift his hand. He touches it to the window. His hand is caressing her cheek, she is thinking, except for the glass that is in the way. She sees him step back then, step back away from the window. His hand is still raised to her. And then she feels her mother come from behind her, now beside her at the window, pushing her aside, asking her who is there. She hears the dog start to bark down at the bottom of the yard. She watches him back away. She feels a tune of deep loss well up in her like a keening. A lament of a melody, in a minor key, is overwhelming her from within, like the crying of a baby. She sees him turn and walk away.

Sean Ban had totally forgotten that Maggie Dan was in the bedroom as well. It had not crossed his mind as a possibility that he would waken the mother. Her appearance beside Annie in the dull darkness of the bedroom had disconcerted him. So much so that he had almost panicked and had had to resist the urge to run. Worse still, their stupid old dog had started to bark. The last thing he wanted was another altercation with Johnny, so he had backed off as surreptitiously as he could, watching her face grow more and more dim at the window until he couldn't make out whether it was Annie or her mother he was seeing. Just the ghostly paleness of a face pressed to the glass, twisted by its unevenness, as if seen through the buckling skew of water.

When he had reached the sand-flats between the shore and Carrickfinn he discovered that he had miscalculated matters slightly. The tide had not, as he had anticipated, started to turn and was still very full in the bay. Although he found this frustrating, he had stood in awe of this beautiful panorama of dusky colours, ultramarine, purple, black and shimmering silver-grey in broad, undulating brushstrokes, swept aesthetically onto a huge, moonlit canvas. There was barely a sound other than the gentle gurgle of the waves as they lapped inquisitively around the rocks at his feet. He had been glad then that he had ample time; there were still four or five hours before the brightness of dawn would creep up behind the Derryveigh Mountains and, rather than get his boots and trousers soaked in risking the long wade out to the Point in the semi-darkness, he had found a sheltered rock to sit upon to wait.

Jacob's return from breakfast brought the additional blessing of a few pieces of soda bread, smuggled from his mother's kitchen table between shirt and jacket, somewhat misshapen as a result but none the worse in taste. Sean appreciated the gesture and this wholesome food, washed down with fresh milk, richly creamy and still warm, from the black cow beneath in its stall. The young Stewart waited patiently for him to finish.

"My father is away with Bobby and Richard on the cart. I told him I wanted to see if I could catch a few fish off the rocks," he explained. "The two boys jumped at the chance and he was happy enough to take them instead."

"That's great. So you have a few hours on your own then?" asked Sean. "What I am going to ask you to do for me is a bit risky and it will take you the most of the afternoon to do."

"I'll do it if I can. But what is it?"

"Can you row me over to Gola?"

"Row you to Gola? Why do you want to go to Gola?" Jacob's surprise reflected in his eyes, his voice.

Sean Ban finished his bread and milk in silence for a bit. He looked at his younger friend.

"I have to get out of the Rosses Jacob. I am planning to go to my sister in Scotland. There's a boat that calls in at Gola most weekends on its way to Glasgow. It ships a cargo of lobsters to the city and there's always somebody coming or going between Glasgow and Gweedore, from what I hear. I'll wait for it on the island somewhere. But I need you to keep it a secret for me. Would you do that?"

"But why? Why are you leaving?"

"I will tell you, but can it wait until we are in the curragh? I'll have plenty of time then; it'll shorten the journey. It's just that the sooner I get on my way, the less chance there is of your mother finding me, do you see? It's going to take you a couple of hours to row me over there, even with me rowing as well; and then you'll be on your own coming back. You'll not have much time for fishing; and you don't want to be caught in a running tide. The sooner we set off, the better the chances are of me getting there unseen and you getting a few fish, do you not think?"

"Fair enough. I'll get the oars. I'll bring a couple of lines too, so you can trail them in the water. The glashen will go for the feathers, so they will. Maybe the odd mackerel too. I could end up with a great catch between here and Gola."

Jacob's enthusiasm was taking a turn for the better.

"You could indeed. We'll do our best anyhow," said Sean.

"You slip out around the side of the barn and keep down low behind the reeds all the way out along the stream. I'll meet you at the curragh in about fifteen minutes. I'll have to think of a way of distracting my mother if she is in the street; and Tilly. I don't want them seeing me with two sets of oars or they'll be wondering what I'm up to, so give me a minute or two. When you hear me whistling it'll be safe to go."

Half an hour later the curragh was afloat, its dark, iconic shape bobbing with graceful ease over the breaking waves. Anyone looking on from the shore would have seen one figure in the little craft, a lithe body bending and straightening with regular, energetic rhythm as it propelled the boat forward. It was an ideal day for the journey and the curragh fairly skimmed over the flat-calm surface of the sea. There was little or no breeze to speak of, an unusual circumstance in this exposed channel at the best of times and even more rare given the season. What little occasional breeze there was came supportively from behind them, from the south-east, the settled weather conniving with Sean Ban's scheme. The swell coming in from the Atlantic was as gentle as anyone could have dreamed of for this particular voyage.

After a bit, the single figure could be seen to be apparently motionless as Jacob untangled the lines and dropped the small weights over the side, taking the feathers and hooks deep into the waters beneath. All the while he was scanning the coastline, on the lookout for anyone who might be taking an interest in his activities. He saw no one however, and the single figure was soon joined by another at the front of the curragh. Fishing as they went, the two young men rowed towards Gola Island. As they did, Sean Ban told Jacob of his predicament.

The story of recent events in his life was painful to relate but Sean covered the gist of it. He thought that if he was receiving this degree of assistance from his friend, as well as his silence, he owed him an explanation. Jacob rowed and listened in silence, his mind trying to understand the forces which play so secretly upon the lives of other people. He could never have imagined that his carefree friend was suffering such pressures, such coercion and such distress. It left him bemused and speechless, struggling to hear in himself any resounding empathy. This was all so outside his limited experience. He could think of nothing to say, no words of consolation, no sympathy, no advice. It was a relief to him every time they had to stop to haul up a line of twisting fish from that invisible realm below because the conversation then switched to the mundane, to something he could understand. The world of Sean Ban's mind was as mysterious to him as the dark, unknown world from which these fish had just emerged. The catch was already growing on the canvas bottom of the ancient craft. Also growing was Jacob's conviction that Sean had made a huge mistake in leaving his home.

The curragh was well out beyond Inishinney, half way to Gola, when he suddenly stopped rowing and turned to stare out over the placid waters of the channel. Sean Ban kept going for a bit, thinking that perhaps his friend had become tired; but then he noticed something in the hunch of his body, the diverted head, the melancholy of his expression.

"What's the matter?" he asked, still rowing towards the sand-spit on the eastern edge of the island.

It took a while for Jacob to find the courage to answer him; when he did, he could barely look at his friend in the eye.

"I think you are wrong," he spluttered out, more disappointment in the tone of his voice than he had allowed for.

"You think I am wrong?" Sean Ban was shocked, having never anticipated that anyone could think about the situation in any way other than how he had come to think of it himself. "I don't think you understand, Jacob. It's a terrible situation I am in. I have thought long about it and this seems to me the only way out of it," he argued.

"Aye, maybe it's the only way out of it alright," agreed his partner, "but is getting out of it the best thing to be doing?"

"It's the only choice I have."

Jacob thought for a while, lifting a beautiful specimen of mackerel from the floor of the curragh below him and examining it carefully, as if for inspiration. He loved the perfect symmetry of the fish, its wonderfully balanced length, the dark stripes on its upper half and the smoothness of its white underbelly. Accusation in its dull, sightless eyes.

"You could stay instead of running away. That would be a different choice," he said softly, still avoiding Sean's fixed glare.

"You think I am running away?"

Jacob pursed his lips. "How else would you describe it, if it's not running away?"

"Alright, so maybe I am running away. What would you do? I don't hear any good alternatives."

"You could always stay and help your father and mother around the farm. You could always ....."

Sean's interruption was vociferous. "I could always what? Marry Annie, is that it? What sort of a life would that lead me into? Stuck in Ranahuel forever, looking after her, looking after a child that isn't even mine. Except all the neighbours will always believe it is mine and blame me for it, and for how the wain turns out in the future, and blame me for Annie's shame, and for Johnny's drinking and for the railway coming and for the price of stout. Don't you see that my life is over here? I am the idiot! I am the fellow to blame! All that has happened is driving me away. All the things that I have no control over; things that are not my fault Jacob. That's why I have to get away. Surely you can see that? There's no future for me here. If I don't leave now, then I never will."

Jacob slowly picked up the oars again and began to row reluctantly on the glassy surface of the sea.

"Aye," he said, "I do see that, I honestly do. But, it's just that I don't like the idea of you running away and leaving your folks. Especially with Frank not well. How do you think he'll take it when he finds out you're gone? How is he going to cope with whatever needs doing on the farm?"

Sean Ban joined him in rowing again and sat quietly for several minutes. With the breeze and whatever tide there was behind them the journey had taken far less time than he had thought, so that now they were only half a mile from the sandy shore of Gola. "My father has been out around the yard lately and he's doing not so bad, now that the worst of the winter weather is past. He will be alright, with the help of my mother. It's not as if there is a huge amount of work to be done about the place; just the animals to look after. Sure I seemed to spend half my time helping Father Dunleavey and the other half out here at the Point with you all."

"There will be potatoes to be planted soon, ploughing to be done first; then there will be hay to be cut and saved. Who's going to help them with that?" persisted Jacob.

"I'm hoping that they'll be able to persuade Johnny O'Donnell to come and do a bit for them before he heads back to the Lagan again in May. That's if he does go back. It's not as if he'll be very busy around their place. And if I can send a bit of money home they might even be able to pay him."

"Do you want me to go up an odd time, just to see how they are getting on?"

Sean Ban stopped rowing briefly and smiled at his friend.

"That would be great," he said. "Would you do that? You could write to me and tell me how things are. Here! I have my sister's address. I'll write it down for you." He took from his pocket the folded sheet and the pencil and scribbled the details at the bottom, the roll and sway of the curragh not doing anything to improve his handwriting. He tore off the bottom of the page and gave it to Jacob.

"How will I be able to read that jumble?" he joked, putting the page in his pocket and taking to the oars again for the final push to the sloping beach of Gola Island.

Chapter 36

Aftermath

In the aftermath of Sean Ban's night-flight there were the predictable reactions throughout the community. The birds in the trees now knew for sure that he was a dirty, immoral dog, and a cowardly one at that; they chirped it far, wide and often. And, as in so many rural Irish contexts, they never let the truth of the matter get in the way of a good story. Rumours concerning him abounded.

Sure had he not fathered another child somewhere down about Dungloe last year?

Him and the poor, innocent Annie amadan would be at it in the sand-hills every time he took her walking to Mullaghdearg beach, it was said.

It was reported that Johnny had beaten him within an inch of his life, so much so that he had owned up and had agreed to the wedding.

Frank, it was said, was so annoyed and embarrassed about it that he had taken to his bed and hadn't been seen out in days.

Brid and Maggie Dan were said to have been crying together ever since, the one as inconsolable as the other.

And Father Dunleavey had ranted and raged from his pulpit the following Sunday so vehemently that he had taken a pain in his chest and had had to get a drink of cold water before he gave Mass.

There was an element of fact about the latter episode. No-one was more annoyed about Sean's disappearance than the pastor of the flock, not least because he would miss the fellow's practical assistance with those woolly 'parishioners' that were so close to his temporal heart. But it was the fact that Sean had gone without any justifiable reason, and after such apparent changes of mind, that really intrigued and annoyed him. The priest had begun to believe in Sean's innocence following the meeting in Maggie Dan's cottage; he had been quite impressed by the quietly determined manner in which Sean had handled himself during those difficult earlier confrontations. Then there had been Sean's apparent change of mind, for which Dunleavey could find no explanation. Confused and disappointed, the old clergyman could sense that there was something not quite right about all this and he determined to get to the bottom of the little mystery. His parish needed the scandal and its associated plague of rumour like his sheep needed an outbreak of foot-rot. And him busy enough with this whole railway thing which had become such an obsession to him. This was such a vital time for the people of this parish, whether or not they could recognise the fact. There were opportunities for employment just around the corner which would put something of a brake on the drain of young men, and indeed young women, who habitually migrated from the Rosses. There were possibilities for the seeds of small businesses to be sown at this time, if only the people could see and seize these chances. He bemoaned the fact that, instead, most of his parishioners were more interested in discussing the ins and outs of the Annie O'Donnell scandal. So short-sighted! So self-content! So beaten down by a history of subservience and suffering that they couldn't lift their gaze over the half-door of their own domesticity, nor beyond the immediate horizon of their neighbourhood gossip. "Good enough folk but a people who know little and think even less," he complained to himself.

Those in the know put about that Sean Ban had probably travelled to Scotland. Maybe to hide in the maze of Glasgow's backstreets, except that these same slums would be too good for him. Maybe gone to his sister who was married and lived over there, somewhere out beyond Edinburgh. If she had any sense of-course, if she knew what was good for her and those wee wains of hers, she would show him the street. Put him out, if she and that Derry man of hers had any wit at all. A pup like that! And him a pet of Father Dunleavey's too. Wouldn't you think the priest would have known better, known the kind of him? Or would have at least some control over him. Or could have advised Maggie Dan to be a bit more vigilant in keeping an eye on the pair of them. After all, with the confessional and all, the priest must have had some inkling of what they were up to.

Some of this gossip spread like the smell of rotting fish and reached as far as the Stewarts on Carrickfinn. There was the same mixture of reaction here as on the mainland; disbelief, dismay, disgust.

"Don't let Tilly or Maud hear of it. Nor Richard either," was the mother's concern. "For they're far too young to be hearing the like of that. And about a fellow we let into this house. It just shows you. You can trust nobody these days."

Jacob had tried his best to keep his head down and say nothing, fearing that his defence of Sean Ban would be so transparent as to implicate him in the whole escape plot. But his mother's condemnation of Sean, founded entirely on the baseless rumours she had been told in the shop in Annagry, really irritated him. He could hold in no longer and he stood up for Sean's honour.

"Mother," he fumed, "you know nothing about it. Don't be making judgements about the fellow when you don't know if those things are true or not. He is not here to defend himself so give him the benefit of the doubt, for goodness sake."

Robert John agreed, though he did not like the vociferous manner in which his oldest son had spoken to his mother.

"Jacob hold your tongue! Don't be giving out to your mother like that, you hear me? And Martha, Sean Ban Sweeney has always been a good friend to this family, to the whole of us, so don't be saying anything about this, either for him or against him. It doesn't help the matter to be spreading it around. It certainly wont help the girl, or her mother. Maybe he has reasons for leaving that we know nothing about. So just keep your counsel, alright?"

Jacob turned away, face looking out to the feeding fowl in the street, afraid that his involvement in the matter might somehow be readable on his face.

Frank and Brid had recovered fairly well from the shock of the empty settle-bed and the letter on the table. Initially both had been horrified, Brid holding her sides and experiencing that sick feeling in the pit of her stomach. Her last child gone from the house. Dermot gone and far away in America, probably never to return to her; Mary, married and living in Scotland, closer but might as well be America for all the chances of them ever returning to live in the Rosses. And now her baby, Sean Ban, gone as well and not a clue as to where. There had been sobbing and then later a low keening sound as she mourned his going and tried to absorb the implications. Implications for herself and for Frank. How were they going to cope, and him with the pains? Implications for Annie, Maggie Dan and Johnny. Would Johnny lose the head again and try to punish them for their son's disappearance? There were wider implications for how they all survived in this community. How would they hold their heads up at Mass, with the people all thinking that their son was such a degenerate character? And him now a runaway.

Frank held her, doing his best to console her. When he thought about it, he was less surprised by Sean's flight than she was.

"Husha, husha, Brid," he soothed. "It is maybe all for the best."

This was not necessarily what she expected nor wanted to hear at that particular moment and she steeled herself against his comfort, so that he felt himself lose her in the rigidity of her body. But he still held on and gradually his words calmed her.

When they went to Maggie Dan's later in the morning, reactions to their news were as predictable as smoke with fire. While Maggie herself moaned and rocked her thin little body in the corner, Johnny had refused to believe the disconsolate couple. He suspected that they were bluffing, that they were behind Sean Ban's escape, that they had planned it and financed it, had forged the note, had hidden him away somewhere. He ranted and raged around the kitchen and seemed to have great difficulty in restraining himself from shaking Frank. Indeed so disbelieving was he that at one point he ran from the room to go to search the Sweeney's place for any sign of Sean. He returned only slightly less wound up and grabbed the letter from Frank to re-read it.

"You'll just have to contact him," he shouted. "Get him back here! Make him go through with this! He promised he would, didn't he? We all heard him! You tell him to get himself back here, you hear me Frank?"

"And how do you suggest I tell him? I don't know where he went. He could be anywhere," was Frank's measured answer.

Johnny went to the door and stood there shifting from one foot to the other, as if undecided about what course of action to take next. He stared glumly across at Annie who was sitting at the table, looking as unconcerned as usual, as oblivious to the implications of all that was going on around her as if the whole sorry plight belonged to someone else. In her hands she had an ancient rag doll which she had resurrected from some forgotten recess of the cottage, her fingers unconsciously playing with the last remains of its discoloured hair.

"Look at her! Sitting there with her old play-doll. And before long she'll have a real, crying, bastard baby to be stroking. While

Sean Ban swans around some foreign part with his arms around some other victim. Well I'll not be staying here to listen to his brat, so I won't."

With this he banged the rickety old door behind him and was gone, inducing further howls from his mother. Frank stood in helplessness while Brid did her best to comfort the grieving woman.

"It'll be alright, Maggie Dan. We will do all we can for the both of you and with the help of God you'll get through this," she said, more faith in her words than she was feeling in her heart. There wasn't much more to be said and the Sweeneys left her to her grief and to her pathetic, silent daughter. On the slow walk back up to their home Frank and Brid discussed Annie's awareness of the situation; both agreed that they were unsure as to how much she understood of what had been said or of how much she understood of the implications of Sean's disappearance.

"Did you see her with that doll?" said Frank. "From the way she was handling it, you would say that she definitely knows she is .... you know, that there's a baby coming, wouldn't you?"

"Frank dear. It's well seen you are a man and have never been pregnant. Of course she knows there's a baby coming. She feels it kicking in her belly half the time. No matter how dull she is, she'll have a mother's instinct about the wain. She knows it's coming, maybe even better than manys a girl who is supposed to have their full wits about them."

"Well, fair enough," smiled Frank, "but I can't work out if she understood that Sean Ban has gone. It's so hard to know with her what's going on in her head."

But later that evening they heard the sound of Annie's whistle drifting down through the still air from somewhere nearby. Brid went out to look and indeed there she was, on the craggy outcrop of rock half way up the hill above their farmstead.

This is where she sits to think of Sean. Where he and she used to play when they were children. She remembers well, so well. But it is a long time since she was up here. Up above his parent's house, up in their very own special play-home between the rocks. There are no old coats now, the way Sean used to bring them up here to spread as a roof over them, stretched out over branches placed between the boulders, with smaller stones set on top to hold them in place. No sticks to make a pretend fire. No soft moss and fresh green ferns that he would gather to spread as a comfortable carpet on the earth below. No blackberries that he would pick for their dinner. No catapult or bow and arrow for Sean to be trying to shoot down any bird foolish enough to fly into the area of their hallowed little home. No make-believe pipe for him to smoke, its bowl childishly fashioned from a hollowed-out rose-hip, its stem a stalk of dried corn, with peat-coom as a tobacco substitute, making him cough and splutter and turn green.

But she still has her rag-doll from all those years ago. Her baby! Sean's baby! And she looks down at it on her lap as she whistles down the dead years.

He is not at home now. Otherwise he would have come up to her. She knows this for certain. She heard the conversation in her kitchen earlier. But she knew that Sean is just hiding. He always used to love hiding. He would leave her in their tent between the boulders, saying that he was going to hunt some animal for their supper. And she would wait for him. But he had hidden somewhere, expecting her to come to look for him. And, if she did, he would jump out at her to scare her. She remembers him once landing on top of her when she had slipped in fright. And he just lay there, his body pressing her down, laughing at her, trying to tickle her to make her laugh. And she had laughed for him, but he hadn't noticed. Because the laugh was drowned deep inside the pool of her. It didn't work its way up to the surface, out to her lips. Like everything else. And he had been annoyed and had given up. Other times he would sneak away from her and pester her by hiding behind a tree or a rock and throwing things at her. She would feel the stones hitting the roof of their play-home, sometimes bringing the roof in on top of her! And she would be annoyed at him for this desecration. Except that he never noticed. How could he have noticed?

Now he has decided to hide somewhere else. Not around the crags. Further away. Maybe on the point, at Carrickfinn, she thinks instinctively. Maybe in the big high dunes beside Mullaghdearg strand where they would often walk, where that old boat sank. Maybe far away at her Granny's place. She doesn't know of anywhere else where he could have gone. Will he come back for her? Maybe! Maybe not! And why did he come to look in at her last night? She is feeling a terrible sense of loneliness like a hurting lump in her chest, a sore feeling, just up above where the baby is lying. Like a wound. Is this the way his face felt when he cut it, she is wondering. Will he be alright? Who will look after it for him?

The tunes merge into one another as she plays. Sometimes jig, sometimes reel, and then again sometimes a slow, painful air. There is a confused feel to the music, like it doesn't know what to be saying. The ornamentations are missing from it; the grace-notes sound half-hearted and trip over themselves; just the bald melody, sometimes staccato and inconsistent, as if it's not really aware of itself, as if earlier conviction has evaporated. But this is how she thinks, with the sound of her whistle, the lilt of the tune, her thoughts struggling up through the twisting undergrowth of her, coming slowly out into the open. He used to understand those thoughts. The only person who did, she is thinking. And she finds inspiration, and plays for him, louder and louder, till the piercing of the whistle is reverberating around in her ears, in her skull. Less of a tune, more of a scream. The sound of loss, and of loneliness, and of "Why did you leave me now, Sean, fair-haired husband of our play-home? Why did you leave us now?"

Brid listened in the yard below. In the clear skies above the girl she watched a dark ribbon of starlings swirl away towards the west, their chittering cacophony resonating eerily, uncomfortably, with the shrill sound of Annie's whistling; the dissonance of this combination seemed to take on visual form, like a musical score etching its wavy pattern on the pastel light of the Spring evening. Until she could stand the poignancy of it all no longer and she went in to her husband and her prayers and her night of tears.

Chapter 37

Railway workers

A few days before the end of Lent a group of men could be seen making their way along a lane through the greening bogland of the Rosses in the direction of Burtonport. It was a day of Donegal wind and rain, coming in from the restless, grey sea; the men's heads bowed into it. The sort of weather that you wouldn't be out in without a really good reason. The thirteen men had such a reason. At their head was the unmistakeable figure of their Parish Priest astride his begrudging Saint Vincent, his dark cloak billowing behind him like the sails of an old schooner in the breeze. His waistline bounced and wobbled like a carrageen jelly in time with with the motion of his mount.

For all the dampness of the day, the spirit within the group seemed to be positive, indeed even jovial at times.

"We're like Jesus and the Twelve Disciples," joked John Joe Roarty. "With him up on that donkey of a thing, all we need is a few branches and they'll think it's Palm Sunday."

Even Father Dunleavey saw the humour of the situation. In his mind he was pleasantly surprised that Roarty knew this much about Palm Sunday.

"I'll keep an eye out for any crosses then," he threw back over his shoulder with the wind. "And which one of you would be Judas?"

"That would have to be you, John Joe," laughed Paddy Cassidy. "You have the shape of him about you."

"Why, who was Judas?" inquired the little fellow innocently, disappointing his priest immediately.

"He must have been a wee runt of a thing, if you're the shape of him," said one of the others in unkind jest. "Look at those skinny wee arms at you. I've seen healthier looking drowned rats, so I have. How on earth do you think you are going to be able for any work on this railway? Sure you'll fall off the end of the shovel."

"Or spend half the day looking for a left handed crowbar," said another.

The men laughed but John Joe was used to this kind of banter and he took it all in his jaunty stride.

"Never you worry about me, Duffy," he countered. "You'll have enough worries of your own trying to stay with me. I'll be laying those sleepers that quick that they'll have to get the rest of you bicycles to keep up."

"Well said, Mister Roarty." The priest was still tuned in to their conversation and stalled his mule to wait for the dripping straggle of would-be railwaymen. "This is the whole idea of the thing," he said. "To get you men off your fat, lazy behinds in Sullivan's public house and get you earning your keep. When I chose you all as the first team of Annagry men to try for jobs with the railway builders, I didn't pick you all for your size or your strength. I am hoping that there will be different types of jobs for you. So John Joe might not do the same kind of work that Paddy does, for example, do you see?"

"That's the way I see it too, Father," Roarty smiled. "They'll likely make me a manager or a foreman or something."

"Or the boy that makes the tea."

"Even that will be weak too."

"Sure he can hardly make his own water."

"Just you wait boys. By the time it's all built and finished they'll be calling it 'The Roarty Railway,'" laughed John Joe. "It'll go down in history, so it will."

"Aye, it'll go down alright," answered Duffy. "If you build it, it will likely fall down!"

Conversation continued in such a manner as the line of prospective labourers wound its way along the muddy lanes of Meenbanad and down the hill towards the port. Paddy Cassidy took the opportunity to move ahead of the pack and walk alongside his clerical benefactor. After some small-talk he raised the subject that had troubled him since leaving the Parochial House in Annagry that morning.

"You didn't think of asking Johnny O'Donnell to come, Father?"

The priest's head jerked away to the south for a bit.

"I've offended him somehow," thought Paddy, "but I don't know how." He was just about to drop back to the others when Dunleavey turned to him with a curtly dismissive, "No I didn't!"

"He'd be good with the shovel, Johnny. His foot and all is well mended up now, so it is. Maybe you'll be thinking of bringing him over for a start the next time? It's none of my business like, but Johnny'll be surprised when he hears we have all gone looking for a job and him back....."

"As you say, Paddy, it's none of your business."

Paddy retreated into his shell like a hermit crab facing a hungry seagull and slowed the pace of his plodding to ease some distance between himself and the grumpiness of the clergyman. The plan did not really work though, because Dunleavey slowed and waited for him. Paddy looked up at him in slight trepidation, expecting some further rebuke. The priest took off his soaking felt hat and shook the rainwater from it, splashing plenty of it around Paddy as he did so.

"Unholy water," thought Paddy, taking evasive action too late.

"The thing is, Paddy," the priest began, "Johnny has disappointed me in the past few months, since he came back from the Lagan. If he was to join you fellows on a work team I'm not sure that I could make promises or guarantees about his behaviour to his employers. If he had too much money thrown at him, for example, how much of it would make its way back to Maggie Dan and how much would end up in some public house somewhere? Do you see what I mean? I have to be able to stand over the references I give you fellows, after me agitating for jobs for the like of you for the last three or four years."

"I know Johnny's hard on the booze but he needs the work as bad as the rest of us, do you not think? It's maybe just what he needs to take him away from it," argued Paddy.

"You might be right but, then again, you might be wrong. I cannot be taking the risk for him. If he really wants to work he'll go back to the Lagan come May."

"It sounds as if you want rid of him."

"Maybe I do Paddy. There's something about the fellow that worries me. Worries me a lot. There's that whole business with Sean Ban Sweeney. There's something fishy about how he left and I want to get to the bottom of it. I have a feeling it might just involve the same Johnny O'Donnell and, until I understand it, until I have my suspicions laid to rest, I will not be recommending him to anybody."

"I don't understand what you mean, Father. Everybody knows Sean ran away because he got Johnny's sister in the family way and then wouldn't marry her. Johnny is the innocent party in all that. You can't lay any blame at his door for Sweeney doing a runner."

The priest scratched his wiry eyebrows and was slow to answer. "So it would seem, Paddy. So it would seem. But.... you see, Sean had sworn blind to me that it wasn't his child. I believed him. Then he somehow changes his mind and says he will marry Annie. Doing the decent thing. We make the arrangements and all. Then he ups and disappears without so much as a reason. There's something about it all that I can't put my finger on. It just does not add up. That's why I am hesitating about Johnny, if the truth be told. That and the senseless amount of drinking he has been doing of late. The fellow has a problem.... it's maybe not all his fault but I cannot take the risk of recommending him. You boys should try to talk a bit of sense into him for he's not going to be listening to an old man like me."

~~~~~~~

On his way back from Burtonport, delighted with his success in having all twelve of his team taken on with the railway building company, Father Dunleavey called with the Sweeneys. He spent a late hour quizzing Frank and Brid about exactly what had happened in the couple of days before Sean Ban left. Initially the couple were very reluctant to give anything other than a vague account of Johnny's role in the events leading up to Sean's flight. But the priest had a way with words and gradually he wrestled the story of that traumatic night from them. Brid was the first to break; he played skilfully upon her motherly instinct to defend her son and this instinct trumped any loyalty to her neighbour and old friend Maggie Dan. As the villainy of Johnny O'Donnell was slowly revealed, Father Dunleavey sat back on his chair and mused, half to himself, half to his hosts.

"So Sean Ban was sort of blackmailed into agreeing to the wedding? The threat of what that rascal would do to you and your home persuaded him to change his mind; it wasn't a sense of his own guilt; nothing to do with his own sense of duty; it was pure blackmail; and then, when he had time to think about the situation, he could see no way out other than to run for it? Is that how you see it Frank?"

"That's how I see it, Father. But," he mumbled uncertainly, "we did not want to be telling you this. Sean wouldn't want it, I know. So we don't want you to be saying anything about it, you understand, not to Maggie Dan or Johnny. Not to anybody Father, if you don't mind."

The priest thought about this. "I understand. It's to your credit, the both of you. And you don't think that Sean is responsible for Annie's condition at all?"

"No I don't. I believe him. It's not his baby. Brid thinks the same. It must have been some other fellow, maybe when she was away during the summer."

"Well, that puts a different complexion on everything, so it does," continued the cleric thoughtfully. "But I wish you had told me that day, before we went through that whole charade of planning the wedding. Mind you, I did think Sean was very subdued at the time...but I just imagined it was because he was embarrassed about how long it had taken him to own up and agree to the thing. Well, well! Poor Sean. And have you any idea yet where he has gone? There's no word from him?"

Brid's voice broke slightly as she answered. "He's with Mary in Scotland. We had a letter from her at the end of last week. Sean arrived on their doorstep in a terrible state. He had walked halfway across the country for he had no money left and couldn't get any work. So Mary has taken him in and he's staying there in the meantime. It's a place called Musselburgh they live in. She's hoping that Pat can maybe get a job for him where he works, once he recovers."

"It must have been hard on the two of you, not knowing."

"It was hard alright, but at least we know now and we're content," reflected Frank. "All we can do now is hope and pray that he gets over it all and that things work out for him."

The priest, rising gingerly, rubbed his behind and shook one leg and then the other.

"I hope and pray the same. He's a good boy at the bottom of it all, even if he did disappear on you. The trouble is... there's not a lot any of us can do about the situation now. It's not going to help Maggie Dan nor Annie. There'll be no father for the poor child and Johnny isn't going to be much of a help to them with the way he has turned out lately. I don't know what I'm going to do with that fellow but one thing is for sure. I won't be vouching for him with the railway company for a job. He'll just have to make his way elsewhere."

"It's hit Maggie Dan badly. She's gone downhill since."

"Do you think so, Frank? And what about yourself? How are you coping with Sean away? How's the rheumatism?"

"Agh, I'm not so bad. And we are managing alright," answered Frank. "Sure there's nothing else for it."

Brid grimaced. "He says he's not so bad, Father, but he's not telling the truth. If you had to live with him and see him suffering when he has done any work about the place you would know different. I don't know what we're going to do if he gets any worse."

"Maybe the warm weather will make a difference to you, when it comes. If it comes," said Father Dunleavey edging towards the door.

"It might," said Frank, "but sure none of us gets out of this alive."

Father Dunleavey nodded at this quaint observation.

"You're right there, Frank," he smiled and with that he took his leave of the Sweeneys and led his weary animal down the hill towards Annagry. As he passed the O'Donnell cottage he wondered how long it would be until Johnny came calling on him.

He did not have long to await the visit.

The following afternoon Johnny arrived in the village to sit on the bridge, as was his wont. He would watch the world go by, his legs swinging against the wall while the coldness of the granite stone numbed his poorly padded hips. Normally he would be joined fairly quickly by some of his friends from the nearby houses but today he had to wait until well into the afternoon before John Joe Roarty lopped into view. As he came closer Johnny heard him sneeze repeatedly, each outburst peppered by squeakily pitched swear words. He arrived beside Johnny and hauled himself painfully up unto the wall, making assiduous use of his coat sleeve to stem a continuous flow of watery mucus from his red nose.

"You sound like you're dying off, John Joe," observed Johnny. "Another change of clothes will do you."

"Aye, if I had another change of clothes," grumped the little fellow. "That's the problem. I got these soaked yesterday on the way over to Burtonport and they haven't dried out yet. Feel them...they're still damp as be-damned."

"You're soaking," said Johnny, running his hand over the old coat. "You should go home and get these dried by the fire. You'll get your death in them, if you haven't already!"

"There's no fire on in the house. We're out of turf, so we are. I thought I'd maybe stand by the fire in Sullivan's. A hot whiskey wouldn't do me any harm either if you're buying."

"You say you went to Burtonport? What took you over there?" asked Johnny.

John Joe suddenly looked a bit uncomfortable and turned his attention to the stream flowing lazily behind them. He was silent and his change of mood immediately aroused Johnny's suspicious interest.

"John Joe," he said, "what are you trying to hide from me? I only asked you what took you to Burtonport? Is there some wee woman on the go that I don't know about? You're looking wild embarrassed and that's not like you."

"Father Dunleavey took us over," replied John Joe, as if to shift the blame.

"Father Dunleavey took.... took who over?"

"It wasn't just me you know. A whole gang of us. Paddy was there too. There was about a dozen of us."

"A dozen of you? But why? What was Dunleavey doing, taking yous all over there?"

"It was for a job, a job on the railway. He got us all fixed up with the railway people. We start at the end of the month." John Joe looked as guilty as if he'd been caught stealing.

Johnny's brows furrowed and he scratched at his ginger hair behind his ear. "Are you telling me that Dunleavey took you over to Burtonport and got you fixed up with a job and he never bothered to tell me about the chance? And big Paddy too? He's got a job as well?"

"Aye, Paddy as well...all of us got a start with them. It's good like. They just asked us a couple of questions and told us how much we'd be getting and asked us if that was alright. That was all that was to it."

Johnny hopped down off the wall as if someone had just lit a fire under the stones.

"I don't believe it!" he said through clenched teeth. "Dunleavey took you and got you a job and ignored me. You, John Joe, for

God's sake. Does he want you to be holding the shovels for the men when they're taking a smoke or what? What use are you going to be on the railway?"

John Joe resented Johnny's taunt and scrambled up to stand defiantly on the bridge, his flared nostrils running profusely, his fists clenched and his arms rigid in an unintentionally comical pose.

"Well Johnny O'Donnell, at least I'll be there and that's more than you will be for he never took you. So put that in your pipe and smoke it."

"Don't you worry! He'll take me yet. I'm away to see him this minute. He will likely want me to go with the next crew he's taking over, so I'll see you on the job. You can hold my shovel for me when it needs cooling down, if it's shaft isn't too hot for you to handle."

And with that Johnny left John Joe to his perch on the bridge and headed towards the Parochial House for a chat with his priest.

"Watch you don't hurt yourself getting down off that wall," he called over his shoulder and continued unaware of John Joe's fingers of scorn raised sardonically after him.

Reaching the priest's house he stood looking at its heavy wooden portal, choosing and organising in his mind the words he wanted to assault Dunleavey with. He banged his fist against the door with too much anger in his action, repenting of the thump of it immediately. Mrs Gallagher came to the door, opened it solemnly and looked somewhat disapprovingly at Johnny's untidy garb. She said nothing.

"Is his reverence in?" Johnny stepped into the hall uninvited.

"Stand there!" she ordered abruptly and limped off towards the depths of the hall. He heard mumbled voices in an unseen room at the rear and the dark figure of Father Dunleavey appeared there in the greyness of the corridor, a cup of tea in his fist.

"Ah Johnny; I've been expecting you. Will you take a cup of tea? Get him a wee cup," he said back to the housekeeper in the kitchen.

"I'm alright, I don't need no tea Father."

"Maybe you'd prefer a drop of whiskey, would you Johnny? Or maybe you're off it for lent, are you? I would doubt that though."

This took Johnny by surprise and put him off his track for a second or two. He was about to respond positively when Dunleavey laughed at him, not without a hint of derision in his mirth.

"Aye, you would take a drop of whiskey off me, so you would. If I was fool enough to give it to you. But that would be irresponsible of a man of my position, wouldn't it? No Johnny, tea will have to do you. And if you had any sense at all, you would be giving up the whiskey altogether and sticking to the tea."

He passed Johnny in the hall and entered the parlour, Johnny following him in as expected, the wind taken out of his sails by the ongoing patter of the clergyman, the sanctimonious tone of the man grating on his ears.

"Aye, the strong drink has started to make a mess of you son, would you not agree? Since you arrived back before Christmas you are seldom out of Sullivan's public house. Don't deny it! And don't think I don't notice. You're becoming a bit of an embarrassment to yourself and to your poor old mother. Her who has a lot more to be worrying about than how you are turning into a drunk in front of her very eyes. It's time you caught yourself on, before it's too late altogether. Do you not think so yourself, Johnny?"

Johnny sat down on the chair indicated to him by the priest. He cleared his throat and tried to think of what to say. His mouth opened and closed a few times before any sound emerged. It was one thing to have an angry question to put to the priest when you were out on the wall with John Joe but an entirely different thing being in here in the spider's parlour, listening to the clergyman's sermon and trying to think of how to defend yourself against his onslaught.

"My drinking is my own affair, and anyway that's not what..."

"Ah, but that's where you are wrong, entirely wrong," interrupted Dunleavey. "You see, your body is the temple of the Holy Ghost and you should not feel it is in your right to abuse it. Your drinking affects your mood; you get all angry and resentful when you have drink taken. Am I not right? And you get the courage to do daft things and say daft things that you wouldn't do or say if you were sober. Am I not right? You take a feed of liquor and suddenly you have the red mist come over you and you think you can change the world into the way you want it to be. So one night you have a feed of the stuff to give yourself the courage you haven't got and you take yourself up the lane to Sweeney's house and stick a lighted torch under their thatch...a crazy thing to be doing! It could have landed you in gaol, for heaven's sake!"

The priest's voice boomed in Johnny's head. He was now squirming in his seat, strongly regretting that he had had the stupidity to come to talk to this cunning cleric. His discomfort was temporarily relieved by the arrival of the Gallagher woman with a cup of tea for him. He took it and sipped slowly, giving himself time to think. There was no point in trying to deny what Dunleavey was saying, but how was he going to get this conversation away from this subject and talk about the railway job? And the priest was still talking.

"You got yourself worked up into such a rage about Annie that you just had to be blaming somebody...anybody! And you picked on the fellow who was your friend for years and blamed him. It didn't really matter whether he was the guilty man or not, you had your victim. And, when he denied it, you could not take his word for it. You had to manipulate him, make him do things your way. Make him take the blame and marry Annie! So you come up with a plan to threaten the Sweeneys, set fire to their house, unless Sean Ban agrees to marry your poor sister. What sort of a stupid, heartless chap are you anyway?"

By this stage Dunleavey's voice had risen to a pitch of fervour that Johnny would not have believed the old man to be capable of. He could barely listen to it without putting his hands over his ears. He made a move forward on the seat, as if to make a run for it. But the priest rose first and stood over him darkly, almost menacingly, and continued his rant.

"Sit there!" he commanded glaring down at Johnny. "The Sweeneys have been great neighbours to you, you know. You might not remember it but when your father was drowned it was Frank and Brid that helped your mother through. They did everything for her, and for you and Annie. Kept the animals. Put food on your table. Spent night after night just talking to Maggie Dan. And that's how you repay them? Imagine how Frank felt, and him a sick man, standing in the middle of the night with you holding a blazing torch to the thatch of his house. They could have gone to the police the next morning, had you arrested, you idiot! And listen! Sean Ban didn't run away because he didn't want to marry Annie. He ran away because he couldn't bear the thought of having you for a brother-in-law. Because of your violence and your drinking. So have a good think about that, Johnny O'Donnell, and then ask me the question you came to ask me."

The cup shook in Johnny's hands. He stared blindly at the floor, at the priest's brown boots. He wanted to throw the tea in his face, punch him in the flab of his over-fed belly, shove him back down into his chair. He did none of these things. He just sat there. After a bit he whimpered, "What question?"

"The question about why I didn't take you to Burtonport along with the others yesterday and get you fixed up with a job. That question. Go on, ask it! That's what you came for, isn't it?"

Johnny shrivelled further and said nothing, internally cowering like a cornered mouse before the claws of a far-too-clever cat. The priest began to pace back and forward in front of the fireplace.

"Alright, maybe you don't need to ask me the question any longer. I've spoken the truth to you and it hasn't been easy for you to listen to. The way you are at the minute son, there is no chance that I would recommend you for a job. Work on the line will start at Burtonport in the next week or two, from what they tell me over there, but unless there's a massive change in your attitude you will not be anywhere near it, you hear me? Take, for example, my own wee flock of sheep. You used to be a big help to me, with looking after them. Then you went away and Sean Ban helped as much as he could. But since you came home, and especially since he disappeared, I have been all on my own with them. If they break out, there I am, at my age, running after them across the heather, over the stone ditches. Where are you? Nowhere to be seen. Likely lying in Sullivan's. You have changed so much since you went to the Lagan. I don't know what has come over you."

"This!" spat Johnny, pointing to his cruelly-shaped nose.

"Agh, get away with you," returned Dunleavey. "That's nothing! A broken nose?"

"Not just the broken nose. It was the beating I took from those bastards. And the damage I did to my foot. And that girl...sort of broke my heart, so she did. But you wouldn't understand that, would you?"

"What I understand is that you had a very tough time. Yes, I understand that you were hurt...in many ways. But the secret of life is that you don't let the bad times get you down. You rise from the ashes. You fight back...and not in the way you have been fighting back. No, no....what I mean is that you rise on top of the difficulties. You swim on top of the waves. You have made a conscious decision to go under them. That's what the drinking is all about. It dulls the pain and then it gives you a double dose of the same pain, do you see? It's not the answer....it's part of the problem. Lots of fellows have had their hearts broken, their pride hurt, their faces smashed. You are not the first, nor will you be the last. But you have got to get over it and move on with the rest of your life. Your mother and your sister need you to do that....rather than drag them down with you."

"And you won't get me a job on the railway?" Johnny's voice had a mixture of deflation, resignation and bitterness in it as he sipped the cooling tea.

"I won't recommend you to the railway company."

"What am I to do then?"

"The man you worked for in Magilligan? What was his name? He was a good man, wasn't he?"

"Robinson? Aye, he was a right good man. Why?"

Father Dunleavey sat down again. "Because I think you owe it to him to go back. Did he not offer you work there if you ever needed it?"

"He did."

"Well, you need it. And after the kindly way he treated you when you were hurt....both times, in fact....my opinion is that you should be going back to him and returning the favour. He must have thought a lot of you. You must have worked hard for him or he would have been glad to see the back of you, with all your bad luck. So, come the start of May, you should get yourself organised and make your way back to him. See if he'll take you on for the summer, what do you say?"

Johnny thought about this. "You might be right," he said very quietly. "He was a decent man; I liked working there, so I did."

"Good. Well, there you are then. And if you want me to write you a reference for him I'll do it."

Johnny was puzzled. "Why would you do that when you wouldn't recommend me to the railway?"

"Two reasons," replied the clergyman. "Firstly, around here you have got yourself a bad reputation, you and your drinking friends. So any money you make will go down your throat in Sullivan's or some other den. You would only make life harder for your mother and Annie. Secondly, that man you worked for had a good influence on you. If you go back and show him the good side of you, rather than hang about here showing everybody the bad side, I think you'd be doing yourself a favour. But my reference, if you want it, will depend on how you behave yourself around here over the next few weeks until May, do you understand?"

"That's fair enough," muttered a subdued Johnny.

"And to begin with, will you come down tomorrow morning and help me to shift these sheep from the meadow up to the hill for there's not a blade of grass left for them down here."

Johnny smiled in spite of himself, thinking, "You sly oul divil! That's how you worm your way around people, for your own ends." But he rose from his chair and said simply, "I'll be there."

"And when you are finished with my sheep," continued the priest as Johnny slid sideways towards the door of escape, "I want you to take your spade and shovel over to Frank Sweeney and finish digging that bit of a garden for him, for he's behind already with the planting of his potatoes. He needs your help. Same way that your family needed his help in times past."

Later, as he trudged his way back up to Ranahuel, the potential embarrassment of a visit to Sullivan's having overcome his intense desire for a drink, it crossed his mind that what the priest had just accomplished with him was, in its own way, a form of manipulation. And not a million miles away from what he had been guilty of with Sean Ban Sweeney.

"We're all of the same stuff here," he thought. "Some use words, some use other methods! I just picked the wrong one. But I'll learn by it! I'll learn, so I will."

Chapter 38

The End of Waiting

During the first week of May Johnny O'Donnell departed for the Lagan for another season of labour. He had every intention of seeking out the Robinson farmer at Magilligan before the day of the Gallop Fair and seeing if he could take up where he had left off last year. Before leaving he had made his peace, in a manner of speaking, with Frank and Brid Sweeney. He had called in at their cottage briefly, telling them that he was going the next day and asking them, as if they needed asking, to keep an eye on his mother and Annie; "Her so big now with the wain." That was all that was said, apart from confirming that he was going to try and get in with the same man as last year and apart from Frank thanking him for the few day's labour he had given several weeks ago when, due to his health, the older man had been struggling to get his turf cut. That and the ploughing of the wee field in preparation for planting this year's potato crop. There had been no query about Sean Ban, no mention of the events of a few months ago. The unspoken memory of those happenings floated between them in the kitchen like the stink of someone's foul flatulence; separating, but not something you were going to make go away by raising it for discussion. Then Johnny had stood up awkwardly beside the older man's chair for a second and, in a gesture which surprised both man and wife, he had stuck out his hand in a self-conscious and jerky manner to Frank. Probably for the first time in his life. Frank had looked at it momentarily, partly in surprise, partly in slowly-dawning comprehension of the underlying intent and significance of the action. His hesitation was brief however, and he took Johnny's hand. Nothing else was said. Johnny had hurried away to the door, eyes diverted to the floor so as to avoid taking in Brid's surprised reaction and was gone before Frank's blessing had finished.
"Slan agus beannachta. God go with you!"
It was three weeks later that Annie's labour began.
On that particular night it was approaching midnight when Maggie Dan came to bed. There was still light in the northern sky and a shimmer of its reflection flickered on the surface of Mullaghdearg Lough below. A wonderfully still and soundless

summer night. The day had been hot and some of its warmth was still in the bedroom. Annie had gone to bed an hour earlier but was still awake, though the tossing around in her discomfort seemed to have stopped. Maggie Dan threw back the spread and lay down beside her. She was immediately conscious of a wetness below her and put her hands down to check.

"Aw, my God; she's wet the bed," was her first reaction but slowly the realisation struck her that Annie's waters had broken. "What am I to do now?" she breathed, "At this time of night?"

She is feeling so hot. It has been like this all day! For the last few days! So uncomfortable, so sweaty and sticky, so heavy and lethargic. She has been sitting in the doorway of the house for most of the afternoon, trying to be in the shade and in the path of any little movement of fresh air that might be circulating between the trap of the kitchen and the wide-open space of the outdoors. But it has been a fruitless exercise. She can hardly get a breath, sitting there. Sitting waiting. Waiting, waiting, waiting! That's all life has been about for the last while. Just waiting. Suil le leanbh....waiting for baby. Can do nothing, think of nothing else. Nothing but this waiting for release. How long it takes. How long it has been. Johnny has left now too, after Sean Ban leaving. They couldn't wait any longer. They could leave. But she is still stuck here in the middle of this waiting land. She cannot leave this waiting land.

It would be easier if it was a cooler waiting land. This heat is here and has come at the wrong time. Driving her round the bend. Arm's sticking to the sides of her breasts. And them so big and heavy and sore of themselves now, heavy and sticky against the skin of her ribs and the skin of where her baby is pressing up against them. And the nipples of her, starting to push out and getting sore and tingly, making her want to massage them and cool them. Her legs bigger on her, and her hips. All pressing together, making her pores flow with perspiration. She would love a bath, a cold pool of water to sit in and cool down, to take the pressure away, to flow around her secret places and bring her cooling, healing release.

She remembers. She thinks of the sea. The great cold sea, near where her Granny lives, the long curving beach and the crystal-cool water flowing around her, the little waves breaking on her thighs and swirling around her hips and the thrill of that freedom. The day she took her Granny's dog for a walk. The day she saw that fellow again.

The baby has not kicked or moved so much in the last few days. He seems stunned by the heat as well. As lazy and tired as she is. Not a leap in him. Not a jig or a reel from him now. More of a very slow waltz, hours between the turns, dragging the notes out as his feet stick in the slimy heat. As the blood thickens in his veins. The complicated tune of her baby. Whoever he is. Or whoever she is, of-course. She just assumes it's a 'he', this baby. She never imagined anything else.

She has been sitting in the doorway today, watching idly as her mother cut more of the tall, lush grass in the small meadow beyond the stone ditch opposite; long slow swipes with the scythe, her body rotating rhythmically from side to side to accompanying grunts of effort; turning the drying hay that she had cut a few days ago, using an ancient-looking fork, bending to pick out the poisonous, yellow-headed ben-weeds which would do her cow no good at all.

The aromatic scent of the fresh hay blending curiously with the stale smell of sweat from her mother makes her stomach turn as she sits at the kitchen table. She is staring without appetite at the meagre meal in front of her. She cannot put a bite across her lips and gags when, at her mother's urging, she tries. She leaves the table and waddles to the half door, leaning her elbows broadly along it to support her weight, the top half of her body flopping out into the evening air. She rocks from side to side to see if she can get relief from the ache in her hip joints but without success.

She is as aware of the baby as if she had him in her arms. His weight has gone from the feeling of pressure around her rib-cage to more of a hanging burden, pushing down, burrowing down into her abdomen. She wants to put her hand under him, to support him, to hold him up, but he is determined to go down, down into dark depths of her. Against her will she finds herself spreading her legs apart in response to the pressure. He must soon come, she is thinking. And she is ready, in her mind, for this tearing release.

She is in her bed early, still awake with the wash of summer light through the four panes of her window. She watches this, a framed portrait of hope hanging against the darkness of the room. She remembers the thrill of Sean Ban coming to look in on her, his shy little tap on the glass, his eyes taking her all in, his nose squadged against the thick pane. She imagines the shape of his blond hair, long and unruly; the clear blueness of his gaze; and the half-smile which he forever seemed to be holding in check in case it should break out into a fit of laughter.

Where has he gone? Why now, when she needs him more than she ever needed him before?

She falls into an unsettled doze. Only briefly though.

Something is happening her!

A flooding sensation, a wetness gushing from her. Fumbling, her hands confirm this and she sniffs the resultant fluid. She lies petrified in panic, eyes staring wildly into the gloom of the room, body paralysed by uncertainty and trepidation. And her mother is getting into the bed beside her now.

Maggie Dan sat by the bed all night, just keeping an eye on Annie, very unsure about what to do and feeling the sense of helplessness as tangibly as if it were another person in the bedroom. Annie did go to sleep, so exhausted was she; it was therefore obvious to her mother that the pains hadn't started yet. Apart from her own two children, this was Maggie Dan's first experience of child-birth and, given Annie's handicap, she had a sense of dread about the whole procedure. She needed the help of her neighbour Brid; she needed the expertise of Bridie Boyle. But both were a distance away, especially Bridie. What was she to do?

She waited for the morning, the blackest of her thoughts swirling around in her head like demented bats. The first rays of morning sunlight slanted in shyly through the bedroom window around six o'clock, as if to see what was going on. A twittering chorus of awakening birds. "Far too joyful, altogether," she thought. "If they only knew the worry that's on me this morning they might have a titter more mercy about them and leave off the chirping."

The idea occurred to her that while Annie was still asleep she should go to see if Brid Sweeney was awake yet. She would ask Brid to find some way of bringing Bridie Boyle over from Kerrytown and then return to look after Annie as best she could till help arrived. So she slipped from the room as silently as possible, closed the door behind her and dressed in the kitchen beyond. Then she scurried up the lane, memories rising in her with the vibrant scent of the fresh growth of grass, of wild mint and cow parsley and whin bushes, and the little hedgerow birds scattering in panic from before her.

There was no sign of Brid, nor indeed of Frank; it wasn't yet half past six; they would still be abed but Maggie Dan's fearful impatience took her to the bedroom window where she rapped the glass until a milky moon of a face appeared from behind the curtain. Brid's eyes squinting, blinking in protest at the light, her mouth a stark gap, like a broken window pane.

"I need you, Brid! It's Annie! Her time has come!"

The panic in her voice, the urgency of that worried face stressing through the bevelled glass brought Brid quickly to the door and Maggie Dan was admitted to rest herself by the kitchen table while Brid dressed. Frank arrived, a folded-over form of a man, his stiffness surprising Maggie Dan.
"I'm like this in the morning," he said in response to her unspoken concern, "till I get myself straightened up. Pay no heed to me. I would go for Mrs Boyle myself but it would take me too long. Brid will be quicker; she'll maybe come across somebody on a horse or a pony. Is Annie doing alright?"
"I'm scared for her. With her the way she is, she can't be telling me how she is feeling, if she's sore or what," confessed Maggie Dan.
"She'll be fine, with the help o' God," assured Frank.
After Brid left her, disappearing at some pace over a hump in the lane, she made her way back to Annie. She found the poor girl in a complete state of terror, her first pains of contraction having come upon her during her mother's absence and not having been helped by this unexplained abandonment.

Her hands reach up intuitively to her mother, fingers flexing and tensing, pulsing with the pain ripping through her lower regions; she grasps at Maggie Dan's arms and pulls her down clumsily onto the bed, on top of her. The tightness of her clutching arms takes the breath away from the older woman and she struggles to free herself from the embrace.

"God help us Annie, let me go. You're going to smother me. Let me up." Maggie Dan rolled herself to her feet, her breath coming in gasps of exertion and frustration. "I was up at Sweeney's. Brid is away to get Bridie Boyle. Bridie will know what to be doing. It'll be alright when she comes, Annie. Just try to be brave till then. She'll not be too long."
But the hours passed and there was no sign of Brid or Bridie Boyle. Annie's pains subsided and rose again, wave after rising wave. Maggie Dan fussed around her, talking constantly as if to spread the memory of her own labours over the rawness of her fear for Annie's.
"I remember when Johnny was born. He came far too early, so he did, and I wasn't expecting it. Your father was away and I was on my own. I had to get myself up to Brid ....." And on and on, driving Annie to distraction in her pain.

Why does it keep happening? Once would have been bad enough. She has no concept of how this works, of how long it is going to take, and why the agony recurs every ten minutes or so, of how this child is going to come from her. She lies back on the bed after the terror of the rending sensation and rests; she tries to hear the tune of the baby in her but it is silent. She is afraid of its silence. She wants to release it, to hold it in her arms, at her breast. She wishes it would come but she doesn't want the opening of herself for its passage from its hiding place out into this world. She wonders about the flow of water which came from her earlier, like a stream breaking out over a childhood dam. Was her baby swimming in this water? How was he breathing in it? What is he doing now, this unknown child? Why are his little arms and legs so still in her, his wriggling stopped? These are the thoughts that are going through her mind during those periods of restfulness, before the breath is driven from her lungs again by the first onslaught of the next wave of agony. And all thought is driven from her as well, replaced by some primeval instinct of survival, of self-preservation in the face of the tearing apart of her human form.

Bridie Boyle and Brid arrived in breathlessly just before ten o'clock. For Brid there had been no fortuitous meeting with anyone on horseback, not at that time of the morning.

For all her renown healing gifts, Bridie herself was suffering from back-ache, a condition she had carried with her since childhood. She had grown far too quickly in her teenage years and, as a very tall gangly girl, had engaged in farm labouring tasks over in the Lagan which were well beyond her physical capacity. The resultant damage to her back was apparently permanent and bouts of recurrent pain and restriction had tormented her for most of her fifty years. People were sorry for her but at the same time there was deep admiration in the community for how she struggled on and for the fact that, groans not withstanding, she would never turn away anyone who needed her. The traditional medicine which she had learned of from her own mother was as much in demand now as it had been for generations past. She had her clientele and would not hear tell of neglecting her role as 'an bhean ghluine', the community mid-wife and healer, when called upon. Bridie's healing gifts were all about natural instinct and unfailing compassion, rather than the inheritance of any special magical charm, as would have been the case with other women of her vocation.

Brid had had to wait for her as she rose painfully from her bed and put herself through a series of stretches and exercises to get the blood flowing, the ligaments loosened and the muscles working. Then she had heated up a strong smelling concoction of herbs and brown sugar and drunk a long draft of the medicine before being helped into her clothes and laced into her tall boots for the long walk to Ranahuel.

The peace, the relief between episodes. The wonderment about where the pain has gone to. How could it be there one minute, spiralling her downwards towards the greyness of death and the next minute have wafted away like the smoke of burning grass. She turns in the bed and her feet search for the floor; then she stands up unsteadily, the two women at either elbow. She makes for the door, gaze focussed, lips trembling. Out into the yard and around the side of the cottage to the primitive outhouse which serves as the family toilet. She is aware of half a dozen red hens which are scrabbling around in the loose earth at its entrance. She stares back into their curious little eyes as they gawk up at her, heads held at strange tangents, feet poised in mid-air as if they have forgotten what they were doing. They scatter sideways, flapping and screeching as Bridie puts her toe to the nearest one. Brid accompanies Annie into the narrow space, holding her arms supportively and speaking soothingly. The smell rises around her, making her gag and her head falls forward into Brid's hands. Before she has finished the next episode of pain is bursting in her stomach, taking her breath away.

"Lift her off that toilet! Get her up, Brid!" Bridie's instructions came from behind the door but Brid found it easier said than done in the tight confines of the outhouse. She half-dragged, half-carried Annie through the door into the yard, the poor girl bent double with the cramping pain.

"Get a kettle on and stoke up that fire, Maggie Dan. We'll need to be giving her a good wash after that; get her cleaned up as quick as we can. Come on now dear! It'll pass in a minute. Through to the bedroom now. Lie yourself down, there you are. Rest yourself a bit now. And you give your hands a good wash, Brid," she commanded.

The hot water came more slowly than was ideal and Bridie washed Annie thoroughly and spread the warm cloth over her abdomen, massaging her stomach very gently.

The contraction eases again and wildness in her eyes is replaced by her more usual look of innocent resignation. The baby is coming, the waiting is over, the baby is nearly here. How she is longing for this to be over, longing for a sight of her baby. Now she doesn't care if it's a boy or a girl; she just wants to hold it, free from her womb, released from her body. She reaches for the whistle on the shelf above her duck-feather pillow. She plays very softly, making up a slow air as she goes along; intermittently; not any great or memorable shape of a tune, just a few repeated phrases echoing from the recesses of her consciousness; the notes form themselves into something akin to a lullaby and she plays them over and over until they take on the quality of a soporific mantra, a therapy which is blocking out all other thoughts, anaesthetising her from the reality of her labour. Until the next contraction overtakes her and she gasps into the whistle and her knuckles buckle white around it and she throws it from her.

"In the history of the world she is likely the first woman to play a tune in the middle of her labour! Did you ever hear the like of it?" whispered Bridie as her body creaked and twisted into position to examine the extent of Annie's dilation. Maggie Dan placed a cold cloth on her daughter's forehead and fought back the tears stinging at the back of her eyes as she saw the silent scream in Annie's face.
"Aye, she's coming on well now, so she is. Maybe three fingers. But it's early days yet," intoned Bridie. "What time is it now? Must be about noon. Maybe half an hour after. She will have another few hours of this yet, being her first time. Go you and make us a drop of tea, Maggie Dan."
When Maggie Dan left the room Brid whispered, "Do you think I should go up to the house for some clean linen, Bridie? There's not much here. I'll get Frank a bite of food and I'll be back in no time."
"Aye, that's a good idea. Go on ahead, there's no rush here and everything seems grand," answered Bridie. "Take your time."
It was an hour before Brid arrived back in the bedroom, a pile of white cloths in her arms. She sensed immediately a hint of concern in Bridie Boyle which had not been present before she left; nothing was said; just a flick of the eyes which contained a

slight shadow of worry for the first time since she had arrived. Her expert hands were running gently but inquisitively over the stretched skin of Annie's stomach, back and forward, reading the signs, gathering clues. Maggie Dan sat at Annie's head, stroking her face and sponging her forehead as before.

Bridie spoke to Brid. "Stay with her there for a minute till Maggie and I get a breath of air." Then to Annie's mother. "Come on Maggie, stretch your legs in the sunshine for a bit. Brid can call us when the next one starts." She led the way out of the room, Maggie Dan following reluctantly. When they reached the yard Bridie turned to her.

"Whenever her waters broke Maggie, was there a bad smell at all, do you remember? Did you get a look at the fluid? Was it clear or was there any sign of colour in it, a greeny colour?"

Maggie Dan's face responded with immediate lines of concern. "No, you see the waters had broken before I came to bed. The bed was wet when I got in, so I don't know. Why Bridie? Why are you asking me that? Is there something wrong?"

"Maybe not, maybe nothing at all. But think, Maggie Dan! What about smell?"

Maggie Dan's eyes screwed up in the act of trying to recall. She shook her head.

"No, honestly, I remember no smell. None at all. Why are you asking?"

"Don't worry about it. If there was no smell that's a good sign. There's likely nothing to worry about. We'll go back in and see how she's doing now. Keep bringing me hot cloths for her." And they re-entered the bedroom to a most unusual sound.

As the latest sear of pain assaults her, Annie O'Donnell's throat opens for the first time since the cries of childhood to utter an animal-like, screeching howl of agony. It lasts for an age. Wolf meets banshee! A shriek from another world! She is astonished herself. Her mother's eyes wide and protruding, frog-like, as she runs to her.

The shocked glance between the two neighbours, and both conscious in themselves of a strangely unsettling tingle running down their spine. As if something alien has just entered the proceedings. A new tension pervaded the bedroom, distressing, virtually tangible. It had a disorientating effect upon the two women, almost paralysing them in fear. They looked at each other and the normal encouraging patter of the midwife dried up in its course, frozen into an arid soundlessness. Hopelessness! Something beyond Bridie's experience, outside the bounds of her wisdom. They were both aware of it, though not a word was spoken. Not that it could have been heard anyway, with the scream of Annie wailing in their ears.

The tightening of her stomach lasts longer this time than any yet. She is conscious of the sound rushing from her mouth and surprised by it, when she has time to be surprised, after the pain has decreased from crashing wave to quivering ripple. She lies back down on her pillow abruptly, her eyes searching out the solace of the rays of sunshine now being refracted through the glass of the four small window panes. She breathes heavily, regularly, noisily. She thinks of nothing but release; of the hope of relief. Bizarrely, a cat runs across her line of imaginary vision; black and glossy, it turns its head to stare at her and hiss. She is hearing Bridie speaking up to the other women from another examination of her nether region; Bridie is saying something about four fingers, whatever she means by that. Is she counting the baby's fingers? Does the baby not have five fingers or what? Maybe one wee hand is out already?

Another hour ticked away, the minutes during pain dragging past, the gaps between seeming to narrow inexorably. Time had begun to rethink its reputation as a linear constant. Brid's concern could wait no longer. She signalled to Bridie to come to the door and spoke to her in a curious and barely audible whisper. "Do you think she is alright?"
"I hope so, but it's the baby I'm more worried about. There hasn't been any sign of movement since we arrived. You'd have expected something, some sign of life, but nothing. I don't know what's wrong. Mind you, babies don't move a lot at this stage of labour. And the trouble is that Annie can't be telling us anything about when she last felt movement."
"Should I be going for more help, do you think? Should I send Frank down to see if he can get the priest to come up?" asked Brid.
"What good would the priest do? Sure he wouldn't come near a birth. And who else is there? And what would they be doing that I'm not capable of doing myself? No, content yourself. It'll be alright, with the help o' God!"

Bridie sounded as if she resented the suggestion and turned quickly on her heel to go back to her patient. Another bout of shouting was imminent.

And so it went on, hour after hour, into the late evening, the space between Annie's bouts of pain narrowing down to a few brief minutes of respite each time, the mother's mumbled rosaries and prayers contracting accordingly.

She is exhausted! She lies lifeless on the bed. Panting for breath. Desperate for this ordeal to end. She hears Bridie's voice as if from another planet. "There's the head starting to appear now! I can just about see it....the dark hair of it. Thank God it's not the wrong way round! The next few pushes should hopefully get the head out!" How many more pushes does she have in her? She feels that her abdomen has shrunken down into a solid, hard ball of lead. She has no sensation of baby any more; the pain is hers and hers alone and has separated her from all consciousness of the child. This is her physical crucifixion, her death throes.

"How's your back holding up?"

"Not good, Brid, not good at all. Can you and Maggie move her down a bit so she gets her feet braced against the end of the bed. And you two stay one at either side of her to help hold her, give her something to push against. Give her your hands to hold."

Bridie straightened and rubbed her back vigorously in anticipation of the next burst of action. Maggie Dan and Brid moved to their positions and took Annie's arms in theirs, ready for her next push.

Her mother is urging. She wants to hit out at her. At them all. They have no idea. She feels close to death! She is not going to make it through this. It is impossible. The baby is too big. Too lazy. It is not helping at all. It is stuck in her circle of bone. The hole is too small. It is impossible! She fights for life, for breath, for energy, for herself, for this child. She is not winning! It cannot go on! Not another ounce of energy can she muster. Spent! And yet a last squeeze is required. She is aware of the Boyle woman shouting at her above the noise of her own screams.

"Push! Push girl, if you want to stay alive at all! Push now!"

She is hearing the words but they are far away from her. She is disconnected from them. They echo from a different world. Some hands are on her stomach pressing down, trying in vain to help but only causing her more distracting agony. It's all so concentrated, so urgent, so much a life in the balance. She feels the spirit draining away from her. Like she is watching herself from the rafters, from the height of her pain. The words, incessant.

"Good girl! Good girl! Keep it going! Push! Just another big push! You're doing great Annie! Come on Annie! Don't give up! Just another big push! Breathe now! Come on, keep breathing, God love you! Don't go on us now Annie! Stay with us! Good girl Annie! It'll soon be over! Just one more big push! Another push Annie!"

But it's fading away! The pain is subsiding again and the chance is missed. She feels rent in two.

Both Maggie Dan and Brid were glad of the respite from the intense grip of Annie's frantically clutching hands and they shook out their cramped fingers, trying to get the blood circulating once more. Maggie Dan reached for the beads again. Anything! Where is the crucifix? Incase....!

"Another good push should have the head out. How's she doing?"

"Put a cloth to her lips, wet them for her. Maybe just a wee sip of cold water, see if it'll revive her."

"She's doing well."

"She's exhausted, my poor Annie. Hail Mary, full of grace, blessed......"

"This next one will be the big one! I hope it arrives on her quick. Give her all the help you can, Brid."

"We're doing our best, aren't we Maggie Dan? And you're doing well Annie. It's not easy, but we've all been through it, so we have. You're not the first."

"Ssh now, Brid; you don't want to annoy her. There, I've counted near enough a minute since the last one, so it should be soon now. Annie, can you hear me? Another big push from you this time. Take wee short breaths and pant between the pushes. It'll soon be over and you'll have your baby in your arms. Give it all you've got girl, you hear me!"

And it rises again like a monstrous sea-swell, a wave like no other, gathering pace and lifting to a terrifying peak of jagged agony in her. It breaks in crashing weight upon her, submerging her and driving the breath out of her lungs so that she is gasping for oxygen. Somehow she finds the presence of mind in the middle of it all to brace her tired body for a final time, steeling her legs against the solid bed-end and pulling back on the arms of her mother and Brid. She does not hear the cries of encouragement, the firm instructions shouted at her. She is in a zone of excruciating wretchedness. The opening rips further apart. Somehow she maintains the frantic pressure and the baby's head makes its slow appearance before the contraction eases back. She is unaware that the baby's head is now stuck out of her and the body still trapped inside. And the baby is still. Its dark hair through the birth mucus near enough matches the shade of its screwed up little face.

"Well done, Annie! Good girl! We're nearly there!" encouraged Brid, close in to Annie's ear.
Bridie began to work her fingers around the head, feverishly, a perceptible degree of panic in her movements.
"Come here, Brid! See if you can... give me a hand here!" she said urgently.
Brid slipped quickly beside her at the foot of the bed.
"God, look at its wee face. Blue as the sea, so it is!" she gasped.
"Ssh Brid!"
"What's wrong with it, Bridie? It's a terrible colour surely?"
"The cord's tight around its neck. Far too tight. There was no way of knowing before the head came out."
"Oh no!" came the grandmother's pleading voice from the other end of the bed. "Sweet Jesus and Mary, help our wee baby! Lord save us!"
"Can you not do something Bridie?" The tears were blurring Brid's eyes.
"I'm doing my best! Look....see how tight it is! I can't even squeeze my finger in between neck and cord."
"Good, look, you're getting it. Can we not cut the cord or something? Go on Bridie, keep trying."
Maggie Dan, staring wildly down the bed at them, stroking Annie's blank face. "Is the wain going to be alright, Bridie?"
"It's not born yet, Maggie Dan," came Brid's tense voice.
"We need another push very quick to get it out. Another pain! The cord... is... trapped.... so... tight!"
She was still striving to free it, red-face, grey words between efforts to loosen the cord, groaning spasmodically as her back protested against the strain.
"It's cutting off the blood supply, that's what I'm afraid of," she murmured.

The harder Annie had pushed, the more the umbilical cord had tightened around the infant's neck. It was touch and go. So vital now that another contraction come immediately and release the rest of the body so that it could be rotated and the pressure on the neck released. The idea of putting fingers down inside the cord was not working. Any attempt to turn the baby at this stage was going to fail. But no contraction came, at least not quickly enough.

Bridie took her sharp knife from its bath of scalding water. She hesitated, still in two minds. Waiting for the contraction.

"Come on! Come on!" she breathed. But no sign yet.

Then she acted. Stretching the cord up as far as her fingers would allow, she sliced through it decisively, a small flow of bloody fluid spewing out on the bed. Fingers into the baby's mouth, trying to clear the airway. Fingers fumbling with the defunct cord, trying to unwrap its coil from the fold of flesh into which it had embedded itself.

"Come on! Come on, girl!"

Still nothing.

"Annie!" she shouted, "As soon as this next pain rises, you push like you've never pushed before! You hear me girl! Here it comes. Here it comes. Good. Now, girl! Give it all you have! Every last ounce of energy!"

She herself was catching the baby's head, turning it slightly, firmly, urgently trying to free it, to draw it from the confines of the birth canal, to give the child a chance of life.

But even as the body came Bridie could tell it was too late.

The colour! A lifeless blueish tinge to it. All over the slimy little torso. A grimness settled on her face. It wasn't the first time she had seen such a delivery. There was no way of knowing beforehand. Except that the baby hadn't been moving around much, perhaps. But that was an unreliable clue. She worked with the child for as long as she could, to give it every chance of taking its first breath. She cleared its mouth and its windpipe as best she could, blowing gently into it, checking to see if she could detect a pulse, in vain. She massaged it, held it upside down and slapped its back, put it in a bath of lukewarm water, rubbed it tenderly, then vigorously. She handed it to Brid to try but all Brid could do was cuddle it and cry. Maggie Dan took it, held it and prayed to all the saints. And then, eventually, as she regained some strength, Annie held out her hands for her lifeless infant. Bridie gave it, hesitantly.

She takes it. She looks at it with as tender a look as she has ever been able to give. She strokes its peat-black hair and curls it in her fingers. Then she lifts her blouse and puts the child to her breast. Stone-blue lips to rose-red nipple. Her first-born son. Her eyes lift to her mother's.

Maggie Dan turned and ran from the room. She continued running, out across the yard and down the lane towards the village and her priest, her bellowed sobs still audible in the stillness of the bedroom across the late evening air.

Chapter 39

In-between

Maggie Dan's journey was a wasted one. She reached the Parochial House in the smudged monochrome light of dusk, moths and the last of the evening's midges annoying her, only to discover that Father Dunleavey was not at home. She stood in despair, the echo of the brass-knocker ringing hollow in hall on the other side of the door.

"No priest there when you need him the most," she thought.

Light from an oil lamp flickered in Mrs Gallagher's window across the street. Maggie Dan made her way to the housekeeper's front door, opened it and called in.

"Mrs Gallagher, is Father Dunleavey not in?"

"He's not," came the woman's response from within. "He's staying the night in Letterkenny. He was at a meeting there all day. Why, what do you need?"

No sound or sign of the woman coming to the door so Maggie Dan, desperate to off-load her sadness onto another human being having walked this far carrying it on her own, stepped hesitantly in through the creaking door and stood behind the back of the woman's chair. There was the pleasant smell of recent baking in the kitchen; soda bread cooling on the table. Mrs Gallagher turned stiffly at the sound of a stifled sob.

"What's the matter, Maggie Dan?" she asked getting to her feet.

"It's Annie! She's had the baby and....and it's dead, the poor wee thing."

Her tears broke out over the top of her reserve and flowed down her wrinkled cheeks in profusion.

"Ah, ta bron orm! I am sorry! Was it born dead?"

"It was, it never got so much as a single breath, as far as I could see," answered Maggie Dan.

"I'm sorry to hear that. And is the girl alright herself?" asked Mrs Gallagher.

Maggie paused for a moment. She suddenly realised that she didn't know the answer to this query, having fled the bedchamber so hastily. She stuttered an indefinite reply.

"I think so. I hope to God she is."

"And what did you want his reverence for?"

The question may have seemed an obvious one to the wizened old housekeeper but Maggie Dan reacted to it in some shock.

"I need him to come and see what he can do," she said indignantly.

"Well, even if he was here I don't see that there's much he could do. If the baby's dead, that's that! There's not much he can do now. He'll likely be back tomorrow evening so I'll let him know of your visit and he will maybe call up and see you before night. You'd be as well hurrying back up to your daughter. If she's on her own with the baby she could be doing with you, I'm sure."

"She's not on her own. What sort of a heartless creature do you take me for? Brid Sweeney and Bridie Boyle are looking after her. I just thought if I could get Father Dunleavey to come he could maybe have baptised the child or something."

Maggie Dan turned sharply towards the door, her chin jutting indignantly as she tried to rein in her temper with every deep breath.

"Not if it was dead already. How could he do that, baptise the wain if there was never any life in it? He's only a priest, you know, not a miracle worker." The woman's callous coldness astounded Maggie Dan and she stomped out of the house without another word passing between the two of them.

~~~~~~~

The still little form of the baby boy lay by Annie all that night, wrapped up in an old piece of linen cloth which had once been white. Maggie Dan went to the settle bed in the kitchen after the two defeated lay-women had taken their leave together.

She has been submerged in a sleep of total exhaustion. She wakens slowly to a blizzard of ice-cold thoughts drifting past her. The disorientation, the weird dreams and visions of the night, the memories of her labour, the dawning realisation that the chill against her skin is coming from her dead child. She manoeuvres her body painfully in the bed to turn so she can see him. She stares blankly at his crinkly form from close range, seeing it out of focus, blurred and contorted, as if seen through the distorting lens of an old glass bottle. She lies in this position until her mother brings a cup of tea and a bowl of steaming porridge from the kitchen. Her eyes follow as Maggie Dan lifts the child, wraps it entirely in the linen and places it reverently on the floor in the corner of the room. She sits up and drinks deep draughts of the warm tea, answering the painful thirst in her throat.

Father Dunleavey arrived at the home in the early evening. His journey back across the mountains from the county town had been tiring in the extreme. He reflected on a sense of resentment and annoyance that the Diocesan meeting he had been attending had eaten up three of his precious days, two of them in travelling to and from Letterkenny. Church politics had never really interested him much, nor had the theological homilies uttered to the gathering by some visiting 'Monsignor' from Dublin.

"Other-worldly prattle of no consequence to those of us living in the real world of poverty-stricken Donegal. I have more important things to be doing on the ground," he had thought as the horse-drawn carriage had bumped its way through the rocky gap in the hills near Creeslough. "And this journey is taking forever. Would to God we had got the go-ahead for the railway back when we should have got it. I'd be flying home to the Rosses in no time, and in style. No more of this bone-shaking trek on roads not fit for any decent Christian traveller."

His mood had not been helped by Mrs Gallagher's stark greeting.

"Annie O'Donnell has had her wain and it's dead."

So his old bones and sinews weren't finished yet.

"Annie! Dear love that poor girl but she had this coming to her," he mused. Annie had held a particular fascination for him for as long as he could remember, had he chosen to remember. Her strangely vacant beauty, even in childhood. Her snowdrop-like innocence; the open-eyed stare in which he could never discern any category of thought, or mood, or reaction; the fact of her muteness.

He had often wondered about the cause of it all and about who the girl was who was locked up in there. What would it take to release this Guinevere from her tower of silence and indifference? Could there ever be a miracle of healing for her? Does Our Lord or His Blessed Mother or any of the hallowed saints still do such miracles? Now that was a question he would have liked to have put to that Dublin theologian. What about the injustice of it all? A silent, handicapped girl in a silent, handicapped west.

She had never been to confession of-course, so he did not know how her mind worked or what her particular temptations were. Over the years she had usually come up for a blessing at Mass with her mother. But there had never been any question of catechising her or preparing her for first communion. All that he had been content to leave in God's hands. Now he wondered if that had been a mistake, especially given her fall from grace. If indeed it was a fall from grace. Maybe some fellow had had his way with her against her will. Probably. He couldn't imagine Annie welcoming sexual advances. How could she, with her simplicity and her silence? There was something about her vulnerability though. A need in her, a naive openness which, if he was being honest, he recognised as a powerful draw. That, coupled with her growing beauty over the past while, a subtly beguiling flowering into full femininity. Girl to womanhood. Chrysalis to butterfly. He had felt mildly captivated by this alluring femininity, even as her priest, something he had freely admitted to himself. To himself alone.

But someone else had experienced the same draw, whoever he was. And now Annie, God love her, was experiencing a harsh judgement on her waywardness. A warning to all the other young girls of the community. Because that is what this death signified to him as priest and shepherd of his flock. And that is the message he would be subtly trying to ensure would come out of this tragedy. A clear lesson for the youth of the parish. Particularly before this railway arrived bringing all sorts of new temptations to lasciviousness.

"Maybe I need to be planning a special mission for them all," he thought. "A pre-emptive strike against debauchery."

He reached O'Donnell's cottage, entered and blessed the house in the customary fashion. Maggie Dan couldn't meet his eyes but, recognising the soreness of his bandy legs and the tiredness of his deeply lined face, she pushed forward a chair for him.

"I am sorry to hear that Annie's baby didn't survive," he began. "I'm sure she had been looking forward to it, in her own simple way. It's a terrible tragedy for her, for you as well."

Silence, as thoughts found no way out into the open.

The priest continued his consolation. "It must be so hard for her, the poor girl. Such a shock. You wonder why these things are allowed to happen, don't you? But maybe it's for the best all the same, Maggie Dan, in the circumstances I mean, with Annie the way she is and.... and no father for the child."

The woman of the house bit her lip for a moment, then, a mixture of astonishment and resentment in her trembling voice, she spoke.

"How could it be for the best, Father? Is life not better than death every time?"

"Of-course it is, of-course it is. I didn't mean that, not at all," he back-tracked. "I'm tired Maggie Dan, after that day of travelling. I didn't mean that. But am I not right in saying that the child was born dead? It never took a breath, from what Mrs Gallagher said?"

"Just because it never took a breath doesn't mean it didn't have life in it," she argued, surprised at the sound of her own audacity and a little pleased by her courage. She could not remember ever having argued with her priest before but he had touched a nerve with his tactless comment about it being 'for the best'.

"It had life in the mother's womb, of-course it had, but that's a different kind of life, isn't it? It is not the same as being a living, breathing soul."

The clergyman was not enjoying this conversation and stood up as if to signify his discomfort, his impatience with this hurting parishioner.

Maggie Dan sub-consciously moved to block the door in case he would leave before she made her request.

"And I suppose that means you will refuse to give the child a decent Christian burial in the church graveyard?"

"Now Maggie Dan! You know better than to ask me that. I can't give it a Christian burial. You know that. And it's not because of who it is, who its mother or grandmother is, who its father is or isn't. It's not even because the child was stillborn. It's because the child has not been baptised. You know that. So does every other mother in the parish. If the child had been baptised that would be different. It would be a member of the church; its original sin washed away in baptism; it wouldn't be a problem."

"Original sin?" she spat out scornfully. "Sure the baby never took a breath. It's as innocent as a newborn....it's as pure as snow, so it is. If anything, it would have more of a right to a Christian burial and to lie in the holy grounds of the church than half the sinners who are buried there, or who will be buried there, myself included."

"That may be but there it is. I cannot do a thing about it. I can pray for it, not that maybe you think that'll do a lot of good, but I can certainly say a prayer for it; now if you want; and for you and Annie as well."

"What will you be praying? That God above takes the poor wee soul straight to heaven? That would only be fair, seeing as it never had any experience of life on God's good earth."

Father Dunleavey found himself noticing, for the first time, the cobweb of fine wrinkles that seemed to have been woven on her ageing skin of late. He shook his head ruefully.

"That I cannot do, Maggie Dan. You know the Church's teaching on this. I'm sure you have heard me going over it before. The soul of an unbaptised infant goes to neither Heaven nor Hell, nor indeed to Purgatory," he intoned. "It goes to an in-between place, a place of peace and happiness....and it's called Limbo. That is where Annie's baby is now. We don't know much about it but that is what the doctrine of the Church teaches. So that's all there is about it."

"Aye, that's all there is about it," she sighed in resignation. "And neither me nor Annie nor anybody else can look forward to seeing it again on the other side?"

"That part you have to just leave to the Good Lord."

"The Good Lord?" she began...

The bedroom door creaks open behind the grandmother. Annie stands there, her eyes slanting down at the dead baby in her arms. There is an other-worldliness about her appearance. A serenity. Her plain white nightdress, slightly blood-soiled from below the waist, framed in the doorway and backlit by the pale shafts of sunlight washing in across the room behind. A down-market watercolour in three dimensions. A very Irish tableau of the Madonna and Child. Mary cradling her dead baby Saviour. But now she is offering it up to her priest, arms extending towards him reverentially. She witnesses the expression of distaste on his face as he takes a step back, the drawing together of his eyebrows, the twist and downturn of his wide mouth. She is not to be discouraged and continues, very deliberately lifting the child upwards towards his line of vision and taking a couple of slow steps into the room. She sees her priest turn away to stare at the fire-less hearth. Her eyes fall vacantly to the stiff little form in her arms and she stands statue-like in that position in the centre of the earthen floor.

"I am so sorry about your baby, Annie," Father Dunleavey said softly to the unravelling remains of the St Bridget's Cross hanging on the wall.
Nobody moved a muscle in the stagnant silence.
"The black hair on it! He didn't get that from Annie. Nor from Sean Ban Sweeney," he thought to himself in the depths of his curious mind.
Annie turned of her own accord and went back into the room, pulling the door behind her with her foot.
"You'll have to get that baby buried as quick as possible," he breathed.
"That's not going to be easy. Who can I get to take it out to the island on Carrickfinn? I have no man, with Johnny away. Frank would help but he's not able, God help him. Sean Ban would have done it, if he had been here. I don't think I could manage to carry it all the way out to Oileán na Márbh by myself, never mind dig a hole for it. And I have no way of leaving her to go and get Seamus O'Donnell to come over with his horse and cart. I am badly stuck here Father," she complained.
The clergyman pulled at his ear for a moment.
"Look, the tide is low for the next few hours. If I leave now I could be over to Seamus and back in time for him to saddle up and come tonight before it gets too dark. You'll be wanting to do the shift after dark, won't you? It saves talk in the parish. Will I do that for you?"
"After dark, is it? As if having a dead grandson was something to be ashamed of," thought Maggie Dan to herself, but she understood that this was the tradition of such illicit burials. "Buried in the half-light! In the half-world between the ocean and the earth, somewhere between Heaven and Hell." she mused. But to Father Dunleavey she said, "Aye, that is maybe the best thing to do. The evening is long with the weather the way it is, so we would have time. Thanks, Father. Would you mind doing that for us?"
"Not at all. The least I can do. We'll be back in an hour, if I can get Vincent to hurry himself up a bit."
He took his leave.

~~~~~~~

She cannot be persuaded to give up her baby and go back inside the house. She is holding it tight, standing in the yard beside her cousin's horse and cart. The black and white mare is stamping its feet as if in protest at being dragged from its stall and re-harnessed at this time of night, after it had imagined its day's work was done. She understands the horse and goes up to its bobbing head, baby in her arms, almost as if to connect, to explain. Seamus watches her, shakes his head sadly but says nothing. Maggie Dan eventually takes her by the arm and leads her to the back of the cart. Her mother helps her as she steps up from an upturned creel with difficulty and lies down stiffly on a bundle of fresh hay which Seamus has thoughtfully brought along. The child she cradles in her arms, adjusting the linen cloth as if to keep it warm as the dusk sucks the last heat out of the day. The horse jerks forward and Seamus' spade which had been set upright against the side-wing of the cart falls over on top of her, striking her on the side of the head. She doesn't seem to notice. Maggie Dan lifts it and places it flat on the floor of the cart. She is conscious of Seamus taking the reins, slapping them against the horse's flank and hears him clicking with his tongue to demand action from his mare.

The three of them in the cart. With the corpse of the child of-course. Out along the almost empty estuary. The tide at its lowest. The crimson blob of the sun clinging onto the rim of the horizon and bleeding red reflections across the westward seascape. In its final seconds of visibility between a stretch of grey-brown cloud and the deep-blue line of the ocean, its dying rays tinged horse and cart with orange light on their seaward side and at the same time cast a gargantuan purple shadow across the undulating sand-flats on the other.
They had met one or two neighbours on their journey. None had spoken to them, turning away from the pain of what they realised was happening, adhering to the age-old prohibitions surrounding such clandestine burials. Nothing was said. No greeting exchanged. Anonymity preserved. Eyes bouncing away from the simple cortege like pebbles ricocheting off a stone wall. A community subliminally barred from entering into the usual supportive practices of waking the deceased and comforting those who mourned the passing.
Jacob Stewart was the only other person who witnessed the burial. He had just finished a peaceful spell of line-fishing off

the rocks at the back of Oileán na Márbh and, deciding to go home, had begun to clamber up towards the grassy plateau above, rod and tackle in one hand and three shining glashen hooked in the fingers of the other. He hadn't heard a sound down there, with the lapping and gurgling of the waves at his feet. So he was more than a little surprised, as he emerged on the summit, to see through the hazy twilight the shapes of two figures standing above him in the island meadow. He ducked back down below the edge of the plateau and watched through the camouflaging fingers of a clump of pink clover as the man began to dig, back bent into his task, arms working quickly and efficiently. But it wasn't the actions of the grave-digger which caught Jacob's attention. It was that of the other figure. He recognised the shape of Annie, silhouetted against the deepening grey of the sky, one or two eastern stars beginning to quiver into life around her head. Her hair blowing back as a sea breeze rose and caught it. She watched the digger impassively, the indistinct shape of a little bundle in her hands.

Jacob had not heard anything about Annie giving birth. None of the Stewarts had. But it was immediately obvious to him what had happened. The sadness of the tragedy he was witnessing above him struck him so forcibly that, consciously dismissing the taboo which would have insisted on him staying where he was and diverting his attention, he rose from his hiding place and made his way across the soft, rich Oileán na Márbh grass to where Annie stood, infant in arms, awaiting its burial. Seamus O'Donnell stopped digging briefly in surprise, looked up quizzically at the newcomer but said nothing. Jacob stood beside Annie.

"I am sorry, Annie. I didn't know," he said simply and slipped his arm around her waist in a gesture of gentle but powerful identification. Seamus began digging again.

Inside herself she is very touched by Jacob's action. But she does not move. Apart from a shiver or two as the chilly night air sweeps up from the surface of the sea. She is glad that her mother could not climb up the rocky path onto the island. Because this is her baby for the grave, her affair, and she doesn't want the complication of her mother keening hysterically as she lays him down in the sandy soil. She hopes Seamus will go and give her peace when he has the hole dug, when the time comes. But now this other fellow is here. She doesn't mind his presence beside her, so close beside her.

Who is he anyway, that he seems to know her? She lifts her gaze from watching the rhythm of the dig and stares out to the west. She sees the rose-coloured shell of the sky above Inishfree and the twinkle of that bright star that always seems to sit above Cruit Island in the evening. Seamus has finished. He is moving away, as if reading her mind. So too is this new fellow. She is alone with the miniature grave and her baby son. She kneels by the hole, mechanically, without any show of emotion. Until, just before laying him in the sand, she unwraps the linen cloth and drops it beside her feet. Then she lifts the tiny naked form above her head and holds it there, looking up at it against the night sky. She remains in this primordial posture until her arms tire and she lowers the child to her cheek for a long final kiss, before wrapping him again in the linen cloth and placing him in the shallow grave. She pushes handfuls of sand over him until he has disappeared into the dry womb of the earth. Then she gets up and walks slowly away, looking back over her shoulder a couple of times as if to check that a miracle of resurrection hasn't happened yet.

Jacob watched this burial in a trance-like state but afterwards his shoulders shook with an unexpected and previously suppressed range of feelings. In his mind he travelled back several months to the occasion when he was digging the grave for that sailor and when he had uncovered the whited, bird-like bones of an infant already in the sand. Annie's raising of her child towards the sky had resonated strongly with his own instinct at the time and he remembered doing something similar with that tiny skeleton. What was it about the corpse of a child which provoked this kind of instinctive reaction, he wondered. Or was it just something special to this place, this un-consecrated ground, which cast an ancient spell over the rites of burial and which demanded a worshipful offering of the innocent remains of such a child to the universe which had given birth to it? Or to the uninvited God who had given it and now taken it so hastily. Church or no church.

The young Stewart returned to the graveside and, taking the shovel in his hands, completed the filling in of the grave himself so that when Seamus materialised through the shadowy darkness the job was finished. Seamus grunted his thanks and followed Annie down the rough track to the beach, to Maggie Dan and the waiting horse and cart.

Before he left Oileán na Márbh that night, Jacob Stewart went again to the grave of that naked sailor, only a few yards away on the other side of the meadow. He tested the turf with his feet, firming it down into place where there had been the inevitable subsidence of soil and sod as the body decayed over the months.

Standing there, he found himself wondering how Sean Ban was getting on in Scotland. It must be four months since he left. He determined in his mind to write to him tomorrow. Of all people, Sean Ban deserved to know about Annie's baby and this unholy burial.

Reluctant to withdraw from the intoxicating pathos of the evening, Jacob eased himself slowly back down from the island. The horse and cart, with its three huddled passengers barely distinguishable, was a mere inky smudge in the dusky quarter-light. Jacob heard it rattling faintly up the stony track at the far end of the beach as it disappeared into the gloom. He meandered thoughtfully along the arc of the shadowy strand, eventually stopping to stare out to the distant meniscus of the ocean, where sky and sea met to console each other at the death of another day.

Delicate ferns of cloud frescoed the darkening dome of the sky to the west. Their underside was still faintly tinged, as in afterthought, with smudges of scarlet and violet by some stubborn rays from the sunken sun. The sea, a pied wash of mercury and silver continents, like an atlas map of the world in the negative. At his feet, the whisper of miniature waves kissing the sand almost in apology for their lack of virility; a repeating swish like the sound of an autumn scythe slicing through the dried-out stalks of well-ripened oats. Somewhere behind him the plaintive, quavering call of a homeward bound herring gull but apart from that, and the ripple of the sea, no other noise to pollute the tranquility of this moment.

"A healing silence," mused the youth, and he waited long in the same pose, draining every last sweet drop of emotional nectar from it, afraid to move in case he should break the enchantment.

Chapter 40

Letters from Home

Over the course of a few weeks in June and early July, Sean Ban Sweeney received three letters from home. The first two contained the same message. One was from his parents. It briefly told him the shockingly sad news that Annie had given birth to a stillborn child. There was little more to it than that. Their mastery of the written Gaelic word did not run to the conveyance of much emotional substance. They were sorry to be bringing him this tragic news of his friend Annie and her baby; they were in reasonable health themselves; they hoped he was content and well; they sent regards to his sister Mary and her family.

The second letter arrived a couple of days later and contained the same news. It was from his old companion, Jacob Stewart of Carrickfinn, and he read it eagerly.

How thoughtful of Jacob to write about Annie. And to think of that strange coincidence that he should be fishing off the back of Oileán na Márbh when the burial was taking place. Credit to him for going to stand by Annie's side as the grave was being dug. You could always count on Jacob to do the supportive thing. Very sensitive of him, given the difficult circumstances and especially as the unpleasant task of digging such a Cillin grave would customarily have been undertaken by the infant's father, and always in secret isolation. Very unusual for a mother to have been present at all. A fine fellow Jacob, if ever there was one.

Sean found his mind wandering increasingly over the following days as he worked. Up until now he had really enjoyed labouring in the open air. He had been fortunate to get a job in the gardens of Carberry Tower, a very grand old mansion of a place near Musselburgh where his brother-in-law, Pat Quinn, had a job as a gardener. Pat had been instrumental in persuading the estate manager to hire his young in-law as an assistant. Sean's arrival in March had been timely, coinciding with the start of Lord Elphinstone's scheme to create some new features in his expansive grounds by digging several lakes and ornamental ponds. A team of strong young local lads had been taken on already, but Pat had not hesitated to stick his neck out and recommend Sean as an additional labourer. The manager had not been disappointed in him. Sean knew how to work. He could stick at a job when others needed a rest and his cooperative attitude had drawn nods of appreciation from his foreman.

In some ways Sean hardly considered the activity as work at all, such was his enjoyment of the experience. The air was clear and much milder than the wet and windy west of Donegal. The ground was easily worked with, entirely different in texture from the boggy, black soil that lay between the rocks and loughs of Ranahuel. When he dug his spade or shovel into this compliant earth he found there was an absence of the clawing protest which tended to happen if he was turning over the sod at home.

The grounds of the old castle were already beautiful but would be so enhanced by this new landscaping scheme. Huge trees abounded everywhere you looked; oaks, sycamores, ash, birch, beech and conifers of many varieties. Many of the species were entirely new to him, several having been imported by past residents of the house, botanical trophies from far-flung foreign climes. His favourite was the mighty Weeping Ash which stood in front of the mansion, dominating the extensive lawn with the massive embrace of its spreading branches; an ancient tree with such character. The exotic scent of roses, border plants, herbs and flowers, many of which he had never heard of before, swept around him wherever he worked. The little garden birds sang, constantly and beautifully; peacocks screeched and strutted; pigeons and doves cooed soothingly; insects buzzed and flitted from plant to plant; the friendly spaniels from the big house came to sniff and bark at him and the most elegant horses and riders he had ever seen paraded past him on their way to exercise along the tracks on the estate.

Sean was enjoying the whole experience. The money was good, more than he could ever have hoped to earn anywhere in Ireland as a labourer. But more importantly, he was his own man here.

It was this freedom from the bind of inevitability and prescription which he valued most of all. He almost celebrated it with every lunge of his pick-axe. Thoughts of home had been draining away from him, like the Scottish rain did when it fell on this loamy earth.

Until now! The image of Annie, standing in the twilight by the shallow grave of her baby, out on that sad Oileán na Márbh.... the picture had etched itself in his mind as he read Jacob's vivid account of the affair and now would not leave him. He was glad that Jacob had been there; of-course he was. He was full of appreciation for the fact that this thoughtful young Protestant had written to him about the matter. But that was only half of his reaction. The other part was a disturbing feeling which he barely recognised and which he had trouble in clearly identifying to himself. Slowly he admitted to a deep-seated and annoying resentment and he saw that he needed to try to analyse the reason for this unhappiness.

It was much more than a sympathy for Annie and the baby. The birds still sang and the earth still smelt the same as he worked but the joy had gone out of it all. Why could he not have been spared this gnawing thought? And what was the nature of this reaction, the cause of his darkening mood, he asked himself.

Gradually it came to him in clarity, and as a surprise. Jealousy! He began to see that he was resentful of the fact that Jacob was there by accident, where he himself should have been there by design. It was his place to have been with Annie, not a fellow that she did not know, however good he was. But his choice had taken him away from her. Deliberately so, of-course. In the midst of all his self-recrimination the irony of the situation was not lost on him. Jacob, who was the one person that he had trusted to help him to escape from Johnny O'Donnell's Ireland, was now the one who was standing in his place as Annie's comforter.

Try as he might to dismiss this pattern of rumination, Sean Ban found himself being swept into a depressive cycle of thoughts and memories. His sister Mary noticed it, as did Pat and the two Quinn children who were starting to find it difficult to persuade Sean to play with them. They had so loved having fun with their Irish uncle on a Sunday or in the evenings when he arrived back to their tiny little terraced house beside the slow-flowing River Esk. He now seemed tired after his day's work and the two mile walk home. Pat and Mary had a good circle of friends, jolly people, some of them Irish and some local. Sean had been part of the group on several occasions, enjoying their company, a bit of fishing or football, a drink or two, a few songs afterwards. They were great homely folk with such humour, such spirit, despite their poverty and the tough living conditions they were having to endure. One or two of the girls in the group had tried to get Sean's attention but, while he wasn't a fellow to turn his back on a flirtatious opportunity, he had never allowed himself to go beyond a one-off conversation. Now he was avoiding this group of good people altogether, choosing to stay in his cupboard-like bedroom of an evening, even when Pat had asked him to come for a pint. His older sister, the woman of the house, was becoming annoyed at him, concerned at his change of mood.

"Are you homesick, Sean?" she asked as he rose from the bones of the herring he had been picking over, the usual evening meal.

He stopped in his tracks and turned from the foot of the tight little staircase up to his room. She saw a heaviness in his eyes as he tried to smile at her question. "Well, that would be a first. Homesick? Sure when I was there I was homesick," he replied. "Sick of home, more like. No, Mary...I'm not homesick. What makes you ask that?"

"You just don't seem as happy as you have been."

"You think?"

"Yes, I do. You seem....different someway. In the last week or two especially."

He just stood there.

"Was it that letter about Annie O'Donnell's baby? Did that annoy you?" she asked perceptively and watched the wince deep behind his eyes as his gaze shifted back to the staircase.

"Aye, well maybe. I was sorry to hear about it. You remember how close Annie and I were... as friends like."

He paused and scratched the back of his neck and she read so much from his bearing.

"You poor fellow," she said coming up behind him and giving him a hug, a motherly hug from a sister, which dispensed with the need for any more words. He didn't turn around but his hand clasped one of hers to his chest for a brief second before he gently removed it and climbed the steep steps two at a time.

The following Thursday Sean Ban and Pat returned from work as usual, arriving in to Mary about seven o'clock on a beautifully warm summer evening. Sean went through the kitchen to the yard at the rear, took off his coat, pumped some cold water from the stand pump there and threw a few handfuls around

his sunburned face. As he rubbed himself dry with a linen cloth Mary appeared at the back door with an envelope in her hand.
"Another letter from home for you Sean," she said, holding it out to him and noticing the eagerness in his grab. He looked at the writing first as he sat himself down on the low windowsill to read.
"Jacob Stewart again, by the look of his hand," he said to Mary's back as she went inside to get the meal on the table. He tore open the somewhat battered envelope. "What's wrong this time? Quite a bit it would seem," he thought looking at the length of the letter and resigning himself to the marathon of trying to decipher meaning from Jacob's spidery scrawl, not to mention his clumsy Irish.

~~~~~~~

<div style="text-align: right">Carrickfinn
Co Donegal
July 6th 1897</div>

Dear Sean Ban,
            This is your friend Jacob Stewart again. I am sorry to be writing to you so soon after the last letter.
I hope you are in good health there in Scotland. I am in good health, as are all the family here in Carrickfinn.
Now I will tell you the reason why I am writing to you again so soon.
You will remember that in my previous letter I told you about your friend Annie and the sad burial of her baby on Oileán na Márbh. A burial which I was able to witness with my own eyes, as I informed you.
Since that night I am writing to tell you of other sadness which I have also witnessed.
Some days after the night I am reminding you about I was fixing the bottom of the curragh with more pitch. It had worn very thin, as you pointed out to me. I was doing this down at the pier in the harbour, across the bay from Oileán na Márbh. As I was working I heard a strange sound. It echoed around the rocks there by the beach. It was the sound of a whistle being played. I wondered where it was coming from and so I followed the sound with my ears until my eyes saw it. Annie was up on top of the island and she was playing her whistle by the grave

where her child lies in the earth. This was fine, I thought at the time. A nice, motherly thing for her to be doing. But later I had finished the repair of the curragh and I looked up at the island again. She was still there. She was just sitting on the rock by the grave. Again I thought that this was not a problem. So I went home. I told my mother. She said that the tide would be coming in very soon so I should go back there and bring Annie off before the water surrounds her. I did this. Annie came with me without a complaint and so I took her to the sand-flats at the bottom of our lane. I pointed her the way home and she went off in the direction of her home. I am sure she is very sad but with her it is hard to tell.

If my story could stop there I would not be writing to you to worry you. But it does not. The same thing happened the next night and once again I did the same thing. I brought her from the island and set her off on her way back to the mainland. This happened a few times. She never resisted in any way and just did as I suggested each time.

But the story gets worse.

Last week my father and I had been working late at the hay crop across from Gweedore. When we arrived back home the sun was set and the air was very still. I stood in the quiet outside looking at the stars in the clear night sky. I heard the whistle again. Long, slow, mournful notes of a tune. So I went to the harbour to look over to see if Annie was there. She was. But what was worse was that the tide was well in. She was cut off from the land. Our curragh had been moved to the north inlet at Poulnapaiste for fishing reasons so it was too far away for me to fetch it to ferry her back. So I waded out through water up to my chest to the island and climbed up to Annie. I took her by the hand to persuade her to come with me to safety. But she was unwilling. It took me a long time of pulling and talking and pointing out the tide to her to get her to come with me. When we climbed down to the rocks the tide was so far in I was afraid it would be above our heads if we waded across. I thought to test the depth of the water first. So I waded out on my own, leaving Annie on the rocks. Before I had reached halfway to the shore I was swallowing mouthfuls of seawater. It was going to be too deep. I cannot swim, as you know, and I thought Annie was in the same boat. (Not that we had a boat, you understand.) So what could I do but turn and try to get back to Annie. The water almost swept me off my feet a couple of times. I was scared to death but I made it back to her. If I had not I could not be writing this account to you.

We were therefore stuck on the island for the night. My clothes were very wet and I shivered badly. Thankfully my mother began to realise that I had not come back into the house. She guessed what might have happened and sent my father out to find me. We heard him shouting from the beach and I shouted back. But then he had to return to the house to get the oars for the curragh and to get Bobby to help him. They ran to the curragh and then paddled around to the island to rescue us.

Annie stayed at our house that night. With the tide full in the estuary we could not get any message to her mother who must have been very worried about her. The next day my mother and father both took Annie back to her home and explained to Maggie Dan what had happened. It seems there is nothing the old woman can do with Annie. She is so determined to go to her baby all the time.

Since that eventful night Annie has been back a few more times to the island but we now keep a watch and make sure she is not trapped there again by the tide. But the danger is always there. Seems she is missing her child so much. In her quiet grief she seems to think the only thing to be doing is to be playing her music to the ghost of the child, maybe to all the children and sailors on Oileán na Márbh.

I am writing to you to tell you this because you may have some ideas about what to do with her. Everyone else, even the priest, is badly stuck for a plan.

I must stop writing because I have exhausted all the paper and it is nearly morning again.

I hope you continue to be well and enjoying your life in Scotland.

Your old friend,
Jacob Stewart

~~~~~~~

Sean sat on the windowsill with the letter in his hand. Mary was aware of the stooped outline of his back from inside for twenty minutes while Pat ate at the table and the children played around the yard. Sean watched the two of them absentmindedly as they hopscotched back and forward on the flagstones but he was far away. In his mind he was in more familiar surroundings; he was in the soft embrace of his winding Ranahuel lanes; smelling the sweet, tobacco-like scent of smoke from his neighbours' turf fires; walking along the open expanse of An Tra Ban with the sea-breeze tingling on the skin of his face; feasting his imagination on the lough-rich landscape of The Rosses, the long, low promontories of Cruit and Owey stretching out onto the Atlantic horizon. All so different from the grimy, limestone confines of a two-up, two-down dwelling in Eskside Road, Musselburgh; the narrowness of the steep staircase, the short little bed and the torn curtain which separated his half of the room from his nephew, the niece having been dispatched to sleep on the floor of her parent's room on the other side of the thin stud wall. He had found it hard to get used to the heavy smell of the choking coal smoke in this place, the greyness of every street, the row after row of dirty slate roofs, such a contrast with the bright warmth of the thatched cottages of home.

At the thought of thatched roofs, a shadow flitted across Sean's idyll. The vision of Johnny O'Donnell, a burning firebrand in his hand and its flames leaping up to the roof of his home needled into his consciousness again and he soured inside himself for a bit. Until it came to him that the only way that he could shift this recurring nightmare was possibly to go back and face it head on. Johnny would be away all summer so if he was going to return this might well be the best time to do it. Anyway, there were more reasons to return, now that he'd read Jacob's letter. He stood up from the coldness of the windowsill and launched a kick at the boy's pig-bladder ball which had bounced to him across the yard, sending it flying over the tin roof of the outside privy and into the no-man's-land of rushes and purple-topped thistles next the river. The lad took off after it through the gate in the back wall like a hare.

"It'd better naw go in the rivir or you're deed," he yelled, his Scottish accent making Sean smile as always.

Mary arrived at the door and said, "Are you not coming in for your tea?"

"Here," he said, handing her the letter without looking at her. "Read that."

And, while he went to eat, Mary took his place on the windowsill to read Jacob's epistle.

"What are you going to do, Sean?" she asked quietly as she came back inside some time later.

"What can I do? I can do nothing from this distance," he replied. "There's nothing for it but go back to her."

"We'll miss you," she sighed. "The wains will miss you."

"It's a big decision to make," observed Pat. "You have worked well since you started at the Tower; they think well of you out there. It could be a job for life if you want it."

"I know. A job for life, if I want it," he repeated. "I don't know what I want. I like it well enough here, I like the work.... and you have been very good to me, taking me in and all. But ....I think it's only right that I go back to her."

"I think it's lovely that you want to go back to her," said Mary, "but it's not just her you are going back to. What about Father Dunleavey? What is he going to say to you?"

"I'm not in a bother what he'll say. It's got nothing to do with him, has it? He can think whatever he likes."

"And the parish? What about the neighbours?"

"What about them? It's none of their business, is it?" he protested.

"No, but you know what they're like around home. They all have an opinion about you and Annie. Some of them will be thinking that you are only coming home now that the baby passed away."

"As I say. It's none of their concern Mary."

"I'm just trying to warn you about what the talk is going to be. You have to be ready for that; maybe to be laughed at; maybe to be shunned by a lot of your old friends; Johnny O'Donnell and his like. I don't want to see you getting hurt," she said.

"Johnny will be away in the Lagan for a good while yet. Don't be worrying about me. I'll be alright."

"Likely you will," Mary persisted, "but will you do yourself a favour. Whenever you get home, go and talk to the priest and tell him the truth. Tell him you are not the baby's father. Make him understand that you are innocent. You need to try to get him on your side. It's the only way to survive in that parish. Promise me you'll do that Sean."

"He already knows I am innocent. I told him once and it's up to him to believe it if he decides to. Anyway, it's not me I'm going home for. It's her," he said and took up his fork.

The conversation dried up as the married couple watched him eat his food in a silence punctuated only by the sound of the children's shouts and laughter from the yard and the faint tick of the clock on the mantlepiece. Mary saw for the first time the lines of her father in his solemnly handsome face and in the slouch of his body at the table. The older man being born out of his youth. "How soon do you want to leave?" The resignation to the inevitable which could be detected in Pat's voice bore no trace of disappointment, nor of annoyance, at Sean's decision.

"What do you think, Pat? Should I be handing in my notice and working as long as they want me to?"

"I'll speak to Forsythe. He'll know what to do. Maybe if I explain the circumstances he will waive the notice thing and let you go as soon as you want. He's not a bad oul foreman, Forsythe," said Pat.

"That'll do; and thanks, Pat. You've been very good to me."

"Not at all," was the reply. "Now, pick yourself up and come with me down to the Crown for a last pint or two. And you're buying for once, right?"

And the two men picked up their coats and caps and left Mary to her pensive dishwashing.

Chapter 41

Oileán na Márbh

'The Mary Ellen' chugged noisily through Tory Sound, rounded the rock-strewn headland of Bloody Foreland and beat its way bravely south-west into the strengthening wind. It was late July but storms in this part of Donegal were no respecters of seasons. And there was no more exposed stretch of water than this, open, as it was, to the full span of the Atlantic where waves could build up in enormity and fury without the interruption of a single island for a few thousand miles. Little wonder that the residents of the most north-westerly of Ireland's inhabited islands, Tory, Inishbofin and Inishdooey, would be cut off from the mainland for several weeks at a time by the mountainous seas created by these recurring gales.

But *'The Mary Ellen'* was used to it, as was her captain of many years, Murray Brownlow. So when one of his more nervous passengers approached him, holding firmly to the ship's safety rail as the vessel bucked and reared over the swell, he listened calmly to the young man's anxious query. In answer he nodded reassuringly; "Aye," he shouted above the combined roar of the sea and the adjacent engine-room, "I still intend to try and put doon anchor in the lee of Gola Island when we reach it. Anither half an hour or so. We'll shelter there at anchor for the night. And if they are game tae send a wee boat oot tomorrow mornin' in weather like this, then you'll be able to get tae Gola. Otherwise," he laughed, "ye'll hae tae swim for it."

Sean Ban thanked him and turned away to go below decks again, relieved that this nightmare of a journey had at least the possibility of an early end in sight. He stumbled against the side of the wheelhouse as the old steamer lurched unexpectedly into a trough between waves.

"Keep a hold of that rail, son!" came the captain's urgent voice after him. "We dinnae want anither man overboard."

Sean Ban took his advice with a smile and grappled his way towards the stairway to below deck. Soon he would be on dry land again. After four days on the road and the sea, the prospect of a warm fire and a decent bite to eat somewhere on terra firma was more than comforting. He had taken the train from Musselburgh to Edinburgh and then to Glasgow, paying the fare with most of what remained of his hard-earned cash, having secreted a small package of money under Mary and Pat's pillow when they refused to accept his offer of payment on the night before he left. Then he had had to wait for a couple of days until he found a boat which was leaving for the west of Ireland. Brownlow's boat was heading to Burtonport, a destination which would have suited Sean fine. But then he heard someone saying that this captain might also anchor off Gola Island to offload occasional Gweedore travellers who wanted to disembark there. This was definitely the boat for him; he couldn't believe his luck and quickly paid the fare, boarded the vessel and found a place to curl up in the bowels of the ship, so as to try to sleep through the threat of sea-sickness in the hours ahead. Luck, however, did not extend to this intention and Sean Ban suffered just as much as he had on his only other sea voyage, that when he travelled to Scotland in a similar boat some months earlier.

He did indeed make it to the quaint little island in the morning, the gale having blown itself out overnight, leaving the waters in the sheltered bay to the east of the place relatively calm. Calm enough for a curragh to bring a load of fresh lobsters to *'The Mary Ellen'*, their claws secured with lengths of string, and to deliver Sean Ban safely to the pier. There was a difficulty however. When he spoke to the locals about the possibility of being rowed over to the Point he found that there was an understandable reticence to take on the journey. Even though it was only a mile across the Gweedore Bay to Carrickfinn, the tail end of the storm was still troubling that stretch of open water and the wise sailors of Gola were not about to risk such a journey.

"Just content yourself for a day or two, 'till this storm has calmed down in the channel, and we'll see about getting you home son," said one of the older islanders, his diamond eyes twinkling out from the folds of his boot-brown face. "You can bed down in the hayloft up behind my house, as long as you promise not to be lighting any fires. No pipe smoking now! And you can call in with the wife for a plate of spuds or a bowl of porridge when you're hungry. I'll tell her to expect you. We'll see what the sea is like tomorrow." And he strode off up the pier without another word or a backward look. Sean followed him nonetheless and took up his offer, on all counts.

It was, however, another two day wait for the homeward-bound traveller. None of his hosts seemed in a mood to take to the sea to row over to the shore of Carrickfinn and pointed to the choppy water and the breakers crashing on the rocks of Inishinny to the south.

"Still too risky!" they mumbled. "Sure it'll not take you long to wait a day or two."

He had no choice but to do just that and he killed the time by wandering over this ruggedly picturesque island. He sat by the tall cliffs at the north end, watching the waves surge through the sea-arches and run up towards the caves deep under the rocks that he was sitting on, the sound of their thunderous thrashing reaching him high above. He found himself studying the flight of gannets and cormorants as they soared on the up-draughts of wind by those sheer rock-faces or dived spectacularly into shoals of mackerel between Gola and Umfin Island. He followed the line of the coast around the steep-sided inlet on the west of the island, a remarkably symmetrical bay into which the huge westerly waves of the Atlantic Ocean drove relentlessly before dissipating themselves in surrender on a deep, resilient bank of wonderfully rounded rocks; he marvelled at how, over time, the power of the sea had graded this bank into clear strata of boulders, stones, pebbles and sand.

Eventually Sean Ban's host appeared on a rise beyond the village and shouted for him to come; it was slack-tide time, the best time to make the crossing, given the strength of the tidal rushes when the estuary was either filling with millions of gallons of water or emptying them back into the ocean. It was a couple of hours until sunset; they would need to leave now so that the men could be back before nightfall.

Two men rowed the boat, their muscular rhythm propelling the sturdy craft across the lumpy surface of the channel with admirable speed. There was little or no chat out of them and Sean Ban appreciated the absence of questions. He offered to take a turn at the oars but was ignored, apart from a half-smile on the bearded face of the middle-aged rower closest to him.

"Sure you'd only fall in," laughed the Gola islander through a mouthful of irregular, brown teeth. "You boys from Donegal don't know the first thing about rowing a boat."

"Boys from Donegal?" thought Sean behind his benign smile of agreement. "Does this fellow think Gola Island is an independent territory or something? Not actually part of the county?"

He said nothing though. He remembered hearing that Tory islanders talk about "going into Ireland" when they leave the shores of Tory for a trip to the mainland. Island mentality was something different altogether, he thought.

Quicker than he had imagined possible, however, he was throwing his bundle ashore and leaping from the bow of the boat unto a natural pier of rock on the northern shore of Carrickfinn. He thanked the rowers, handing them a handful of coins to divide between themselves and watched them push off the rocks again to begin the journey home, wordless and mechanical.

Sean stretched himself and looked around. Owey Island in the west looked as familiarly solid as ever. Daylight winked at him through the ruined windows of Kincasslagh Tower on the other side of the bay. The Stag Rocks stuck their rocky fingers over the horizon in a welcoming wave. The orb of the sun was just above the northern tip of Inishfree and was casting silver and golden rays up into a cloud formation that looked for all the world like a giant swan, settling itself on the lake of the sky. He drank in the piquant tang of the sea-spray. How good to be back in his own place. Picking up his bundle, he slung it over his shoulder and began to walk across the luxuriant summer grass, surprising one or two dozing cows as he went. Stewart's well-fed shorthorns, of-course. He wondered should he call in with his friends at the clachan of cottages below the hill, just to give his thanks to Jacob for his thoughtful communications. But on reflection he decided to walk on home on this occasion; he had people to see and things to say that were, in his mind, more important, more urgent than thanking Jacob. That could wait.

He climbed up and away from the growl of the sea and onto the highest part of the terrain. As the pervasive noise of waves breaking on rocks and sand fell away behind him he was conscious of the warbling song of three or four skylarks as they danced in the cooling air high above him. A few squawking seagulls carved swirling circles against the blue of the sky and a black and white wagtail flitted and bobbed in front of him, as if to guide him along the overgrown path towards home. He reached the highest point on the peninsula and saw ahead of him the dip in the hills which contained the harbour in an exquisitely horseshoe-shaped bay of unique tranquility. It was the kind of vista which demanded attention, uninterrupted attention. So Sean stopped to take it in. He stood motionless above the path of the setting sun, now red as a splash of spilled pig-blood in the saucer of the bay. He waited in the still air of his home-coming evening.

And, wafting to his listening ears, like a delicate and much-loved scent to the nose, he heard it. Against the low, bassy rumble of waves, fusing with the soprano trills of larks and the tenor squeals of gulls, he heard it.

The sound of a whistle.

Gentle as the tickle of bog-cotton; curling up to him like the last wisp of smoke from a dying ash-wood fire; drifting softly over the meadow grasses and flowers, the pink clover, the blue Hare-Bells, the yellow Bird's Foot, the purple Orchids and mingling with their fragrance, all the way from Oileán na Márbh, beyond the harbour.

The sweet sound of Annie's whistle!

Sean took off and ran with the energy of a young bull released from its stall. Headlong down the sandy path towards the harbour, up over the rocks and along the beach, his feet splashing exuberantly in the small waves.

She is with the baby. The tune of the child is in her, morose and pitiful. A 'fonn mall', an ancient slow air that she has heard a piper play when she was much younger. She has stored it away in the depths of her complex mind. For such a time as this. Its intense sadness she has never forgotten and now retrieves it. Relives it. For her baby. For herself. And for her poor distraught mother. A lament in memory of what might have been. She plays it with all the slow, expressive emotion of her loss. Every long, quivering note a tear that she cannot cry. Every snatched breath a lonely keening. Each phrase of the melody a sigh of what she had imagined, hoped for, lost.

She sits, cross-legged, on an outcrop of cold granite, her skirt tucked around her legs for warmth, her shawl tied at the front. Her hair floats in front of her bowed face. Her eyes see little of her surroundings. Only the still face of her boy.

She hopes that the local fellow will not come to disturb her this night, nice and all as he is. It is too beautiful to be here, too important to be close to her son, to play him these lullabies. The thought of her unwanted protector prompts her to lift her head involuntarily and she scans the shore for his presence. She does not see him and she is glad. But, before she resumes her lonesome serenade, a movement in the hills high above the harbour catches her eye. She focuses. There is a figure there. A man. He has her full attention, for some reason. He is waiting, looking around him. He is familiar, she is thinking, even from this distance. Could it be .....?

As she watches him, she is surprised to see him begin to run. A bundle bounces up and down on his back. He trips and falls once and, as her whistle comes to her lips again, she sees him scramble to his feet out of the tall marram grass.

She plays again. The lament has given way to something more like a waltz, tentative and less assured than her usual masterly standard. Because she is feeling unsure. And she is preoccupied by this running, leaping, tumbling figure who has now reached the beach below her. He is about to disappear from her line of vision below the rim of the island. She rises from her rocky seat and moves quickly to the edge of the cliff where she can keep him in view. The waltz stutters and stops mid-stanza. Annie stares down from the island at the splashing figure in the waves below. She knows the shape of him running. She sees him running on the bog roddens of Ranahuel in the sharpness of her memory. Her face is impassive as ever but inside herself she feels her heart race and thump like she has never felt it before. She hears her name being called.

"Annie! Annie! It's me!"

And she knows that voice. She has always known it, like she has always known her mother's voice. She cannot remember a time when that voice was not as much a part of her as breathing. And, if she can remember such a time, in the sand hills near her granny's, she wants to forget that time. She has heard that voice in her dreams every night since he left. For the first time in a very long time, she wishes that she had a voice to call to him her welcome home. If any voice could rise to the pure joy of it!

Instead, as she watches him clamber across the seaweed-covered rocks to reach the island, she turns the slow waltz into a flat-out jig of delight and plays it with a vengeance on those lonely months without him. She sees his head appear now and then among the huge boulders which guard the approach to the island's summit and he clambers up onto the flatness of the meadow. She does not come to meet him. As the jig reaches its final cadence she retreats with short, backward steps to the sandy scar in the grass. She stands beside where her infant lies beneath her feet and waits for him.

She sees the rush drain out of him. He comes to her reverently, slowly, at the end. He stands opposite her and takes her two hands in his. She drops her whistle inadvertently.

"I am so sorry, Annie," she hears him say.

After a short hesitation she squats down to retrieve her whistle and sits, head down, hair veiling her face characteristically. She leans on one hand, while the other scoops a handful of dry sand from the roughened surface and lifts it. She watches the grains slip slowly, so slowly, through her fingers onto the grass until none remain. He joins her and they sit on the sward, the damp of the dew chilling to their hips, the grave lying between them. The grave bringing them together. He says nothing. Just sits patiently watching her. The whistle comes to her lips again and rests there. But she does not play. Several silent minutes pass. Shared, wordless communion. In time she raises her head and her sad, dreamy blue eyes focus on his.

They looked at each other until Sean Ban could bear the question of her gaze no longer. He stood to his feet and raised her gently by the hand, before leading her very slowly away from her baby's resting place towards the rocky descent to the strand and down into the darkening shadow of Oileán na Márbh. The sky flared to rusty crimson above the island's sleeping body. The tide was still low as they ambled along the beach, Sean's hand lightly on her waist. The waves here in the protection of the bay sighed gently to rest at their feet and a few scavenging seabirds took to flight as they approached. Several red-legged oyster-catchers paused temporarily in their supper quest and scurried away in front of them.
"Stop a minute, Annie," said Sean, turning her around to face him by the water's edge. "I have so much to tell you, and I will tell you, bit by bit, as time goes by. But the main thing I want to tell you is.... well, I don't know how to say this, but.... you and me? Do you not think that you and me are meant to be together? Look, I know I ran away off, like the fool idiot that I was! I didn't mean to hurt you....it wasn't you I was running away from. Maybe it was myself....I don't know. But what I'm saying is....it took me to be away from you in Scotland for a while to realise... to realise that there is no other girl I could love but you, Annie. And I think I'm guessing right that you love me too, even though you never got round to telling me," he laughed. "You must know inside yourself that I love you. I suppose I always have loved you, for as far back as I can think. Remember when we used to lie in our play-house up by the rock? I was your husband and you were my wife, in our own wee home, made from branches and rocks and stuff. Well, now I think it's time to move on up a step to the real thing.... So we'll

go to Father Dunleavey tomorrow, will we, and see about a wedding? What do you think?"

She does a funny thing. A funny and unexpected thing, for her. She moves. She takes a step in closer to him. Just that. Nothing else. Hardly even looking him in the eye. Just steps into him, so the whole length of her body is touching his, face on, for the first time ever. And she stands there, so close to him, pressing closer against him. She smells the fresh sweat of him from his exertions. She senses his masculine urge but she is more moved deep inside herself by the intensity of his tenderness. She feels his arms go around her. Feels him pull her in so close to his body that her breath is forced from her chest and she gasps. And he gasps too. And then she realises that his is not a gasp exactly. Her head nestles on the strength of his shoulder, her hair soft against the stubble of his cheek, her eyes looking away back across the sand to the dark silhouette of Oileán na Márbh, that sacred island, resting place of strangers and nameless children.

ABOUT THE AUTHOR

David Dunlop was born and raised in North Antrim, N Ireland. He spent many years in education, both as a teacher and as a school leader; in those roles he exercised his passion to bring together young people from across N Ireland's various divides so as to encourage a shared understanding of history and appreciation of culture. To that end he wrote and directed several stage musicals with historical and cross-cultural themes and which drew on his experience of various musical genré. "Oileán na Márbh" is his first novel.
He now lives in West Donegal with his wife, Mary.

email- dadunlop50@gmail.com

For additional information see the following video presentations;

David Dunlop's promotional video, 'Oilean na Marbh- Island of the Dead', at http://vimeo.com/81494239

Donal Haughey's television production for TG4 entitled 'Oileán na Marbh; island of the dead' at http://youtu.be/olpqFUsulZI

Printed in Great Britain
by Amazon